BRIAN STABLEFORD

THE
REVELATIONS
OF TIME
AND SPACE

THIS IS A SNUGGLY BOOK

ISBN: 978-1-64525-030-2

The cover shows *Lagoon Nebula (Messier 8)*,
provided by NASA, ESA, STScI.

THE
REVELATIONS
OF TIME
AND SPACE

Brian Stableford's scholarly work includes *New Atlantis: A Narrative History of Scientific Romance* (Wildside Press, 2016), *The Plurality of Imaginary Worlds: The Evolution of French roman scientifique* (Black Coat Press, 2017) and *Tales of Enchantment and Disenchantment: A History of Faerie* (Black Coat Press, 2019). In support of the latter projects he has translated more than a hundred volumes of roman scientifique and more than twenty volumes of contes de fées into English. He has edited *Decadence and Symbolism: A Showcase Anthology* (Snuggly Books, 2018), and is busy translating more Symbolist and Decadent fiction.

His recent fiction, in the genre of metaphysical fantasy, includes a trilogy of novels set in West Wales, consisting of *Spirits of the Vasty Deep* (2018), *The Insubstantial Pageant* (2018) and *The Truths of Darkness* (2019), published by Snuggly Books, and a trilogy set in Paris and the south of France, consisting of *The Painter of Spirits*, *The Quiet Dead* and *Living with the Dead*, all published by Black Coat Press in 2019.

SNUGGLY BOOKS

for Brendan

THE REVELATIONS OF TIME AND SPACE

PART ONE

THE SEVENTH GENERATION

I

Corcoran was sitting on a bench on Marine Parade overlooking the Thames Estuary, feeling the breeze on his face and the grass beneath his feet, breathing in the strange multi-scented air, minding his own business, when the kid came to stare at him.

As soon as he saw that stare, Corcoran knew that his mother had been unable to help herself talking. The news would be all over the neighborhood by now, and every time he stepped outside the flat he would become a focus of attention. He was, alas, recognizable. His picture had been splashed all over the news, and everyone who knew his mother would have paid particular attention to it.

He'd managed to avoid TV, and the few interviews he'd been badgered into giving to web journalists while captive in the hospital in Greenland had been masterpieces of inarticulacy, of a kind that only someone as far along the autism spectrum as he was could possibly contrive, with the aid of a little malicious stubbornness, but still, he was recognizable.

He'd been back on Earth for more than a month, so the return of the mission was old news by now, but even though the handsome captain of Olympus Five, Chris Kemmering, had got the lion's share of media attention when it landed, Corcoran had been second in line, having been the man who had actually tried to talk to the Jovian cloud-whales. Even if he'd only been four-teenth in line, as the only Brit on the crew, his return would have been big news on home turf. In terms of local gossip, his arrival back in England was sensational.

He couldn't blame his mother. She was old enough to ap-preciate any reflected glory she could get and she had never sym-pathized with his enthusiasm for hiding. She had always wanted him to "get out more" when he was a child, and she still thought of him as a child, even though he was in his thirties now and had left home fifteen years ago. Since leaving rehab, however, Corcoran had thought it a good idea to stay with his mother tem-porarily, because he had not yet made any firm plans to reinsert himself back into earthly existence.

During the month in rehab he had had plenty of time to think about where he might go when he was allowed out, but the prospect of actually finding a place to live had seemed like hassle best postponed. After a seven-year stint away, almost all of it taken up by the long journeys there and back, and all of it living in a tin can, he had enough credit in the bank to buy or rent a flat anywhere in England, and fit it out as he pleased, but actually doing something about it was something still out of psychological reach. He was out of rehab and certified physically fit, but mental recuperation was a different matter and a much slower process, if "recuperation" was a word that could even be applied to a life like his.

He knew, therefore, that the kid was only a symptom and a beginning.

I should have stayed in the flat, Corcoran thought. *I knew it.*

But it wasn't that simple. He had been away from Earth for seven years, living in a tin can, and had spent the last month in a hospital in Greenland. Coming back to England was something that required a special kind of reacquaintance, which hiding in his temporary room in his mother's tiny flat couldn't supply. On the other hand, he could at least have stayed in hiding until Denise had arrived and that particular element of the reacquaintance process had been tackled.

His sister was coming out from London that afternoon specifically to see him, and she would probably be at the flat when he went back. That was an encounter to which he was actually looking forward, but that didn't mean that the prospect wasn't challenging and its anticipation charged with anxiety.

He and Denise hadn't been close before he went away—indeed, he had found her presence almost as discomfiting as that of other people—but he and she had spent a lot of time talking on-screen while Olympus Five was heading back to Earth, getting closer all the while, and he felt that he knew her a lot better now. He felt, too, that he had changed while he had been away, that that mission had taught him a great deal about how to tolerate and interact with other human beings. He was certainly looking forward to seeing his sister—in his own way, he felt now that he was genuinely fond of her—but that very fact created the possibility of disappointment, and of failure. He couldn't be certain that all his old awkwardness might not come flooding back now that he was back in England, back in the cauldron of his childhood, of his flawed making.

He didn't know how Denise was going to feel when the crucial moment came, either. On-screen closeness was one thing, but she too might well have problems when the relationship had to change gear, and venue.

In consequence, he had been nervous all morning, and had felt the need to get out of the flat. And the weather had been so tempting! The day was sunny and calm, and not too hot, even though it was August. Nothing in the sky, nor the stately flow of the river, gave any indication that the world was still teetering on the brink of destruction—provided, that is, that he kept his eyes resolutely facing eastwards, avoiding the sight of the ruins of Canvey Island, which had not been "restored," the way that much of London and its environs had been after the Great Flood, but left to rot. So he had come out, to do what ought to have been the most normal thing in human life, even nowadays, and take a walk.

Now, though, the kid was staring, and Corcoran felt a prickling sensation in his spine that he hadn't felt for years, but which, he remembered, had once been all-too-familiar.

The staring kid looked too young to be out on his own, Corcoran thought. He was no expert at judging children's ages, but the little monster couldn't have been more than eight. For a moment, he wondered why the brat wasn't in school, and then remembered that schools still closed down in August, out of respect for ancient tradition. When he glanced around, however, he saw that the kid wasn't on his own. His mother was standing thirty feet away, holding a leash whose other end was attached to an impatient dog—some kind of terrier—watching her little treasure like a hawk.

Well, if you're that scared, Corcoran thought, *why did you let the little wretch come to stare at me?*

Finally, the kid plucked up his courage. "You're the man who went to Jupiter," he said.

It wasn't a question, but Corcoran reminded himself that he was a changed man, and didn't have to revert to his old habits just because he was back on Earth again. He could continue to be the man of Olympus Five. He could make conversation if he had a mind to. But he didn't.

Corcoran didn't answer. He hoped the kid would go away. No such luck.

"My Mum knows your Mum," said the kid.

My Mum knows practically everyone for half a mile around, it seems, Corcoran thought. *Very chatty, my Mum. If heredity worked backwards, I'd wonder where she got it from. Even Denise isn't chatty . . . at least, she wasn't. Not with me. But maybe that was just with me . . .*

His mother had always wondered incessantly, and aloud, where Corcoran got his taciturnity and laconism from, although she didn't call it taciturnity and laconism. She called it being bloody-minded. And even though she wondered aloud about it herself, if anyone else had commented on it, she would have instantly said: "He gets it from his Dad."

His father had been an engineer. He'd been considerably older than his wife, who had been pushing forty herself when she had given birth to the child that some crazy whim had led them to call Zephaniah. "Thirty-nine's not that old these days," she had doubtless said, defensively, at the time, and must obviously have said the same, whether or not she thought it, when she's had Denise at forty-two. In all likelihood, Corcoran thought, her eggs had all deteriorated over time, and so had his father's sperm. Not that that explained anything, especially as Denise could pass for normal with apparent ease.

The kid had finally cottoned on to the fact that Corcoran didn't reply to statements, and decided to go for the blunt question.

"Are you resting up because your bones are weak from having been in zero-gee for so long?" the kid asked.

Corcoran was startled. He had expected something vague and dumb like "What's Jupiter like?" or, even more likely, "What's Chris Kemmering like?"

"No," he said, pulling himself together and trying to restore his new self to control of his conduct. "The ship was accelerating or decelerating for much of the journey, so there were only brief periods of weightlessness."

There you go, he thought. *You can be chatty too, if you try.*

"I forgot," said the kid. "That's the whole point of the matter-annihilation engine. Weren't you in zero-gee when you were orbiting Jupiter, though?"

Corcoran didn't know whether to increase his estimate of the kid's age, whether he was dealing with some kind of prodigy, or whether all eight-year-olds were routinely taught nowadays about the matter-annihilation engine and its implications.

"No," he said, "it was a powered orbit. We had to get close to the atmospheric surface to maneuver the drones."

"Did you manage to talk to the cloud-whales?"

And there it was—the big question.

"I can't say," he replied, glibly.

"Why not?"

Another hard one, if taken seriously—which he had no intention of doing, for the moment. Life was difficult enough. One step at a time.

"I signed a confidentiality agreement," he said.

That was true. He didn't like lying—he found it difficult, in fact, although he certainly seemed to be getting better with practice—but there were some truths that made excellent shields, and could be hauled out in virtually any circumstances. It seemed a little mean to use that one on a curious eight-year-old, though . . . if the kid really was eight. After all, the kid didn't know that he was a seeming monster, did he?

The child's mother had edged a lot closer, evidently intent on hearing what Corcoran was saying to her treasure.

"Are you going to go back?" the kid asked. "To space I mean."

That was an easy one. "I don't know," said Corcoran.

"You don't know whether you want to, or you don't know whether you'll be allowed?"

"Both."

He knew that if Chris Kemmering had turned in a bad report on him, or the computer analyses of his physical and social per-formance had been poor, his space-traveling days would be over for good. Not that he had any reason to think that Kemmering would bad-mouth him. The captain had always treated him with kindness and respect—but he had treated everyone with kind-ness and respect; that was his style. What he thought privately, Corcoran had no idea. Nor had he any idea what the computers would report, even though the joke had been made more than once that he seemed to have more empathy with machines than people. Nor was he sure that even if the International Space Agency strategists came to him on bended knee, which they probably wouldn't, the captain and the computer analyses having certified him fit, he would actually want to go back into space. The experience had proved far more comfortable than he had feared when momentary madness had inspired him to agree to the ISA's unexpected offer, but even so . . .

"Are you going to go back to the future, then?" the kid persisted.

That was another kettle of fish entirely. He had an appointment to see Walter Halleck at eleven o'clock the following morning.

Halleck had called him numerous times at the hospital, urging him to come back to the Institute, but Corcoran had kept putting him off, telling him—without lying—that he really hadn't made up his mind yet what he wanted to do, and was determined to finish rehab before he even started thinking about it in earnest. Now he was out, though, and no longer in Greenland, he was going to have to face his former collaborator in the flesh, as well as his sister, and if seeing Denise was enough to make him a little nervous, the prospect of seeing Halleck was enough to cause real fear.

At the time, Halleck had considered Corcoran's acceptance of the ISA's offer to be a rank betrayal and justification for wrath, and even though he had been striving hard to be as nice as pie during their recent on-screen interactions, and to assure him that no hard feelings had survived the seven years of their separation, Corcoran wasn't sure that he could believe him. Like him, the physicist had always been a man who found it difficult to lie, but like him, he had had seven years to retrain himself and practice. Who could tell whether he was still the same man as before? On the other hand, Corcoran thought, it would be interesting to find out exactly what he had been doing for the past seven years, and what kind of fruit their old collaborative endeavors had continued to bear in the meantime—all the things that Halleck and he couldn't talk about over an unsecured phone link.

"I don't know," Corcoran told the kid, honestly. He was able to leave it at that verbally, but not mentally. Innocent as they were, the kid's questions were stirring things up, and Corcoran really wished, now, that the boy would give it up and go away.

Would he go back to the future, given that Halleck seemed to be so desperate to send him? On the one hand, he had enough money saved up to live for five, ten or even twenty years without doing anything at all. On the other hand, how could he possibly stand doing nothing at all? On the third hand, if there were such a thing in metaphorical parlance, he didn't even know for sure whether Halleck had somehow fiddled an adequate budget refresher out of some client or other actually to provide him with employment for years, or even for months. It was possible that

Halleck's apparent desperation was the result of the fact that he, the Sling and the Institute, like civilization itself, were suspended on the edge of oblivion.

"How long will you be staying?" The kid seemed to be harboring the notion that this stilted interview might be a real conversation, perhaps even the beginning of some kind of weird friendship.

"Not long," Corcoran said, the statement being sufficiently meaningless not to qualify as a lie whatever the truth eventually turned out to be.

The kid's mother had finally had enough. She came to collect her treasure.

"I hope Luke's not bothering you, Mr. Corcoran," she said, as she pulled the boy toward her, against his will. "My name's Emily Saverne. I know your mother."

There wasn't a question in there, but she was looking at him quite hard, as if she expected a comment or acknowledgement of some kind.

Corcoran nodded his head.

"Give my regards to your mother, then," the woman said. "Just tell her Emily. She'll know who you mean."

Corcoran nodded again.

The woman hesitated, as if there were something else she would have liked to have said, but she thought better of it and let the terrier drag her away, dragging the little boy in her turn.

Damn! thought Corcoran. *I must have come across like a real social incompetent. I'm going to have to do better than that in future. But kids are disconcerting, and anyway, it's over now.*

Corcoran's relief was short-lived. In the distance, Denise had already turned the corner on to Marine Parade, apparently having decided that she would take the initiative and not wait meekly for her brother to return to the flat in his own time.

For an instant, his heart leapt with something that, he assumed, must resemble joy. But he realized, as he came to his feet and took a step in her direction, that she wasn't alone.

There was another woman with her. The other was about the same age, not as pretty, very soberly dressed, with short-cropped brown hair that didn't make the most of her face the way that Denise's long, straight, blonde hair did. She was taller than Denise, but not tall enough to seem intimidating—not, at least, to anyone but Corcoran.

Although he wasn't at all sure that it was logical or reasonable for him to feel that way, Corcoran felt deeply upset by the presence of that stranger, and deeply upset with Denise for having brought her—or, at the very least, for tolerating her presence during what was supposed to be a significant, and personal reunion.

Denise hadn't seen him for seven years, after all, and even though they'd been talking on a regular basis on-screen, Corcoran felt that she too ought to have thought that their reunion in physical space ought to be something at least a little bit sacred, something that she wanted entirely to herself, not something to share with a friend . . . assuming that the short-haired brunette was just a friend . . .

Whether she thought the moment sacred or not, Denise was either genuinely delighted to see him or felt obliged to put on a show for her mysterious friend. She ran the last fifteen yards or so that separated him, threw her arms around him and kissed him on the cheek.

Corcoran weathered the contact, and even tried to like it, as he knew that he ought to do and perhaps, if he were able to suppress his stupid autonomic flinch, actually could. The suppression was imperfect, though; Denise felt the flinch, broke off the hug and moved away, uncertainly and apologetically.

Corcoran cursed himself. Doubtless aided, if not actually obliged, by the presence of the stranger, Denise instantly slipped into formal mode.

"It's good to see you, Zeph," she said, in a polite and carefully distanced fashion.

His mother and his sister were the only people in the world who called him Zeph, although his full forename had inevitably been splashed all over the web when Olympus Five had returned.

Neither Halleck nor any of the tech staff at the Institute had ever called him anything but "Corcoran." On Olympus, too, protocol had demanded that all the crew address one another by their surnames, and no one on the ship, for seven years, had ever called him "Zephaniah," let alone "Zeph."

"It's good to see you, too, Nise," he replied, mechanically, uncomfortably aware that he sounded even more formal and distanced than she did. He was busy looking at her companion, silently asking the question of what she was doing there.

Denise had the grace to look more than slightly guilty. "This is a colleague of mine, Zeph," she said. "She was extremely keen to meet you. Marie, this is my brother Zeph; Zeph, this is the Reverend Marie MacLaughlin."

Corcoran's eyebrows twitched, but he didn't verbalize his surprise. He remained frozen in position, though, awkwardly aware that it must seem impolite for him to do so.

Denise responded to his astonishment with a strange smile. "Marie is attached to the college Chaplaincy," she explained, although it was one of those "explanations" that wasn't really an explanation at all. Corcoran did realize, however, that if Denise's friend was a priest, that might explain why it had been difficult to refuse her request to accompany her to see him. Even an atheist—even an atheist who taught evolutionary biology at Imperial College—might find it a trifle difficult to tell a politely pleading priest to go to hell.

But what on earth does a priest want with me? Corcoran thought.

Marie MacLaughlin did not hold out her hand to be shaken, but simply favored him with a smile and a nod of the head. Perhaps she'd been warned, or perhaps her pastoral duties routinely brought her into contact with people with autism spectrum disorders. She was working at Imperial, after all, where you couldn't throw a stone into a Senior Common Room without hitting an asp.

"Mum's invited Marie to tea," Denise said. "She thought you wouldn't mind." Corcoram knew perfectly well that their mother hadn't thought any such thing, but Denise didn't have her brother's qualms about lying. She did it with ease and style, as befitted an intelligent, attractive and socially competent woman in her early thirties.

Corcoran's gaze flicked between the two women, comparing them and wondering what their relationship was.

"Marie is working on a PhD thesis in Theology, Zeph," Denise said. "Do you know what Natural Theology is?"

"William Paley," Corcoran answered, almost reflexively. "The watchmaker argument."

"In fact," Marie Maclaughin put in, "I prefer William Derham's term *Physico-Theology*. Have you heard of him too?"

"The author of *Astro-Theology*," said Corcoran, quoting the title of another of Derham's books, and feeling a slight thrill of satisfaction at not having been caught on the intellectual hop.

"Good," said Denise. "So you can see, then, why Marie is interested in my work, and why she's even more interested in yours, can't you?"

"No," said Corcoran, bluntly, and honestly—although he had a sneaking suspicion that if he'd wanted to think about it, he would surely have been able to work it out.

"My thesis isn't purely historical," Marie MacLaughlin said, obviously launching into another of those so-called "explanations" that wasn't an explanation at all, "although it has to start with some kind of historical study, because that's what PhD theses do. Derham's ancient enough to be academically respectable, and although his ideas are unfashionable nowadays, they're not necessarily heretical—and Anglicanism is a broad church anyway, so we don't have the Catholic allergy to heresy. I'm not attempting to resurrect physico-theology, exactly, but, at least as a kind of hypothetical exercise, I'm intensely interested in the question of what recent scientific discoveries might tell us about the being and attributes of God. Imperial is a real gold mine, from my point of view, obviously, and Denise has been very helpful—but no one there, or anywhere else, has the kind of experience you have, and the kind of insight you've achieved. If you'd be willing to talk to me, you could be immensely useful."

"It doesn't matter that you don't believe in God," Denise put in, helpfully. "Will you do it, Zeph?"

"I've signed a confidentiality agreement," Corcoran said, reflexively, although he knew as he said it that it wasn't going to work on Denise.

"I'm perfectly willing to confine my questions to material that's already in the public domain," the Reverend hastened to say.

"Some of your colleagues," Corcoran observed, "think that I'm the Antichrist."

"Not my colleagues," Marie MacLaughlin said. "I don't say that the word hasn't been bandied about here as well as in America, but that's not the view of the Church of England, and it's certainly not mine."

"Others think I'm insane," Corcoran added. "A fantasist subject to schizoid delusions."

"I don't think that either. Honestly, Mr. Corcoran, I'm not going into this with any kind of prejudiced predisposition."

"That's a lie," said Corcoran, flatly, although he knew that he was overstepping the line.

For an instant, as might be expected, the woman seemed distraught, and deeply offended—but she was an intelligent woman. It took her less than three seconds to realize what he must mean.

She shook her head. "No, it's not, Mr. Corcoran. To you, the fact that I take the existence of God for granted might seem like a prejudiced predisposition, but that doesn't mean that I'm lying when I assert it. Quite the opposite, in fact. If I were to state that my faith were a mere prejudice, or a hypothesis, *that* would be a lie."

Corcoran nodded, tacitly conceding the point.

"You haven't answered the question, Zeph," Denise put in. "*I've signed a confidentiality agreement* isn't an answer."

"I'll think about it," said Corcoran, falling back on the Plan B of all-purpose shields.

"I'll hold you to that," said Denise. "You can think about it while we have tea. Then you can give Marie an answer before we drive back to London. I think you should do it, Zeph."

Corcoran met her eyes, although it wasn't something he liked to do. She was challenging him to ask "why?" but she knew full well that he had no intention of doing so. It wasn't that he couldn't; indeed, with practice, he'd become tolerably good at it over the years, but it wasn't his style.

Denise reached out and put a hand on his shoulder. He didn't flinch. "I think it might be good for you," she said. "I'm not talking about conversion, just about conversation. I think it might be good for you to talk about it all, to help you explore what you think about it. I know that you and I have been doing that, talking on-screen, and obviously, we'll continue, but I'm your sister, and it's a trifle incestuous. I really do think that you might benefit from talking to her."

You need to get out more, Corcoran thought. *Et tu, Brute?*

He had been all too well aware that his reunion with Denise carried an innate risk of disappointment, but this . . .

"I'll think about it," Corcoran repeated, doggedly, backsliding ignominiously.

Denise tried to contrive a smile. "We'd better get back to the flat," she said. "Mum's waiting, and we can't leave her on her own. I've come to see her too, you know."

Corcoran nodded. He looked at Marie MacLaughlin. She was studying him with interest, like a specimen: not a specimen of the Antichrist, presumably, or even like a bug under a microscope, but studying him nevertheless, as if his mere existence might be able to reveal something to her about the mysterious workings of the mind of God.

"They're not beetles," he said, testing her. "Whatever the popular press says, the third and fourth generation aren't beetles, or ants, and certainly not praying mantises."

She smiled, with an odd delicacy. She evidently knew the Haldane quote about a lifetime's study of nature having informed him that God had an inordinate fondness for beetles.

"Shouldn't you be using the future tense, Mr. Corcoran?" she suggested.

It was, Corcoran had to admit, a fair point. But it was an insoluble problem. From the viewpoint of his personal experience, the Dancing Rats, the Inverts and the Megaplants were all coexistent with him, or in the past, and it was perfectly natural for him to talk about them in the present or the past tense, even though they weren't scheduled to exist for billions of years.

"Oh, for God's sake call him Zeph," said Denise. "And you, Zeph, can call her Marie, if you ever get round to addressing her at all. Let's pretend we're friends, shall we?"

Shall we? Corcoran wondered. *And what, exactly, does that 'we' imply?* Again his gaze flickered between the two women. He didn't want to jump to any conclusions. He knew that wasn't his forte. Meekly, he began to walk toward the corner, keeping discreetly behind the two of them.

"It's a nice view," Marie MacLaughlin commented, with a backward nod at the estuary. She was facing east, not looking at the wreck of Canvey.

"Wonderful," said Denise. "Mum swears that on a clear day you can see Gravesend from the top of the hill, but I think it's just Tilbury. Not that it matters—one set of cranes is pretty much the same as another. We get wonderful sunsets here too, as the air pollution from the Reconstruction of London mingles with the dust from the Ring of Fire eruptions gradually falling back from the stratosphere. Can't complain, though—rumor has it that the increased albedo due to the pollutant particles is all that's keeping the second installment of the final catastrophe at bay . . . but not for long, if Zeph's Dancing Rats can be trusted, and Zeph is reading their messages right."

Halleck had assured Corcoran that the AIs had managed to collect a lot more from the Rats during the seven years he'd been away, so the possibility that the vision of their world that the Slingshots had developed was just some kind of delusion on Corcoran's part had surely been dismissed long ago, even by the hardiest of deniers and conspiracy theorists, but Corcoran didn't object to his sister's implication that he was somehow personally responsible for the revelations of the oracle.

As they were going up the hill, Marie MacLaughlin turned to look at Corcoran and moved to one side, tacitly inviting him to draw level with them. He didn't.

"I don't suppose it's any consolation you, Mr. Corcoran," she said to him, "but for every American preacher who's convinced that you, Dr. Halleck's Institute and the ISA are the minions of the Devil, there's at last one who thinks that you're a genuine prophet, an authentic Zephaniah."

"More like Jeremiah," muttered Denise, presumably thinking that she was being witty—but Corcoran knew, and knew that Marie MacLaughlin must know, that the Biblical Zephaniah and Jeremiah had been contemporaries, and probably even acquaintances, who must have compared notes and had serious discussions, over a pint of whatever people in Jerusalem used to drink in those days, about the exact shape of the catastrophe and Day of Judgment to come.

"All prophets are prophets of doom," the Reverend pointed out to her atheistic friend, mildly. "It's a basic qualification. If doom is what lies in wait for us, the honest prophet is bound by honesty to tell us so. Except that the Biblical Zephaniah, again like all honest prophets, assures us that beyond the catastrophe, beyond destruction and judgment, the kingdom of God still awaits us."

"Not humans," Denise observed. "Not according to Zeph and Walter Halleck."

Denise had met Halleck several times. She didn't like him. That wasn't surprising; Halleck was a difficult man to like—and most people thought the same about Corcoran, or had, seven years ago.

"Some argue that it's a matter of definition," Marie MacLaughlin said, countering Denise's argument—not as a point of principle, Corcoran judged, but because she was trying to impress him, trying to convince him that she was a genuine scholar with whom he could have serious discussions. "Humans as a biological species might be doomed, but souls are immortal . . . and if all beings endowed with souls and sentience are made in the image of God, whether their physical resemblance is vaguely to rats, insects, plants or clouds and whales, the narrative takes on a different complexion."

Corcoran—who, in spite of his promise to Denise, hadn't actually been thinking about it at all—wondered then, on impulse rather than as a matter of desire or rational calculation, whether it might perhaps be a good idea to talk to Marie MacLaughlin, and make a genuine attempt to answer her questions. The comparisons with his Biblical namesake left him cold, but "the narrative takes on a different complexion" seemed to him to be not only a well-turned phrase but an interesting sentiment. The *complexion of the narrative* might be something in which he could take an interest.

And as Denise said, it might even be good for him. Just because his mother thought he should get out more, it didn't mean that the opinion was wrong. But then, reflexively, he pushed the matter to the back of his mind, out of the way.

II

Tea could have been easy enough. Family meals had been relatively comfortable in the past, before he had left Earth, because his mother and sister had always been able to talk to one another, as mothers and daughters did talk, and they were well used to Corcoran's non-participation. His taciturnity hadn't bothered them, even if his mother, at least, thought that it was really bloody-mindedness; he had been able to sit back and let them follow their own comfortable flow. In the days when his father had been alive and they had lived in the old house, further inland, it had been just as easy, because his father had been equally taciturn—or equally bloody-minded—and two absences were as easy for his mother and sister to accommodate as one.

Complications had arisen, however, both before and after his father's death, if ever there were other guests. That had, admittedly, been very rare, but not entirely unknown. Other presences could upset the equilibrium.

Denise and her mother tried hard not to let that happen on the present occasion, of course, by including Marie MacLaughlin

24

in their conversation, but they weren't entirely successful in that, partly because they were, after all, mother and daughter, who didn't see as much of one another as they might have, and who had all kinds of catching up to do that didn't easily accommodate a third wheel, and partly because Denise's mother seemed slightly uneasy about the presence to the newcomer in question.

Corcoran wasn't entirely sure of the nature of that unease. It might, he thought, simply have been the fact that the chaplain was a clergywoman. His mother was an agnostic rather than an atheist, who didn't exactly believe in God, but didn't exactly not believe in Him either, and thus found the presence of a Reverend at her table a trifle challenging, and perhaps even intimidating. It might, on the other hand, be something else.

Corcoran knew that his mother worried about him, and always had, but he had never really considered the possibility that she might worry about Denise too, and about the possibility that, although she clearly wasn't as abnormal as her son, she might nevertheless not be completely "normal." He considered it now.

Corcoran wasn't particularly surprised that Denise was still unmarried after the seven years that he'd been away, because he knew that she had always been primarily focused on her career, and that she was too intelligent to be led astray by temporary infatuations. Statistically speaking, it was not unusual for women of thirty-two to be still unmarried, and even forty years ago, their mother had been well over thirty when she had tied the knot. Corcoran had never enquired about his sister's sexuality, and would not have cared in the least had it turned out to be in any way unorthodox, but he knew that his mother might not see things the same way, or, at least, might not be able to suppress nagging suspicions and anxieties entirely. Nor would she be able entirely to set aside popular myths and prejudices regarding clergywomen.

Whatever its cause, however, the net result of that slight unease on his mother's part was that, in spite of the efforts of forced politeness, she focused her attention far more intently on Denise than on her guest, and left Denise little scope to remedy the relative neglect, thus encouraging, if not actually forcing, Marie MacLaughlin to attempt to strike up her own parallel conversation with Corcoran.

Perhaps naturally, that was an opportunity that the theologian was keen to exploit.

"I hope you won't think it indiscreet of me," she said to Corcoran, while Denise and her mother were otherwise engrossed, "but I can't help being struck by the contrast in your Christian names. Zephaniah and Denise seem so oddly out of tune. Do you know how that came about?"

Corcoran resisted the temptation to remark that the forenames weren't Christian names, because his parents weren't, strictly speaking, Christians. "I think my father had a double standard," he replied. "He wanted his son to stand out, to have a distinctive name. He didn't want that for his daughter. He wanted her to blend in. It seems to have worked."

"You mean that if he had registered you under the name John you might have become an accountant?"

"Who can tell?" countered Corcoran.

"But Denise is exceptional too, isn't she?"

"Is she? There are more women than men teaching in universities nowadays, even at Imperial—at least in the biological sciences. It's only in maths, physics and computer sciences that we asps still rule the roost."

"Asps?"

"It's a contraction of Asperger's Syndrome, although the term is obsolete now and was on the way out even when I was a child. The middle of the imaginary Bell curve of mental aptitude used to be described as 'neurotypical' way back when, which was sometimes flippantly shortened to 'newt,' to set up a cute contrast of sorts. I used to be behind the times even before I set off on Olympus."

"That sounds bizarre, coming from a man who's famous for venturing billions of years into the future . . . and a pioneer who's been further away from Earth than any human had ever been before."

Corcoran ignored the subtle flattery and took refuge in pedantry.

"Olympus Five was the third fully manned Jupiter mission," Corcoran pointed out, scrupulously. "And the first Saturn mission was already beyond Jupiter's orbit when I arrived there. I was just following in the footsteps of others, and not going as far as the farthest travelers. Even aboard Five, I was just following Captain Kemmering's orders."

"True," she conceded, unapologetically. "But you went a great deal further than anyone else by means of the Sling."

"*Further* might not be the correct term," he argued. "In my . . . excursions previous to the Jupiter mission, I never left London—in fact, the Institute is within easy walking distance of Imperial College."

"It's conventional to speak of time in terms of distance," she countered, seemingly no stranger to pedantic games. "It's perfectly acceptable to speak of the near or remote past, and the near or remote future. No one before you had made contact with the second generation, let alone the sixth. All the other human registers that Dr. Halleck has employed have been following in your footsteps. And to return to the starting-point, *behind the times* is something that you definitely were not."

But I was, Corcoran thought. *Existentially, I've never looked like catching up with the present moment, let alone getting ahead of myself.* But that wasn't a direction in which he wanted the conversation to go, given that he seemed to be trapped in it. Gathering his resources, he set out to deflect it on to safer ground.

"According to some of Walter Halleck's colleagues—or rivals, as he'd probably think of them—the idea of time as a linear dimension is just an artifact of our senses; from a purely mathematical viewpoint, they tell me, time has neither direction nor duration."

"But you don't have a purely mathematical viewpoint, do you?" the chaplain countered.

"No," Corcoran admitted.

"And according to the Institute's findings, so far as they've been placed in the public domain or leaked, even though the entities of the five further generations have additional senses that humans don't, the species with which a degree of communication is possible still seem to think in terms of past and future, near and remote."

"That was my impression," Corcoran conceded, "but some commentators think that it's merely something I was reading into the rapport I felt that I'd obtained, a product of my own prejudice. If I did have a purely mathematical viewpoint, I might be better able to make objective judgments."

"Or you might not be able to make any judgment at all. Dr. Halleck, at least, was convinced that you have a very particular talent, and that the rapport you established, at least with the Rats, and probably the Insects too, was immensely useful. He managed to convince others of the fact, too. That's why the ISA recruited you to go to Jupiter, isn't it?"

"That is the vulgar version of the argument," Corcoran agreed. "Because I have no empathy with human beings—allegedly— it leaves scope in my serpentine brain to develop empathy with unhuman beings: Dancing Rats, antlike Inverts, Megaplants . . . or Jovian cloud-whales. Others think I'm simply delusional."

"Why do you say *allegedly*?" she asked, in a soft tone that belied the fact that she was pouncing like a cat on a point that intrigued her.

"Because it's alleged," he replied, stubbornly pedantic. "It's a cliché. People supposedly displaced along the so-called autism spectrum are routinely said to be incapable of human empathy— like psychopaths."

She nodded, sympathetically. Corcoran assumed that Denise must have told her something about his views on asp/newt mythology—the views he'd had seven years ago, at least. Exactly what Denise might have told her, he didn't know, and it had doubtless been polluted by Denise's own opinion on the matter, but Marie MacLaughlin obviously knew that he considered that the representation of alternative sanities as a simple "spectrum" was drastically oversimplified, and that in his arrogant opinion, mind had at least as many dimensions as spacetime. But given that he was the ace temponaut, the man who thought he could communicate with at least two of the five post-human generations, he would think that, wouldn't he?

She looked him in the eyes, and he managed not to look away. "Will you allow me to interview you, Mr. Corcoran? Earnestly and in depth? It really would be very valuable to my research."

"I was under the impression that you were already doing that," Corcoran said.

She laughed. "And I was under the impression that we were just chatting politely over tea. But you're right—I'm being too intense. A degree of obsession tends to come with the vocation . . . but you know the feeling, don't you?"

That seemed to Corcoran to be an interesting provocation, given that it was tantamount to an invitation to empathy.

"I know my own feeling," he said, scrupulously, "but as to how it compares with yours . . . that would be guesswork."

She smiled, almost as if he had made a joke. "Taking your previous answer as an assent, then," she said, "may we discuss some precise arrangements? I'm perfectly happy to come out here to conduct the interviews, or to meet in London, at Imperial or elsewhere. Which would you prefer?"

"I don't know what my schedule is going to be," Corcoran said. "I have an appointment to see Walter Halleck in London tomorrow morning. I don't know yet exactly what he has to offer me, because he couldn't go into detail on-screen for security reasons, but he certainly wants me to go back to work at the Institute, seemingly with some urgency. If I accept the offer he makes, that will determine both my timetable and my future location. I'm not in a position to make any firm arrangements at the moment."

"I understand," she said, although Corcoran guessed that she probably thought that he was just being evasive. "May I phone you tomorrow evening, then, in order to fix a time and place for an initial meeting?"

"I don't have a phone," Corcoran told her. "I didn't need a personal phone while I was in the hospital and I haven't bought one yet."

"But I can contact you here via the flat's devices—you will be coming back here to sleep, I assume?"

"Yes," Corcoran agreed. "I don't know what time I'll get back from London though. It might be late."

"I'll try again if I can't contact you the first time," Marie MacLaughlin assured him, "and keep trying until I do." He believed her.

Denise must have been eavesdropping with at least a fraction of her attention, because she was quick to turn away from her gossipy chat with her mother to say: "Have you made your arrangements with Zeph, Marie?"

"Not exactly," the Reverend replied, scrupulously. "But we've made arrangements to make arrangements, haven't we, Zeph?"

Corcoran knew that the question wasn't entirely rhetorical, that she was looking for confirmation of his commitment to the loose agreement into which she'd badgered him, and of what that implied for his future cooperation with her project.

"Yes," he said, taking the question literally, and intending no implication with regard to the longer term—if it were even appropriate to think of time in terms of length.

"We'd better be making a move, then, Marie," Denise said. "If we leave it any longer the traffic on the 127 will be horrendous."

Already? Corcoran thought. *But we haven't even said hello, not properly.* And he found himself in a state of utter confusion, knowing that his old self wouldn't have been in the least concerned about a social occasion being cut short, and would probably have been relieved. He could sense the temptation of that old, familiar pattern of thought . . . but he could also feel the determination that the new man forged aboard Olympus Five had cultivated, and he felt profoundly let down by Denise, who had held out the tantalizing prospect, during their recent on-screen conversations, of something resembling what old-style newts would doubtless have considered to be a "normal sibling relationship."

Denise stood up as she spoke, and Marie MacLaughlin stood up too. This time, she did offer her hand to be shaken, apparently still looking for some symbolic sealing of a pact. At least, Corcoran thought, it wasn't a pact with the Devil.

After a moment's hesitation, he took the proffered hand, and shook it with what he hoped was sufficient firmness.

Denise insisted on kissing him again. She had a license for it, and she seemed to be feeling pleased with herself, because the mission she had undertaken on her friend's behalf had not failed—yet.

"Thanks, Zeph," she whispered—although the whisper could hardly have been inaudible to others, given that all four of them were still standing around a relatively narrow table. "It really is good to see you again, safe and sound. We'll catch up properly, I promise—soon."

Safe? Corcoran couldn't help thinking. *Sound? Soon?*

But why shouldn't she think him safe and sound? And why shouldn't he? But what did "soon" mean?

"I have to ask, though," Denise added, loudly, obviously addressing Marie MacLaughlin as well as him, "what's Chris Kemmering really like? Surely he can't be the artificial PR puppet he seems to be in webcasts?"

"No, he's not," said Corcoran, automatically. "He was a really good captain—monumentally efficient, and expert in maintaining the spirit of the crew. We got on very well. I liked him."

"There you are," said Denise, this time addressing the chaplain directly. "Even Zeph's under his spell, a victim of hero-worship. That's the ultimate test of indomitable charm."

"That's a bit harsh, Nise!" Corcoran protested. "It's not a question of spells, charms or hero-worship. When he's not performing for the cameras he's all business, and very efficient."

"And you really did get on very well with him?"

"Yes. Do you really find that so implausible?"

The sense of injury must have been evident in his voice.

"Only joking, Zeph," she said. "It's just that . . . well, Captain Kemmering has become something of a worldwide joke these last few weeks. I'll explain it to you next time I see you." She glanced sideways as she said it at her mother, as if the joke were something that she couldn't explain in Mrs. Corcoran's presence.

Corcoran couldn't begin to imagine what she meant, but he thought it a shame, if it were really true. He really did like Chris Kemmering, and the American really wasn't the "PR puppet" that his job had forced him to be when momentary celebrity status had been thrust upon him after the return of the ship, even though he'd performed that task just as efficiently as all the others required of him during the mission.

When Denise and her guest had gone, the first thing his mother said was: "She seems like a nice girl."

Corcoran experienced a slight shock. "My God," he said. "You don't think she's trying to *fix me* up, do you? With a *vicar?*" He knew that he was failing his normal standards of pedantry, because he knew perfectly well that a vicar was an incumbent of a parish, and Marie MacLaughlin was merely attached to a college Chaplaincy, but he overlooked the laxity.

"Don't be silly, Zeph," his mother said. "You know that Denise wouldn't do anything like that."

Do I? he thought. His mother had made feeble efforts in that direction once, and would have been perfectly willing to recruit Denise's assistance in those days. But he decided, on reflection, that it was extremely unlikely. Even if Denise had taken the view that it would do him good to have some sort of sexual relationship, she would surely never have dreamed of inflicting him on one of her friends.

Anyway, he was over that particular existential hurdle now. It was a long way to Jupiter and back, and the extreme tedium of space flight had been conducive to intimacies that would probably never have broken through the barriers of his inhibition on the surface of Earth.

In any case, it seemed that that wasn't the question toward which his mother had been groping, in her tentative fashion. "You don't think she and Denise . . . ?" she followed up.

"Don't be silly, yourself," Corcoran retorted, even though the idea had been the first to cross his own mind. "The Reverend is no more interested in Denise than she is in me, even though Denise is much prettier. She seems very focused on her . . . vocation."

"But she's C-of-E," his mother pointed out. "She's not a nun, is she?"

Corcoran did not bother to call attention to the *non sequitur.*

"No," Corcoran agreed. "But that doesn't necessarily make her a lesbian sex-maniac."

"Oh, Zeph!" his mother protested. "What are you like?"

What indeed? thought Corcoran, although he knew full well that he wasn't really entitled to think that he had had a hard day simply because he had been stared at by a precocious kid, kissed by his sister and grilled by a C-of-E clergywoman who probably wasn't a lesbian sex-maniac. He was out of rehab now, and had to cope with the real world again: its gravity, its air, its space and its people, and he had to take the rough with the smooth.

"Are you still in touch with Captain Kemmering?" his mother asked then—which seemed to Corcoran to be a peculiar question, even though his former shipmate had been a topic of conversation only a few minutes before.

"I have his phone number," he confirmed, warily. "He was the first to be transferred home out of Greenland, so I haven't actually seen or spoken to him for the best part of a month, but you can't spend seven years in a tin can with thirteen people without forming a special bond. I suspect we all regard one another as still being *in touch* . . . although, after seven years' close confinement in a tin can, I don't suppose any of us feels any urgency about getting together for a drink and a chat. I'm sure the Captain and I will be in touch again . . . but I don't know when. Why—do you want me to introduce him to Denise?"

"Certainly not," his mother replied, as if mysteriously offended by the suggestion.

Corcoran shook his head. Thus far, his readaptation to everyday life in England wasn't going very well. Even his mother was still a puzzle to him. It obviously wasn't going to be as easy to be a new man as he had naively hoped. He had a growing suspicion that he was really going to miss Olympus Five, and that he might soon be hoping desperately that the ISA might consider him seriously for future space missions.

If only he had managed to get along with the cloud-whales as well he had with the Dancing Rats. . .

III

Walter Halleck looked a good deal older, fatter and considerably more haggard than when Corcoran had last seen him, seven years before. Halleck had never been one to go in for keeping fit, let alone cosmetic somatics; he lived in his head, and was proud of it. He had no objection to being instantly identifiable as a great man of science, whose brand of sanity was not that of the common run of humankind. He seemed to be wearing his fifty-some years proudly, and probably thought that his gray hairs made him look more dignified.

"Thanks for coming, Corcoran," the physicist said, sounding genuinely relieved that Corcoran had actually kept the appointment. "How are you feeling, now that you're back from the wilderness?"

"Very well," Corcoran said, blandly. "But Greenland isn't a wilderness. Since the glaciers melted it's a green and pleasant land, and it's undergoing an economic boom, thanks to all the refugees resettled there. The ground's a little unstable, in spite of the adherent effect of the permafrost, but the tremors are very minor."

"You obviously liked it," Halleck sniped, "since you were in no hurry to get back."

"Not my choice," Corcoran assured him. "I was still under contract to the Space Agency until I was officially out of rehab, and they were insistent on carrying out the debriefing there. As you can imagine, my debriefing was a lot more complicated than my colleagues'."

"I can," said Halleck, dryly, who had spent a great deal of time and effort "debriefing" Corcoran back in the hectic days when they had been pioneering the far future.

"I got the impression that they'd have liked to keep me under wraps even longer," Corcoran said, "even though we really had run out of conversation on the subject of the cloud-whales."

"About which you still can't talk to me?"

"I've signed a confidentiality agreement," Corcoran said, and smiled. Between the two of them, it was practically a joke.

"Apart from what your confidentiality agreement forbids you to talk about, how was Jupiter?" Halleck asked, presumably trying in his inexpert fashion to break the ice that remained between them, even after seven years and numerous on-screen communications.

"Dark," said Corcoran. "Slow. Big. Cloudy."

"Stormy?" Halleck prompted, pretending that it was a game.

"Sometimes."

"And cold?"

"The temperature was very low," Corcoran confirmed, "but it didn't feel cold. Surrogates don't have nerves capable of transmitting sensations of that kind to their hosts." Halleck knew that, of course, but Corcoran wanted to demonstrate that he could play games too, and pedantry was one of his favorites.

"You felt quite comfortable with the surrogates, then? Even in an alien atmosphere?"

"The atmospheres in which the future generations exist isn't identical to the one we live in—or did, until we fucked it up," Corcoran pointed out.

"No, but it's still fundamentally an oxygen-nitrogen mix, with impurities. The Jovian atmosphere is basically solar: hydrogen-helium with trace compounds. That must make a difference."

"Yes, but maybe not as much as you'd think, in terms of how it feels. Again, the surrogates aren't kitted out to be chemically sensitive. They take the Jovian atmosphere for granted, much as we take ours—or did before we . . . etc. The big difference, in terms of the host's sensations, is temporal."

"But you were in tight orbit. The signal lag can't have been more than a second or two."

"A second or two is very tangible when you're trying to react to the environment, let alone trying to communicate with entities that might or might not be sufficiently sentient and intelligent to respond. I shouldn't exaggerate, though. It's a big, slow planet, and that helps to adapt to the lag problems."

"And the moons?"

"Not uninteresting, although Ganymede became tedious after we'd been there for a couple of months. Very drab."

"But you had solid physical presence, in the planetary atmosphere and on the moons," Halleck said. "The ghosts are physical too, of course, but it's not the same, is it? That solid presence must have been something to appreciate." There was no enthusiasm in the observation. Halleck wasn't a man to appreciate solid physical presence, actual or surrogate.

Halleck was fishing for something, Corcoran knew, but he couldn't find it in his heart to hold it against the physicist. It was just the nature of the beast. Halleck was an angler, and would never be anything else. He had been fishing for Corcoran ever since the Jupiter mission touched down, and even though Corcoran was now in his office, he hadn't landed him yet, and wasn't even sure that he had taken the bait. He wasn't hurrying, because he thought that time was on his side now that Corcoran was sitting in front of him, but he was still anxious to get the job done—to get the hook firmly embedded in Corcoran's gullet, and reel him in.

"Solid physical presence is overrated," Corcoran said, mildly, although he didn't really care whether the remark struck a chord or not.

"Especially in the Jovian atmosphere, where the native life-forms are vaporous, smoky or aerosol," Halleck agreed, although he could only speak hypothetically. "To them, our surrogate fish must have seemed utterly bizarre. When human biotech advances to the point of building surrogates of the same type and texture as the cloud-whales, someone like you might be able to have a real conversation with them. Until then . . . well, you can't tell me, but I suspect that I know exactly how it is. There's still a lot of data for the computers to analyze, but how many needles there are in the haystack, and whether you can find them . . .

"It's the same here, of course. We're still getting data-dumps from the Dancing Rats, although they seem to have got distinctly snotty since you left, even when we use human registers instead of AIs—but the budget starvation has slowed down our analysis as well as spacing out the shots. Things have really gone to hell since you left, Corcoran. I don't mind telling you . . ."

Corcoran let him ramble on, although he'd heard the plaints before, more than once. In fact, when he'd made his own remark, he hadn't been thinking about the giants he'd manipulated by means of his expert telepresence in the depths of Jovian atmosphere, which he'd always thought of as birds rather than fish, or the walkers he'd paraded around the desolate landscape of Ganymede, or the divers he'd employed in the liquid cores of the ice-moons. Nor had he been talking about himself, given that he really was fully tuned-up for quotidian Earthly existence. He had been thinking about the "fresh air" that he had unwisely left the flat in order to savor on Marine Parade, the infinitely varied foodstuffs, punctuated by "treats" with which his mother insisted on plying him, the pavements and the fumes, and the estuary itself, with its acres of mud when the tide was out, the ragged trees on the slope down to the marina, and its shabby yachts. And that was the nice part. As for London, even the carefully "Restored" parts . . .

The Rats are right, Corcoran thought, while Halleck went through his whining litany. *Even though we've cleaned up our act a little since the Crash . . . the first phase of the Crash . . . we're still the dirty monkeys, the first generation, the ones who got it all wrong, the slapdash clowns.*

He still wondered, sometimes, what the Megaplants thought of the Mammal and Invert generations, but the Plants had stretched his supposed empathy with the unhuman to the limit, and perhaps beyond. He was still convinced that they really had been aware of the presence of the ghosts projected by the Sling, but they hadn't really shown signs of that awareness capable of convincing a skeptical investigator. All of his missions to the world of the fifth and sixth generations had been look and learn—good practice for Jupiter and Ganymede, in a way, but by no means as much fun as jigging with the Dancing Rats or semaphoring with the antenna-waving Inverts.

Bringing his attention back to Halleck's account of his own woes he picked up mention of the term "progress," in the context of the difficulty of making it.

"We can still make progress," Corcoran said, trying to be upbeat. "In spite of everything, including the impending Day of Judgment, we can still make further progress with the Jovians, and the future generations—even the Megaplants. We're not done yet, and we're not going to throw in the towel while we still have breath in our lungs and cash in the bank."

"I'm very glad to hear you say that," said Halleck—who was, of course, following his own train of thought, "because that's exactly what I want to do. Now that the ISA has relaxed its claws, I need you here, Corcoran. I know I've told you that on-screen, but I wasn't able to tell you exactly how badly I need you. We both know that nobody else can hold a candle to you. You're ready and willing to start right away, I hope?"

Corcoran didn't thank his former employer for the compliment. "I'm not sure yet that I want to start," he replied, feeling compelled at least to pretend that the new man he was could strike a hard bargain. "I have seven years' back pay in the bank. I can go anywhere I want, do anything I want. I don't need a job—not right away, at any rate."

Halleck's eyes narrowed, but he didn't lose his self-confidence. He obviously thought that he knew his man. He obviously thought, too, that he had maggots enough in his bait-tin to overcome any mere wriggling on his star temponaut's part.

"Where are you staying?" Halleck asked, suddenly.

"With my mother, for the moment, until I decide where to go next."

Halleck opened his desk drawer and pulled out a key ring with two keys attached. He dangled them from his right forefinger.

"First floor flat in Kensington," he said. "Fifty yards from the Gardens, and within easy walking distance of the Institute. Fully furnished. It's yours for as long as you want it. You'd have to be a billionaire to get a better one."

Corcoran was impressed, but he didn't reach out to take the keys. "My sister works at Imperial," he commented, in a neutral tone.

Halleck took it the wrong way. "She knows you—she isn't going to be dropping round every five minutes, or asking to borrow it for her extra-curricular sexual adventures."

"She's my sister," Corcoran observed. "She has a license for dropping in, and she's not above using it."

"I met your sister back in the day," Halleck reminded him. "She struck me as a perfectly reasonable human being. She isn't someone from whom you need to hide. I know I can't tempt you with money, so this is the only bribe I have to hand, but if you want me to get you a flat somewhere else, just name the place. I'll take care of everything. I figure you're worth it."

Corcoran was tempted to make some smart remark about Halleck being good at figuring, being the smartest mathematician in the world, at least in his own estimation—and he was slightly tempted, too, to blow him off completely, just to have the small satisfaction of throwing his current calculation into confusion. One of the side-effects of his current state of mind, after the long journey home, much of it spent in virtual reality because the real reality of space travel was distinctly tedious, was that he couldn't bring himself to give a damn about flats in Kensington with a view of the Gardens and the Palace . . . but he knew that Halleck was lying about not having any other lures to set out.

"What is it that you need me to do?" he said. "When I let the ISA poach me, I really did think that it was a good time to move on. The Board were considering suspending the use of human registers completely, and if they'd reached that decision, I'd have been out of a job anyway."

"I would never have let them do that."

"I wasn't convinced that you had the power to stop them. You were the resident genius, not the holder of the purse-strings. There were people on that Board that regarded you as a problem, not a golden goose—and they gave me the definite impression that they thought the same about me."

"They were a bunch of clowns."

"But they were running the show."

"Bullshit. They had delusions of grandeur even greater than their delusions of competence. Anyway, they're out of the picture now. They still exist, but they're utterly toothless."

"Really? Who's running the show now then?"

"I am," said Halleck, flatly—but Corcoran could tell that it wasn't true. Even thought he wasn't supposed to be able to read people, and Halleck wasn't supposed to be able to lie, he knew that Halleck's delusions of control were just that. But it still left open the question of who might actually be running the show . . . and why.

"To tell the truth, Walter," Corcoran said, "I wasn't at all sure that the skeptics on the Board were wrong. We'd reached the limit, after all, with the sixth generation. There was nothing left to do but repeat and retrench—and from a personal point of view, I thought I'd reached my limit. I thought I'd done what I could, even with the Rats and the Inverts. I thought that the Board members who were arguing that time travel ought to be work for AIs henceforth had a point."

"You were depressed," Halleck said. "You weren't thinking straight. And the ISA dangled the carrot of the cloud-whales. I was angry at the time, but I understand now. Anyway, it's water under the bridge, and you're back now."

"But you have got by without me for seven years," Corcoran pointed out. "The project is still going, still producing data—faster than you can analyze it apparently, where the Rats and Inverts are concerned. I can't help worrying that you're overestimating me a little, expecting more from me than I'm actually capable of delivering. Your AIs must have improved a great deal over the last seven years. I'm really not sure that I have any real advantage over them."

"I'm sure," Halleck said, with conviction. "AIs are brilliant in their own way, but fundamentally stupid in others: the ultimate *idiots savants.* You can put machine minds through a million generations of natural selection in a matter of months—days, now—but if you start with dumb inorganics you end up with dumb inorganics, however supersmart and supersane they may be. It took me a long time to talk the Board round, but I did, even in your absence. We resumed using human registers long ago—but they're not you, Corcoran, and the more we used them the more obvious it became that you really were unique. The ISA's advisers realized that too. Are you really trying to convince me that you're corroded by self-doubt? That's not the Corcoran I knew . . . he was an arrogant bastard, just like me."

"I'll take that as a compliment," Corcoran said, blandly, "although I know people who'd shudder at the comparison. None of my replacements could step into my shoes, then? They didn't live up to your hopes?"

"Not by a long chalk. They didn't even live up to my expectations, which were modest to begin with. I really do need you, Corcoran. Otherwise . . ."

He left it there, although it wasn't obvious to Corcoran what inference he was supposed to take. Otherwise, the project was doomed? But why? It was still bearing fruit, and if the Institute's Board had been rendered toothless, someone must have inserted cash over whose flow they had no control, so someone obviously had confidence in it. Surely that confidence couldn't be dependent on his re-recruitment. Or could it?

Whatever the "otherwise" threatened was, however, Corcoran was well aware of the responsibility that Halleck was trying to load on to his shoulders. But if he couldn't measure up to the hopes of his new employers either . . .

"Do you really think I might be able to make some headway with the Megaplants second time around?" he asked.

Halleck put his hand in the drawer again and pulled out a piece of paper.

"Sign it," he said, bluntly.

Corcoran scanned it. It was a standard confidentiality agreement. "I haven't agreed to take the job yet," he pointed out.

"I know. And in order to convince you that you have to take it, I need to tell you something that I can't tell you unless you sign the confidentiality agreement. So just sign it, and I'll tell you the bottom line—why I need you and you need me."

Corcoran shrugged. He didn't mind signing confidentiality agreements—quite the contrary, in fact. He signed the piece of paper with the pen that Halleck held out to him.

Halleck put it back in the drawer, and didn't even wait to be asked the question.

"I think we might have tuned in to the seventh generation," he said.

IV

There had been a time in Corcoran's life when that affirmation would have made him sit bolt upright with shock and caused his mind to boggle, and then some. He looked exactly the same now as he had in those days—people who went into space had no alternative but to resort to drastic somatic engineering, and the cosmetic modifications came with the package—but he was a great deal older inside, and a great deal older subjectively than mere years could make him. He considered himself, in any case, to be immune to the psychological effects of mere years; the Sling had hurled him across billions of them. The long haul out to Jupiter and back, and steering the birds in the long glides into the Jovian atmosphere, had probably corroded his mind's capacity to boggle, but he preferred to think of his present unshockability as an internal evolution, a kind of growing up . . . or at least sideways.

He consented, however, to nod his head as a tokenistic acknowledgement of astonishment. "You told me seven years ago that was impossible," he reminded Halleck, mildly. "You told me that we'd gone right up to the margin where the Sun was getting sick, ready to erupt and turn into a red giant, scorching and then swallowing up the Earth in the process. If you'd been able to tune the Sling with sufficient accuracy, you'd have sent my ghost out to watch it happen, but witnessed or not, it was bound to happen. No more Earth, no seventh generation. You were quite definite about it."

Halleck shifted uncomfortably in his chair. He didn't like making mistakes, and he certainly didn't like admitting that he'd made one. If he'd had a short-range dirigible time machine instead of the wayward Sling he'd probably have spent his life editing his life and twisting his existence into paradoxical knots in which he was always right.

"Either we underestimated the secondary plant-descendants—which wouldn't have been difficult, given that they wouldn't let us get the slightest taste of their fruit—or someone else intervened," the physicist told him. "In matters of Coincidence, we're in the infancy of the science. The sun will turn red giant, bang on schedule, give or take a few hundred million years, but the Earth won't be swallowed up. It will undergo an orbital adjustment. It will survive—and, apparently, thrive."

An "orbital adjustment," Corcoran thought. As simple as that—not even a tacit exclamation mark. Someone or something will move the Earth, so that it won't be swallowed up when the sun blows up into a giant. Maybe life will have to lie dormant for a while, waiting out the upheaval—the pupation of the sixth generation, if it makes any sense to talk about plants pupating—but once the big red sun has stabilized, springtime will come around again. Out will pop the seventh generation. The third Megaplant generation, presumably . . . if it still makes any sense to talk about plants. The third plant-descended generation, to be pedantic.

Except, of course, that it couldn't be as simple as that from the viewpoint of first-generation anglers, because Halleck, who had something of a reputation as a pedant himself, had only said that he "thought" he "might have" tuned in to the seventh generation—which implied doubt, which implied other possibilities. The "someone" or "something" that had moved the Earth to a new orbit might not have been the descendants of the climax community of the sixth generation but someone or something else. Obviously, the AIs inserted into the new ghosts that Halleck had contrived had not been able to bring back much in the way of useful inferences, and whatever images the ghosts had been able to form must have been enigmatic as well as blurred.

Corcoran was struck by a sudden idea. "Before I left," he said, "it seemed to me that the Dancing Rats and the talkative Inverts both had some awareness of the future generations even before I gave them the news that they were eventually due to be replaced by the Invert generations, and then the Megaplant generations. We discussed it, and hypothesized that at least one of the extra senses that the future generations have might be connected to Coincidence phenomena—that even though they don't seem to have Sling technology *per se*, they do have some kind of pseudosensory window into the future. So, if the Dancing Rats have been dumping data on you for seven years, they must have given you some indication of the extent and shape of their future awareness. Do they know about a seventh generation? And if so, what do they know?"

"We don't know," said Halleck, bluntly. "Maybe there's something in the data they've dumped and maybe there isn't, but you know what a difficult exercise it is trying to decipher that grimoire. We've certainly tried to ask, but . . . we'll, as I say, they've become a trifle snotty of late. They miss you, Corcoran. If you were to ask . . . but hopefully, that won't be necessary. Hopefully, we can find out for ourselves . . . or you can."

Again, Corcoran felt the weight of the responsibility that Halleck was so enthusiastic to load on to his shoulders . . . but he also felt the attraction of the lure, the magnetism of the mystery.

"What makes you think that I'll be any more effective in dealing with the seventh generation than I was with the fifth and sixth?" Corcoran asked, while his eyes wandered mechanically around Halleck's office, from the big screen above the desk to the various hand-held devices on the shelves—Halleck wasn't a man to send his dead electronics to Silicon Hell—to the tokenistic pictures adding "decoration" to the white-emulsioned wall: a Klimt nude and an old photograph of his daughter, aged seven. Ever faithful to the cliché of the scientist with asp tendencies, Halleck had learned to hate both his ex-wives, but he still adored his daughter, who was five years older than Denise and now had two kids of her own—both boys, and hence, in Halleck's sexist view, potential mathematicians of genius.

"I don't think that you were ineffective in dealing with the Megaplants, in spite of the limitations," Halleck said. "I remember our old discussions about them quite fondly, and although we scrupulously restricted ourselves to hypothetical elaborations, I've since come to believe that your intuitions were sound—perhaps even more so than you dared to think yourself, at the time. In any case, I'm by no means certain that the seventh generation is a third plant-descended generation. I won't say that I favor the extraterrestrial hypothesis, because that would be scientifically irresponsible, but I'm certainly prepared to take it seriously. I think we could have some very intriguing discussions based on what you discover or intuit—in fact, I think we might be able to begin those discussions while you're still in the Sling—live, as it were."

"You've managed to fix up some kind of substitute voice-link allowing you to maintain a dialogue with a human register?"

"I think so. It's untested, but in theory, it ought to work. I've never stopped moving forward, you see, in spite of all the difficulties. Now you're back . . . the old team . . . things will go further and faster."

Halleck's desperation was naked, but Corcoran couldn't measure its exact nature. Evidently, however, the physicist thought of the possible contact with the seventh generation as a final roll of the dice of fate, so far as the Project and his personal future—or his legacy—were concerned.

"And of what practical relevance do you think it might be if the seventh generation turn out to be extraterrestrial colonists, who've politely waited to take over the Earth until its own generations were finished with it?"

"Who can tell?" said Halleck. "But it's not impossible that they might be even more like us than the Dancing Rats, and even more communicative."

"If that's the carrot that you've dangled for your new investors, it's one hell of a long shot," Corcoran observed, dubiously.

"I haven't dangled any dodgy carrots," Halleck assured him. "They came to us . . . to the Institute, that is. I haven't even met them, so you can't accuse me of any kind of enticement. They have faith . . . in the Sling, in me, and in you."

"But who are they?"

Halleck looked slightly embarrassed. "I can't tell you," he said.

Obviously, the physicist had signed yet another confidentiality agreement—but Corcoran couldn't help wondering whether he even knew.

"You say they have faith in me?" he said. "Does that mean that their continued funding of the project is conditional on my re-recruitment?"

Halleck's embarrassment increased. "Nobody's said that to me," he said. Corcoran took that to mean exactly what it said, and nothing more.

"Look, Corcoran," Halleck said. "You can understand my position. As I say, I don't believe that you failed with the Megaplants. It's not your fault that the interface didn't attract their attention, or that they chose to ignore it if it did, and your insights were valuable regardless. Anyway, that doesn't matter; whatever we're dealing with now is an entirely unknown quantity. Quite frankly, the machines haven't brought back anything worth a damn. You might. You have the contacts, the experience, the intuition and the empathy. If you hadn't already been on your way home when we got the touch, I'd have sent word all the way to Jupiter begging you to come back. You know how hard I tried to get through to you while you were in rehab, and you can see how hard I'm trying now. I'm prepared to beg now, if that's what you want. Please, Corcoran. I need you."

Corcoran wasn't surprised that Halleck was still addressing him by his surname, even while telling him that he was prepared to get down on his knees and beg, and even though Corcoran often addressed him as "Walter." It would have rung false if Halleck had called him Zephaniah, let alone "Zeph." Halleck wasn't the kind of person who used first names in his speech or his thinking; for him, names were just labels, and the only time a surname was inadequate to the job was when he had to distinguish between two people with the same one. He was *able* to use first names, or even nicknames, when he thought it useful or necessary to bait a hook, just as he was *able* to use flattery, but when he did so it was always conspicuously artificial, and always rang horribly false. There was nothing intuitive or empathetic about Halleck. Halleck was a certified mathematical genius, but one reason that he hated AIs was that he was very nearly as rigid in his thinking as they tended to be, and just as dumb, in his own saccharine supersane way. That was why he thought that he was buttering Corcoran up by crediting him with intuition and empathy as well as experience and his biotech wiring.

Corcoran reached up, reflexively, to scratch the back of his neck, although his contacts weren't itching. They never itched, in any literal sense—but still, even after all this time, they were an alien presence in his flesh, a bridge allowing his brain to link up with machines, by means of direct neuronal connection or wireless. Thanks to them, he was capable of operating all models of surrogates by means of telepresence: humanoid surrogates, non-humanoid material surrogates, and even ghosts, which were mere agents of Coincidence, refracted through time. With regard to temporal ghosts, he was the ace, the expert, the artist.

In fact, Corcoran liked to think that he was more than an expert, perhaps even more than an artist, and he was glad of Halleck's endorsement of that estimation, even though Halleck had no appreciation of art and a purely statistical appreciation of expertise.

Although his contacts never itched in any material sense, however, the impulse to scratch them was still there in Corcoran's subliminal consciousness, as if they were somehow afflicted by the ghost of an itch . . . or maybe the intuition of an itch.

"Okay, Walter," said Corcoran, blandly. "I'm on board. Why not?"

Halleck blinked, probably not because Corcoran had taken the job, but because he'd said "Why not?" Devoid of empathy as he might be, Halleck had known Corcoran well enough back in the heyday of Sling to know that he had been the kind of man to tabulate reasons pro and con, with a modicum of sagacity, enthusiasm and ambition, but never the kind of man to do something merely because he wasn't doing anything else.

But Corcoran had been to outer space since then, and it really had been very dark inside the atmosphere of Jupiter—and even though his surrogates hadn't been equipped to feel the intense cold, the ghost of the chill had leaked into his bones and brain alike. Corcoran was a new man now.

As soon as he had blinked, though, Halleck sighed again, with relief.

"Can you report for work tomorrow?" he asked, immediately.

"When can I move into the Kensington flat?" Corcoran counted.

"This afternoon, if you like."

"I have to pack first. I don't have much, but what I have is at Mum's, and she won't want me just dashing in and dashing out again. I owe her the evening, at least—she is my mother. I can move in tomorrow morning, but I'd rather not have to report for work instantly."

"Fine—I'll even give you the afternoon to settle in, stock the fridge and do any other necessary shopping. You've been away a long time; there are bound to be lots of things you need."

Halleck handed him the keys to the flat and two slips of paper, one bearing the address and the other the security code for the main door. "Burn that after memorizing. Report at nine Thursday morning. Your old salary, adjusted for inflation, plus fifteen per cent?"

"Fine."

"You'll have to train on the new equipment, and make all the necessary adaptations, but that shouldn't take long. I'll bring you up to date personally with a summary of the last seven years' findings, and brief you fully on the information we have regarding the new target. We should be able to power up the Sling for an initial test run in a matter of days—you can go to see the Rats first, to renew your old acquaintance. We'll decide then what the next step should be, but at present I'm thinking in terms of at least one more test run, to Invert world. There's a lot of fine tuning to be done and it's been seven years. We have to take things one step at a time, to make sure we get it right, but I've no intention of dragging it out. Let's just hope there are no hitches. Okay?"

"Fine."

"What's your number?"

"I haven't had a chance to buy a new phone yet."

Halleck reached into his magic drawer again and pulled out a phone, still in its shrink-wrap. "It's pre-paid for three months in advance. After that, it's easy enough to top it up. The protocols have only changed slightly in the last seven years." He cracked the plastic wrap and switched the phone on. As soon as he got a display on the screen he made a note of the number. Then he handed it over.

Corcoran looked at it briefly, and then slipped it into his pocket.

"Do you need a tablet as well?" Halleck asked.

Corcoran couldn't help glancing at the drawer again, wondering what else might be hauled out if he confessed a lack, but he shook his head. "Had to get one the day I landed," he said. "Wouldn't have survived rehab otherwise. It was gratis, though— I'm continually astonished by the willingness of people to give me things for free now that I'm a little bit famous. I left it at Mum's, but I'll send you an email as soon as I get back, and you can send me the hook-up information to integrate it into your network."

"You left your tablet at the flat? You survived the train journey without it?"

"I've been in space for seven years," Corcoran reminded him. "After seven years locked in a tin can, real reality is all new to me again. I won't need distraction from it for at least a week—maybe two."

Halleck stared at him, as if wondering whether he was joking. "You've changed," he said.

"Everybody changes," Corcoran told him. "Even people with minds like ours. Nothing stays the same."

"There you go," said Halleck. "Corcoran waxing philosophical. I never thought I'd see the day."

"Your memory is letting you down. I was always capable of philosophizing. It's not five minutes since you were getting nostalgic about our old hypothetical debates about the Megaplant noösphere. But you're right—seven years of space travel does seem to bring it out. Nothing like nothingness to make latent seeds of thought germinate."

"Well, don't let it get out of hand. I need the Corcoran I used to know and trust. I need the temponaut, not the space traveler, and I need him at the very top of his game. This one really is the last throw—for both of us. This is the crown of all our endeavors; there won't be anything to cap it."

Corcoran sketched a thin smile. This was the man who was complaining about his having caught a mild case of philosophy? The words "pot" and "kettle" came to mind.

"I'll see you the day after tomorrow, then," he said, getting to his feet. He paused before going to the door. "You really don't have any idea who's funding this, do you?" he asked, curiously.

"I can't tell you that."

Corcoran shook his head. "Do you even care?"

"No. I just work here. My concern is the Sling—and you. See you Thursday, then." A slight frown creased Halleck's age-wrinkled forehead, exaggerating the hint of gray in his bushy eyebrows. "I knew I could count on you, Corcoran," he said.

50

He was trying to be affable, presumably because he thought he ought to make the effort. Seven years ago, Corcoran suspected, Halleck wouldn't have thought that—but he had changed too; time had had its effect, even though he was the kind of old dog who wasn't supposed to be able to learn new tricks. Halleck had thought he ought to make an effort to be polite; he probably hadn't felt any inclination, and he probably didn't really understand what it was that he was doing, but his long, if desultory, studies of the mysteries of human social life had given him a crude appreciation of the mechanisms of propriety, if not their rationale.

Shit, thought Corcoran. *He's right—this philosphizing is getting out of hand.*

He sighed, and put out his hand. Halleck took it and shook it. That was one of the few social routines with which the physicist felt almost comfortable. "It's good to see you again, Walter," Corcoran said, although it was sailing rather close to the mendacious wind. "We are old friends, after all."

Halleck smiled at that. He had always seemed to like the idea that he might have friends, even if he probably didn't know what it ought to involve.

V

"Are you going back to work for Mr. Halleck?" Corcoran's mother asked, when he got back to the flat. She was making tea again. Even seven years ago, nobody had made tea any more except people of her generation, who still clung to the formalities that the first restabilized post-Crash generation had reinstituted, not because they were nostalgic for some imaginary pre-Crash English Golden Age, but because they had suffered from a collective Post-Traumatic Stress disorder that had made a need for formality and routine pathological. His mother had never quite got over that, Corcoran knew. He never criticized or tried to break any of her slightly eccentric habits; he knew that his job had always been, and still was, merely to drink the tea and eat the biscuits.

"Yes," he told her, waiting patiently to pick up the tray and carry it into the living room for her, for feigned politeness' sake rather than because she wasn't perfectly capable of doing it herself. "I start on Thursday, but I'll have to spend tomorrow moving into my new flat."

"What flat?" she asked, her face falling.

"The Institute's letting me use it. It's handy for the labs, and only a short walk from Imperial. Denise will be able to pop round after work if she wants to. I'll come back here to see you at weekends, if that's okay."

"Of course it's okay. This is your home." In fact, his mother's flat, designed for single occupancy, was a trifle crowded for two, but the widowed Mrs. Corcoran was appreciating the company, at least for the time being, and she must have known perfectly well that the likelihood of his coming to see her at the weekends on a regular basis was slim.

"You're lucky to be able to walk into a job so soon after getting back," she observed, probably meaning that he was lucky to be offered a job at all, in this day and age, when he'd only just left something called "rehab," especially at his age, when there were so many younger and better-educated people desperate to get on to the employment ladder. She knew that he was supposed to have unique talents, but she had never understood exactly what they were or why anyone would be willing to give him money to employ them. She was proud of him for being slightly famous, for being "the man who had been to Jupiter," but she put it all down to luck.

"Luck had nothing to do with it," Corcoran said, for form's sake, as he picked up the tea tray. "It was pure Coincidence."

"You know I don't understand jokes like that," she said, with a sigh, following him along the short corridor. "To me, coincidence is no different from luck. Why your friend had to go and name a new branch of mathematics after it is beyond me—it just confuses things. And as for all the stuff about elementary particles retaining relationships when separated . . . I just can't make head nor tail of it."

"To tell you the truth, Mum, neither can I," Corcoran said, putting the tray down again in the sitting room and taking a seat by the window, which was open to let in the supposedly fresh air. "When I left Earth seven years ago, rumor had it that there were only three people in the world who understood Coincidence Theory, but if you'd said that to Walter Halleck, he'd have taken offense and demanded to know who the other two were supposed to be."

"But *you* have to understand it," his mother said. She was his mother, after all; it was inevitable that she should overestimate his intellect, if not his ability to land a job. "You've been millions of years into the future," she added, blithely unaware of the *non sequitur*. The "been" was an overestimation too, although the "millions" was a drastic underestimation.

"No, I really don't have to understand it," he told her, with a slight sigh. "I just have to trust Walter to be able to get his calculations right. And the Sling isn't the kind of time machine that can actually *send* me, or anything material, into the future. As you say, it makes use of the fact that subatomic particles—or, rather, the underlying fields that produce them—are independent of time. In a sense, they're what *create* time. That allows machines that can set up vibrations in the here and now to generate resonance effects with the same field/particle systems at other times, and use that linkage to warp the fabric of space into a kind of lens capable of gathering a certain amount of information from transitions and collisions."

"There you are," his mother said, sipping her tea triumphantly. "You *do* understand it. It's all just gobbledegook to me—but I think I understand that you're not actually *going* into the future, just *seeing* into it through your lens."

Momentarily, Corcoran contemplated making an attempt to explain that the Sling's "lens" didn't even allow particles or radiation to "travel" through time, and didn't create any kind of net energy deficit or surplus either in present or future time, when the account books had to be settled, because it was always respectful of the sacred conservation laws, but that it nevertheless contrived, with the twisted ingenuity of an expert tax advisor, to permit a "register" in contact with the lens to obtain impressions Coincidentally from the interaction of its "surface" with both electromagnetic and sonic waves in the Resonant Nucleus. Having thought about it, however, he figured that it was neither necessary nor desirable to go into that kind of detail. Anyway, his mother was absolutely right. It *was* just gobbledegook.

"Didn't you say before you went off gallivanting in space that Mr. Halleck's project had finished?" his mother persisted. "That there was nowhere further to go because the sun was going to blow up, and that you couldn't talk to the smart plants anyway?"

"That was then," Corcoran told her. "This is now." He didn't add anything further. He had signed a confidentiality agreement.

On due reflection, however, while he sipped his tea, he realized that his mother was right. He *was* lucky that the Project was still going and that Walter Halleck still felt such an urgent need for him to be part of it. Any other man might have stopped fishing, having reached the point that the Sling program had reached seven years ago, but not Walter Halleck. Having mastered his Sling, more or less, that fat little David was never going to stop before he had hit Goliath smack on the head. And now, it appeared, he might have done exactly that. It seemed that the Earth had somehow acquired . . . *would* somehow acquire . . . a new lease of life, beyond the metamorphosis of the Sun. Somebody had moved it, apparently . . . *would* move it, billions of years in the future.

How?

He had no chance of understanding that.

Why?

That might be another matter.

"But you are going back, aren't you?" his mother said. "All the way?"

"Forward," Corcoran corrected. "But yes, all the way, it seems. As far as the Sling can hurl me."

"And it's dangerous, isn't it?"

"The equipment uses high energies," he said, "but no, it's not really dangerous. Because it's just Coincidence, nothing actually travels through time."

"You're just saying that," she said. "You wouldn't tell me even if it was dangerous, but you don't actually know, do you? You don't *know*."

Corcoran shrugged his shoulders. He could hardly affirm that he did know.

His mother shook her head. "You've only just got back!" she complained. "For seven years you've been riding in a spaceship with that weird engine that creates antimatter by God only knows what infernal trickery and then blows it up. And now you're off again, without even waiting a week."

"I worked for the Institute for five years before I went to the ISA," he reminded her. "I made hundreds of Slingshots without getting a scratch. I'd be taking a far greater risk commuting to London every day along the 127. Denise definitely takes a greater risk commuting from Kilburn to Kensington, and you're probably at greater risk of killing yourself slipping on the soap in the shower. There's never been a single fatal accident with the Sling in its entire history."

The old woman wasn't convinced. She had had little or no conception of what had been involved in going to Jupiter and participating in the exploration of its atmosphere and its satellites, even though Corcoran had tried to describe the various experiences to her in slightly more detailed terms than "dark" and "tedious." Her imagination wasn't as flexible as his, although it had a more highly developed visual component than Halleck's. She had even less conception of what was involved in Slingshots. He could hardly blame her for that. It was essentially mind-boggling, and he had signed confidentiality agreements that put a severe limit on the kinds of explanation that he could give her, even if her imagination had been able to make the effort.

"Well, I can't see the point," she said. "No matter how far you see into the future, it'll still be going backwards, won't it?"

Corcoran had tried to explain to the author of his being on more than one occasion that the future evolution of life on Earth, as revealed by the Sling, was a matter of progress, not of degeneration, but she couldn't or wouldn't see it that way. To her, the fact that the second generation of intelligent life would be descended from present-day rats, the third and fourth from present-day invertebrates of some kind, and the fifth and sixth from present-day plants, meant that the pinnacle of perfection represented by humankind had been passed—deservedly so, given the recklessness that had caused the Crash and the apparent imminent inevitability of its renewal—and that everything subsequent could only be a tragedy, a decline, a slide into oblivion.

She wasn't alone in that. The pedantic Halleck had never wanted the terms *rat, insect* and *plant* to be popularized with regard to their highly intelligent and scientifically sophisticated descendants, but he hadn't been able to stand against the bitter desire of the human public to diminish its eventual successors, and to remain in denial of the all-too-evident fact that those successors would, in fact, be smarter, saner and more scrupulous than mere dirty monkeys with delusions of grandeur could ever be.

Corcoran had sometimes wondered whether the plant-descended intelligences had never acknowledged his ghost's existence not because they were unaware of it, as Halleck had stubbornly insisted at one time—although he seemed to have modified his conviction somewhat—but simply because it was beneath their dignity. The Dancing Rats and the Inverts had been enthusiastic to establish and employ the minimal communication that Coincidence permitted, not least because they believed that it was they, not humans, who had established the Coincidental link, and that they were the anglers, not the fish. At any rate, they had been curious, as eager to obtain insights into the world of their remote forebears as their forebears were to haunt theirs Nor had the rat-descendants ever been openly contemptuous of the monkeys who had failed so dismally to make use of their hard-won intelligence as to have condemned themselves, and hundreds of thousands of other species, to ignominious extinction; in communication, they were always respectful, always glad to give credit for the science that humankind had managed to bequeath to its successors via its artifacts, saving them hundreds, if not thousands, of years of methodical groping.

Corcoran couldn't help pulling a face as he bit into his biscuit, which was sugar-coated and packed with shriveled imitation raisins. Nobody ate such things any more, apart from people of his mother's generation and the people they invited for tea. Synthesizers using the products of artificial photosynthesis automatically paid due respect to the principles of nutritional economy and balance—but while the market was still there, the product would continue to exist, and while the habit wouldn't die, neither would the market. That was the monkey way.

Corcoran looked out of the window, wondering whether there might be any Coincidental ghosts watching the road, marveling at the primitive nature of monkey transport—although, so far as Halleck had been able to tell this far, Slingshots were a one-way technology, which only worked forwards. If he was wrong, though, and there were Coincidental ghosts in the present, there was no way for any mere mortal to tell; detecting ghosts was every bit as difficult as Slinging them. Corcoran took that as a license to wonder. His imagination teased him with the idea that there might be plant-descended ghosts in the sloping field at that very moment, sending back transmissions that would allow their surrogate operators to feel a twinge of strange sentiment on contemplating a poppy, or a hawthorn hedgerow.

That was taking fancy a little too far, he decided; if the plant-descended generations had any familiarity with Coincidence Theory, and the use of senses based in Coincidence phenomena, neither of which seemed particularly unlikely, the use they made of them was likely to be far more subtle and sophisticated than the Slingshot's crude hurling and the contrivance of ghosts—and in any case, if Halleck's mathematics could be trusted, any such sense or usage was likely to be forward-looking, not backward-looking. Even the Megaplants might have to rely on a Sling like Halleck's to give them a viable link to the past.

But who could tell? Not a mere dirty monkey, in all likelihood, and certainly not a dirty monkey whose personal mathematical abilities didn't extend much beyond trigonometry.

"You're away with the fairies, again?" his mother pointed out, presumably thinking that she was being helpful in bringing him back again. She had always referred to his reveries in those terms, and when he had tried to explain to her, ten years ago, what riding the Slingshot was like, she had simply accommodated the notion to the same phrase. For her, half his life—the more important half—was lived "away with the fairies." Even the trip to Jupiter, in her estimation, was probably just one more excursion to Faerie, even if it had required a tin can to transport him.

"Yes, Mum," he replied, dutifully. "I was having tea with Titania—but hers isn't as good as yours, so I don't know why I bother." It wasn't a lie. Talking to one's mother, one could say anything one liked, and it was just humorous banter. Truth was neither here nor there.

"Nor do I," she said. "You should get out more."

"I can't. Ever since you spread the news around that I was here, little kids come and stare at me, and ask me impertinent questions."

"Oh, that's just Luke—don't mind him. I can have a word with Emily, if you like."

"No, I wouldn't want to get in kid into trouble. He can't help being a monster."

"No, he can't," his mother agreed. Corcoran imagined her adding: *any more than you could,* but she didn't say another word.

"Anyway," he said, "I'll be leaving tomorrow. I'll be living near Kensington Gardens—I can go for walks there. And there's no better place to be away with the fairies, if J. M. Barrie can be believed."

"When I used to say that you should get out more," she chided him, "I didn't mean away with the fairies—and I certainly didn't mean a million miles away . . . in your head or in the outer planets."

"Well, I'll only be in London, for a while. As I say, I'll come back to see you, and Denise will be right there to keep an eye on me. I'm sorry about drifting off just now, but I have lots to think about at the moment, thanks to Walter Halleck. And to take up the point you made before I drifted away, you really shouldn't think of further evolution in terms of 'going backwards.' The Megaplants really are very advanced, I'm convinced of it."

"A rose is a rose is a rose," she quoted, probably without the slightest idea where the quote originated, or what she actually meant by saying it in the context of the present discussion.

"True," he said, with a sigh.

And maybe, he thought, *we are entitled to doubt the notion of perpetual progress, in an evolutionary as well as a social sense, given that, in the fullness of time, entropy will bring everything to an ignominious conclusion. And maybe everything that happens in the meantime is just monkeys and rats dancing, insects twitching their antennae, and roses being roses being roses . . .*

"But are the aliens whales or clouds?" she asked, following her unsteady train of thought, "because I really don't see how they can be both." Her tone was strangely anxious.

Corcoran realized that the anxieties that his adventures had stirred up in her, and that the prospect of his future adventures were stirring up now, were real, even though she had no idea how to express them coherently.

"The idea of a life form that's not solid is a trifle odd," he admitted. "But Jupiter's a strange world—more like a cold sun than a planet. Everything there is strange."

"And now that we know that we're not alone," she said, "we have no idea what else might be out there, and how strange it might be, do we?"

Corcoran's mother obviously knew that the conventional wisdom, when she had been young, had been that humans *had* to be alone, according to the logic of the Fermi paradox. She knew, too, if only from popular reportage, that the Sling experiments had tended to support the view that whether we were alone or not, there didn't seem to be any clear evidence of extraterrestrial interference in future earthly affairs, but that hadn't set her mind at rest. Why should it? No one had ever quite believed, in their heart of hearts, that we were alone, whether they had an imagination flexible enough to grasp the true size of the universe or not, and one thing the Sling experiment certainly showed was that life was exceedingly variable and exceedingly ingenious. Everyone—or almost everyone—had suspected, or intuited, or even merely hoped, that other life forms *had* to be out there, even before the discovery of the cloud-whales. For one reason or another, the extraterrestrials didn't seem to be in a communicative mood, just like the plant-descended intelligences of the fifth and sixth generations of Earthly life, but that didn't mean that they weren't there . . . just that they weren't like dirty monkeys.

"No, Mum," Corcoran admitted. "We still have no idea. But with luck, we might yet find out."

"Luck," his mother countered, getting her own back, "has nothing to do with it. It's fate."

His pedantic instinct told him to contradict that, but he didn't get a chance. The wallscreen buzzed to indicate an incoming call. Corcoran got up and answered it. It was Marie MacLaughlin. She seemed glad to see him, evidently having feared that he would refuse to take the call.

"You promised to fix an appointment for an initial interview, Mr. Corcoran," she said.

"Promised" was a trifle strong, and "initial interview" a trifle presumptuous, but he let it pass.

"I'm moving into a new flat tomorrow," he said, in a neutral tone that he hoped might convey a hint of feigned apology. "I start work again at the Institute the following morning, so I fear . . ."

"Where's the flat?" she asked, bluntly.

He felt a slight sinking feeling. "Kensington," he admitted.

"You've rented a flat in Kensington?" she said, evidently amazed, although he wasn't entirely sure why.

"Not exactly," he said. "The Institute is letting me use it, while I'm working on the current project."

He half-expected her to ask him what the current project was, so that he could trot out the standard shield, but she caught him on the wrong foot again. "Are you free tomorrow evening?" she demanded.

Confused, he could not contrive anything less honest than: "Yes."

"What's the address?"

Still off-balance, he gave it to her.

"Seven o'clock," she said. "I'll be on time,"

He wondered if the chaplain had been coached by Denise on how best to handle her evasive brother. He found it difficult to believe that a Church of England chaplain would ever have been so assertive without prompting. He had no opportunity left to bring any further armor into play, though.

"All right," he said, weakly.

When the connection was broken he turned back to his mother. Back on home ground, she smiled with ironic malice. "She had you there, didn't she?" she observed.

"Well, I had agreed, in principle, to talk to her," Corcoran observed, feebly, thinking to himself that he really ought to have a stern word with Denise next time he saw her.

VI

By five o'clock Corcoran had finished distributing his meager existing belongings around the flat, and had taken delivery of his initial consignment of necessary supplies, including a couple of mixed cases of so-called wine, and the additional purchases that seemed most urgent. He was still negotiating a path through the unexpectedly tricky virtual world of shopping for things that lay on the margin between things he could not do without and things that, although not strictly necessary, would make life easier, when the doorbell rang again.

By now, fortunately, he had taken enough deliveries to have worked out how to get an image from the front door's spy-eye and how to operate the mechanism for opening the front door without actually leaving the flat and running downstairs, so it only took a few seconds to recognize Denise and let her in, and then a few more for her to climb the stairs and locate the door to the flat. He opened it before she arrived to save her the trouble of knocking.

"My God," she said, after taking a long look around. "I could hardly believe it when Marie told me, but it's actually true. You've joined the social elite. Do you know how much a place like this costs?"

"Yes," said Corcoran. He had looked it up.

"Right," said Denise, after a slight pause to see whether he was going to add anything further. "This is where, assuming that you aren't going to give me a hug, you invite me to sit down in one of those nice leather armchairs and offer me a drink, and I say that even though it's a little early I've had a hard day and could really use a glass of wine—but you know that, don't you, because the social cripple act you've been putting on since you reached puberty is mostly a sham?"

Corcoran was slightly startled. He had changed, but Denise was still Denise, evidently and although she'd been on her best behavior the day before because she was with company, she obviously felt free to revert to type now. He realized that she'd also been behaving slightly artificially during their seemingly intimate on-screen conversations because people always did behave artificially on-screen, because they knew that no electronic connection was really private, if anyone cared to hack the records. Even so, her attitude seemed more than a trifle disappointing.

"I have got some wine," he confirmed. "It arrived half an hour ago."

"I'll get it," she said. "Don't worry."

Somehow, although he hadn't shown her round, she seemed to know instinctively where the wine rack was, and found the glasses at the first attempt. The theory of modern household ergonomics evidently had no mysteries for her.

She unscrewed the cap of a bottle of synthetic claret, poured two glasses without consulting Corcoran, and brought them back into the room where he was waiting, uncertainly.

"Sit," she said.

He sat down in an armchair. She sat down on its twin, carefully positioned at a social distance that was polite without being intimate. Immediately, however, she leaned forward to reduce that distance.

"First of all," she said, "I owe you an apology. I could say that in unleashing Marie on you I was being cruel in order to be kind, but it wouldn't be true. She has a forceful personality, and she knows how to get her own way. I'm sure you'll be able to stonewall her, though, if that's what you want to do. She'll probably come at you hard, but she won't keep battering her head against a brick wall if you decide to play the immovable object. Will you forgive me?"

Corcoran realized that he had probably been wrong about Denise having coached Marie MacLaughlin before the previous day's phone call. Apparently, it was a matter of natural talent, or perhaps careful research. The archives of the web were doubtless full of advice on how to handle asps, if one could only be bothered to search for it.

"It's okay," he said. "No forgiveness necessary."

She looked relieved. "So you have changed," she said. "The Institute gave you this flat as a sweetener in order to entice you back, did they?"

"So it seems," he admitted.

"They must really believe in you—now. They must really regret having let the ISA poach you. Do you know what changed their minds?"

"No," said Corcoran.

"Would you like me to tell you?"

Corcoran raised an eyebrow. "Do you know?" he countered, surprised.

"Not for certain, but I can work it out. I can work out a great many things—have worked out a great many things, I mean, thanks to the all-pervasiveness of news and rumor, and a little scrupulous scientific logic. For instance, I know why you accepted the ISA's offer, even though the Institute, and Walter Halleck in particular, must have been utterly gobsmacked. Would you like me to tell you that?"

"Please do," Corcoran said, contriving a heavily ironic tone, as if he doubted her.

"I will, then. But first, I want you to know that I have good reason to be seriously angry with you. You've caused me some real inconvenience. In fact, you'd caused me a great deal of inconvenience even before you went away, and you'd doubtless have continued to do so even if you hadn't joined the Jupiter Mission, but that was the final straw. You don't owe me anything, just because we came out of the same womb and share half our genes, of course, but even though the act is mostly sham, I believe that you genuinely don't know what an awful inconvenience you've been. Am I right?"

"Well . . ." Corcoran prevaricated, but it took him too long to gather his thoughts, and Denise was already moving on. He noticed that she had already consumed half her glass of wine, whereas he had only taken one tiny sip. He wasn't sure how she had managed that, give than she had been doing all the talking. There was obviously a knack to it, but he couldn't imagine how or why she had cultivated it.

"I'm an evolutionary biologist," she stated, although that was hardly news. "I'm supposed to be an expert on how the ecosphere has developed over the last three billion years, able to explain all its mutations, the patterns of its diversification and apparent progress from the simple to the complex, from the inert to the relatively smart. I'd like to be thought competent, even respected, in my field. And I'm lucky, or at least I seem to be, because, by an outrageous several-billion-to-one coincidence, my big brother is the one person in the world who seems—and I emphasize the word *seems*—not only to have made the first ever breakthrough in the anticipation of the future evolution of the ecosphere, but, in a mere matter of years, while I was still finishing my PhD, has filled in the entire picture of that future evolution, from now until far more than three billion years in the future. That is what we in the business call a privileged resource.

"Now, some of my elders, and even one or two of my peers, don't believe a word of it. They think you're a fantasist, or a con man. Others think it's the greatest leap forward in human knowledge ever—and I mean *ever*. Mostly, they don't know. And who do you think they want to consult, if not for an expert opinion, at least for a little inside knowledge?"

Corcoran recognized the rhetorical question, but he felt an atypical desire to get a word in edgewise, so he said: "You."

"Exactly. Because I'm supposed to be privileged. I'm your sister. I'm supposed to know you. I suppose I do know you better than anyone else in the world, but that really isn't very well, is it? And everybody knows that I'm your sister, because, when you became briefly famous, or at least notorious in the days before Olympus Five set forth, your life became an open book. Everybody's life is, nowadays, thanks to the way the web automatically stores information, but it's only when people attract public attention that anyone ever bothers to read the damn book. So everybody knew that you were an asp, that you didn't like to be touched, that you had difficulty forming social relationships, that you were chronically shy, ridiculously obsessive, and all the other aspects of your personality that you exaggerate so carefully and so deliberately. But I'm your sister. I was still expected to have the inside track. So can you begin to imagine, Zeph, what an embarrassment it was to me, seven years ago not only not to have that inside track, but to get up one morning and discover—*from the news*—that you'd just become famous because you'd signed up to go to *Jupiter*?"

"They asked me," Corcoran observed, weakly. He was remembering, belatedly, one of the reasons why he had not given his little sister the "inside track" that she apparently resented not having had. He had been scared of her—terrified, even. He wondered, briefly, how he had somehow managed to commit that to forgetfulness while he had been away, and had allowed their recent on-screen friendliness to obscure the memory completely.

"So they did," she said. "And for once in your life—the one time, in fact, that logic and everyone who knew you even slightly would have predicted that you would take immediate evasive action, you didn't. You said yes. Would you like to know why?"

"Because they needed me."

"Don't bullshit me, Zeph. You might think I don't know you at all, but I do. You did it because you couldn't stand the pressure that was building up around you at the Institute. You did it because you couldn't stand the notoriety and the controversy consequent on the Slingshot results going into the public domain. You did it because you're a coward, and you were so frightened of what was happening to you here on Earth that you thought that, however terrifying the thought might be of being locked in a tin can with thirteen strangers and traveling six hundred million kilometers to the outer solar system, it looked like the safer option. That's it, isn't it?"

Corcoran shrugged his shoulders and took a longer sip from his glass. "If you like," he said.

"Oh God," she said, reaching for the bottle in order to fill her own glass again. "Now you're going to sulk." She paused before adding: "What I would like to do right now is give you a hug, and tell you that I don't mean to hurt you, and that I love you because you're my brother. But you wouldn't like that, would you? Or, at least, you'd feel compelled to put on a show of not liking it rather than drop out of character. After all, we're not on a spaceship, are we?"

That surprised him. "What's that supposed to mean?" he asked, sharply.

"You really shouldn't try to hide your head in the sand, Zeph. Even ostriches don't actually do that. You might have thought of your little excursion on the Olympus Five as the ultimate escape, and the perfect hiding place, but if you'd bothered to adjust your news-filters more rationally, you'd have known that it was a seven-year sideshow in which the social dynamics of the crew were studied with minute care and attention. Nothing that happened aboard that ship was private. A vast amount was censored from the public domain, but the world is full of hackers and the target was too juicy. Everybody in the world who cares to search out and go through the data with sufficient attention and assiduity knows exactly which three female crew members you screwed, how many times, when, and exactly where the experience registered on the embarrassment scale."

"What!" Corcoran had to put his glass down. He was trembling. There wasn't a mirror handy in which he could look at himself, but he imagined that he must have gone as white as a sheet as the blood drained from his face—or at least a dull shade of gray. He felt dizzy. And nauseated.

"Oh, God!" murmured his sister. "You really didn't know, did you? That's the trouble with filtered information. We all live in our closeted, custom-designed little information-world, keeping everything we don't want to know at bay. I'm sorry, Zeph. I, of all people, should have been able to break that gently . . . I guess I hadn't quite realized how much resentment I'd stored up. Maybe even helping Marie get to you was more malicious than I thought. And it's not as if I'm entitled, after all. It's just that . . . well, to go back to the beginning, I'm an evolutionary biologist, and you . . . well, you didn't even try to help me out. How do you think that made me look? How do you think it made me feel? Although that, of course, is a stupid question . . ."

To gain time she reached for the wine bottle and made as if to top up his glass, but he put his hand over it, and she abandoned the attempt.

"I'm sorry," he said.

"For what?"

"For everything. For not talking to you about . . . what I found in the Slingshots. But it happened so fast, and there was so much, and I could hardly begin to understand it . . . except for the Dancing Rats, and even then . . . I didn't know what it said about me that I thought I could understand the Rats, let alone the Inverts. You're right—I was scared half to death. I ran. From everything. But you're right—I should have thought about you, put myself in your place, realized the position it put you in, and how you would feel . . . and I won't say I couldn't, because that's too easy, too textbook, even though it's a bit over the top to tell me that I'm just putting on an act. I let you down . . . not as badly as I let myself down, but . . ."

He flinched in advance, anticipating the scathing accusation of self-pity, but Denise swallowed the impulse, emptied her glass again and filled it up for the third time.

"Okay," she said, "Let's say that I've vented now and got it out of my system, and let's start again."

"Just a minute," said Corcoran. "Do you really mean that the intimate details of my sex life, such as it is, are public knowledge? That it's not just precocious kids who'll be staring at me every time I'm recognized, but *everybody?*"

"Oh—no, it's not that bad. I mean the data can be accessed, by anyone clever enough and who has a reason to pry. I had a reason, but to be quite honest, nobody else cares . . . about you, that is."

Enlightenment dawned. "That's what you meant about Chris Kemmering having acquired worldwide fame?"

"And how. *His* exploits really did go viral."

"Poor guy."

"Poor guy? I know you liked him, and thought he was a good captain, but hell. *All of them?*"

"You don't understand. You don't know what it was like aboard the ship."

"Of course I do. Everybody does. It was a sideshow—and thanks to your handsome friend, it became a pornographic sideshow."

"No," he said. "You *really* don't understand. Trust me. On-screen and face-to-face are different worlds. You know that— that's how we've been the best of friends in the last few months while I was still on the ship, but as soon as we're really together, you've reverted to being a bitch again."

She seemed startled by that—not because it wasn't true, but because it wasn't in character for him to say it. Not the character she knew.

"Okay," he said. "Now we've both vented. Can we have that hug now, and *really* go back to the beginning?"

She nodded, put her glass down and stood up. He stood up too, and they hugged. "It's good to see you again, Nise, after all this time," he said.

"It's good to see you, too, Zeph," she said.

And they sat down again.

"Now," he said. "Before we got sidetracked, you hinted that you might know something about why the Institute and Walter are so desperate to get me back on board. What have you heard?"

"Well, it's not exactly common knowledge, but anyone who's interested enough to dig has known for years that Halleck and the Institute have been kicking themselves because they let you go, and couldn't stop you, not having realized early enough how unique you are and not having got around to stitching you up with a tighter contract. The machines and the other contact men who were working alongside you way back when haven't come through. Rumor has it that the Rats are actually asking for you, insofar as they're capable of making any kind of request comprehensible, and that even the Insects are showing what might be signs of annoyance. No headway has been made with the Plants, and now the Seventh Generation has come up . . ."

"You know about that?" Corcoran blurted out.

"As I've just explained," she said, "the world is an open book. Data can be sealed, but whatever can be sealed can be unsealed, if anyone clever enough is interested enough to try, and smeared all over the web in a matter of seconds. I'm at Imperial; I'm not actually a member of the Circle, but I know people who are, and I'm close enough to the periphery to get any item of news they think might interest me. By definition, anyone who is interested in the finer points of the Slingshot Project is clever enough to hack it. Various rumors have been flying around for two years. Walter Halleck is by no means the only man on earth who's been eagerly awaiting your return. Your lips will doubtless be buttoned, as usual, but it won't prevent the information leaking. Not that we know that much, and no one can really be sure how much more

Halleck might think he knows, but the word that's going round is that if the Slingshot data can be trusted, the Earth isn't doomed to be swallowed up when the Sun expands. Its orbit will be adjusted beforehand and its surface prepared to withstand the holocaust. Something will survive, or at least move in—something active, but weirder even than the Megaplants. It's a tantalizing idea."

Corcoran shook his head, trying to adjust his thought processes to the cataract of new information—new, at least in the sense that it had never crossed his mind that Denise knew any of it. He thought about asking her whether she knew where the Institute's new finances came from, but thought better of it. If she didn't, she'd be bound to start trying to find out, and if Imperial's hacker Circle started prying, it would be obvious that he'd talked out of turn.

He frowned. "Have you talked about this with your friend the chaplain?" he asked.

"Yes," said Denise. "Marie knows everything I've just told you, and she and I have discussed it, quite avidly. But I have told her to tread carefully, and that you take confidentiality agreements very seriously. She is sometimes reminiscent of a bull in a china shop, but if she tries to bully you, you have adequate defenses."

"Are you and she . . . ?" Corcoran left it there.

It was Denise's turn to look surprised. "An item? Good God no. I haven't changed that much in seven years, and she's as straight as a die. If you fancy your chances, by all means feel free to have a go—but don't expect too much. She is a vicar, after all."

"No she's not," Corcoran couldn't help saying. "A vicar is an incumbent in a parish. She's just a chaplain."

"And a PhD student. Do you have any idea how competitive the C-of-E is nowadays?"

"Not really," Corcoran admitted. "I know that organized religion had a big resurgence when the first phase of the Crash hit hard and the *mea culpas* started flying thick and fast, and that it's still riding the wave, but internal Church politics is a world far beyond my filters."

"Well, if anyone thought that women attaining a majority within the clergy was going to soften things up, they were mistaken. Where the Church and Academia overlap . . . well, it's not exactly dog eat dog, but there are claws enough for 'you stroke my back and I'll stroke yours' to be a risky business. Marie's ambitious, and intends to make bishop by the time she's forty. She thinks I'm her ticket—not because of my brilliant intellect and deep insight, alas, but because I happened to pop out of the same womb as you. She thinks that there's a chance that you've seen the authentic face of God—or might, if the latest Slingshot works—and the fact that you're an atheist and won't recognize Him when you see Him just makes her task as a potential interpreter that much more vital."

"And Mum thought she was such a nice girl," Corcoran observed.

"Oh, she is. Probably too nice for her own good. If she were less scrupulous, she'd probably screw you just to get the news of the Seventh Generation hot off the presses, but she gives every indication of taking chastity seriously. If you try, though, do let me know how you get on."

"I won't," Corcoran said bluntly, meaning that he had no intention of trying rather than no intention of informing her.

"I know," she said. "In spite of your denial, I do have some inkling of how the special circumstances of the Olympus Mission—the carefully planned and scrupulously monitored special circumstances of the Olympus Mission—succeeded in breaking down that particular barrier, and I understand, or think I do, how difficult everything will become again now you're back on Earth. But for what it's worth, if you do want to extrapolate your sex life, it really would be as easy as pie. You're famous. Not very, but enough, and in all the right places. Marie's a serious chaplain, and out of bounds, but there are plenty of PhD students over the road who aren't, and I can give you the numbers of at least three who are fully paid-up members of the PT and would be only too happy to add your name to their dance-cards."

She looked at him enquiringly, in case his news filters had screened out the fact that "PT" was shorthand for "Promiscuous Tendency." They hadn't. Earthbound society had reacted in many and various ways to the awareness that the End of Civilization had already begun, and was only suspended for the moment, but one of the most obvious reactions was that the birth rate had fallen steeply among the urban middle classes, as considerable numbers of young women had decided that bringing children into an ending world was unkind as well as pointless. Not all of them, but a significant proportion, had also taken the view that if time was limited and there was no longer any point in seeking stable long-term relationships, then the logical life-strategy, for as long as it might last, was to cram in as much sex as possible with as many partners as possible.

Corcoran was only momentarily surprised that there were PhD students at Imperial who were "fully paid-up members of the PT." It was, after all, largely an urban middle-class phenomenon. What surprised him more was the way that Denise's enquiring glance persisted for far longer than it should have done, once he had failed to ask for a clarification of the term.

"Oh God," he groaned. "You think because of what happened on the ship, *I* might have . . . come on, Nise!"

"I just thought you might have ambitions," Denise said, less apologetically than he would have liked. "Having been corrupted by the good captain's example, I thought . . ."

"I was *not* corrupted by Chris Kemmering's example!" Corcoran snapped. "And what happened aboard Olympus Five was *not* promiscuity, whatever it looked like to the prurient minds of prying dirty monkeys on Earth. You do *not* understand, you hear me?"

"Wow! Didn't know it was meltdown material. Sorry for any offence caused. I get the message—your sex life isn't a suitable topic for sisterly chat. Subject closed. I'll start again—again. Are you scared, Zeph?"

"Of what?"

"Take your pick. Not being able to deliver when Halleck fires you into the far future. Of the possibility that the balance of scientific opinion might tip in favor of the thesis that you're a con man who's pulled off the greatest scientific hoax in history? Of convincing yourself, however reluctantly, that it's all been a delusion and that you belong in a padded cell? Of anything and everything. Or am I just being stupid, wanting to know how you feel, because I have the idiotic delusion that if you do feel scared, I might be able to say something that will make you feel slightly better?"

Corcoran thought about it for a few seconds, and then sighed, and said: "Scared to death, Nise. God, I miss Greenland . . . and Olympus."

Denise seemed to think for a few seconds, too. Then she said: "Well, for what it's worth, I believe in you. I know you're not a con man, and I don't think you're crazy, and I'm morally certain that if any man alive can draw any conclusions at all from whatever tenuous ghost Halleck has contrived to construct in a world where it ought not to be possible for any ghost to exist, it's you. And I love you like a brother—unconditionally."

Corcoran knew that simply saying "Thanks" wasn't adequate. He got up, and hugged his sister again, hoping that she didn't think that he was just going through the motions.

"I needed that," he confessed.

"The hug?"

"No, the expression of faith."

"You're welcome." Denise glanced at her phone, checking the time. "And if that's all you need from Marie, you can probably double your score in half an hour or so. She believes in you too, and doesn't even have the excuse of shared genes. By the way, I was really impressed that you'd heard of William Derham, and so was she. What the hell is astrotheology and how come you know what it is?"

"When you spend seven years locked in a tin can with thirteen people who are all certified geniuses and mostly certified oddballs, you discuss a lot of strange subjects, as well as getting physically closer than you would ever have done in less confined circumstances, and working out social and psychological means to handle that unusual proximity. Even talking about the weather becomes intellectually high-powered when you're talking about the solar wind, ultra-high energy snow and ex-cometary hail.

"You apparently have a far better idea than I do about how carefully it might have been planned, but there was an even balance on the ship between atheists and deists of various stripes. I didn't actually read the book, mind—it's a collection of sermons, for God's sake—but as I understand it, it adds up to an elementary textbook of physics, geology and biology, in which the complexity, orderliness and sheer wonder of life on Earth is construed as evidence of the enormous ingenuity and artistry of the creator. According to the deists on Olympus, Paley was just reprocessing second-hand materials from a century before, and the true originators of natural theology in Britain were Derham and John Ray—although, intellectuals of the spacefaring stripe being what they are, they naturally found its original roots in Plato."

"I know a bit about John Ray, obviously," Denise observed. "You're prepared, then, for the line of argument that Marie is trying to develop? You've heard it all before?"

"Not only have I heard it all before," said Corcoran, proudly, "but I've heard it while cruising through the asteroid belt, with a view of the stars that . . . well, let's say that it adds an extra dimension of persuasion to astrotheology, in the broadest sense."

"But you're still an atheist?"

"Yes. I couldn't help wondering, though, what idea the cloud-whales might have of God, living as they do in a cold, deep solar ocean, probably devoid of any sensory apparatus that allows them to perceive anything beyond its vague surface."

"Probably? But possibly not?"

"Deep philosophical waters there. I didn't actually manage to start much of a conversation. Cloud-whales do dance, apparently, in an oddly distinctive way, but if it's communication, I couldn't make head nor tail of it. The AIs might, given time."

"But you did make some sort of contact? And you did achieve . . . well, empathy and intuition are both loaded terms, but you did obtain some vague inference of their existential situation? And don't give me the usual confidentiality bullshit."

"I honestly don't know. We have objective evidence that they're alive, that they communicate between themselves, that their behavior occasionally lends itself to the interpretation that they're at least as smart as crows, maybe cats, maybe whales and . . . well, you're familiar with the difficulties. But yes, for what it's worth, I did have the feeling that they had minds—souls, if you like—and feelings of their own. But what that's worth, I don't know. Lots of people are said to feel the same way about their pets, their cars and their computers. The old Radical Asp thesis holds that all supposed empathy is delusion and projection, that we see nothing in other human beings or the objects around us but displaced fragmentary reflections of our mistaken awareness of ourselves. If I'm deluded, I wouldn't know it, would I?"

"Me neither," his sister replied, getting to her feet. "Look, I've got to go, Zeph—Marie will be here in a few minutes. She's very punctual. Don't forget to offer her a drink, and order something to eat if she hasn't already eaten—and something for yourself, anyway. Don't let her bully you, but don't bully her either. Be nice. Remember that what you say and do reflects on me too. And I'll be back. Now that you're within walking distance of the office, the pressure of expectation will go up a notch. Whether I get an inside track or not, I'm going to have put on a show. I'm sorry if that makes you uncomfortable."

"It's okay," Corcoran told her. "You have a license for it. Come round any time—but I'll probably be tied up at the Institute all day and half the night until I've trained on all the new equipment, got my contacts properly in tune and brought myself up to date with all the information that they think they've kept secret. Don't expect too much, and not very often."

"Good line," she said, as she went to the door of the flat. "That should work, even on Marie. I'll see myself out. Thanks, Zeph."

"For what?" he asked, slightly surprised.

"For the toleration," she said, as she closed the door behind her, and disappeared.

VII

Marie MacLaughlin was, as his sister had promised, punctual, but Denise had been careful to give him a good ten minutes to pull himself together before the scheduled time of her arrival. Had he been quick enough off the mark, he had had plenty of time to tidy away the open wine-bottle and the two glasses—only one of which was empty—but he never gave a thought to that. He was still sitting in the armchair, hardly having moved, when the doorbell rang again.

The Reverend seemed just as impressed with the flat as Denise had.

"Yes," Corcoran said, wanting to seize the initiative in the conversation, "I do know how much these places cost, and how lucky I am. Would you like a drink?"

His guest's eyes immediately settled on the bottle and the glasses. "Is there any left?" she said.

She was probably being ironic, but Corcoran decided to take it literally. "I'm sure I can squeeze another glass out for you, if that's what you'd like," he said. "But if you'd prefer tea, coffee or a different kind of alcohol, that would be fine. I've had time to stock up."

"I'll take the wine, as it's open," the Reverend said. "Denise?"

"Yes. You've just missed her. Sit down."

Obeying the injunction, Marie Maclaughlin said: "I thought about not telling her about the appointment we'd made, but it wouldn't have been fair—and I thought that you probably would anyway. I expect she apologized profusely for foisting me upon you, and advised you as to the best way of getting rid of me in the shortest possible time."

It wasn't a question, but Corcoran was making an effort.

"She's angry with me," he told the priest. "She came round to tear me off a strip. She couldn't do it yesterday because you were there."

"Really?" said the chaplain, evidently surprised. "Why on earth is she angry with you . . . if I'm not being indiscreet?"

Corcoran refrained from pointing out that she certainly was being indiscreet, and must be aware of it.

"She thinks I left her in the lurch when I agreed to go on the Olympus Mission. She had seven years of accumulated rancor to vent, which she didn't feel that she could vent on-screen . . . but I think it's okay now. I think she's forgiven me."

"Forgiven you? I've known her for two years and she never gave me the slightest inkling that there was anything to forgive. I've rarely encountered such an extreme case of hero-worship."

Corcoran reacted before noticing the sharply inquisitive gaze that the woman was directing at him. "What?"

"You didn't know? I wondered yesterday, when I saw you together. Given my position, I suppose I should be extra-careful about using words like 'idolize,' but . . . well, I suppose I shouldn't be surprised that she's able to put on a show of being angry with you. Emotional displacement. We've talked about you a great deal. Did she tell you that?"

"That's only natural," Corcoran countered, warily, "given the nature of your interest in her work. Have you eaten?"

The Reverend seemed surprised by the question. "No," she said. "I was planning to get something later . . . afterwards."

"I'm hungry," Corcoran stated. "Do you mind if I order something for us?"

"Not in the least. It's very kind of you, I didn't . . ."

"Obviously not," said Corcoran, "as you seem to have imagined that Denise came here to advise me on how to get rid of you."

Marie MacLaughlin blushed. "I'm sorry," she said. "That was stupid of me."

"In fact," Corcoran said, carefully not lying, "we discussed astrotheology. She was pleased to find that I'd be prepared for the kind of argumentative line you might take."

"I'm glad," the Reverend said. "Perhaps I was foolish, but I wasn't entirely sure that she wanted you to help me. I thought I had to work quite hard to persuade her to introduce me to you, and I was afraid that she might be regretting having yielded to the pressure. I thought . . ." She stopped.

Corcoran didn't bother to attempt to draw any speculative inference as to what Marie MacLaughlin might have thought. He went to the sideboard, collected the menus from local delivery firms that he'd found in his mailbox when he arrived, and handed them to her.

"Take your pick," he said. "I'm happy with anything. After seven years in a spaceship and a month in hospital, I have a lot of culinary reacquaintances to make, even if most of it is synthesized."

"Tempura?" she suggested. "The fish will be real, and probably genuinely fished—not the product of intensive aquaculture I mean."

"Fine," said Corcoran, and went to the wall-unit to place the order.

"It's very kind of you to grant me this interview, Mr. Corcoran," the Reverend said, a trifle tentatively, when he sat down again. She seemed out of her depth now, and perhaps even out of her element. "Or may I call you Zephaniah . . . or Zeph?"

Corcoran thought about that for a good seven seconds, trying to decide. "All right," he said, finally, "You can call me Zeph."

"And you'll call me Marie?"

Corcoran reached that decision in half the time.

"Yes," he said.

She seemed relieved, evidently thinking that she was making progress. "This means a lot to me," she said. "Theological disputes might seem like storms in a teacup to you, but . . . you've heard of astrotheology? Not just in the general academic sense, but in Derham's sense . . . The physicotheological sense."

"Yes," said Corcoran.

"And you've discussed it before?"

"Yes. On Olympus Five."

Her face cleared slightly. "Ah!" she said. "Seven years on a spaceship is a long time. The situation, and the people . . ."

"Yes," said Corcoran. "You get around to all sorts of things that you probably wouldn't have got around to in the course of affairs on Earth."

She blushed slightly, evidently having discussed Corcoran's time on the spaceship with Denise, even if their discussion hadn't extended to astrotheological contemplations.

"That's helpful," she said. "You know where I'm coming from. But you weren't converted?"

"The crew members were scientists, not evangelists. Nobody was trying to convert anyone. It was polite, hypothetical discussion."

"I'm not going to try to convert you either, Zeph. Perhaps it's my duty, in a sense, but that's not the purpose of my wanting to talk to you. I know that I've been a trifle bullish in getting this far, but I really do want to handle the matter with kid gloves from now on. I simply want to investigate your opinions and . . . well, your feelings . . . and I'll be careful to stick to material that's in the public domain. I don't want to compromise you in any way. Will the people at the Institute mind if you talk to me?"

"I don't know," Corcoran said. "I haven't told them yet. But I doubt it. I don't think they have any anxieties about the Church of England . . . not, at any rate, about a chaplain at Imperial working on a PhD in physicotheology."

Marie MacLaughlin smiled, wryly. "No," she said, "I'm a very small cog in the cosmic and academic gears. I won't be delivering sermons in St. Paul's any time soon. I hope you're right, and that your employers won't raise any objection . . . but I hope you won't mind if I try to take full advantage of the period of grace before you put the matter to the test?"

"Feel free," said Corcoran.

The doorbell rang then, and he went downstairs to collect the food. By the time he got back, Marie Maclaughlin had laid the dining-table, evidently having had no difficulty in locating a tablecloth and all the necessary accoutrements.

"Shall I open another bottle of wine?" he asked.

"Just water for me, if you don't mind," she said, without adding any superfluous explanation.

He fetched two glasses of water, and they sat down.

"Do you mind if I launch into the matter in hand?" the Reverend asked.

"Feel free," said Corcoran, again.

"Can we start at the beginning, with the species that the popular news outlets call Dancing Rats?"

"For once," Corcoran observed, "the popular press isn't far wrong. So far as I could gather—and this is the one instance in which the machines and other human registers have gathered abundant data, they really are the eventual descendants of the common European brown rat, our natural, and perhaps inevitable, heirs. As for the dancing—well that's an artifact of the communication difficulties inherent in the use of the ghost. It is material, so it's sensitive to both light and sound, although it doesn't have eyes or ears—but actually translating its sensations into quasi-visual and auditory form requires the efforts of the Coincidence Computer, which I can't begin to understand. Anyway, the upshot of it is that exchanging information visually, let alone verbally, is fiendishly difficult, and has to begin with gesticulation. Hence, the first communication we established with the rats was a matter of frenetic sign language—or, in terms of the fuzzy pictures that the media were able to extract from the computer synthesis, what appeared to the naïve eye to be dancing."

She nodded. He had known that she knew all that, but he had spelled it out anyway in order to get into the groove and build up a little momentum.

"But once you got to the stage of more sophisticated exchanges—once you began to develop a language, you were able to get some idea of what they'll think of us, themselves and their existential situation?"

"Vaguely, yes."

"And you think they already thought of themselves as our heirs before the contact—as our *inevitable* heirs? You think that they'll see the human world, as we now experience it, merely as a phase in an evolutionary process of which their species is the natural and inevitable culmination?"

"Yes. But they're grateful to us. They don't regard us simply as a vanished rival. They seemed to me to be well aware of the fact that their own evolution received a tremendous and crucial boost from the artificial environment that human civilization provided for their ancestors. That much, they've said—but there's a lot more that I've . . . let's say inferred. They know that we didn't do it deliberately, obviously aware that it was an unintended side-effect—and they know, too, that humans spent a lot of time trying unavailingly to purge their cities of rats, but they don't hold that against us. Without the selective pressure that humans put on rats by means of poisons, traps and engineered diseases, their ancestors would never have developed the robust constitutions and cunning instincts that laid the physiological foundations for their eventual development of self-consciousness and intelligence. In their view, the human species was the chisel in the hand of the sculptor that formed them—a sharp and mordant instrument, but one whose action eventually led to the creation of something magnificent and beautiful."

"Did they seem beautiful to you?"

It was not the question that Corcoran had expected. "In fact," he said, "yes. I know that when the computer-generated images were first published, lots of people were horrified, dancing or no dancing, because they provoked a kind of primitive gut-reaction of repulsion, just as the kind of rats we know often do. But they didn't have that effect on me, ever. Perhaps it was primarily the effect of surprise, or the triumph of achievement, but they always seemed to me to be beautiful. And as the dancing developed—although I've never been entirely sure whether they're demonstrating one of their art-forms for my benefit or indulging in a peculiar private joke referring to our first attempts at communication—I certainly found that very beautiful. I think they knew that, and were pleased; they seemed to regard me, eventually, as something of a valued connoisseur."

"You liked them?"

"When I got to know them . . . or thought I was getting to know them, yes, certainly."

"Some people thought at the time, and still think, that they were lying to you, even manipulating you. Is that possible, do you think?"

Corcoran hesitated. Finally, he said: "I don't know . . . but I'd like to think that if they were deceiving me, they had good reasons."

"What do you mean?"

"Well, there are some very tricky questions, very fundamental questions, that arise in connection with the idea of the transfer of information through time. Put crudely, by talking to us, the Rats might be risking changing their own past, and might perceive a real danger in that, however paradoxical the very notion might be. That might provide the Rats with a very strong incentive for censoring, or even distorting, the information that they transmit backwards through time. If the Sling worked differently, and permitted us to communicate with our own apish ancestors, I think we'd want to be very careful about the information we gave them, if only because of having read a lot of clever fiction about time travel and time paradoxes."

"But according to the published accounts, the Rats aren't overly worried about that—or say they aren't."

"That's correct. The Rats seem to regard our extinction as something that's already happened, and would probably think of the idea of it being alterable as absurd. If that's right, then our extinction is inevitable and their own ascent to replace us is, indeed, the natural order of events. They don't seem to have the kind of anxieties that so many old time travel stories broached and explored. They know they exist, and take that existence for granted—but they regard the Coincidence established by the Sling as the discovery of a window through time that is fascinating to them, because it allows them to peer into an era of which almost all trace has been obliterated by time."

"If they see the human species as the chisel that sculpted their ancestors into precursors of their own species, how do they see the sculptor?"

That was the question that Corcoran had been expecting earlier. "That's far more difficult to determine. One thing that can be ruled out, so far as I was able to judge, is that they imagine a God made in their own image, a kind of rodent Yahveh employing the great chain of being as a means to perfect the Rat species. They didn't seem to me to have that kind of idea at all. They seemed to me, in fact, already to have a consciousness of their own inevitable supersession, their own inevitable doom, and to be resigned to it.

"It's a delicate question, obviously, and there was a lot of discussion at the Institute, reflected in the media, as to what I and other human registers ought to tell the Rats about the discoveries we made about the third and subsequent generations—but I'm convinced that they already knew. They hadn't invented a Sling of their own and they really didn't seem to be very interested in acquiring information from us as to how to build one. I thought, when I was in contact with them, that they already had, or believed they already had, a means of anticipating the future, albeit in a vague and distant manner. My impression was that they already knew the broad shape that the Invert generations, and perhaps the Plant generations, would take."

"You think they have prophets, and took them seriously?"

Corcoran saw what she was getting at. It wasn't as if humans had ever been short of premonitions and warnings of doom, or even the knowledge that the species would one day reach a terminus and disappear. But humans had always been great filterers of information, eager to stick their heads in the sand.

"That's one way of looking at it," he said. "But they're smart. They know the score, in terms of the pattern of evolution—and perhaps they aren't as perversely expert as fudging it as our forefathers were."

"If they know—will know—about the Insect and Plant generations, do you think they know about the seventh generation too?"

That was an awkward question. After what Denise had told him, there was no reason at all to be surprised that the chaplain had caught wind of Halleck's supposed discovery, but it was a question he couldn't answer, and not because he'd signed a confidentiality agreement.

"I really don't know exactly what they thought, or on what basis they formed their thesis. I just had the strong impression that they were aware of their own ephemerality as a species, that even while they had, so to speak, stepped into the human ecological niche, they didn't think of themselves as the dominant species, the rulers of creation. If they believe in any kind of deity, it isn't any kind of deity that favors them especially. I think theodicy is a non-issue for them. I suspect that they don't have to juggle questions of the incompatibility of the creator's omnipotence and benevolence, because I don't think either notion would make any sense to them. But there we really are straying a long way into the realm of impression and speculation. You have to remember the limitations under which registers work. You probably can't imagine how difficult it was actually to talk to the Rats, to establish a kind of translatable sign-language. Believe me, communicating with an alien species via dance, gesticulations, grunts and crude line-drawings is no easy matter."

"Which is why human registers are so important—why some kind of empathy is vitally important?"

"That's the theory," Corcoran agreed. "The notion on which my notoriety rests, as the man who can empathize with aliens . . . because he can't empathize with his own species."

"Allegedly," she supplied, obligingly.

"Allegedly," he agreed.

"Are you still in contact with the other crew members of the Olympus Five?" she suddenly asked, out of the blue.

"Of course," he said, warily. "We weren't all together in rehab, after the first few days, but I have all their phone numbers. We all intend to keep in touch. When you share an experience like that, it creates a bond that can last a lifetime."

"Undoubtedly," she said. "But will you actually bother to phone one another? Will you get together if two of you happen to be in the same city?" She didn't go so far as to ask whether those members of the crew who had slept together on the ship were ever going to sleep together again, but Corcoran could see the direction in which her thoughts were tending, and why.

"I don't know," he said. "Time will tell, I guess. It's not relevant to the matter in hand, is it?"

"No, it isn't," she admitted. After a pause to change mental gear, she asked: "Do you think that the Rats have more senses than we do?"

"I suspect so. The Inverts certainly do. That's another complicating factor. But if you're wondering whether the Rats' ideas about the future, and about their situation within the temporal pattern, emerges from some kind of sixth sense—a sense that a few humans have possessed but which is undeveloped in most of us—that's tricky ground."

"The Insects do have extra senses, though?"

"I certainly got that impression, and there's some objective evidence. It's difficult to be sure what's going on with regard to the fourth generation, but the third were great antenna-twitchers, as well as whistlers, and I think I contrived a good rapport there, with some kind of collective hive mind as well as the individuals they actually posted to monitor the stabilized ghost. The standard theory is that they're the ultimate descendants of ants."

"You sound skeptical."

"I am. Analogy doesn't prove descent. I'm not even convinced that the so-called Insects are really descended from Insects. They're invertebrates, obviously, and they have six limbs, although they generally walk on four and use the front pair as arms. Some of them are winged, too, in a fashion reminiscent of insects—but all of that could be due to convergent evolution. We'll need far more anatomical information than we've so far been able to elicit before we can locate the origin of their branch of the tree of life with any certainty."

"But the fourth generation are the descendants of the third, or kindred species of the sentient members of the third?"

"That's the standard view. I have no reason to doubt it, and it seems perfectly reasonable. To be perfectly honest, Denise is probably more familiar with the hard data than I am, and she has the expert knowledge to sort through it. She can advise you better than I can on the likely ancestry of the Inverts."

"It's not the implication of the hard data that I need from you, Zeph. Did you get the impression that the Insects—the third or the fourth generations—were aware of their own ephemerality, as the Rats were?"

"The third, yes I did, definitely; the fourth, I'm really not sure, but it would seem to be a natural assumption . . . and, to tell the truth, I did get a vague impression that they not only knew that they were going to be superseded by the plants, but . . . well, that they were actually trying to achieve that result."

"You think they were trying to bioengineer their successor species?"

"That was the impression I got."

"Why?"

"Good question. But if it's true . . . well, the narrative takes on a different complexion, as you put it so neatly."

"Yes, it does," she said, pensively, doubtless trying to fit it in with her own preliminary narrative. "And is that awareness, according to your impressions, associated with some sense of ultimate purpose, some notion of an eventual evolutionary end?"

"That might be stretching it a little too far, Reverend MacLaughlin. I can see why you'd like to reach some such conclusion, but my impression only suggested that there was something odd about the relationship between the fourth generation Inverts and the fifth generation Megaplants . . . a kind of . . . let's call it complicity . . ."

She fixed him with her blue eyes. "Marie," she said.

"What?"

"You agreed to call me Marie." She actually seemed to want to hold him to the promise.

"Sorry, Marie. As I said, it's beyond anything I was able to infer."

"But you're going back, aren't you? If only for practice, the Sling is going to throw you back to the stabilized ghosts with which you've been linked before—before it tries to hurl you all the way to the companion of the red giant?"

"Probably," Corcoran conceded. "I haven't discussed a schedule, and when I do . . ."

"You've signed a confidentiality agreement. I understand. I'm not in any position to ask favors of you, Zeph, and I don't want to overstep my own mark. I'll stick to the public domain from now on, as promised . . ."

"Actually," Corcoran cut in, "it's getting late, and I'm tired. I'm still adapting to the pattern and pace of real life. I think I'd like to call it a day there, if you don't mind."

She pursed her lips very slightly. "Of course," she said. "Which brings us, I suppose, to the big question. Can we continue the conversation another time?"

"Yes," said Corcoran, in no danger of lying because she had said *can*, not *may*, "but I'm going to be very busy for a while. May I call you when I know what my schedule is going to be, when it will be possible to arrange another meeting?"

"Of course," she said, again—but her lips were still slightly pursed. "May I use the bathroom?"

Corcoran nodded.

Several minutes passed before she came out again, giving him time to clear away the detritus of their dinner. She seemed to have eaten heartily, as he had. The fish had, indeed, been genuine, and the rice had probably come from a paddy-field rather than a SAP-field. The sauces were a different matter.

"I'll leave you alone, for now, then," she said, as she prepared to leave. "Give my regards to your mother."

"And give mine to Denise," Corcoran said.

"Not your love?"

"All right, then," said Corcoran, mildly. "Give her my love."

She was still studying him, and only edging imperceptible toward the door. Then, as if making a decision, she said: "Thank you very much, Zeph. It's been very helpful, and it means a lot to me."

"You're welcome," Corcoran replied, figuring that it didn't commit him to anything.

She didn't attempt to kiss him, but she didn't offer her hand to be shaken either. She reached out quite deliberately, and touched his cheek lightly with her fingers. "Good luck with the new venture, Zeph," she said. "I hope it works out, whether you can tell me about it or not."

"Thanks," said Corcoran.

"Marie," she reminded him, gently.

"Thanks, Marie," he said.

And she left.

Corcoran thought about calling Denise for a full three minutes, in order to give her a report, but he didn't.

IX

When the technical staff began the painstaking business of hooking Corcoran up to the machinery—to the future ghost—the process was no different from what the parallel tech crew had done for him in the Jupiter orbiter. In fact, he observed that the internal environment of the Institute's Slingroom looked bizarrely similar to the feeler-pods aboard the Olympus Five and the orbiter, although it was much larger, space not being at such a premium in London as in outer space, even in Kensington. When the hood was placed over his eyes, the sensation of similarity didn't increase any further, though. His own weight and the atmosphere he was breathing were different, and tangibly so, so once the visual cues were removed, the slight sense of interplanetary *déjà vu* lessened rather than being augmented.

Corcoran was surprised how impatient he felt, having thought that he'd lost the capacity to feel impatience while making the long trip to Jupiter and the seemingly longer—but actually slightly shorter—trip home. In all fairness, however, he had already been kicking his heels for some time while Halleck tried to tune the machine, and him, continually dissatisfied with the set-up, as only an obsessively scrupulous person could be.

"Let's just *get on with it*," Corcoran had eventually said, more than once.

"It's not as easy as that, alas," Halleck had told him. "I wish it were, but there's a delicate balance to be struck, even before we can begin to hook you up. If you knew how complicated Coincidence calibration is . . . let's just say that your role is the easier one."

Now, at least, he was on the brink. Surely it couldn't take more than a few more minutes now that he was inside the hood.

"Seven years ago," he observed to the invisible Halleck, "someone told me that there were only three people in the world who understood Coincidence theory, but there must be hundreds by now, mustn't there?"

"The other two were probably lying then," Halleck assured him, "and if there are hundreds making the claim now, ninety-nine out of every hundred are surely bluffing. Trust me, Corcoran, you're in the only safe hands there are. We're the ultimate team, you and I. I'm not sure there'll ever be another like us, this side of World's End."

Considering that the Crash was only in suspense, still hanging over the entire species like the sword of Damocles, that didn't seem to Corcoran to be an excessively boastful claim. And given that neither the Dancing Rats nor the third- and fourth-generation Inverts had shown the slightest interest in wanting to build Slings of their own, it might well be true for all eternity, so far as Earth was concerned.

But surely, somewhere else in that vast universe that had seemed so imposing out there in the asteroid belt . . .

"Hold on a while longer, Corcoran," Halleck's voice said. "This isn't quite right. I've got to get everything in perfect balance, or we might miss the shot."

"Let's take a stab, for God's sake," Corcoran retorted, with an altogether atypical recklessness. "We're not going to miss the shot—I'm only going a few million years, to see old friends. It's not as if we're aiming long range, and you're not even trying out the new voice-link, so it's all familiar stuff. The faster we get it over with, the faster we can get on to the real deal. Life's too short to allow preliminary trials to run on forever."

Halleck didn't bother to remind him that nobody knew, any more, how short or long human life might turn out to be, given post-Crash advances in medicine. Corcoran knew, however, that although his mother probably wouldn't make it that far past a hundred, he and Denise might easily manage two hundred, all being well—which would make his current age a mere extended youth. On the other hand, the chances of all being well, and the ecosphere lasting that long without the ecocatastrophe going into hectic overdrive again were surely no better than ever and perhaps a lot worse, which made the likelihood of Corcoran, Denise and Marie Maclaughlin witnessing the end of the human story uncomfortably high.

The physicist contented himself with saying: "We're not in the trial-and-error phase any more, Corcoran, but it's a matter of getting the adjustments dead on, and the results guaranteed. It's been seven years, and there have been subtle changes, in the machinery and in your contacts. Just sit tight for a few minutes longer and let me get the adaptations perfect. You used to be so calm and collected—what happened to you out there in Jupiter orbit?"

Corcoran knew full well that it wasn't what had happened to him "out there" that was making him nervous now. Readjusting to surface life had proved to be more stressful than he had anticipated. He was physically rehabilitated, but mentally, he felt even worse today than he had when the kid had started staring at him down on Marine Parade, and in spite of the fact that Denise's visit the previous day, after a distinctly sticky start, had provided some valuable moral support . . .

Mercifully, Halleck was finally satisfied.

"It's a go, lads and lasses," he said to the four-person crew. "Priming in three, two, one . . ."

There was no explosion, of course, and nothing much seemed to happen at all for a few seconds, although Corcoran lost the sense of his own gravity, the sensation of life in his body. It was as if his mind—his soul—were being gradually detached from its corporeal envelope.

As the apparatus that would put him in communion with the far-futuristic lens geared up for the Slingshot, however, the differences between the time-leap he was about to make and the finger-exercises in surrogacy he's undertaken on the Olympus Five, the Jupiter orbiter and the various satellite bases became clearly manifest to his consciousness. The knot in space formed by the Slingshot, at a "distance" measurable in mind-boggling multimillions of years, didn't feel anything like a physical surrogate, and the preparatory process of what Corcoran liked to think of as "mental transfiguration" was something quite distinct, quite unique.

It was, however, more like "coming home" than he had expected. The familiarity hadn't decayed completely, even in seven years.

The attenuated surrogate really did feel like a ghost, conscious of its own immateriality, its own implausibility, its own impropriety.

After a long stint inserting his mental presence into the variously shaped atmosphere-divers adapted to explore the gaseous realms of Jupiter and the various environments of the gas-giant's satellites, assuming the personality of a time-displaced ghost again was a metamorphosis into something impossibly light, but not frail, impossibly agile, but not frivolous, impossibly unhuman, but not alien. As he settled into the pattern of supplementary neuronal linkages augmenting his brain, it was by no means an unwelcome feeling, as it had been way back at the beginning, before making his first contact with the Dancing Rats. It was comfortable, and surprisingly facile, certainly a matter of "coming home" if not of recovering an "old self."

Corcoran still had time before the dataflow began in earnest to chide himself for that foolish sentimentality, and to remind himself that, at the end of the day, a ghost was a ghost was a ghost . . . something dead, not truly human, never a true *self* in the way that human surrogates sometimes came to seem.

That, Corcoran thought, was probably part of his problem. He had spent too much of his life being dead, and preparing to be dead, and analyzing the wages of death. On the other hand, pretending to be a bird soaring through the Jovian fog or a *flaneur* taking the exotic air on Ganymede hadn't actually proved to be an antidote, any more than the long months of the journey home had, much of it having been spent in virtual environments not much different in existential texture from the environments into which he intruded his professional telepresence, in spite of being adapted for human use, human pleasure and human satisfaction.

Corcoran wasn't certain that he was any longer capable of human satisfaction, if he ever had been and if such a thing were really possible. The rat-descendants would probably have denied that it was—but then, the insect-descendants, if that's what they were, probably didn't believe in rodent satisfaction either, and probably etcetera all along the line, if the plant-descendants gave such matters any thought at all.

Corcoran kept the silly train of thought going, because he had the illusion that his contacts were itching, and knew from long experience that an imaginary scratch wouldn't solve the problem, because life wasn't that fair.

Halleck, of course, wasn't interested in satisfaction. If people were capable of satisfaction, where would be the spur to drive progress? He probably wasn't interested in pleasure either—which meant that he probably had more in common with Corcoran, and perhaps with the ultrasmart plant-descendants, than any of them would have liked to think.

The data was flowing now, though, almost at torrential level. Corcoran forced himself to pay attention, knowing that he should now be able to see, and perhaps to hear, assuming that there was anything at the far end of the Slingshot to see and hear.

There was—and that, too, was a matter of coming home.

The Rats had set up a permanent monitoring station around the stabilized ghost, their window to the past. Corcoran assumed that it was manned twenty-four hours a day three hundred and sixty-five days of the year, if the day still had twenty-four hours and the year three hundred and sixty-five days. Probably not, even in the latter case, given the Moon's steady gravitational toll.

The Rats were already dancing. They were excited. Corcoran had not the slightest doubt that they recognized him. They had been asking for him, he knew. He had been away for seven long years in his own estimation, and it wasn't just Denise who had felt neglected, and perhaps a trifle resentful, even though the duration from their viewpoint might have been quite different. They were dancing even while they were making telephone calls to summon their friends to the ball—and he gesticulated in his turn. They exchanged greetings visually and aurally. The Rats even attempted a few meaningful words before their machines kicked in and started talking directly to the machines controlling and monitoring the ghost's Coincidence. That was in binary, obviously, and its full import wouldn't be clear, at either end, until it was all analyzed and repackaged for Human and Rat consumption and cogitation.

In the meantime, however, Corcoran could "see" via the ghost's lens and other computer-aided pseudosensory apparatus, and he could make himself seen. He could also "hear" and make himself heard. Most of all, though, he could move. The ghost's powers of perambulation were limited, especially now that it was fully stabilized, but he could mime; he could gesticulate; he could dance.

So he danced, knowing that he couldn't make it beautiful, but knowing that the Rats would appreciate his efforts anyway.

More Rats arrived.

They switched on some kind of phonograph, playing what was presumably music, and danced to that. This time, he was sure, it was a work of art, not just a kind of in-joke. It was something they had prepared long before, something they might have been itching to perform for months. They wanted him to like it—and they were confident, at least, that they could impress him.

They did.

It was quite a ballet. The rats wore clothing, gray on the part of the rats who had been "on watch" when the Slingshot operated, but more brightly colored on the part of the newcomers.

For his part, Corcoran tried to explain to the Rats where he had been. They seemed to catch on without too much difficulty. They had astronomy; they knew about the planets. Space travel was not an alien notion to them. Even so, the news that Corcoran had been to Jupiter seemed to boggle their minds slightly. They were impressed. They asked for further information. And Corcoran realized—or, at least, guessed—after half a minute or so, that they were asking for specific information. They were asking about the cloud-whales. They were imitating the movements of the creatures of the Jovian atmosphere.

But how could they know that Jupiter was inhabited, and by what kind of species?

Corcoran tried to ask. The rats seemed surprised that he had to. It evidently seemed obvious to them that they would know.

As Corcoran studied the ballet more carefully, he became fully convinced that the Rats really were mimicking the cloud-whales—the cloud-whales that he had visited, not their descendants millions of years later . . . unless their descendants millions of years later were essentially unchanged, at least physically. Was that possible? Corcoran wondered.

Why not? he thought. Earth was a tiny, solid, rapid world; Jupiter was a vast, vaporous, slow world, albeit a trifle stormy. Changes probably happened there at a slower pace. Evolution probably happened there at a much slower pace.

Then the ballet changed, and the Rats started asking about something else, forcing Corcoran to concentrate on the new topic.

What were they mimicking?

Could they possibly be asking about other alien life forms? Inhabitants of Saturn, or Titan, perhaps, or . . . was it possible that they were wondering about plasmatic intelligence within the Sun itself? He could not tell, and did not know. He tried to signal his ignorance; the Rats tried to inform him. Now, if ever, was the time for his intuition to come into play, for his supposed empathy with the unhuman to do its bit. There was something to be learned here, if only he could grasp it . . .

But the Rats were already beginning to bid him farewell. They were already telling him how glad they had been to see him again, and asking him to come again soon. They knew before he did that the Slingshot was losing its impetus, that Corcoran's consciousness was about to tumble back into the abyss of time, to be lost in darkness, leaving the ghost inert. He was amazed. The time had flown by. He had not had nearly enough time. Even though it was only the temporal equivalent of on-screen conversation, and not the real intimacy of face-to-face, it felt very intimate . . . even more intimate, in its way, than his conversation with Marie MacLaughlin, and perhaps even more intimate than his fraught confrontation with Nise.

He didn't want to go—and that fact, of itself, convinced him more than a ton of philosophical argument that the empathy he felt with the Rats was real. He knew them. They knew him. And they were all glad to have met up again.

How on Earth had he been able to tear himself away, seven years ago?

Frantically, he tried to signal to the Rats, while he still could, that it was not them he had left, not them he had fled, but all sorts of things of which they, mercifully could not know anything.

If the ghost had been able to weep, Corcoran would have wept, but it could not and he did not want to mime weeping, because he did not know whether the Rats shed tears, or, if they did, what they signified.

As the ballet ended, he thought that it had been beautiful, and meaningful, and precious. But most of all, he thought that it had been welcoming. He wondered whether the Rats had understood that he was not in control of his visits, whether they realized that if things had gone slightly differently in the human world, neither he nor any other human register would ever have come to inhabit the ghost again, and that the ghost itself might have evaporated, deprived of the support of Halleck's transtemporal fishing line.

He thought that they probably did, and that that had been part of the reason for their pleasure.

Then he found himself back in his own body, possessed of its familiar solidity and weight.

That didn't feel like coming home. Perhaps he had been alone too long.

The connections were detached from his contacts; the hood came off. The lights seemed harsh and bright, but it only took his eyes a matter of seconds and a little furious blinking to adapt.

"How did it feel?" Halleck asked, while he checked the dimensions of the data-dump that the Rat's computers had transmitted to his own.

"Good," said Corcoran. "The Rats were pleased to see me. They asked about the cloud-whales."

"What?" Halleck looked up, startled.

"The Jovian cloud-whales. They asked about them."

"But they don't have space travel . . . at least we didn't think so. If we're wrong . . ."

"They asked about other entities too—other alien intelligences, perhaps."

"Saturn?"

"Maybe."

"Or?"

"Maybe the Sun."

"The *Sun?*"

"Maybe. I don't know. Maybe they were just speculating—but they actually mimicked the cloud-whales."

Halleck shrugged, but it was a nervous shrug, far less laid-back than his usual gesture. "Don't worry about it," he said, in the uneasy tone that people who are worried use when saying *don't worry about it*. "That's something we can ask about through the machine. We're communicating well enough now to make concepts of that sort clear . . . I think . . . particularly if they know about the cloud-whales. That gives us a toehold. Damn! If the Rats have space travel, or had it in the past and have given it up . . ."

"I don't think they do. In fact, I'm pretty sure they don't. Not in the time at which the ghost is stabilized, at any rate."

"Some other avenue of communication, then?"

"I think so."

"Right. That's more likely, I guess. I think we can ask about that, too. If it pans out . . . well, it'll prove to the Board that I was right, that we need you . . . *you*, not just any hopeful idiot with a set of contacts. That's a great relief, believe me, Corcoran."

Corcoran believed the assertion that his presence was a great relief—but it was obvious from Halleck's manner that it wasn't by any means a complete relief. Halleck was a worried man, and now that the intense concentration required by the Slingshot was no longer keeping him focused, he was letting it show in his stance, his tone and his movements.

"What's the matter, Walter?"

"Matter? Nothing's the matter," Halleck retorted, in the tone that people who are worried use when saying *nothing's the matter*. "Everything's going as planned—but there's still a lot to do."

"Okay," Corcoran conceded. "When do we go tomorrow?"

"Tomorrow?" Halleck seemed surprised. "I won't be ready to go again tomorrow. Monday at the earliest. I've got to go through this stuff, check all the machinery, compile a report. Probably Tuesday."

"But that will only be another short-range shot—to the third generation. It'll take months, at that rate, before you can attempt to send me long distance."

"No, no, certainly not months. We'll be able to accelerate, skip at least one step, maybe two. Believe me, I'm every bit as anxious to get you all the way to the seventh generation as you are to go, but we're scientists, not cowboys. There's a lot I have to check and double-check . . . and there's the voice-link to perfect and integrate into the machine. I'd like to test that on the next shot, so I certainly can't go before Monday. Be patient—and be grateful that you don't have to deal with all the bullshit I have to deal with, on top of all the calculations and calibrations. You have it easy, believe me. And even if it does take ten days or two weeks before you make it to the world of the red sun, it'll give you longer to settle down and readapt fully to Earthly life—which you probably need, because, quite frankly, you're not your old self yet. I need you in tomorrow, all day, but I think you can take Sunday off. Go see your mother by the seaside. Relax. Come in Monday morning fully refreshed, and if I can get the voice-link hooked up and the apparatus ready to go, you can go say hello to the Inverts."

"I suppose I could give my Reverend another interview," Corcoran said, with a slight sigh, but no hidden agenda. He was slightly surprised when Halleck's expression darkened.

"Are you sure that's wise?" he asked.

"I have permission," Corcoran pointed out. "From you. You agreed that it couldn't do any harm."

"To the project, yes. But I'm worried about you. Are you fucking this woman?"

"She's a clergywoman!" Corcoran protested. "Of course not."

"No, I suppose not. Silly idea. But be careful, Corcoran. Something's gnawing away at you, and I can't tell what it is. Okay, it's not the vicar . . ."

"She's not a vicar," said Corcoran, automatically. "She's a chaplain."

"I stand corrected," said Halleck, unrepentantly. "How's your sister?"

"Fine."

"No trouble there?"

"None," Corcoran assured him, wondering why Halleck, after all these years, had suddenly felt obliged to put on a show of concern regarding Corcoran's personal affairs.

Halleck appeared to take his word for it. "Beats me, then," he said. "You haven't heard from the ISA, have you?"

"Only routine messages."

"The crew of the Olympus?"

"A couple of COAs. Nothing personal."

"Must be just the air and gravity, then. Let's give it time. Take my advice and take Sunday off. For now, go home and rest. I'll call if you're needed, but I can't see anything urgent coming that can't wait for tomorrow's meeting."

And with that, Halleck plunged back into full concentration mode, seemingly oblivious to the fact that Corcoran was still there.

"I'll be on time," Corcoran promised.

X

As soon as he was outside, Corcoran headed for Kensington Gardens. There, after walking around pensively for ten minutes, he sat down on a bench and called Denise.

"Can you meet me for a drink?" he asked.

"What, now?"

"If possible. If not, later. Dinner, if you like."

"You're inviting me out to dinner?"

"Yes."

"I saw Marie today, and she said you'd told her to give me your love. Is that true?"

"Yes."

"Without prompting?"

"Well, no," Corcoran admitted, "but I did mean it."

"That's a relief. I thought for a moment that I or the world had gone mad. Yes, I can meet you for a drink, if you like . . . we can see about dinner, later. What's the matter?"

"Why should anything be the matter?"

"Come on, Zeph, don't play the fool. Is it Marie?"

"No," said Corcoran, surprised. "Why would it be Marie?"

"Work, then? You've just done a Slingshot. Did it go wrong?"

"No, the shot was fine . . . the Rats were glad to see me."

"But?"

"Something's going on, and I can't tell what it is. Halleck's just . . . well, I don't know what it was. Emotional displacement, your friend would probably call it. He was manifestly redirecting his own anxieties at me, projecting them, for some reason. You seem to have your finger on the rumor pulse. I thought you might have heard something, or might be able to find out."

"Oh. Well, in that case, you'd better give me half an hour. Where are you, at the flat?"

"Kensington Gardens."

"Okay. You might as well stay there. I'll pick you up and we can go to a wine bar . . . if you don't mind the possibility of being recognized and pointed out."

"Do you?"

"Hell, no. It won't make up for seven years of neglect, but it's a step in the right direction—but I don't want you to be put out. If you'd rather I came to the flat, say so."

"No, it's okay. I'll wait here. It's a pleasant evening."

"Where, exactly?"

"I'm on a bench near the *Physical Energy* sculpture."

"Aptly incongruous. I'll see you in half an hour or so. I'll find out what I can."

"Thanks."

"No problem. I think I might know how the Rats felt."

"I'll be interested to see you dance, then."

"Not this side of World's End," she assured him, and broke the connection.

Corcoran actually felt relaxed, sitting on the bench staring at the Watts statue that was supposed to symbolize "the restless physical impulse to seek the still unachieved in the realm of material things." He understood what Denise had meant by "aptly incongruous," but he didn't agree with the judgment. He was, after all, not merely a temponaut but a man who had been to Jupiter. Who, in London, had a better claim to a restless physical impulse to seek the as-yet-unachieved in the material realm? Was he not preparing to set forth on a journey to the end of that world . . . and a belated end of the world at that? What had the cavalier shading his eyes ever done to compare with that? What could he possibly have imagined to compare with that, back at the beginning of the twentieth century?

And yet, he really did feel quite relaxed, as if he were gradually easing back into earthly gravity and London air, and the pleasant mildness of the evening. It was Halleck who had been on tenter-hooks, accusing him unjustly of being at odds with the world.

He tried to recall the dance of the Rats—not the specific steps, which would have been impossible—but the general impression, the beauty of it. To be able to generate that kind of excitement, that kind of apparent pleasure, at a distance of several million years, possibly tens of millions, was surely something, surely a compliment. Surely it proved his empathy with the unhuman, his special talent, his freedom from delusion.

He was sufficiently absorbed in his thoughts that he didn't notice the man with the hat pulled down over his eyes approaching the bench until he paused directly in front of him, cutting off his view of the statue, and said: "Hello, Zephaniah."

It was only a month since he had last heard the voice, and yet it seemed to come out of the depths of time. Corcoran got to his feet, not so much out of politeness as because of a strange notion of obligation—although, obviously, it had never been conventional aboard Olympus Five to leap to one's feet when the captain spoke.

"I'm sorry," said Chris Kemmering. "I don't mean to startle you. May I sit down?"

He sat down without waiting for any sign of assent, taking the permission for granted. He was the captain, after all, although he didn't seem very commanding at present. Indeed, the way he was wearing his hat, evidently trying to avoid the possibility of being recognized, to the extent that that might be possible, made him seem distinctly shifty.

Corcoran sat down again too.

"How have you been, Zephaniah?" Kemmering asked. "Not easy to get used to all this again, is it? This is a nice place, though. Nice building—restored after the Great Flood, obviously, but they've done a good job."

They had. There were whole areas of London that had simply been bulldozed and replaced, but there was a core of national monuments that was held to constitute the heart and soul of British identity and pride, and every effort had been made to put them back exactly as they had been before the Flood. Kensington Palace was one, Imperial College another.

"We don't have anything like that in the States," Kemmering added, when Corcoran did not speak. "We have history, of course, but not that kind—no palaces. Who's the statue over there?"

"Watts," said Corcoran, inarticulately.

"Excuse me?"

"Sorry. The statue's by a man named Watts. It's nobody in particular; it's symbolic."

"Of what?"

"It's called *Physical Energy*." Corcoran thought the short version adequate to answer what was presumably an incurious remark made in an attempt to grease the wheels of the social interaction. He was still a couple of questions behind, though, so he added: "I'm fine. Readapting slowly. How about you?"

"Having a rather difficult time, truth be told. For a week or so, my entire career was hanging in the balance—you understand, don't you?"

"I heard about the sex tapes. I haven't tried to look at them. Mine are out there too, apparently, but nobody's interested."

"But you *understand*, don't you?" Kemmering, adding the emphasis.

Corcoran did. "Yes, of course. I was there. I understand what the circumstances necessitated. We all did. And you were the one with the responsibility—to maintain and massage crew morale, and do everything possible to stifle the development of potentially harmful jealousies and resentments. You had to organize our private subculture in order to maintain its harmony . . . a kind of mini-utopia. And you did it brilliantly. I don't think anyone else could have done as well. But people down here don't understand. They don't know what was at stake, and they can't imagine the circumstances."

"Thanks," said the ex-captain of the Olympus Five. "I wasn't just doing my duty, though . . . it was all sincere; I loved them all. You know that, don't you, Zephaniah."

"Absolutely. We all did . . . do."

"Thank God for that, at any rate. I'm sorry I didn't call, but there's no such thing as an unmonitored phone call any more, and I needed to talk to you off the record. Would you care to take a little drive with me? There's someone who'd like to meet you."

"Where to?"

"Not far: the American Embassy. The car will bring you back to your apartment, or anywhere else you'd prefer. It won't take more than an hour."

Corcoran blinked, utterly bewildered. The American Embassy? Kemmering wasn't here on behalf of the ISA, then?

"I can't," he said. "I'm meeting my sister. She'll be here in a few minutes. We're going for a drink."

"Denise? The biology professor?"

It wasn't particularly surprising that Chris Kemmering should know Denise's name, even though Corcoran couldn't recall having mentioned her in conversation with the Captain during the seven years of the Mission. He was the captain, after all. He was supposed to know his crew.

"That's right," said Corcoran, warily.

"Actually, that's convenient. Bring her with you. As I say, it won't take long, and I'll drop you again anywhere you like."

"What's this about, Captain?"

"I'm not a captain any more. It's just Chris now. And my . . . superior will want to tell you himself."

Corcoran suppressed an impulse to laugh. "You've signed a confidentiality agreement," he observed.

"Actually," Kemmering said, "it was a little more serious than that. I'm not a captain any more, but my oath of allegiance still holds. Like you, I'm on a new mission now. I'd ask you how the Slingshot went if I thought you were allowed to talk about it, but we'll get the report tomorrow, so there's no need . . . oh, don't look so shocked. There are no secrets any more. We try—my God, we try—but everything leaks eventually. All confidentiality wins you these days is a little time. Ironic, no?"

"Is it?" Corcoran queried, all at sea.

"In the sense that time is running out? The end of the world is nigh, and all that? Too subtle? Sorry, Zephaniah."

Kemmering had never called him Zephaniah on the ship. There, it had always been Corcoran. Rigid protocol. He suspected that Kemmering hadn't even called the female crew members by their first names when he was sleeping with them. He made a mental note to ask Denise, who, according to her boast, could give him every last detail of every last episode. Then he crossed out the mental note. He didn't want to know. The point was that if Kemmering was calling him Zephaniah now, it must mean that a different set of protocols was in force.

"You're working for the American government?" said Corcoran.

"Of course," said Kemmering. "Indirectly, so are you."

Corcoran suspected that Denise's research had just become redundant. Halleck's refreshed funding was coming from the US government—but not directly. That might be ticklish information, diplomatically speaking, but Corcoran didn't suppose for a moment that the British Government didn't know, unofficially if not officially. And the two were supposed to be on the same side . . . but everyone was supposed to be on the same side now, united against the threat of imminent World's End. Officially, at least.

Have the US built their own Sling? Corcoran wondered. *Are they trying to poach me? But if they've put money into the Institute, and are effectively funding the Seventh Generation shot, why bother?*

He knew that there was no point in asking. He would probably find out soon enough, if Denise was willing to make a little excursion to the American Embassy before they got their drink. He didn't imagine for an instant that she'd refuse. This lent a whole new dimension to the idea of having an inside track.

Denise appeared then, bang on cue.

"Denise," he began, "this is . . ."

"Captain Kemmering," said Denise, reaching out to shake the American's hand. "I recognize you from the photographs. It's a great privilege to meet you. Zeph didn't tell me you'd be here."

"I took him slightly by surprise, I fear, Professor Corcoran," the ex-captain said, oozing charm. "I'm very sorry to interrupt your plans, but I've been asked at rather short notice to invite Zephaniah to call in at the American Embassy for a brief meeting. To be honest, the fact that he was waiting here to meet you is something of a bonus, because it would probably be in everyone's interest if you were included in the meeting, rather than your brother filling you in at second hand."

Denise looked at Corcoran. She didn't seem to have been thrown out of her stride at all. Indeed, she seemed to be matching Kemmering's charm with a similar quantity of coquetry. Was this the way she always behaved around handsome men, he wondered? Had she too joined the PT, or at least begun to test the waters? It didn't seem likely, but he had been away for seven years, and how well had he known Denise even back then?

"That's very kind of you, Captain," she said, with what was almost a simper. "Will I have to sign a confidentiality agreement?" Her tone was impish; she knew that Kemmering wouldn't get the joke. Even though Corcoran had already used a weak version of it, he didn't.

"Naturally, we'll ask you both to keep the details of the meeting confidential," Kemmering replied, "but we prefer to rely on your word. And, as I was just explaining to Zephaniah, I'm no longer a captain."

"But his oath of allegiance still holds," Corcoran put in, thinking that if Denise wanted to be mischievous, he ought to support her. Even though Denise wasn't an alien, he got the strong impression that her research hadn't been fruitless, and that she already had some inkling of what this was about. At least, he hoped that she wasn't smiling seductively at Kemmering because she had suddenly turned groupie.

"Well then," said Denise. "We'd better not keep your superior waiting, had we? He must be a busy man."

Kemmering smiled. "The car's this way," he said. "Illegally parked, I fear, but with diplomatic plates . . . we're still notorious for taking liberties, I believe."

"You do have that reputation," Denise agreed, and fell into step with the ex-captain as if it were the most natural thing in the world. Corcoran didn't know whether she was simply adapting to American notions of appropriate social distance or whether she was following some hormone-driven instinct. He fell into step alongside her, keeping slightly more distance than might have been reckoned conventional between a loving brother and sister.

The drive to Grosvenor Square didn't take long. Corcoran kept hoping that Denise would find an opportunity to whisper something that would give him a clue as to what on earth was going on, but she didn't even seem to be trying. He was profoundly glad that she was there, though, and taking the lead in whatever tricky negotiation he'd been sucked into. He had no way of knowing how adequate she might be as a shield, but as long as she was prepared to get between him and the enemy that was fine.

Except, of course, that Chris Kemmering and he were supposed to be the firmest of allies, having been fellow missionaries beyond the frontiers of Earth only a few weeks before. And what kind of coward hid behind his little sister anyhow?

The carpets in the Restored Embassy were plush, the corridors broad and high-ceilinged, with a quasi-religious atmosphere befitting a cathedral of diplomacy—although Corcoran was vaguely aware that it must have been built some time before it became a little slice of American soil, and must originally have been a Temple to some purely British form of worship.

The room to which they were taken was on the seventh floor, but Corcoran was suitably impressed by the smoothness of the elevator.

He had expected an office, but they were ushered into a small reception room with a view over the Square. Corcoran took instant note of the fact that four armchairs had been placed around a low, square table, although Kemmering hadn't made any call to announce the unanticipated presence of an extra guest.

The man who stood up from one of the armchairs in order to greet them was in his sixties, and was instantly recognizable as the American Secretary of State, Stefan Jablonski. Kemmering introduced him anyway. There were handshakes all round. Corcoran had to steel himself even more than usual.

"Thank you for coming, Mr. Corcoran," Jablonski said. "And you too, Professor. I'm sorry to spring this on you at such short notice, but I'm not in the country for long and I have a very full schedule. I was very keen to make time to meet you, however. I'm a great admirer of your work."

"Oh," was all that Corcoran could manage to say.

"Mr. Kemmering speaks very highly of your contribution to the Olympus Mission," the Secretary of State went on, "and I've recently had occasion to reappraise the work you did beforehand at the Institute . . . and, of course, the project in which you're currently involved. I'll be extremely interested to discover the result of your attempt to contact the seventh generation." He paused, but this time, Corcoran couldn't even break the silence. He glanced at Denise, but she was waiting, looking at the statesman with naked interest—but not, in this instance, with the slightest hint of lust or contrived seduction.

"You might think that the Slingshot project has no political interest," Jablonski went on, smoothly, "that it's what used to be called 'blue skies research' in my grandfather's day. And many people still think the same of the space program: that it's something very expensive, of no practical value, on which world governments shouldn't be spending billions while the world is allegedly on the brink of annihilation. You might even have been subjected to protest demonstrations and online abuse since you got back, as Mr. Kemmering has?"

Again, he paused, but it wasn't really a question, so Corcoran didn't feel any obligation to answer it.

"I was the captain," Kemmering put in, "so it's only natural that I took the heavy fire—and the British are more civilized in that regard."

Little does he know, Corcoran thought, but still didn't say anything.

"The point is, however, that neither I nor the President take that view," said the Secretary of State. "We think that the work that you've done, and the work that you're doing at present, are not merely interesting, but vital. And that's why we want to offer you employment. Not right away, I hasten to add—we want you to finish the current project first. We're very eager to know what you might be able to deduce from Walter Halleck's latest ghost . . . but I didn't want to wait until then to make our position clear. Regard this as a kind of pre-emptive strike, if you wish."

Phrases like "pre-emptive strike" still rolled easily off the tongue of an American Secretary of State, even in these sternly pacified days.

"According to . . . Chris," said Corcoran, finally finding his voice, "you already employ me."

"We have, indeed, made a substantial contribution to the funding of the latest series of experiments, with the permission of your government. Nevertheless, you're still employed by the Institute, which is an independent body. On the other hand, the present funding is a short-term matter, and the likelihood is that you'll be free of contract again in a matter of months . . . perhaps weeks."

Weeks? Corcoran thought. *I've just signed a contract for five years!* But he knew that the contract in question was entirely dependent on funding. If the Americans cut off the funding, it wouldn't, as the proverb had it, be worth the paper it was written on. He now understood why Halleck had been so agitated . . . and why he'd asked whether Corcoran had heard from any members of the Olympus crew.

"You want me to move to America?" he queried, warily.

"We would want you to do that," Jablonski confirmed.

"To work on an American Sling?"

Jablonski and Kemmering exchanged a brief glance. "I'd rather not go into specific details at the moment," the Secretary of State said. "Obviously, though, we'd like to recruit you because of your particular expertise and proven experience. Salary is literally no object, and we'll do everything we can to make the relocation as smooth as possible."

Denise finally judged that the moment had come to intervene. "And where, precisely, would Zeph be required to move to?"

"Well," said the Secretary of State, "as you obviously know, during what you in Britain refer to as the Crash, the States took something of a battering—considerably worse than your beautiful little island. But the increase in atmospheric temperature worked wonders in Alaska, and it's become the economic boom state, where many of our new enterprises are based. And I'd like to add at this point that the offer to relocate is open to you too, Professor Corcoran. We'd like to offer you a senior position at one of our finest universities."

"Fairbanks?" queried Denise, instantly.

Jablonski didn't blink. "Indeed," he said. "We think you'd fit in very well there, and would be very happy. Imperial is one of the finest institutions in the world, of course, but we're very proud of Fairbanks, and we believe that we could put together a very attractive package for you."

"Just as a sweetener to help you persuade Zeph to relocate?"

"Not at all," said the statesman, smoothly. "We consider you to be a very valuable asset in your own right. Although, having said that, we have been thinking of the arrangement as something of a package deal."

Denise nodded. She didn't smile. She was being businesslike now. She wasn't making eyes at Chris Kemmering any longer. "I see," she said. "We'll need time to think it over, obviously, and discuss it between ourselves. It would be a major step for me, as you'll understand. Zeph is quite an adventurer, having volunteered for the Jupiter Mission, so a move to Alaska is obviously something he could take in his stride, but we'll still need to talk it over . . . and consult our mother too. So, unless you'd like to give us more details of exactly what it is that you want Zeph to do for you, we'd better not take up any more of your valuable time."

The Secretary of State still wasn't fazed. The ghost of a smile might even have crossed his lips, possibly a smile of recognition in acknowledgement of a gifted amateur.

"I'm not in a position at present to spell the situation out exactly," he said, "but I do want to stress that we—the President and I—consider your brother to be a person of great value, whom we'd very much like to involve in research that I'm sure he'd find interesting and challenging. As I say, money is no object. Please do discuss the matter carefully. Mr. Kemmering will be in touch. Thank you for coming. It was a great pleasure to meet you both."

The Secretary of State stood up. Everyone else did likewise. There was another round of handshakes. Then Kemmering escorted Corcoran and Denise back to the elevator.

"Where shall I ask the car to drop you?" he asked.

"Don't bother," Denise said. "We'll walk. It's a nice evening."

"I look forward to seeing you again soon, Professor," the ex-captain added, as the elevator reached the ground floor and they began the walk toward the Grosvenor Square entrance. "And I really do hope that we'll have the opportunity of working together again very soon, Zephaniah."

"Being locked up in a tin can for seven years wasn't enough, then?" Denise interjected, her eyes drilling into Kemmering's face.

He laughed, although Corcoran couldn't see the joke.

"You'd be surprised, Professor, how much camaraderie an adventure like that can produce. There was a time, quite recently, when people thought that being cooped up together like that might drive people mad, or at least develop social tensions to the point of generating hatreds—but the Jupiter missions have proved that, at least with a modicum of careful planning, the opposite effect can be produced. Your brother did very well on the mission—very well indeed. We all did—and I say that without boasting, because any extra credit due to me as captain is minimal."

"It's very modest of you to say so," said Denise. "You make the prospect seem quite attractive, though. Perhaps I'll have a chance to try it myself some time."

Kemmering was oozing charm again. "It's not impossible, Professor," he said, smoothly. "Although I doubt that it's an opportunity you'll have at Imperial—one more reason why you might well be tempted to relocate to Fairbanks."

There were more handshakes when they said goodbye, promising to keep in touch.

XI

Denise glanced briefly at the gardens, and then dragged Corcoran away in the direction of Oxford Street, where she stopped at the first wine bar they came to and told Corcoran to grab a table while she ordered a bottle of expensive Burgundy.

"I'll pay," she assured him. "It's a special occasion."

Once she'd poured the drinks, he said: "God, I'm glad you were there. I could hardly open my mouth, and I hadn't a clue what was going on. I hope you won't take it amiss, but I've never been so thankful in all my life that I have a sister."

"A sister that loves you," Denise pointed out, taking a long swig from her glass, "and whose supposed inside track to your dubious affections has just won me by far the largest bribe I'll ever be offered in this life. It's me who should be thanking you."

"They're not dubious," said Corcoran, a trifle resentfully. "I just . . ."

"Have difficulty expressing them. I know—let's skip that. What are you going to do?"

"Do? You mean, am I going to take this crazy job offer?"

"Exactly."

"Do I have a choice? I mean, I know it was all smiles back there, but I got the distinct impression that we were being made an offer we can't refuse."

"They're not the Mafia, Zeph, or even the CIA. Those times are over. They certainly aren't going to make any threats against you, and if they have people watching you they probably have orders to take a bullet for you, if necessary. But yes, they do seem determined. Not just the Secretary of State for God's sake, but carefully dropped references to the President. That's serious enthusiasm."

"But why? As the man said, what I'm involved with, even if I'm not delusional, is blue skies research. Or have the Rats finally come through with some technical information that's worth its weight in political gold? Have they sent us specifications for a machine to switch off the global catastrophe? Are the Americans suddenly desperate to monopolize communications with them?"

"That is one possibility," Denise conceded.

"But not the only one?"

"No. I suppose, if it were something of that sort, and the Americans weren't satisfied just to have taken financial control of Halleck's sling, they might well be thinking of constructing their own Sling and trying to open their own hotline to the rats. But did you notice who was missing from that meeting?"

"Walter Halleck."

"Indeed. And the handsome captain sidled up to you in Kensington Gardens rather than going to the Institute, or even phoning you."

"But even Halleck doesn't think he's the only man in the world who understands Coincidence Theory any more. He thinks that ninety-nine per cent of those who make the claim are bluffing, but that leaves one per cent, at least one of whom is bound to be an arrogant American who thinks he's an even bigger genius than Halleck."

"True. But there's nothing on the grapevine about the Americans building their own Sling, and if they were . . . well, you can't keep a project like that completely under wraps in this day and age."

"But they're building something in or near Fairbanks?"

"More things than one. As Jablonski said, Alaska is the new Wild West, the new frontier. It's where everything is happening, thanks to the aftermath of the Big Thaw. Among other things, it's where they're building their principal Survival Enclave . . . the impervious dome where all the important people are going to take refuge when the Crash goes bang again."

"And they think we're important enough to offer us a ticket to that Enclave?"

"Maybe, but I suspect they have something else in mind— and although what I got out of your buddy Kemmering wasn't exactly a confession, it was the kind of hint that can crush toes when carefully dropped."

"I don't understand."

"I'm not entirely sure that I do, either, but it's a hypothesis worth serious attention. And there has been gossip . . . not just recently, but for years."

"About what?"

"Think about it, Zeph. Why do you think you were recruited to the Jupiter Mission, given that, seven years ago, it would have been hard to think of a less likely astronaut, on all the normal criteria?"

"Because they wanted me to try to make contact with the cloud-whales, and even though my reputation was slightly dubious at the time, there were enough informed people who thought it was worth a shot."

"And why did they want to make contact with the cloud-whales?"

Corcoran was slightly surprised by the question. "Well, because they're there. They're the only semi-intelligent extraterrestrial aliens we've found . . . and for years, the orthodox view had been that we were alone. We're not—and it's only natural that we should do our utmost to open communication with them, just as it was only natural that we should try to open communication with future generations, once the Sling had proved that Halleck not only wasn't crazy but that he actually could construct ghosts. And the hope of achieving some kind of practical advantage, of receiving useful scientific and technical knowledge, is still alive and kicking, in spite of the initial frustrations and the paradoxical anxieties."

"That's certainly the orthodox argument," Denise said, teasingly, "and the official one."

"But?" asked Corcoran, impatiently.

"There's an alternative thesis suggesting that the cloud-whales were only an excuse—that the true purpose of all the Jupiter missions, and the current Saturn mission, is to carry out a minute analysis of the capacity of humans to tolerate long periods of isolation, and the processes of social and psychological adaptation involved . . . the ones you told me, so patronizingly, that I don't understand."

"And you think that's why they collected all the data whose leakage permitted you to know who I'd slept with, etc.?"

"Exactly."

"Data that might be very useful for post-catastrophe survival even on Earth in the Enclaves, but which would be absolutely vital if anyone were seriously thinking about the possibility of post-catastrophe survival *off* Earth?"

"Exactly."

"So they're investigating the Jupiter and Saturn satellites systems looking for potential colonization sites?"

"Among other things."

Corcoran finally twigged. "And Fairbanks, or somewhere near there, is where the Americans are building their fabled starship!"

"So it's rumored."

"And they're not offering us tickets to the Alaskan Survival Enclave—they're offering us tickets to the starship?"

"They're offering *you* a ticket to the starship," Denise said. "All Kemmering said to me is that it *wasn't impossible* that I might get a chance to sample the delights of tin-can life—which is diplomat-speak for 'don't hold your breath.' But you must really have impressed him aboard Olympus, even if they have been a bit slow off the mark since the landing. Even Americans have to go through committee stages, I guess—but I suppose they knew you were as good as captive once they'd got a financial stranglehold on the Institute."

"Wow!" murmured Corcoran, a trifle overwhelmed. "I mean, obviously, the matter-annihilation engine is theoretically capable to taking a ship to another solar system, and if it can contrive something akin to a steady acceleration of one-gee, and then decelerate at a tolerable rate, it wouldn't take all that long . . . but it would still be decades. We're already in our thirties; we'd be old by the time the ship got anywhere, if it ever did."

"By today's longevity standards," Denise pointed out, "which might no longer apply even to us. Not that there will necessarily be an *us*. You're the one they want, remember. You're the one who might be capable of talking to aliens."

"If they're that keen," Corcoran observed, "I could probably get your ticket to the post-holocaust world bumped up from steerage to first class . . . if that's what you want."

"I don't even know whether I want to leave Imperial yet. This is all a bit sudden. But I'm touched that you thought of it."

"You're my sister."

She didn't point out that she was the sister who'd learned that he'd signed on for the Jupiter Mission from the web news. They'd cleared that out of the way.

Denise refilled their glasses.

"It's one hell of a gamble," Corcoran observed. "The starship, I mean. It has to be reckoned a long shot. Even if it can actually get somewhere, we have no idea where there's anywhere worth going within twenty light years. It can certainly head for a system known to have a planet in the Goldilocks zone but God only knows what it will find if it reaches it. Any serious student of probability looking for a long life, if and when the Crash goes bang, would be far wiser to put their money on an Earthbound Survival Enclave."

"That's true," Denise agreed. "But if you take the offer, I'm not sure that you'll be able trade in one ticket for the other."

Corcoran thought about it carefully for a full minute, while sipping wine faster than his habit. "You seriously think that they want to recruit me for the starship?"

"It's just a guess. Weigh up the probabilities for yourself . . . or wait until Kemmering gets in touch again, and see what he's willing to tell you and when."

"If it is true, what do you think we ought to do?"

"You're asking for my advice?"

"No, I'm consulting you, because it seems that we're in it to-gether. What I do affects you . . . even if your involvement is just a sweetener."

"I don't know, Zeph. What do you want to do . . . for yourself?"

"It would be a hell of a gamble . . . if that really is what they want," Corcoran repeated.

"Yes, it would."

"And there's no point in even wondering whether it's the only starship project under way, because the odds would be just as long in any event. The choice is yes or no, not which."

"Rumor has it that the Americans are the only ones with both the money and the drive. The ISA has too many cooks watching over its international broth, and the Chinese don't have the same philosophy. If the stars are the way to go, the US project is probably the only viable game on the planet. But as you say, compared to the survival enclaves, or even the possibility of extraterrestrial colonization within the system, it's a long shot—a gamble strictly for heroes. But you have your diploma already, heroism-wise."

"I signed on for Olympus Five. Two full crews had already made the trip, as well as the test flights. Every aspect of the mission was proven."

"But that's not why you signed on, is it?"

"No," Corcoran admitted. They'd been through that too. After a pause, he added: "If in doubt, hesitate. We don't have to decide anything right away. It's going to take Halleck days . . . maybe weeks . . . to get the Sling ready to send me all the way to the ultimate ghost. I really don't know what difference it might make if I find something there, or what it might be . . . but that's the object on my personal horizon at present. I can reasonably postpone any kind of decision until after that. Jablonkski and Kemmering are aware of that . . . they just want me to think about future possibilities beforehand . . . *vague* future possibilities."

"True."

Corcoran thought about those future possibilities while they finished the bottle of wine. As they got up to leave, in order to walk along Oxford Street in the direction of Marble Arch, in search of a proper restaurant with a decent menu—money, it seemed, no longer being any object to either of them—Corcoran said. "Marie MacLaughlin told me that your attitude to me is one of hero-worship. She even went so far as to use the word *idolize*."

"That's the way she talks," said Denise. "She's a priest, it's just the jargon of the profession. Idolization, certainly not. Worship, ditto. But hero—you have the diploma. You're every bit as much a hero as Chris Kemmering, and more so. Don't get swell-headed, though—no man is *really* a hero to his sister. Marie was just trying to butter you up."

"That's what I thought," he admitted. It wasn't *exactly* a lie.

"Are you going to see her again?" she asked.

"Do you think I should?"

"This sudden mania you've developed for asking my opinion is flattering, in a way, but it could get tiresome really quickly. She's my friend, but I really don't care one way or the other."

"So why ask?"

"You brought the subject up, not me. I assumed that you had a reason. And now you're being sensitive, so you obviously had. You're not going to fall in love with her, I hope?"

"I don't think so. Although I am just back from seven years in outer space, during which I completed my initiation in the mating game, so an independent observer might think I'm in an unusually vulnerable situation, and even my sister thought that I might be looking to join the PT. And the fact that she's a clergy-woman, and essentially unobtainable, might add an extra twist to the possibility of fascination . . ."

"All right," Denise conceded, "you can drop the sarcasm. I never thought I'd miss the old act but . . . anyway, Chris Kemmering has just passed you sane enough and sufficiently well balanced to justify a US government contract, so my bet is that you can hold out. I can still give you those other numbers I mentioned, if you want. And you didn't answer the question."

"I know," he said. "I really have changed, haven't I? With a little more practice, I could probably pass for normal."

"You're preaching to the choir," Denise told him. "I've always thought that the incompetence was just an act. You're a certified hero now—you don't need it any more. So when are you going to continue Marie's tutorial on the Inverts and the Plants?"

"I can do Sunday, I suppose," he said, "if she's free—although I suppose it's not a good day for her."

"For you," Denise opined, "she'll make time."

XII

"I'd like to ask you more about the Invertebrates, before we go on to the Plant Intelligences," said Marie MacLaughlin. Corcoran had agreed to meet her in the university chaplaincy, where she was, in some peculiar sense that he didn't really understand, "on duty." The room was Spartan trying unavailingly to seem more welcoming than it actually was to the eyes of potential clients. The walls were papered with floral patterns, and there were sofas instead of stiff-backed chairs, arranged in such a fashion that the chaplain and her guests could have one each, while still facing one another, but not quite close enough to allow them to reach out and make physical contact.

"Fire away," said Corcoran.

"I'm particularly interested in the concept of a hive mind, and the intuitions you obtained when you established communication with . . . the creatures analogous to ants."

"In my view," Corcoran said, "it's an idea that carries too much of a hangover from its crude formulation way back in the nineteenth century. There's certainly a sense in which an ant-hive can be considered as a dissociated body, in which workers, soldiers and so on are more akin to specialized cells than biological individuals, and the so-called Queen is more analogous to a reproductive organ than any kind of monarch. It doesn't follow from that, however, that the aspects of ant behavior that seem mentally organized and purposive reveal the existence of some kind of supersoul possessed by, or possessing, the entire hive—

especially if one bears in mind that workers, insofar as they're analogous to the cells of a complex body, are merely acting on impulses and instructions originating elsewhere."

"Where?"

"That's an awkward question. Probably nowhere, and the illusion of mentality and purpose are just a reflection of mindless complexity. But the point I'm trying to make is that analogy becomes even weaker if one tries to transfer it to the third and fourth-generation entities. They certainly seem to be hive organisms—dissociated bodies—and they certainly seem to have a mentality that's capable of rational and purposive behavior, but it's still a conceptual error to see it as some kind of general supersoul.

"My impression, in fact, is that one of the third-generation castes, and perhaps more than one of the fourth-generation castes, are, in effect, the specialist brain-cells of the hive, which simply send instructions to other castes as our brains send orders to body cells via the nerves. Except that, as I see it, the Thinkers, if I can use that term for the castes in question, are more flexible than human brains, because they're versatile: they can function as individuals, as more complex individuals can, but they can also come together and form a network—a network partly formed by purely physical pseudo-neural connections, partly by communicative connections, primarily the twitching antennae, and . . . well, that's where I run into my gray area."

"Another sense, which resembles telepathy more than what you call antenna-twitching?"

"Another sense—but the analogy with the traditional idea of telepathy might not be helpful."

"Empathy, then—feeling transmission, rather than thought-transmission?"

"Same problem."

"But there is another analogy available—another explanatory resource, isn't there?"

The Reverend was a smart woman, and she'd done the reading, but Corcoran could tell that she wanted him to broach the subject without being prompted.

"Yes," he agreed, "it's certainly possible that the extra sense in question relates in some way to the phenomena of Coincidence. It's highly speculative, but yes—sometimes, when I'm operating through a ghost, I do get the impression that I'm addressing and being addressed by other 'ghosts,' albeit solid ones."

"By which you mean entities whose guiding intelligence isn't necessarily contained, at least not fully, within their individual neural networks?"

"Perhaps."

"And how far would you like to take that analogy, Zeph? Not by way of scientific conclusions, I hasten to add, or even vague intuitions? How far do you take it in speculation, in the realm of imaginative possibilities? Do the hive minds of the fourth generation Inverts extend across time as well as space. And if so, what of those—or *that*—of the sixth generation Megaplants?"

"That's not where my supposed expertise lies," Corcoran countered. "It's outside our present remit."

She pouted, but dropped it, for the moment.

"Well, can you say more about the Plants in a more general sense, then?" she asked. "Both the fifth and sixth generations? Officially, all we have from those ghosts are images, which are open to interpretation—but whether it's outside your remit or not, you're on record as having expressed your conviction that the plants are purposive in their behavior, that they exert a very high degree of control over their environment, and that what might at first glance seem to be animals living in parallel with them are really aspects of the plant species."

"That's not just an opinion," Corcoran said. "The motiles can be seen budding from the sedentary structures, and fusing with them. They don't really eat the plants; they draw their energy supplies entirely from plant saps that they absorb, but it's more closely akin to babies suckling at the breast, or the body supplying individual tissues with chemical energy supplies. That's accepted. What's slightly more contentious is the assertion that the fifth generation still represents an evolutionary phase of competition and natural selection, in which multiple species exist, while the sixth is a post-selection era in which there is, in effect, only one single species, and perhaps only one single organism, occupying the Earth's entire surface, with a mind that constitutes what Walter Halleck used to be fond of calling a noösphere: a sphere of thought analogous to the biosphere."

"But you can't be certain of that, because the ghost isn't mobile, and its viewpoint is very limited? So that really is a matter of your intuition, not the interpretation of the data sucked up by the computers?"

"True," Corcoran admitted.

"And in any case, that does seem to you to be the natural endpoint of the evolutionary sequence as you've mapped it out—just as it seemed to the man who invented the idea of a noösphere back in the twentieth century? You know, of course, that that was a Churchman—a Jesuit?"

"Yes—Teilhard de Chardin. But the term became generalized thereafter, and Walter Halleck uses it in a non-religious sense . . . or thinks he does."

"But either way, the idea of the ultimate Megaplant, whose body constitutes the entire biosphere and its mind the entire noösphere, does seem to many people, including you, to be the natural culmination and climax of the Earth's evolutionary story? And that's why you were ready to interpret your intuitions of the sixth generation in that way?"

"Now you're playing Devil's Advocate," Corcoran said, slightly surprised.

"Of course I am," she said. "I'm a PhD student, a serious theologian. I have to look at both sides of the question—but I don't really want to believe that your interpretation of the sixth generation is simply a displacement of your own prejudices. What I'd really like is for you to give me a reason to reject that hypothesis. Can you?"

Corcoran squirmed in his sofa, which, although its softness seemed superficially attractive, actually had too little firmness to provide the foundation of a comfortable seating position.

"I don't think I can," he admitted. "I've always resisted the Radical Asp hypothesis that all empathy is illusion, and that all newts can do is delude themselves that they understand one another by projecting their own feelings, and only manage to make as many correct inferences as they do because newts are essentially boring people who are all pretty much alike. I've never taken refuge in that kind of cynicism—but that doesn't mean that I have a secure defense against it. I really can't be certain that all the empathy I think I feel with the Rats, the Inverts, and even the plants, is anything more than a delusion . . . a displacement of my own ideas, and hopes.

"It did seem to me, seven or ten years ago, that Walter's ideas about the noösphere, which he was certainly ready to impose on the reports I brought back without anything to go on but esthetic prejudice, had a certain seductive logic to it, as a narrative to which the entire series of generations could be fitted. I did have the sense, back then, that the sixth generation represented a kind of terminus: the achievement of a particular kind of unity . . . but looking back now, I'm more suspicious of myself, and my supposed gift."

Unlike the Americans, it seems, he thought. But he wasn't sure whether to put that down to innate cultural optimism, the frontier spirit, or the Promiscuous Tendency of ideas, rather than to any genuine conviction.

"But if the sixth generation really is a biological unity," Marie MacLaughlin integrated, "you really did get the impression in confrontation with it that it's a unity with a mind . . . an intellect . . . even though you couldn't institute a recognizable dialogue with it?"

"That was my impression—but it might be the most hazardous of all my impressions. I'd fallen for the seeming esthetic neatness of the pattern of evolution that Walter and I had sketched out in speculative discussion: the narrative in which the feverish mammals pave the way for the calm insects, which pave the way for the contemplative plants, which combine into the ultimate organism. Not that I read any teleological element into that, even then—I never thought that it was *fated*, that it was following some kind of divine plan . . . although I can understand why someone like John Ray or William Derham might have jumped to that conclusion."

"Someone like me, you mean?"

"I suspect so."

"Delicately put. But when you say that all that is what you thought seven to ten years ago, do you mean that you've changed your mind, or that you're simply less insistent in your conviction."

"The latter, I suppose. I haven't transferred my intuitive allegiance to an alternative narrative."

"But you'll be going back to the sixth during the new series of shots?"

"I certainly hope so—after the crucial shot, if Halleck doesn't include it in the test runs . . . provided that . . . but I can't talk about that."

"All right, let's go back to your loss of conviction . . . what you said just now implies that it's just an effect of the lapse of time. Your fundamental intuition still remains the same?"

"Well . . . that's tricky ground. Let's just say that certain doubts have been amplified."

"Doubts plural?"

"Yes."

"Not just the fact that Halleck thinks that he's found a seventh generation, then?"

"That might be unimportant in itself. Just because the evolutionary narrative seemed to have reached a logical terminus of sorts doesn't mean that it couldn't have begun over—and might have had to, if the plant-descendants were destroyed by a catastrophe. What seems odder to me is the fact that the Earth's orbit will apparently be moved. I can't imagine how entities like the sixth generation Megaplants, or Megaplant, could have contrived that. Obviously, there's an element in the plot that my old narrative scheme hadn't considered."

"More than one, since you have plural doubts?"

"Yes."

"Can you talk about the others?"

"I guess—vaguely, at least. One is the cloud-whales. They also complicate the picture: another stray element."

"It would be interesting to build a Sling in Jupiter orbit," Marie MacLaughlin mused. "If we could build up a picture of the broad pattern if Jovian evolution, from its origins to its own terminus . . . but that's definitely outside our remit. What about the others?"

"One other," Corcoran corrected, automatically, although what he really meant was that there was only one other item of the list he'd drawn up as potentially communicable to the Reverend.

"One other," she acquiesced. "What?"

"The possibility we've already broached, and has been floating around for years, that one or more of the additional senses possessed by the future generations might employ phenomena of Coincidence. That might, if true, help to explain why I've had the impression that even the Rats, let alone the Inverts, already know something about their own future generations . . . that, as you put it, they have prophets and take them seriously."

"But you knew that long ago, and didn't think it was particularly important."

"No, I didn't, but I do now."

"Why?"

Because it isn't just temporal, he thought. *If it's true that the Rats already knew about the cloud-whales before I tried to get the idea across to them, and if Coincidence effects, or something similar, can work across interplanetary space . . . then the plausibility of the idea of a Cosmic Mind, as an eventual product of cosmic life goes up a notch.* But he couldn't tell her that, even though he was sure that she'd be delighted were the narrative to take on such a complexion. That was covered by his confidentiality agreement. It wasn't in the public domain, although it might well be hackable, given that Marie worked at Imperial, as Denise did, and had an overlapping circle of friends.

"It's just something that seems more significant now than it did then," he hedged.

124

"It seems particularly significant to me, too," she said, "for reasons you can probably understand." She meant that if humans had such a sense in embryo, more developed in some than in others, experiencing it as a kind of intuition, then the plausibility of prophecy within a religious context went up a significant notch.

"Perhaps you ought to talk to Walter Halleck," Corcoran suggested. "If Coincidence theory can offer any special insight into the mind of God, he's the man who can explain exactly what it might tell us. Except that his firm opinion is that while we have mathematics, we don't need God . . . or that Mathematics is God."

"It's not a new idea," the chaplain observed.

"I'm sorry," Corcoran said. "I know we don't seem to be getting very far, because we're bogged down in so much confusion . . . I am, at any rate . . . but it's getting late again, and I'm tired. Can we call it a day?"

"Of course," she said, apparently feeling more confident about the prospect of coming back to him with more questions since he'd phoned her to offer her the present appointment. "I'm sorry that I can't return the favor you did me last time, but even though the lack of demand for my services is painfully obvious, there really is a sense in which I'm on duty, and won't finish my supposed shift for hours. Thanks very much for dropping in. I know it's difficult for you."

He had to stretch his limbs after rising from the treacherously soft sofa, but it only took a few seconds to restore their flexibility, by which time she had opened the door for him.

She came out of the room behind him and escorted him all the way to the door of the chaplaincy. She was just being polite, but she reaped an entirely unexpected reward when she saw the man who was waiting outside the chaplaincy door. For a second, she must have thought that he was a client, and she stepped forward eagerly to offer him a good Christian welcome—but then she recognized him, in spite of the fact that his hat was pulled well down over his eyes, and not because the evening sun was unduly troublesome.

"Oh!" she said, startled. "You're . . ."

"Yes," Chris Kemmering admitted, "but I'd be obliged if you didn't shout it out. I . . . heard that Mr. Corcoran was here, and thought I'd wait, as I didn't want to disturb you. He and I are old friends, as you know." He smiled, positively dripping charm.

"Yes, of course," said Marie MacLaughlin, blushing. For a moment, Corcoran actually thought that she was going to simper, but she pulled herself together in time to save the dignity of the cloth. "I'll leave him to you, then." She bowed imperceptibly, and withdrew.

"Walk with me," Kemmering said to him. Corcoran obeyed, meekly.

"I'm sorry for springing Jablonski on you the other day, Zephaniah," the former captain said, as he led the way, "but he's an old bird and his habits are a trifle antediluvian. It's a wrench going back to being a mere aide after being captain of my own ship for such a long time, but needs must. Your sister worked it out, didn't she? She figured out why we want you?"

"She put forward an interesting hypothesis."

"Let's go this way—back toward the Gardens. We'll be more comfortable there. And you've had a chance to talk it over with Denise?"

Corcoran was still following, half a stride behind, having to make an effort to keep up. "We've talked," he admitted.

"And how do you feel?"

"About signing on for a ride on an untried starship to an unspecified destination? Come on, Captain, you know I'll need a lot more information than you've given me before I can make a rational decision."

"Of course I do. You can imagine that I needed a hell of a lot more myself before I said yes, and I'm still under orders. I don't really have a choice."

"Do I? Really, I mean?"

"Yes, of course. Nobody leaned on you about joining Olympus Five, did they? And I think you realize now how keen we were to have you aboard. If you say no, we'll respect it. These days, even

Americans can say no to the President. But do you really want to say no? It's a nice night, to be sure, not too torrid, even for August, but we both know that it's the calm before the storm. You Brits have a lot to be thankful for, being an island, with the prevailing wind still blowing from the west. You're about as far from Hell as anyone, except maybe deepest Scandinavia . . . and Alaska, although it has the rest of the States attached to it like an economic ball-and-chain. I can see how you might be able to look around here and now, and think that things really aren't so bad, in spite of all the damage done by the Great Flood. Lots of people do, and I certainly can't blame them. But you know the score. So does your sister. What does she say?"

"She's thinking about it?"

"And what conclusion will she reach, when she's finished?"

"I don't actually know her that well."

"Don't play that game with me, Zephaniah. What will she decide?"

Corcoran sighed. "She'll want me to go," he said. "She loves me. Even if she thinks she ought not to go herself, she'll want me to have the chance . . . not so much the chance to escape, because she knows what a gamble it will be, but the chance to be a hero—again."

"And do you think when the time comes to cast your ballot, that you'll be able to bring yourself to let her down?"

Corcoran hadn't looked at it from that angle before. *Would I?* he wondered.

"Probably not," he admitted, and then amended it to: "Of course not."

"That's what I figured. Jablonski won't pressure you until you've made the crucial Slingshot, but once that's out of the way, he won't want the grass growing under your feet. He's a nervous man—all senior statesmen get up every morning shit scared that something's going to happen that will topple them from their pinnacle. It will ease his pain if I can tell him that you're agreeable in principle, even though I'm not supposed to have told you what you're being asked to agree to. Politics, eh? Imagine how much more straightforward things will be when I'm the captain again. I'm kind of hoping, by the way, that that will be a thought that might reassure you rather than putting you off."

"It's certainly not a negative," Corcoran conceded. "I suppose I'd never forgive myself if I chickened out . . . and nor, as you so cunningly point out, would Denise. About which I'm surprised to realize how much I care."

They had reached *Physical Energy*, but Chris Kemmering didn't show any inclination to sit down on the bench.

"I'm sorry, Zephaniah," he said. "In an ideal world, there'd be no hurry, but that's not the way things work now. Are you in? I need your word. I know that I can trust it as much or more than any contract the bloody lawyers draw up. We're shipmates, after all."

"You can drop the flannel, Captain." said Corcoran, wearily. "Of course I'm in. I'll work out later exactly what I'm in for . . . and exactly what I ought to demand for Denise."

"For what it's worth," said Kemmering, "I'd quite like her to be aboard myself. She's impressive."

"And she simpers at you like a little girl—but they all do, don't they? Even clergywomen, very nearly."

The ex-captain smiled wryly. "Well, I'm not going to tell you that it's a curse—but I can't claim any credit for it. It's Nature's gift. I'm not addicted, though, and whatever the world thinks, I'm not promiscuous. Say the word, and I won't lay a finger on your sister."

"If I did, that's something else for which she'd never forgive me. You know, I really didn't give a damn about things like that, once. Being cooped up on that bloody ship for seven years has ruined me." But he said it with a smile, and he knew that Chris Kemmering knew exactly what he meant.

The captain clapped him on the shoulder, unrepentant and glad to be. "Just think what thirty years is going to do to us, shipmate."

XIII

When Corcoran got back to the flat, Denise was sitting on the doorstep. She stood up as he approached.

"I thought of coming to find you in the Gardens," she said. "I'd have laid odds that you'd have headed for *Physical Energy*. But I decided against it and came here instead."

"Marie phoned you," Corcoran inferred, as he opened the door and they headed for the stairs, "the moment she was back in her office. And you were at work—even though it's Sunday?"

"Of course she did. It's not every day you find Chris Kemmering lurking outside your door, trying feebly to maintain his incognito with a ridiculous fedora pulled down over his blond hair and eyebrows. And of course I was at work. Imperial doesn't have a Sabbath, no matter what the organizers of the shift system at the chaplaincy think. So, what did you decide?"

"I had to tell him yes—for myself. I didn't commit you, though. I left you out of the deal, for now, until you make your own decision."

"You can't," Denise pointed out. "It's polite of you to wait for guidance, but you know that you're the one who holds the cards. If you don't use your pull, I get left behind."

"Fair point," Corcoran agreed, as he opened the door to the flat. "But you still have a choice. Whatever you tell me to do, I'll do. We might not have as much time as we thought, though. As soon as Halleck shoots me to the surface of the relocated Earth, I think they'll shut Slingshot down—and I suspect they're already on Halleck's back, trying to get him to hurry up. They know something we don't . . . about the fall of the sword of Damocles, that is."

"So rumor has it. It's all over the web, even public access channels. The clock has been moved up to five minutes to panic stations, although nobody seems to know exactly what triggered the alarm bell. We're lucky here, it seems, not to have seen the signs in the skies. The fine weather is deceptive—the storms are coming."

"A drink?" Corcoran asked. "To toast my new career . . . or the end of civilization as we know it."

"I suppose so," his sister replied. "Probably not much point worrying about liver cirrhosis or putting on weight. But order us some food, will you. Whatever you like. I need company, and if you turn me down I'll have to go over to the chaplaincy and let Marie try to convert me."

"Sure," said Corcoran. "Italian?"

"Fine. Thanks. Sorry—got to use the bathroom." She disappeared. Corcoran had plenty of time to place the order, set the table, and open the wine. In fact, the time dragged on for so long thereafter that he was reduced to reading the small print on the label of the wine bottle, which gave vague implications as to how the product had been synthesized, while insisting that the original genetic imprint of the organic materials really did come from authentic antique grape stocks.

Eventually, Denise reappeared. "When Halleck gave me the keys to the flat," Corcoran remarked, "he assured me that, even though it's so close to your office, you wouldn't be dropping round every five minutes."

"Well, he doesn't know me, and I will be. It could be worse."

"I suppose it might be, if we end up locked in the same tin can for thirty years. On the upside, though, you'd get to screw Chris Kemmering."

"Along with every other woman on board? I've seen the secret interplanetary porn tapes, remember. No thanks. I haven't joined the PT yet, and even if I did . . . Anyway, I haven't got a ticket."

"I'm pretty certain that you'll get one if I refuse to go without you."

"And you'd do it, too, wouldn't you?—out of sheer bloody-mindedness, of course, not filial affection."

"Maybe—but it's a shitty thing to say, even so."

"I didn't mean it. Sometimes, you know, people don't."

"So it's rumored."

Denise frowned with embarrassment, evidently regretting having lost control of the tone of the conversation. Corcoran felt that it was up to him, as the person who had made the accusation, to smooth things over, but he had no idea how to do that. He realized that the new intimacy that had been established between himself and his sister was still artificial, and rather fragile, and wished that he wasn't so reliant on her to maintain its integrity. After all, if they really were going to spend thirty years together on an American starship, perhaps as the only Brits aboard . . .

Fortunately, the food arrived. Corcoran deliberately didn't ask himself how it could possibly have arrived so quickly, given the time that it would have required to cook the ingredients had they actually been what they were pretending to be.

"Do you know where the British Survival Enclaves are?" he asked, when they had both sat down and started eating.

"Of course. As secrets go, that one's not so much open as positively gaping. The biggest is in Yorkshire, but there's one in Snowdonia and one in the Scottish Highlands. The problem, of course, will be getting there when the shit finally hits the fan, even if the helicopters are all on standby. My guess is that the locals will be laughing, whether they have tickets or not, but you can bet that when the new Houses of Parliament follow the old ones to the river bed, there won't be a single Minister at his desk. Anyway, if we were here, we'd be able to watch the catastrophe unfolding across the continents for weeks until it reached this sceptered isle. If we're in Fairbanks, we'll have a website seat for months, maybe years."

Corcoran was glad to see that she had relaxed again, and that things seemed to have been smoothed over of their own accord. "If?" he queried

"When we're in Fairbanks."

"You've decided, then?"

"No, you've decided. Not that you had any choice. Nor do I, realistically speaking. Even if I had a ticket to the Yorkshire bunker, do you really think I could stand the company? Even in Alaska we'd get a better class of neighbors than that."

Corcoran raised his glass. "To our new life, then."

"Amen. Speaking of which, how did you get on with Marie?"

"I found it rather frustrating, to be honest—no, don't look like that. *Intellectually* frustrating. She asked questions to which I knew answers that I couldn't give her . . . questions that have been tormenting me a bit, to tell you the truth."

"But you can't tell me, either."

"Technically, no, and given that the flat's probably bugged, I probably shouldn't, but I've just signed on to take a thirty-year ride on an untried starship headed for God only knows where, if it actually gets to take off before civilization collapses, so what the hell."

"I feel privileged. For me, my saintly brother is going to break a confidentiality agreement. The world really is turning upside down. Drop it on me, then. What's occasioned the crisis of conscience?"

"The Rats know about the cloud-whales."

"Shit—I was expecting something interesting. Did they tell you that?"

"They not only told me, they danced it—and they mimicked the cloud-whales with uncanny artistry. When I say they know about them, I mean that they really *know*. At first, I thought they'd just been told about them, either by a data-dump or one of the human registers, during the time I've been away. It would be a natural topic of conversation, after all. So I've checked back . . . very quickly, obviously, but as I knew what I was looking for . . ."

"And?"

"Yes, the fact that Jupiter is inhabited has been mentioned during the interchanges, several times . . . even before I went away. But it was the Rats who mentioned it first, not us. I overlooked it at the time, obviously, and the various people monitoring and analyzing the transmissions could easily have mistaken the references to hypothetical remarks . . . but on the other hand, it's not impossible that someone picked up the inference as long as ten years ago, and jumped to the conclusion I've only just reached . . . maybe because they were already looking for it."

"You're not talking about the Institute's computer analysts—you're talking about hackers?"

"Of course."

"American hackers?"

"With the aid of recent hindsight, it seems probable. Even if I'd noticed the Rats referring to Jupiter back then, I wouldn't have thought that it was anything significant, or even the cloud-whales, given that they could have been mentioned in one of our attempted data-transmissions—but when I saw that dance, or, to be strictly accurate, afterwards, when I really thought about what it implied . . ." He paused, groping for the right way to explain what he had thought.

"You had a feeling," Denise supplied.

"Yes, of course," he said, a trifle impatiently. "That's why I'm going to the stars, remember. People have faith in my intuitions."

"Fair point. Okay—so what?"

"Think about it, Denise. Think about what it implies."

"It might only imply that there are documents in the Rat world left over from the pre-Rat era that record humankind's discovery of the cloud-whales in some detail, including images."

"Exceedingly improbable."

"Okay. You and Halleck have both broached the hypothesis, way back when, that the Rats know about the future genera-tions—the Insects and the Plants. Halleck suggested that it was a Coincidence effect, adding further weight to his theory. So they probably know about humans by the same route . . . including our discovery of the cloud-whales."

"Possibly. We can be reasonably sure that if such a Coincidence sense exists, it would give them a measure of forward insight, as it gives us, but we don't have any theoretical basis for backward insight—and until we generated the ghost in their world, all they seemed to know about humans, let alone other species about which humans might know, was what the ruins told them."

"Okay—so what does it imply, according to your hasty re-search, scrupulous logic and magical intuition?"

"Well . . ."

He was interrupted by the buzzer indicating that there was someone at the front door. Whoever was leaning on it was using an unnecessarily heavy hand.

Corcoran and his sister exchanged a glance that said, with manifest clarity: *Who the hell is that?*

Corcoran went to the spy-screen, blinked and pressed the release to let the visitor in. Then he turned to Denise and said: "Halleck."

"Halleck? And he was assuring you that I wouldn't be dropping round every five minutes?"

"Halleck doesn't *drop round*," Corcoran told her. "Something's wrong."

He went to the door of the flat in order to let the physicist in.

Halleck came in like a whirlwind, already beginning to say: "You'll never guess . . ." but stopped dead when he saw that Corcoran wasn't alone. The first expression momentarily etched on his face was astonishment, but it was rapidly followed by anxiety.

"I'm sorry," he said, in a completely different and conspicuously stilted tone. "I didn't know you had . . . company."

"You remember Denise," Corcoran said, guessing that Halleck hadn't.

The physicist's face cleared. Obviously, he had been imagining possibilities compared with which the fact that Corcoran was having a quiet Sunday dinner with his sister was a great relief. "Oh, Denise! Yes, of course I remember. It's been a few years . . ."

"You were wrong, you see," Corcoran couldn't resist saying. "She *is* going to be dropping round every five minutes now I'm so close to her office. Would you like a drink, Walter?"

"No thanks."

"Well, sit down anyway. We'll be finished in a few minutes, but don't feel obliged to bottle it up in the meantime. What's wrong?"

Halleck was still looking at Denise, but no longer with relief. He didn't want to talk in front of her.

"Walter," said Corcoran, softly. "Denise works at Imperial, where the Computer Science department has some of the best hackers in the world. She's very interested in what I do, because she's my sister. Believe me, I have absolutely no secrets from her, even though I'm normally very scrupulous about confidentiality. She knows more about me than I do. So if there's any urgency about what you want to tell me, just spit it out."

Halleck didn't even bother to think about it. The cue was all he needed. "We're in trouble," he said. "They want to close us down—the whole project."

"They?"

Halleck looked slightly embarrassed. "I didn't tell you this," he said, "but the new funding we got . . ."

"Came from the US Government in some kind of under-the-table deal. I know."

Halleck's gaze immediately flicked to Denise. She raised her hands. "It wasn't me who told him," she said. "It was Chris Kemmering."

"Who the hell is Chris Kemmering?"

Corcoran was amazed. "The Captain of the Olympus Five," he prompted.

At least that clicked. "Oh yes—the front man who looks like a film star. The ISA have been on to you, then? Already?"

"Kemmering was only on secondment to the ISA for the duration of the mission—as we all were, technically. He's in the US Armed Forces, and went straight back on duty, even before getting out of Rehab. He seems to be currently functioning as an aide-de-camp to Stefan Jablonski."

"Who's . . . oh, I know, he's their government's blusterer-in-chief, always jetting all over the world to pose for pictures with heads of state. Jesus, I didn't realize the orders were coming from that high up the food chain. I thought it was just their scientists figuring that it was easier to steal my equipment and ship it off to God knows where rather than build their own Sling. Hang on . . . did you *know* that they were going to close us down."

"No, I didn't . . . and for what it's worth, I don't think Chris Kemmering knows either. I saw him not much more than an hour ago. So far as I could tell, they were actually quite keen for the experimental series to proceed, at least until we make the

Slingshot inserting me into the new ghost. Admittedly, Jablonski was only talking about weeks, but . . ."

"So you *did* know! And not only that, but you've been talking to the US government behind my back. Damn it, Corcoran I trusted you!"

Denise, having abandoned her dinner unfinished, had her tablet out and was tapping furiously. Before reacting to Halleck's ire, Corcoran looked at her questioningly. She met his gaze, but only to say: "I'll have to use your wall unit, Zeph."

"To do what?"

"To find out what's causing the worldwide panic, of course— to discover exactly how big the bang's going to be and how soon we need to duck, assuming that there's still time to duck at all. The Circle's already formed—no wonder there was so much buzz on campus on a lazy Sunday in August . . . but I can get in on the periphery, especially if I drop your names. Don't go anywhere, Mr. Halleck. Two geniuses at my elbow gives me even more clout than one."

Corcoran turned his attention back to Halleck, who was now completely at sea. "What's she talking about?" he asked.

"She's talking about using her connections at Imperial to try to find out what the new revised timetable for the end of the world looks like. If Chris Kemmering still didn't know less than two hours ago, given his connections, the situation must be developing literally by the minute. When did you get the news that the Americans are shutting you down?"

"About an hour ago. I was at the Institute, making adjustments to the apparatus for tomorrow's trial . . . except that it seems that there isn't going to be a trial tomorrow."

"Ah!" said Corcoran. "You mean shutting us down just like *that*. Instantaneously?"

"Worse. They want us to fire up the shot tomorrow, but they don't want it to be the planned trial. They don't want any of the planned trials. They want me to send you all the way, immediately. They want your report on the seventh generation. Really, they wanted it yesterday . . . they've been on my back since day one, before you even signed the contract. Incidentally, did you read that contract?"

"Sort of," said Corcoran. "Who reads contracts? I suppose I should have had a lawyer check it over . . ."

"Famous last words. I didn't read mine, either . . . and the lawyer who checked it over . . . well, it's possible that he might not have had my interests primarily in mind. But I was over a barrel anyway. You have no idea, Corcoran, what it's been like—not just these last few days, or the seven years when you abandoned me to go hiking in the outer system, but from the day the Institute first agreed to fund experiments to test and explore the implications of Coincidence Theory. You were just a hireling, then, but even when I realized how important you might be . . . long before anyone else cottoned on . . . I wanted to protect you from all that. I wanted you to be able to focus, just as I'd have liked to be able to focus myself. I understand how the obsessive mind functions, you see, Corcoran, and I didn't want you to have to suffer the kinds of distraction that were raining down on me like king-sized hailstones . . ."

"Very kind of you, I'm sure," said Corcoran, the fraught situation allowing him to lie without a twinge. "Let's get back to the point. The Americans are insisting that you skip all the preliminaries and do the climactic Slingshot tomorrow—and they've stitched you up so tightly with your contract that you can't refuse?"

"Yes," Halleck confirmed, calming down somewhat. "I literally can't. If I refuse, they'll bring someone else in—and no matter how good he is, or how arrogant he is, he's likely to foul the whole thing up. At best he'd simply fail, and at worst he'd kill you and blow the apparatus to kingdom come. I can't let that happen . . . for your sake, Corcoran. Without me, believe me, you'd be in real danger . . . but I've only just got the voice-link wired up, and I haven't had a chance to test it yet, and I need at least two trial runs with established ghosts before attempting to insert you into the new one. This isn't the ABC of telepresence, Corcoran—it's not like hooking you up to some kind of kite flying in the Jovian atmosphere. This is *serious*."

"So," said Corcoran, "to cut what you're insisting on making into a long story to more sensible dimensions, you feel obliged to do as you're told and make the shot they want you to make, because you want to protect your apparatus . . . and me, of course, being the great humanitarian that you are."

Halleck had already moved on. "How much influence do you have with Jablonski?" he asked, suddenly.

Corcoran laughed. "Precisely none," he said. "If you think they've got you over a barrel, you should see the one they've got me over. The chances of my being able to talk your puppet-masters into extending your timetable are zero."

"The bastards!" said Halleck. "The utter bastards!"

"Actually," said Corcoran, "they're not. Quite the contrary. They believe, perfectly sincerely, that they're acting in my interests as well as theirs and those of the human race, and they have a good case. Unlikely as it might seem to you, I think they probably think the same about you. Have you got a ticket to one of Britain's Survival Enclaves?"

Halleck's eyes shifted uncomfortably. "If you mean, am I on the Ministry of Science's list of important national assets, yes I am. I've got a packet of sealed orders to be opened in case the government declares a triple-red state of emergency. I am the world's leading expert in Coincidence Theory, after all."

"The Ministry doesn't seem to have got round to issuing mine," Corcoran observed, finding the sarcasm coming surprisingly easily under stress. "That's why it's genuinely kind of the Americans to step in. They want me to take a few risks in exchange, but that's only reasonable—a fair exchange. After all, my unique expertise still has a question mark hanging over it." He turned to Denise. "Any progress?"

"Lots," she replied briefly, "but things are happening too fast to get a clear picture. Might still be a storm in a teacup . . . and even if it isn't, we're still talking weeks rather than hours. If the world does go to triple-red, there'll be time to activate the programs, although whether they'll actually be workable in the ensuing chaos is a different matter. And whether the Survival

Enclaves are in a fit condition to seal their domes and hunker down is even more uncertain."

"But do you know what's actually triggered the panic?"

"Yes. A massive methane eruption in the north of Greenland, about six hours ago. Half the territory's been devastated. Lucky you left the hospital when you did . . . if you were still there, you might not have got out at all. It's still fairly low down on the disaster scale, seen individually—there've been half a dozen Ring of Fire eruptions that have done more immediate damage—but the real danger is the threat of a chain reaction. Even if it just ran around the remaining permafrosts in Canada and Siberia, it could be a billion-killer. If it were to trigger the release of the clathrates on the bed of the Arctic Sea . . . well, that's been the bookies' favorite world-killing scenario ever since the ice cap disappeared. Burning that kind of methane release would drop the oxygen pressure in the atmosphere way down. Nothing with our kind of lungs could breathe without a private supply."

While Corcoran had been in Rehab, during the few fleeting hours of near-darkness that overtook those latitudes in summer, it had often been possible to see a colored glow on the northern horizon, compounded out of the Aurora Borealis and the spontaneous combustion of methane leaking out of what had once been named permafrost, but whose label only survived ironically. Such leakage had been taking place for a century, slowly thus far . . . but the possibility of a rapid acceleration had been on the cards for generations. Nobody was any longer foolish enough to think that such processes followed smooth curves.

"It'll be another false alarm," said Halleck, defiantly. "You've been away, Corcoran. If you knew how many ends of the world have been announced in the last seven years . . ."

"Only one, Mr. Halleck," Denise put in, dryly. "And we've been living through it throughout my lifetime, and yours too. Nobody now alive has lived in a world that wasn't ending. The only question is, how fast is the process unfolding? Yesterday, we all thought we had weeks or months in hand, at least, to finish whatever we happened to be doing. Tomorrow . . . well, let me get on with eavesdropping on the Circle, and I might be able to tell you whether we have to start thinking about hours. Do you have your packet of sealed orders with you, Mr. Halleck?"

"No—it's at the Institute."

"Well, at least you can lay your hands on it in a matter of minutes, and the directions it will give you might not even require you to leave London. At the most, you'll be off to Snowdonia or Yorkshire. Zeph and I will have to wait to see whether our American friends actually have a means of collecting us and transporting us to Alaska."

"You're going to Alaska?" Halleck queried.

"Actually," Denise retorted, "we're going a hell of a lot further than that, if the plans still have time to unfold. To be honest, given the panic levels currently being registered, I'm a little surprised that the Americans are still insisting that you make a Slingshot tomorrow. They must really want to know the result. What do they know, do you think, that Zeph and I don't?"

Halleck still seemed completely at sea. "I have no idea," he said. "Mine has always been what they used to call blue skies research . . . an addition to human enlightenment with no practical value whatsoever."

"But they didn't always think that, did they?" Corcoran put in. "Twelve years ago . . . probably twenty, long before you recruited me . . . the funding you got was in anticipation of the possibility that a means of seeing through time might actually pay off big rewards, in cashable terms."

"Well, yes," Halleck admitted. "I never lied to them, though. I didn't bluff them just to get the finance, the way some people I could name did. I was always straight. I always explained to them that it couldn't and wouldn't be a matter of reading tomorrow's newspaper. I told them that the minimum interval for stabilizing a ghost, according to my calculations, was measured in hundreds of millions of years. To be perfectly honest, I think I was the only person in the world who actually thought the Sling might actually work, but it was a time of crazy gambles. When I succeeded in stabilizing the first ghost . . . well, there was an explosion of enthusiasm, only slightly tempered by our first sightings of the Rats . . . but that enthusiasm began to drain away soon enough, even though the experiment, in purely scientific terms, went from strength to strength. Even I didn't expect that I would be able to stabilize four more ghosts so rapidly, let alone the kinds of images they would send back. And I never imagined that the human factor would have any importance at all, with all due respect to you, Corcoran. That was just bizarre. And if everything since then has boggled my mind, can you imagine what it's done to the minds of the cretins trying to evaluate it all without even being able to understand the mathematics . . . ?"

"I can and do," said Corcoran, dryly.

"Well, there you go. And you're supposed to have more insight than anyone . . . apart from me, obviously."

"Obviously."

"And then we reached a phase where the only people getting excited about our results were evolutionary biologists and philosophers, and there's nothing that puts a dampener on grant applications more than that."

"Yes, there is," Denise put in, still busy at the big screen. "You're forgetting theologians."

Halleck waved his hand dismissively, as if theologians, from the viewpoint of a mathematician like himself, were so far along the spectrum of irrelevance as to be unworthy of a moment's thought.

"Well, anyway," he said. "You get the idea. So, the funding dried up, as you know, and you went off like a rat leaving a sinking ship . . . all the way to bloody Jupiter, for Christ's sake!—and I thought I'd be back in the realm of pure math for good, and was consoling myself as best I could with the idea that that was where I had always really belonged, when the Americans started taking an interest. Why, God alone knows. Maybe they noticed something in the data they'd pirated that I hadn't. Maybe some hotshot young mathematician who thinks he's mastered Coincidence theory thinks he's found further possibilities in the math. Either way, they haven't told me. I'm just a hireling, it seems. Has your friend the captain given you any clue, Corcoran?"

"Not directly . . . but I do have an inkling as to why they might be so interested in me, and why they're so keen for the last experimental run to take place before civilization crumbles . . . or, if things go bad tonight, while it's actually crumbling."

His phone buzzed. His first impulse was to switch the call to voicemail, but he only hesitated for a moment before taking it.

"Marie," he said.

"Oh, thank God!" said the Reverend Marie MacLaughlin. "I thought everyone in the world had stopped answering their phones. I've been trying to get through to Denise. Something's going on, Zeph, and I have no idea what. I've been stuck here at the chaplaincy all day, on my own . . . I mean, people rarely come, but there's literally no one . . ."

"You can come round to the flat if you like, Marie," Corcoran told her. "Denise is here, doing her level best to keep track of what's happening. We can't tell for certain yet, but it might be very bad, and we're trying to keep up with the news behind the news. Unless you'd rather be with your own people, at St. Paul's or wherever . . ."

"You're a lot closer," the chaplain said, with an alacrity that almost made him doubt her faith. "I'll be there in fifteen minutes, if that's okay?"

"Fine."

Denise was looking at him quizzically. "That was . . . kind," she said.

"Yes, it was," he replied, in a neutral tone.

"Who was it?" Halleck asked, still lagging behind.

"The Reverend Marie MacLaughlin."

"The priest who's been talking to you about the future generations?"

"The priest who's doing a PhD in physico-theology," Corcoran confirmed.

"And you're inviting her round?"

"I could hardly leave her on her own. If the atmosphere really is about to catch fire, even you wouldn't want to be on your own, confronted by an endless stream of answerphone messages. If it comes to the moment when there's nothing left to do but pray, we might actually be grateful to have a priest to show us how."

Halleck looked at him as if he were mad. It wasn't the first time that Corcoran had seen that expression on his face. It almost made him feel nostalgic.

All Halleck actually said, though, was: "It's just another false alarm. In the morning, we're all going to feel foolish for being scared."

"We won't have time to feel foolish," Corcoran told him. "In fact, I'm not sure that we even have time to feel scared. Wouldn't you be better off at the Institute, getting everything as ready as it possibly can be for tomorrow's shot?"

Halleck stared at him for a full minute before saying: "I did everything I can do tonight before coming here. I don't know whether the voice-link will work, but I can't test it until we actually try the shot."

"By voice-link, you mean that you've rigged the apparatus so that you can talk to me while I'm animating the ghost, and you can somehow read my brainwaves in such a way that I can talk back?"

"Yes."

"Why couldn't you rig something like that up years ago?"

"I tried, as you know very well. Technical hitches. As I say, I don't know yet whether they've been overcome."

"And there's nothing else you'd rather be doing over there, on your own, instead of hanging out here with mere mathematical morons?"

"You've changed, Corcoran," Halleck complained. "Time was when you didn't understand what sarcasm was."

"Time was when you didn't either, Walter. We've both grown older, and more perverse. How's it coming, Denise?"

"Still on tenterhooks. Colossal rescue operation in Greenland. No shortage of heroes there. No one anywhere else has announced a full state of emergency yet. Everyone's monitoring the situation, standing by with their fingers hovering over the panic button."

"Told you so," said Halleck. "False alarm."

"Not for half the population of Greenland," Denise snapped. "Casualty figures in millions. So much for the finest of the new promised lands."

"It's not even raining here."

"Shut up, Walter," said Corcoran. "If you don't want to be in the lab on your own, the least you can do is play your part in the shared anxiety. If you don't want to bond, go away."

"You can't throw me out," said Halleck, peevishly. "It's not your flat."

"No," Corcoran agreed. "It's the US government's."

Corcoran's phone buzzed again. Again, he answered it. "Captain," he said. "I've been expecting your call."

Kemmering didn't waste any time in idle chitchat. "Are you up to date?"

"Trying to keep up. Denise is here, using her resources—and Halleck brought me the news about the change of plan."

"Yes—sorry about that. Caught me on the hop too. Can you do it?"

"The Slingshot, you mean?"

"Obviously."

"We don't know that it will succeed, but we can certainly try, if the Institute's still standing in the morning."

"It will be. I'll be there. With luck, it'll just be a matter of observing."

"And without?"

"If necessary, we'll have a copter on standby. You should ask Denise to come and observe as well. You don't need Halleck's permission. For the moment, it looks as if you'll be able to go home afterwards. We might even be able to give you and Halleck another chance to use the Sling . . . but if not . . . well, I know you don't have any substantial luggage to pack, but you'd better suggest to Denise that she put the absolute essentials in a bag, just in case. Got to go—see you soon."

Kemmering closed the connection without waiting for Corcoran to say goodbye.

XIV

"Well?" Denise was swift to demand.

"The Americans don't expect the world to end tonight, and they're still relentlessly optimistic about tomorrow—but he wants me to bring you along to the Slingshot, and suggests that you have your most precious items about your person, just in case."

"Wait a minute!" said Halleck.

"And he says I don't need your permission," Corcoran added. "He'll be there himself. If things really do go bad, you might be glad of that . . . provided that we can squeeze you into the copter. Whether they'll let you on to the jet for Alaska, though, I can't say."

"You're really going to Alaska?"

"Yes. I assume we'll take the polar route, in which case we might actually be able to watch the sea boiling beneath us as all the methane bubbles out. Could be a bumpy ride, though, even at thirty thousand feet."

"You're not serious?" said Halleck, uncertainly.

"Yes, I am," Corcoran countered. "It might be a false alarm, as you say—ninety-nine chances out of a hundred say that we'll be able to go home—but I'm deadly serious, even so. Kemmering says that you might even get another chance to use the Sling, if you're lucky. Are you feeling lucky, Walter?"

Corcoran was beginning to enjoy himself, much to his surprise. Seven years aboard Olympus Five seemed to have immunized him against common-or-garden cowardice. Stress was actually bringing capacities out of him that he hadn't known he had.

The door-buzzer announced Marie MacLaughlin's arrival. He let her in. He didn't have a chance to introduce her to Walter Halleck; she ran straight to Denise, in search of information.

"So far so good," Denise told her, "but we're not off the hook yet. If you want to pray, pray. It's probably a good time. Every minute that goes by without the triple-red being called reduces the probability. On the other hand, if you'd rather have a drink, you know where the wine rack is."

"I can do both," said the Reverend.

"So can I," said Denise. "Pour one for me too."

"I have to use the bathroom first," the chaplain said, and disappeared.

Walter Halleck took out his phone, but he was only checking the time. "It's a false alarm," he said, stubbornly.

"We don't know that yet," Denise told him, equally stubbornly, "but as I told Marie, every minute that goes by makes it more likely, and it really is a good time to pray."

Corcoran went over to her, and only hesitated for a moment before putting his arms around her.

After half a minute or so, she eased herself out of the hug. "That was kind," she observed.

"No it wasn't," he said. "I was being selfish."

"And that's kind too," she added.

A few more minutes passed before Marie MacLaughlin returned carrying two glasses of wine. She handed one to Denise. "You don't mind me leaving you to get your own, do you?" she said to Corcoran.

"No," he assured her, but didn't make a move toward the kitchen.

Denise took a deep draught of the alcohol, and then looked around, weighing the silence. Her gaze, finally, alighted on Marie. "Well, look on the bright side," she said. "If the world does go bang tonight and we have to join the PT in order to spend our last moments as profitably as possible, at least you'll get to screw Zeph in the bedroom. I'll have to settle for Dr. Halleck on the sofa."

Corcoran assumed that he was not the only one looking at her as if she might be mad.

"Joke," she added.

Nobody laughed.

"Oh, all right," she said. "You're all as bad as one another. What about that inkling, Zeph?"

"Sorry?" said Corcoran.

"Before this long series of interruptions started, you were about to explain to Dr. Halleck and me why the Americans have changed their attitude to you and the Slingshot. And don't raise a shield just because Marie's here. You invited her, and you've already broken confidentiality for my sake—and anyway, as you so correctly remarked, what the hell."

Corcoran glanced at Halleck, who simply shrugged his shoulders. "You don't need my permission, it seems. So tell me—what have I been missing all these years?"

"The Rats know about the cloud-whales," Corcoran told him. "When I gave them my news on the test shot, they already knew, just as they already knew about the Invert and Plant generations. They danced a cloud-whale dance, so when I say that they knew, I mean they *knew*."

"We've already done that," Denise complained. "Move on."

"I'm bringing Walter and Marie up to date," Corcoran told her. His gaze was flickering from one to the other. He saw enlightenment dawn on Walter Halleck's face, but it was Marie who suddenly said: "I knew it! I knew it! I knew that I only had to find the evidence, and I knew that you must have it, even if you didn't understand what it meant. But you do know what it means, don't you, Zeph?"

"I think I can guess what you think it means, just as I can guess why the Americans think it might be a good idea to give me a berth on their starship . . . but I'm not sure that my reading corresponds with yours, or theirs."

"Oh, fuck!" said Denise. "Am I the only moron here who can't put two and two together?"

"The math is a lot more complicated than that," said Walter Halleck, "and I suspect that your brother's understanding is probably no better than Miss MacLaughlin's. It'll take me a while to work it out . . . and if some American hotshot thinks he's got there ahead of me, he's undoubtedly jumping the gun. At least, I hope so . . . At any rate, I can see now why they're so keen to send you to the repositioned Earth. The fact that the ghost can be constituted at all is weird enough, but if you really can establish some kind of communication link, however impressionistic . . ."

"You'll be talking directly to God," said Marie MacLaughlin, "and you won't be able to doubt it."

"I suspect that you're underestimating my capacity for doubt," said Corcoran.

"God has nothing to do with it," Halleck put in. "It's just a matter of mathematics . . . the underlying configuration of the universe."

"Which is to say, *God*," the chaplain insisted.

Denise was practically in tears. "I can't work it out," she complained. "Please, just tell me." She was talking to Corcoran, but Marie Maclaughlin had the wind in her sails.

"If the Dancing Rats are not only aware of the existence of life forms on Jupiter," she said, "but sufficiently aware of their nature to imitate their communicative behavior convincingly, then the sixth sense that informs them of the existence of species as-yet-unevolved isn't just a matter of temporal awareness—it's a matter of spatial awareness too. I can't begin to understand the intricacies of Coincidence Theory, but I know that it has to do with the fundamental relationship that persists between elementary particles after their separation. The ghosts that the Sling configures at various points in future time can only be generated because the particles composing them are still linked by Coincidence with the particles composing the Sling and, more importantly, the human register operating in conjunction with it. Am I right so far, Mr. Halleck?"

"Yes," the physicist conceded, a trifle grudgingly.

"Now, there's no particular difficulty, once you've accepted the basic principle of Coincidence," Marie MacLaughlin went on, "in understanding how ghosts can be constituted in the future, employing what are, in essence, the same material particles that once made up the body of the machine and its rider, which can't have moved very far within the Earth's gravitational field in the interim—even an interim of billions of years. No matter how many times they've been recycled through other bodies, they're still associated. The same applies to a hypothetical sense exploiting the phenomenon of Coincidence. It's not implausible that it might provide vague intuitions regarding the distant future, although their utility isn't immediately obvious. Right, Zeph?"

"I'm with you so far," Corcoran agreed.

"But for the same sense, or a related one, to provide the Dancing Rats . . . and, we're encouraged to hypothesize, not just the Insects but the Plants, with an awareness that extends across interplanetary space rather than earthly time, it must be drawing on other past Coincidental associations than the ones involved in the recycling of Earthly matter. At the very least it must be going back to associations that formed during the origins of the solar system . . . but it's entirely possible that the associations go back way beyond that, all the way to the initial formulation of matter in the aftermath of Creation—or, as you'd probably put it, the Big Bang. And if that's true, it means that the entire universe is still bound together, intimately, by associations that minds . . . not ours, apparently, but the minds of the Rats and the species that will replace them . . . are capable of sensing, and translating into feeling and thought. What it means, in brief, is that the universe as a whole has a mind as well as matter, that the universe *is* a mind, rather than a mere accumulation of matter in motion. What it means is that God, indubitably, exists."

Denise glanced at Corcoran. "No," he said. "That far, I wouldn't go. As Walter says, it proves that the mathematics of the configuration of the universe are more complicated and more peculiar than we thought, but it doesn't prove any more than that. On the other hand, if you can forgive me for looking at things from a more selfish viewpoint, it might also make me a more complicated and more peculiar freak than even I thought."

This time, Denise was eager to catch on quickly. "You mean," she said, "that there's something of the Dancing Rat about you— that you have embryonic traces of their special sense . . . the sense that gives them a kind of empathy with the entities of the future generations?"

"Oh, we already knew that, years ago . . . or at least suspected it. The point is that the empathy in question might conceivably extend spatially as well as temporally. If it can be developed, coaxed with practice, in the way that the planners of the Olympus Five mission apparently tried to do by introducing me to the cloud-whales . . . well, if the Rats are aware of the cloud-whales without the kind of proximity that the Jupiter orbiter gave me, maybe—and it's a long shot, but maybe—I can develop a longer distance sensitivity too, which might, in principle, extend beyond interplanetary distances."

"Ah!" said Denise, with a sigh of relief. "The Americans don't just want you aboard their starship on the off-chance that if it ever ends up in another inhabited system, you'll be able to help establish communication with the locals. They want you there because they hope . . . even though it's a long shot . . . that with the right kind of assistance, you might be able to detect alien intelligences over interstellar distances, and even obtain information about their nature?"

"That's right," said Halleck. "And the reason they want me to associate Corcoran with the ultimate ghost is because, even though the computers can't see anything much except blurs, if he really does have a mind potentially capable of responding to Coincidence phenomena, he might be able to do something similar through the ghost, in the exceptional circumstances of the repositioned Earth."

"Or, to put it another way," Marie MacLaughlin supplied, "the special circumstances might enable him to communicate directly with the mind of God. They might allow him to become an authentic prophet."

"Americans being Americans," Halleck supplied, bitterly. "I wouldn't put it past them to think exactly that. But in all probability, they just want to put him to the acid test, to see what, if anything, he can deduce or intuit about the world of the relocated Earth. If I had to guess—and I do, because the bastards don't tell me anything—I'd suggest that they really do think that their stupid starship is going to save the human race from the wreck of the Earth, allow it to thrive and evolve elsewhere, and then come back and save the Earth from being swallowed up by the Red Giant, for old time's sake. I suspect that they're fishing for some clue that their particular brand of wishful thinking can interpret as evidence that the American Dream isn't doomed, that it can push on beyond the sciencefictional final frontier forever, to move and redeem worlds."

Denise looked at Corcoran again. "It's possible," he said. "Until I've taken the shot, I can't even make a guess—but tomorrow could be very interesting, if it actually arrives. How's the Arctic Sea Bubble, Denise?"

Denise still had one eye on the big screen, and her fingers were still periodically busy.

"Still in suspense," she reported. "Thus far, Hell is restricted to northern Greenland. We're not out of danger, by a long way, but at the risk of the repetition becoming tedious, every minute that passes brings us closer—and if you say 'It's a false alarm' once again, Dr. Halleck, I'll slap your face. The world might not end tonight, but this alarm is very, very real."

Halleck raised his arms, as if no such thought had crossed his mind.

"Thank Heaven you invited me round," said Marie MacLaughlin. "I really wouldn't have wanted to be on my own. Thank you all."

"You'd get a better class of prayer at St. Paul's," Corcoran observed.

"That's not the point," the chaplain retorted.

Corcoran saw Denise's lips move to form a joke that would probably have been in exceedingly bad taste, but she suppressed it. He caught her eye and remarked: "That was kind."

"I suppose so," she conceded, "but for what it's worth, let me echo Marie's sentiment." She raised the wine glass that the chaplain had brought her, which—remarkably, Corcoran thought—still had a little wine in it. "Thank heaven I'm here, and thank you all for being here too." She drained the glass.

Halleck looked at Corcoran, to see whether he was going to echo the sentiment. Corcoran contented himself with a smile. Halleck settled for a scowl—but it wasn't sincere. It was getting very late—long past midnight—but no one made the slightest move to leave. Corcoran took note of the fact that the armchairs were, in fact, quite comfortable, but wondered whether he ought to be chivalrous, and if so, whether he ought to offer Denise or Marie the use of the bed.

He decided, on due reflection, that even though he had to work in the morning, what he really needed was a drink.

The bottle that Marie had opened was still on the worktop in the kitchen beside the rack. Corcoran poured himself a glass and then took the bottle into the sitting room in order to offer Marie and Denise a not-very-generous refill.

"I can open another," he said to Walter Halleck.

"No you can't," said Halleck. "In fact, I'd far rather that you didn't drink that one. Tomorrow . . . today . . . is going to be difficult enough without your mind being clouded."

"You're the one who's got the difficult job, Walter," Corcoran pointed out. I just have to sit there and intuit, and all Denise and Marie have to do is watch and wonder. You have to make it work. In fact, do you want to use the bed to get some sleep . . . if Denise and Marie don't mind."

"Not me," Denise assured him.

Marie nodded assent.

Halleck thought about it for a moment or two, and then said: "You're right. I do have the difficult job. So yes, I'll take the bed . . . but get some sleep yourself, if you can. I'm sure your sister can wake you up if anything terrible happens . . . anything more terrible, that is, than what's already happening."

Denise conspicuously failed to offer to accompany him into the bedroom in order to help him relax. "He's right, though," she said, when Halleck had gone. "You should get some sleep, if you can. Marie and I will keep vigil. We'll wake you if need be. Trust us."

"I do," said Corcoran. The words tripped so easily of his tongue that he thought that he must mean them.

XV

When Chris Kemmering came into the Slingroom the following morning he frowned at the level of crowding. He took Corcoran aside and whispered in his ear.

"I told you to bring Denise along," he said, "but the chaplain?"

"It's Judgment Day," said Corcoran. "Would you really have wanted me to tell a priest that she couldn't attend?"

Kemmering hesitated for a moment, and then decided to laugh. "Fair enough. The copter's still standing by, but things are a lot quieter now. It looks as if the holocaust will be limited to Greenland—this time. Canada and Siberia are on high alert, but the Arctic patrols are signaling all quiet. That part of the judgment looks to be suspended again. I can't give Halleck any more time, though. He looks like hell. Do you think he'll be okay?"

"We all look like hell, Chris. A couple of us tried to sleep, but I don't think any of us got more than a couple of the proverbial forty winks."

"You look okay, though—that stint on Olympus has steeled you for irregular hours and quick catnaps. How do I seem?"

"As perfect as ever. For God's sake don't smile at either of the female techs, or they'll be wetting their knickers."

"I'll try not to. How about the pastor?"

Corcoran assumed that it was a joke. "Feel free."

The American went over to Halleck and addressed him in a louder voice. "I'm truly sorry, Dr. Halleck, but the orders stand. I wish I could give you more time, but the brass have got the wind up. Do you think you can do it, given that this might be your one and only chance?"

If Halleck had been a basilisk, Kemmering would have turned to stone, but he was still smiling as the physicist replied: "I'm the one man on Earth who can. But you know that, or you'd have someone else standing here in my shoes. If the math is correct—and I'd bet my life on that—the shot will work. Ideally, I would have taken a week and a couple more practice shots to tune Corcoran's contacts to the supportive machinery, but the first shot worked very well, so there's every reason to hope that this one will."

"What about the voice-link?" Kemmering asked. Obviously, the project had no secrets from him.

"I don't know," said Halleck. "Your people seem to know the apparatus and its results better than I do. You've obviously got more out of the Rats' transmissions than the Institute's analysts could, or at least you've taken wilder guesses, so you tell me."

"I know how you feel, Dr. Halleck," the former captain said. "It was no picnic commanding Olympus Five under the aegis of a need-to-know policy, believe me, and the ISA are pussycats by comparison with my present bosses. Men like us just have to do our duty and be content with the knowledge that we're the real heroes, right?"

Corcoran couldn't believe that such brutal flattery would work, but it seemed to soften Halleck up at least a little. It must have been the first time in his life that someone like Chris Kemmering had included him in the phrase "men like us."

The ex- and future captain then went to take up an unobtrusive position, insofar as any position in the cramped room could be considered unobtrusive, between Denise and Marie MacLaughlin. Corcoran almost expected him to put his arms round both of them.

Corcoran climbed into position, and tried to make himself as comfortable as humanly possible for the tedious preliminaries. Halleck was all business now, functioning like a machine, snapping out instructions and demands for information, seemingly imposing his own automatism on the techs.

Finally, though, it was over. Before the hood sealed him away from the real world for good, Corcoran saw Halleck flash him the faintest hint of a smile. He seemed confident, now—indeed, he seemed triumphant in advance. For all his prudent protests, little David was utterly convinced that he was about to hit Goliath smack on the head. Corcoran didn't know whether to be glad about that or worried.

"Are you comfortable, Mr. Corcoran?" Halleck asked, a few minutes later.

As soon as the physicist he had received an affirmative answer, the Sling went into operation, and Corcoran was divorced from the present, psychologically if not physically.

After a minute or two, Halleck repeated the question—and Corcoran could still hear him, even though the voice wasn't traveling through the air. The voice-link was working, inwards at least. Again, Halleck had addressed him as "Mr. Corcoran" to emphasize the formality of the occasion, not so much for the benefit of the present watchers, as for the benefit of everyone else who would be able to access the pseudosensory record and the commentary dialogue in future.

"I'm fine, Walter," Corcoran replied, seeing no need to follow the same protocol. He had only subvocalized the answer, and was amazed to hear his voice come back to him over the link. It was thin and high-pitched, but the computer had synthesized it from the thoughts that the ghost had picked up within the brain that he had left behind countless billions of years ago, by means of the linkage. That was a long step beyond anything that Halleck had achieved before.

"Can you see anything?"

"Not much—but I *can* see. It's foggy—as if the billions of years were blurring my vision. Are you reading my subvocalizations clearly? The synthesized voice sounds weird to me."

"We have sight, sound and voice," Halleck confirmed. "The recorders are functioning and the computer is processing; you should be able to see more clearly by now."

Halleck sounded understandably anxious. The thought that he might have made a mistake, after all that calculation . . .

Corcoran suddenly had the oddest sensation of having opened his eyes, although he knew perfectly well that he hadn't. It wasn't just that the "fog" he'd mentioned to Halleck had cleared; there really had been a transition, as if an inner eye he hadn't known he possessed had suddenly elbowed his other eyes out of the way, rather rudely.

At any rate, he could see. He could see the sun.

Halleck hadn't bothered to tell him exactly how big the transformed sun ought to be, or how far away from it the future Earth's new orbit was, or how the combination of those figures would translate into the apparent size of the solar disk visible from the planet, but Corcoran had half-expected something spectacular, maybe filling half the sky, and he wasn't too disappointed. Had the entire disk been visible it wouldn't have filled half the sky, but it wouldn't have been that far short.

At first, Corcoran couldn't tell whether the sun had just begun to set or hadn't quite finished rising. Nor could he decide whether the blotches on its surface were clouds in the Earth's atmosphere or sunspots of some kind, or both. He knew that he would figure it out before long, however, and was content to focus his first impressions on matters of color. The colors were supposed to be authentic, in the sense that an actual human eye situated in the remote future where the ghost was situated would have seen them in the same way, although the machines to which he was neuronally linked had to do a great deal of work to resynthesize that authenticity for the benefit of his present-day brain within the hood. At any rate, the sun was mostly crimson, as he had expected, and the sky was mostly purple, as he had also expected. So far, so good.

The ground on which the ghost appeared to be standing was blue, which he had not expected: not pale blue, but a combination of darker shades, ranging from royal blue to indigo. There were interruptions of various shades of brown, but they seemed to be mere arbitrary streaks, not structures or patterns. There were no greens, apart from the occasional touch of dark turquoise. Corcoran didn't know whether to be surprised by that or not. If the blue surface was photosynthetic, time or the new conditions of solar light had obviously favored the evolution of a replacement for chlorophyll, but not one that resembled the black artificial photosynthetics that humans and their rat-descended successors had employed.

The dappled blue surface wasn't entirely flat, but its undulations were gentle, and reasonably smooth—it wasn't sufficiently choppy to be suggestive of a frozen ocean, but the unevenness had an aggression about it suggestive of growth-processes going on as well as erosion by wind and water. Nor were the protuberances motionless, although Corcoran wasn't sure that their movement was really significant of activity rather than mere instability. The most prominent undulations didn't resemble marine waves at all; they were more reminiscent of tremulous blisters, sometimes swelling very gradually, sometimes diminishing at a similarly leisurely pace.

"Talk to me, Corcoran," said Halleck, dropping the "Mister."

"If it is alive," Corcoran observed to Halleck, "it's disappointingly passive." There was to need to report on what he saw and heard, because Halleck would be able to see that on a screen and hear it through a microphone—and had probably seen and heard it all before, at least momentarily, with AI assistance during the flash tests, although he hadn't played Corcoran the tapes. Subtler impressions never came across in flash tests, though.

"Can't judge on the basis of such a restricted sample," Halleck countered, reasonably. "Give it time."

Corcoran knew that one glimpse was insufficient to judge a world, but even if the present sample turned out not to be representative, it was still disappointing. The scene wasn't as boring as the surface of Ganymede, but it wasn't as varied as any other Earthly landscape he'd ever seen in the course of his extensive time-tourism. There was nothing that looked like an edifice, monkey-style, rat-style or invert-style. That was disappointing, but it wouldn't have been the first time he'd hit wilderness, with wondrous cities perhaps beyond the horizon. Even as wilderness, however, the blue blistery landscape seemed lacking in variety.

There were no dendritic forms even faintly reminiscent of the fifth-generation sedentary intelligences, nor anything that bore a strong resemblance to their remote ancestors of earlier generations. There were fuzzy patches here and there, which a flexible imagination might have been able to find reminiscent of grass, but Corcoran didn't want to be making an imaginative effort to find something that might be more interesting than a quivering encrustation of lichen. He wanted clear evidence of complex life of some kind, if not of industry.

Nothing seemed to be moving rapidly or independently: nothing at all that made Corcoran think "animal." The silence wasn't absolute, but all he could make out, with the computer's aid, was a kind of susurrus of white noise, devoid of any perceptible identity.

The ghost was capable of deformation in a quasi-human fashion, just like its analogues in earlier futures. Corcoran was able to reach down and touch the ground. Although primarily orientated to reproduce pseudo-sight and pseudo-sound by means of the impingement of various sorts of waves on "his" surface, the machines could also synthesize a measure of touch sensation.

"It's tingling," he reported to Halleck.

"Vibrating, you mean?" Halleck's voice was little more than a whisper in his ear, but it was quite distinct.

"Maybe—or maybe the tingling sensation is in my fingers, induced by some aspect of the surface that doesn't quite translate."

"Can you take a step forward?"

Corcoran took note of the fact that Halleck had said "Can you" and not "Will you"—which implied that there might be a difficulty. It transpired that he could, though, as easily as he had done a hundred times before, and he did.

The stride felt normal, but that didn't necessarily mean that the gravitational attraction of the displaced Earth was identical to that of the Earth of the first generation. The "gravitational attraction" he felt via the ghost was an artifact, a necessary illusion assisting him to move.

"No problem," Corcoran reported.

"Good," said Halleck—implying that something else might have happened, and presumably had to at least one of the AI-connected ghosts.

Corcoran took another stride. The surface over which he was "walking" seemed securely solid, but a trifle elastic. He moved cautiously toward the nearest "blister," to take a closer look.

"Be careful," Halleck said, scrupulously not telling him why he needed to be careful—especially given that it was supposed to be impossible for Corcoran to suffer any harm.

Nothing happened. He touched the surface of the blister. It tingled . . . or, in some mysterious way, caused the machines to which Corcoran was hooked up to reproduce a tingling sensation in his own flesh. He looked around again, in case anything new had come into view by virtue of his change of position.

"It's like standing on the skin of a gargantuan toad," he said to Halleck, knowing that the physicist wouldn't complain, although he would never have made any such comparison himself. It was part of Corcoran's job to make such comparisons, to record subjective impressions. The whole point of not being an AI was that he had subjective impressions—although he couldn't imagine that there was anything useful in that particular remark. Whatever the members of the seventh generation were descended from, if they really existed, it wasn't toads. Toads hadn't survived the monkey holocaust.

He looked at the sun again, able to do that even though his ghost wasn't equipped with sunglasses. It did have spots, but there were also clouds in the new Earth's atmosphere. Corcoran thought that they were cirrus clouds, although he wasn't sure that ancient meteorological categorizations still applied. He wasn't even sure that the slow and sullen wind he thought he could feel was real. He turned around through three hundred and sixty degrees, in order to give Halleck a panning shot of the entire horizon.

"And no birds sing," he whispered, more to himself than to fulfill his professional duties.

Then he bent over again, to investigate whether there was any visible vibration on the surface of the blister.

There wasn't—but the blister, which had been dark blue until he touched it with his ghostly hand, changed color. It turned silver—silvery enough, in fact, to function as a mirror. For a split second, Corcoran half-expected to see his own face, albeit distorted by the convex surface—forgetting that, in the far, far future, he didn't have a face, because he was a ghost. Indeed, he was a sufficiently intangible presence that he shouldn't really have been able to see anything at all, except maybe a very slight blur. At first, indeed, he couldn't even see that . . . but some inkling made him keep looking, and after a moment or two, he did indeed begin to see a blur, which rapidly became more violent than it should have been.

He felt a surge of triumph. The color change might have been any kind of reaction, but *this* was surely more than anything merely physical or chemical. This was biological, perhaps even intelligent.

This was the seventh generation, or else the alien.

"Have you seen this before, Walter?" he asked, as the pattern in the "mirror" swirled, as if trying to make up its mind what it wanted to be.

"No," Halleck replied, curtly.

"But there've been reactions before, with the AI-guided ghosts, in spite of the brevity of the shots?"

"Not this one," Halleck said, evasively.

A different one, then, Corcoran thought. *Even so, a reaction is just a reaction. It* could *be passive—not necessarily aware, let alone intelligent.*

Again, he reached down to "touch" the surface of the blister. The tingling sensation was not reproduced. Instead, the surface seemed warm—although that could not possibly be a straightforward reproduction—and somehow *gentle*.

That kind of subjective impression was exactly what no AI could ever experience or report; it was for exactly that kind of sensation that the project needed a human register, and not just any human register but one with Corcoran's sophisticated and experienced contacts. Corcoran had no idea how to report it, though. If he told Halleck that it "seemed gentle" Halleck would ask him what he meant—and he didn't really know. He didn't know, in fact, whether he was feeling anything at all—even the warmth—or whether it was a mere figment of his imagination.

He didn't trust himself.

He was mildly surprised by that. He'd always trusted himself before, even on Jupiter and the satellites. What had changed?

Concentrate, he instructed himself, sternly. *Mind on the job.*

In the meantime, the blur in the mirrored surface of the blister was still becoming denser, more like a cloud—as if, Corcoran thought, the blister were trying to organize itself as an eye, actually trying to *see* something, even though there was nothing to his presence but a slight distortion of the fabric of spacetime.

Obliged to report, Corcoran said: "It's almost as if the blister were trying to see through the lens, in the same way that I'm seeing through it. It's almost as if it were trying to form an image of me—not the lab, but me."

"Keep talking," Halleck murmured.

"It's not like it was before," Corcoran reported, letting himself ramble. "When we established communication of a sort with the rat-descendants and the insect-descendants, we knew that they'd detected the lens and knew what it was . . . and, for that very reason, knew that they couldn't look through it. We knew that their signals were signals, because they did their utmost to make it obvious. This is different, not just because they seemed, at first, to be holding up a mirror to reflect back at me what the future intelligences could see . . . if, in fact, that's what's happening, rather than some purely coincidental—ordinary coincidental, not Coincidental with a capital C—phenomenon that I'm misinterpreting by virtue of my preconceptions . . ."

"But you think that they have detected you?" Halleck said, trying to cut to the chase. "They're not like the members of the fifth generation and sixth generation, who didn't even seem to know that you were there? And they detected you instantly, as if they expected you . . ." He too was rambling. Corcoran knew that Halleck had to be excited, although his voice was flat and still conscientiously low.

"Do you think they're trying to figure out what kind of signal to display?" Corcoran asked.

That reminded Halleck of his role. "I don't know," he said, flatly.

"Has this happened before, with the test-probes? I know you don't like to tell me such things in advance, for fear of spoiling the innocence of my perceptions and reactions, but if you know anything—especially given that you think I need to be careful . . ."

"Just keep talking," Halleck told him, dutifully—but he relented slightly. "It's new. Could be anything. Keep looking—and touching . . . but be careful."

"Come on, Walter! Careful of what?"

"Try not to get stuck," said Halleck, reluctantly. Obviously, a previous ghost had "got stuck." Did that mean that it had been immobilized completely, Corcoran wondered, or merely that it had got bogged down?

Corcoran was about to ask that very question when his hand was *gripped*, even though he knew, and could see, perfectly well that he had no hand that was solid enough to grip, and that nothing visible was actually resting on the blister from which he was endeavoring to obtain touch sensations.

"Too late," he said to Halleck, dryly—but the grip was not in any way severe; it was gentle, as if his hand were being clasped affectionately. He didn't have the impression that he couldn't pull away. Nor, oddly enough, did he have the impression that he wanted to.

Dutifully, Corcoran issued a correction to his hasty remark. "No, it's okay; I'm not *stuck*—at least, I don't think so. But this isn't just reaction, Hal; there's definitely intelligence in it. Someone or something here is aware of the Sling, and has probably learned from other shots you've made. I think there's a possibility of communication here, and that they're trying to act on it. Whether these are DNA-descendants or something alien, we've hit the jackpot. It really is the seventh generation, and they're not as standoffish as the fifth and sixth."

"Steady, Mr. Corcoran," said Halleck. "Let's not get carried away."

That proved, in the circumstances, to be an unfortunate turn of phrase. At that moment, the "blister" burst, explosively. Corcoran's ghost was suddenly flooded by a deluge of black liquid, which covered it without going through it, although that shouldn't have been possible, and somehow *gripped* it.

At the same time, the pre-existent grip on his hand tightened, affectionately—and *pulled*.

Weirdly, before he lost consciousness—which was not supposed to be possible—Corcoran had the strangest but quite distinct impression that he was not being pulled in anger or brutality, or even vulgar curiosity, and that, if possible, no harm would be done to him . . .

XVI

"Walter?" said Corcoran, as soon as he became conscious of himself again, thinking that time had passed, and not merely thirty seconds or a minute, although he couldn't be certain. "Are you there?"

Obviously, Halleck wasn't, for the moment—but Corcoran heard another voice, which he remembered having heard before, but to which he couldn't put a name, shouting words he couldn't quite make out, because they were being shouted too far away from the microphone.

It seemed that several minutes passed before Halleck finally got to the apparatus. In the meantime, Corcoran dutifully took note of what he couldn't see—because, apparently, his ghost had been drawn into some tomb-like vortex of black liquid, which had robbed him of his ability to move it and manipulate it at will.

This has to be psychological, not physical, he told himself. *They can't actually make physical contact with the remote past. All they can do is play subtle games with time-independent particles and fields. They're messing with my mind, not the surrogate . . . which is, in its way, just as boggling.*

"Corcoran?" Halleck said, sounding like a man who has just woken up and has not yet managed to sort out the saliva in his mouth. "You're conscious?" It was not like him to ask for confirmation of the obvious; he was obviously under stress.

"Yes," Corcoran said. "I can't see anything, or hear anything except you. Presumably I'm back—but why am I still in the hood? Are the neuronal connections still in place? How long was I out? Why didn't you just disconnect me?"

Halleck cleared his throat, and then said, ominously: "It's not as simple as that."

Corcoran felt sure that his heart would have sunk, if he had been able to experience any such sensation. He couldn't feel any bodily sensation—or, come to that, any ghostly sensation. He felt as if his consciousness were in some kind of limbo, lost in space, lost in time—and, as the ancient poet had put it, in meaning.

He was, however, able to feel afraid. He was perversely glad about that. It seemed to be better than nothing.

"What happened?" Corcoran asked.

"We were rather hoping that you could tell us," Halleck retorted.

"I blacked out."

"That's what our instruments showed, but . . . well, we're in uncharted waters here. We're not sure how far we can trust the in-strumentation. At least we have you . . . alive, if not . . ." Halleck trailed off, obviously unable to find the right word. That, too, was atypical.

"If not what?" Corcoran demanded, reflexively, although he knew that it would be futile.

"According to our monitors," Halleck said, "things inside your body—especially your head—have gone a little crazy. We're sure that it's psychosomatic, but beyond that, we don't know what's happening, how, or what to do about it. Given that you're im-mobilized anyway, it might seem silly to say that we think you're paralyzed from the neck down, but that's what the encephalo-graph readings suggest. Are you consciously aware of anything weird going on in your head?"

"I feel a little fuzzy. No hallucinations, if that's what you mean. And I can't see anything through the lens any more, although I suppose that might be down to the deluge of black liquid. You did see the black liquid on the monitors, I suppose?"

"Yes—but it's not like paint. The seventh generation obviously has far more sophisticated control of Coincidence than the second, third or fourth. That figures, I suppose. However they moved the Earth they didn't use anything as simple as a lever or a block-and-tackle. They must have a degree of control over the fundamental fields that's beyond the reach of my current theories."

Not *our* current theories, Corcoran noted, but *mine*. Halleck had always been reluctant to admit that even the rat-descendants or the insect-descendants understood Coincidence Theory better than he did, but now he was definitely an also-ran, and knew it.

"You're telling me that you *can't* take me out of the hood?" Corcoran said, just to make sure.

"I'm telling you that we *daren't*. The future still has some kind of grip on your consciousness, and hence on your body. We're not convinced that we can pull you back without damaging you. If we're lucky, they might just be observing, after their own fashion. Like the Rats and the Inverts, they probably think they fished you out of the remote past rather than our slinging you forward. The fundamental resonance is effectively instantaneous, but once the link is made their observation process has to go on in real time, sequentially, just like ours. If we're really lucky, they'll respect the principle of *quid pro quo*, and when they've finished whatever they're doing, they'll give us something in exchange, even if it's only the seventh generation equivalent of a cheery hello and a picture postcard."

"Luck," Corcoran muttered, "has nothing to do with it." He knew that Halleck would fill in the second part of the judgment mentally with the old joke about Coincidence, but he wasn't thinking along those lines at all. He wasn't thinking about fate either; he was thinking about the possible motives and ambitions of the seventh generation, whether they were Earth-life-descended or not.

They were trying to handle him gently; he was sure of that, although he wasn't quite sure how he could be sure. They didn't intend to harm him—why would they? But that didn't mean that he couldn't come to harm, and might, indeed, already have come to harm if Halleck had panicked and pulled him out of the hood while he was still connected by some mysterious non-neuronal—and presumably non-material—thread to the remote future, and the Earth that was no longer in the same orbit as of old.

Do they have any idea what they're doing? he wondered. *Or are they just groping in the dark, like us?*

He felt a touch then. He still couldn't hear anything, or see anything, but something simulated the sensation of touch within his brain. Except that it didn't really feel that it was *his* body that was being touched, or even the ghostly simulacrum of it feigned by the Slingshot. It felt like a very different kind of body: gigantic, cumbersome and approximately spherical.

That didn't feel as odd to Corcoran as it would have done to most other people. He had handled some strange surrogates in his time; he was good at adapting himself to exotic corporeal forms via telepresence and had proved that even before he joined the Institute. That was part of the ostensible reason that he had been recruited to go to Jupiter, and why he hadn't been entirely surprised when the ISA had asked him to join the mission.

"Something's happening," he told Halleck, dutifully. "I think they're fixing up some kind of relay between the lens and some other surrogate—something substantial. It's passive, but the pseudosensory information is beginning to come through."

"We can detect that," Halleck told him. "It's registering on our monitors. It's vague, though, for now."

"Give them a chance," Corcoran said. "As you said just now, this is a real-time operation. I can't hear anything, but I'm getting a glimmer of light."

It was, indeed, just a glimmer, more reminiscent of the kind of effect produced by pressure when human eyelids are closed, or of phantom phosphenes, than anything that open eyes might see—but it was changing; it was evolving. There was a distinct splotch now, and other dots.

"It looks vaguely like the sky, as seen from a spaceship," he said. "Big sun, little stars, no atmospheric scattering, no depth perception."

He had, of course, seen the sky from a spaceship, on the way out to Jupiter, and then again, more than once, on the way back. He had done more than that, in fact; he had *felt* space, using his contacts to hook into the ship's sensors—including the deflectors that protected the swiftly moving projectile from particles of dust. Not that there had been much dust, even while they were passing through the supposedly matter-rich regions between Jupiter and Mars—just enough to produce a slight strange tingling sensation . . .

"That's what I can feel!" he said. "Only more so—and getting more so by the minute."

"You're not making sense, Corcoran," Halleck told him, a trifle resentfully, "and all the monitors are giving us is static."

"It's not static," Corcoran murmured. "Quite the opposite. Holy shit!" He knew that he ought to explain; indeed, he wanted to explain, but whoever or whatever was manipulating his ghost-consciousness billions of years in the future was getting the hang of it now, and the experience was unfolding rapidly, like a flower beginning to bloom in his brain.

The impressions were coming too fast, and too densely packed, to give him pause for reportage. Experienced seer as he might be, this was new. It wasn't painful; it still seemed, in some mysterious way, affectionate—but it *was* overwhelming. In time, he thought, he would be able to talk, but not yet.

The sensation he had in the "skin" of his gargantuan body wasn't the same kind of tingling sensation that he'd felt when the tiny particles in the not-so-hard vacuum of interplanetary space had been deflected from the spaceship's long-range armor—not similar enough, at any rate, to be instantly recognizable—but it was, he was sure, a related phenomenon. The new surrogate into which his consciousness was being gradually eased was traveling through space. What looked like the sun and the stars, seen from space, really were the sun and the stars, seen from space, and what felt vaguely akin to the impact of dust particles intercepted in the surrogate's progress really was the impact of dust particles . . . not the cushioned impact of their deviation and deflection by a space-warping shield, but actual impacts. The surrogate wasn't armored, and it was experiencing a *lot* of impacts—which meant that it was either moving very fast indeed, or moving through space that was considerably more matter-dense than the so-called asteroid belt.

There might, of course, be a time lag between event and perception, of which I'm not aware because I'm not trying to interact. Maybe the signal's coming from way out in the system . . . except that . . .

Corcoran had told his mother the truth when he had said that he didn't understand Coincidence Theory at all, beyond the elementary ABC, but one thing he did understand was that the resonant particles, or their generative fields, had to be the *same* particles or generative fields, at different spatiotemporal standpoints. The Sling could link present Earthly matter to what was in essence, "the same" future Earthly matter, but not—at least, not so far as they had so far thought—to extraterrestrial matter. Mind might be a different issue, but as far as raw particles were concerned, the ghost had to consist of particles that had existed on Earth in his own day.

At least, it had if he was still associated with the same ghost—but ever since the black flood, he had been in unknown conceptual territory.

As far as he could judge from past experience, however, if what the enigmatic members of the seventh generation were trying to link him to was some kind of deep-space probe, it had to be an Earthly space probe, and it had to contain at least some matter that had once been the matter of his own body and the machinery surrounding it. The ghost really did have to be *his* ghost, and the Sling's.

As far as he could judge . . .

Maybe those rules don't apply any more, he couldn't help thinking. *Maybe there's a way around it for more advanced theorists and practitioners. Or maybe . . .*

The flower of consciousness reached full expansion then, and brought knowledge—or at least conviction—as well as sight. He knew what the surrogate was into which he was being linked,

168

and knew why he felt gripped by it instead of being able to grip it as he had gripped so many other surrogates. He knew why the relationship was inverted, leaving no doubt at all that he was no longer bait but fish. He even knew why the seventh generation felt something for him that his own mind translated as affection.

He understood, at least vaguely—or at least thought he understood—what Earthly life had become in the fullness of time—and *why* . . .

Briefly, at least, it all seemed to make sense.

For a further moment or two—or maybe longer, in real time—he looked through the eyes of the seventh generation, at the world of the edge of time, and gloried in it. Then he got back to the job, with the hypothetical tongue that he was able to move again with his mind.

"Halleck!" he said aloud. "Are you still there?"

"Where the hell else would I be," the physicist retorted, intemperately. His voice was no longer quiet. "Talk to me, damn it—the machines are giving me shit." Corcoran had never heard him so out of control.

"I think they're hooking me into a bigger ghost," Corcoran said, dutifully conserving a measure of objective doubt, although he had none personally. "You've only ever managed to connect me to a thin network of the particles that are presently part of me. They're trying to build me up, and they're succeeding."

"But the particles that are presently part of you must be spread all over the . . . oh!"

"Exactly," said Corcoran. "They're hooking me up to the entire planet. They're giving me the entire Earth—or its ghost, at least—as a surrogate body. How that involves sensations of sight and touch I'm not sure, but it makes perfect sense. They have to be able to see and hear, not just for themselves but . . . anyway, it does *see*—the Earth, I mean, not just its inhabitants. I can see the sun and the stars, and I can feel . . . where is the Earth now, by the way? This might sound crazy, but it doesn't *feel* as if I'm in local space, unless the asteroid belt is a lot more matter-rich than it was in our day . . ."

Which was, Corcoran realized, not an unlikely hypothesis. The members of the seventh generation had moved the Earth. Shuffling tinier particles of matter was probably child's play. Unlike the ship in which he'd traveled back and forth from Jupiter, the future Earth wasn't being shielded from impacts with dust and more substantial meteorites—quite the opposite, in fact. Somehow, the Earth's far-future inhabitants were actually drawing matter into the planet's path, in a gradual, measured and very determinate way. But why?

His own thoughts—if they really were his own in any objective sense, became temporarily so insistent, so *loud*, that they drowned out the scrupulously mathematical reply that Halleck was giving him, relating to the dimensions of the future Earth's orbit. Whatever had a grip on him was too busy with him to allow him to pay immediate attention to Halleck.

Now that Corcoran had a reasonably clear idea of what was happening to him, he could see reasonably well, because he could interpret the information his "eyes" were receiving. He could see the turbulent sun quite clearly, and even make out a hint of its redness. He could feel the dust that the Earth was sweeping up in its orbit . . . but now the experience was moving beyond that. He was becoming conscious of more things.

The silence was still absolute, apart from Halleck's temporarily meaningless jabbering. The entities of the seventh generation couldn't—or perhaps didn't want to—talk to him in any language he could understand, or even offer him a bleep or two to test that part of his pseudosensory apparatus. They were trying to do something much more ambitious than merely have a chat.

They were trying to make his new ghost self-conscious: not self-conscious in the trivial, Cartesian sense of thinking and therefore being, but far more fully conscious of his vast-ghost body. They were trying to make him—or, at least, allow him to—think the thoughts of the planet, or the thoughts of a seventh-generation individual hooked by means of sophisticated telepresence to the hyperconscious, active and purposive flesh of the planet.

That was not something for which Corcoran had very many experiential reference points. To be sure, he had felt his heart hammering in his present-day body a time or two, and felt various parts of him aching, twingeing, itching, and performing a few of the other tiny shocks to which flesh was heir. All of that, however, was a mere matter of alarms and warnings, the organic equivalent of clanging bells and wailing sirens. He had never been conscious of his flesh in any broader sense, nor that of any surrogate.

No wonder they're groping, he thought.

The groping was succeeding, though. Halleck's voice began to come through clear and meaningful again, although all that the physicist was saying, at present, was: "Talk, damn it! I can't make head nor tail of the raw data. For God's sake, tell me what you're seeing and feeling! Corcoran? Are you even bloody *listening*?" His voice was loud now, edging toward the hysterical.

"Their consciousness differs from ours," Corcoran reported, able now to be tranquil and meticulous, almost as if his innate monkey madness had taken a shower in mathematical sanity. "It's totipotent. They're conscious of everything that's going on in their bodies—the functioning of every organ, maybe every single metabolic transaction—and not only their own, but the entire planet's. They're trying to give me the ghost of some such sensation . . . it's the *quid pro quo*, I think . . . the picture postcard . . . but it's not easy. Damn, I feel weird. I could probably cope with extended consciousness of a human body . . . my own body . . . but this . . . have you ever tried to imagine what it might be like to be a planet, Hal?"

"Are you sure," was Halleck's suddenly thoughtful response, "that you really mean *they*?"

Corcoran had no difficulty seeing which way Halleck's train of thought was running. They had talked about the possibility many times before, as he had explained to Marie MacLaughlin while she was quizzing him in the Chaplaincy. In the old days, before the disappointment with the uncommunicative plant intelligences that had finally come to the fore when the meek really had inherited the Earth, Halleck had been quite keen on the hypothesis that the eventual destiny of life on Earth was what he called a *compound noösphere*: a single planetary mind, whose body was the entire planet.

Corcoran remembered, with exceptional clarity, that he had raised the objection that organic matter was only an infinitesimal fraction of the Earth's mass and that a "living planet" could never be any more than a thin carbonaceous envelope wrapped around a vast stony mantle and an even vaster iron core, but Halleck hadn't been so sure.

"The ultimate alchemical marriage," the physicist had said, "will be between the organic and the inorganic. We're already laying the foundation for an ultimate convergence between nanotech and silicon computer technology and organic technology. Fusion might be impossible, but we know that efficient hybridization will make enormous progress during the Invert generations. In the same way that the scientific progress we made wasn't lost with our extinction, the progress the insects made will be passed on to the plants. I suspect, in fact, that plant intelligence could never have developed without that legacy . . . that the fourth generation laid the groundwork for the fifth generation and the sixth generation precisely by means of that kind of hybridization. One day, that hybridization will reach perfection . . ."

That day had not come by the time the sun metamorphosed into a red giant . . . but that cataclysmic event had not marked the end of Earth's story, or the story of life on Earth.

Corcoran had asked Halleck more than once whether he had ever tried to imagine what it might be like to *be* a plant-descendant, perfectly hybridized with its own intrinsic and extrinsic inorganic components, awash with its own surrogates, perhaps able to make elaborate use not merely of the kind of surrogacy of which humans were capable but something far more sophisticated, perhaps based on minds that could not only comprehend Coincidence Theory but apply it, naturally and internally.

"It would be pointless," Halleck had told him, mournfully. "It's beyond the scope of human imagination—even mine."

Corcoran had not doubted the judgment then, and did not doubt it now, but he also knew that the question had suddenly become urgent, and that however far his own meager imagination might fall short, he had to make every effort to extend it as far as he could.

He had to make as much sense as he could of the sensations that the entities of the seventh generation were attempting to give him, generously, in order to allow him to feel, sympathetically. And if he couldn't make sense of it, he had to try to feel it, to sense it, to get in touch with it at some deep psychological level within the unconscious sector of his mind.

The Americans were right, he realized. This was the acid test, not so much of what he could do as a temponaut, but what he might become, with the right encouragement, the right help.

This wasn't a matter of logical and mathematical calculation; it was a matter of personal evolution. It was the opportunity of a lifetime, and perhaps not just his lifetime, but the lifetime of the planet.

So he tried to imagine, now, on his own behalf, what it might actually feel like to be an intelligent organism that was more than an organism, but a hybrid, equipped by its own processes of growth and evolution not only with its own internal nanotech but its own external megatech, with a whole scale of permanent and natural surrogate existences stretching all the way from the molecular level of its own metabolism and neurochemistry but to an identification with all of its own kind and to the entire planet that they inhabited . . . and perhaps, with the aid of senses based in Coincidence phenomena, even further than that.

He was groping, with no real chance of success, but he had to try, and he tried, hard.

XVII

"Yes," Corcoran said, eventually, belatedly answering Halleck's question. "I do mean *they*."

"You have to give me more than that, Corcoran," Halleck said, plaintively. All his efficiency had crumbled; his confusion had reduced him to helplessness. He even went so far as to add: "Please."

"I'll do my best," Corcoran promised. "But I think this might be one of those occasions when you have to be there. This time, I think, you might to have to get contacts fitted and hook yourself up to your own apparatus if you really want to understand me."

They both knew that there was no chance of that happening—not with monkey civilization already in its death throes and the Americans calling the shots. In any case, Corcoran knew that Halleck would have never put himself through the intricate surgery required to fit him with contacts, even if Judgment Day hadn't been nigh. It simply wasn't in him. That required a special kind of person, of which Halleck was not one, and Corcoran was. Halleck might be one of only a handful of living human beings who understood the intricacies of Coincidence Theory, but he was a physical coward as well. What was more, Corcoran thought, it was possible that the kind of understanding of Coincidence Theory that Halleck had might be more of a handicap than an advantage in this particular situation, and that he, Corcoran, was better equipped than his employer, and maybe anybody, to do what he was being asked to do.

"Just give me what you can, Corcoran, please," the physicist said, resignedly.

Corcoran didn't feel rejuvenated, but he did feel proud. He felt that he had a purpose. He had a sneaking suspicion that it might be a borrowed sensation, but what did that matter? If he had to borrow a sensation in order to feel, where better to borrow it from than billions of years in the future, and not merely from the supersane hybrid inhabitants of that remote era, but from the entire planet?

At any rate, he was determined to try to explain it to Halleck, to the extent that it was humanly explicable, because if he could do that, he might be able to get a better imaginative handle on it himself, and secure the ghost of a remarkable, active and affectionate consciousness within his own numb feeble mind—even if it was only a picture-postcard version, and not the real thing at all.

He started out by thinking that it ought not to be too difficult to identify with the future Earth, given that he had a good idea of what a planet was like, in terms of its crust, mantle and core—but he had to abandon that kind of primitivism very quickly, because the surge of sensations that was assailing him now, confused as it was, gave the lie to that. That was the Earth of the present day; the Earth of billons of years hence was a great deal more complicated than that, in terms of its internal structure, its transactions with its environment, and its sense of purpose, its mentality, its philosophy, its emotions . . .

Corcoran was trying so very hard to imagine what it might feel like to be a planet, that he couldn't be entirely certain that the image he eventually formed of the seventh generation was anything more than a product of his imagination, but he was sure that it wasn't a pure product, because the flow of pseudosensory information was real, insistent and making an effort of some kind to enlighten him.

He couldn't be certain of anything, but he formed some strong impressions. They were tantalizingly out of reach of his full consciousness but nevertheless sufficiently proximate to be tantalizing, seemingly *wanting* to be grasped.

Eventually, he felt able to make his attempt.

"They didn't come from somewhere else," he reported to Halleck, his own voice now little more than a whisper. "They're not extraterrestrial. The Megaplants knew what the future had in store for the sun, the planet and their own descendants, and even though they were plants, or maybe *because* they were plant-descended, and not the offspring of flibbertigibbet animals, they weren't content to sit around and enjoy the mellow sunshine while it lasted. They had a lot of work to do, but they had had a long time to prepare, and a much closer relationship with their technology than even the second Invert generation had ever contrived. They had prepared for their survival of the sun's inflation, and for what would happen afterwards. They went underground . . . and never came out again . . . at least, they haven't yet, although they haven't finished engineering the surface, by any means. Anyway, they're DNA-descended, still our relatives—distant, admittedly, but not as distant as a brief glance at the family tree might suggest.

"Yes, plants and animals branched very early, and yes, it was the animal branch that had to develop intelligence first, because that's the way natural selection works. Yes, the mammals had to do the pioneering work, we monkeys as well as the Rats. But then it was the Insects' turn, and the Insects had had an intimate symbiotic relationship with flowering plants from day one—and I feel certain, now, that the Inverts of the third and fourth generations really are insect-descended, just as the seductive ant-analogies suggested.

"Given time enough, and sufficient genetic flexibility, symbiosis tends toward fusion, as in the case of the fungi and algae that fused to become lichens. The fifth generation was only partly plant-descended; they were insect-descended and machine-descended too, at least in their peripherals. Motile intelligence was the seed of sedentary intelligence, and it permitted sedentary intelligences to take motile entities aboard. Maybe it was fate and maybe it was just the way it happened to work out, but there's a rationale to it."

"All this we've been through before," Halleck put in, sounding somewhat aggrieved. "Never mind the recapitulation—move on."

"I know what you already know, Walter," Corcoran replied, "but I'm taking things in order, getting the story straight in my own mind, so that I can feel its narrative thrust. Bear with me.

"We monkeys couldn't ever have done what the sixth generation did in adapting themselves to survive the solar metamorphosis. Neither could the Rats, or the Insects. It had to be the Plants—but plants enriched by four generations of appropriate animal intelligence—an intangible seed far more valuable than their own DNA. If anything was going to survive the sun's metamorphosis, things had to go the way they did. We're not an irrelevance, a suicidal evolutionary dead-end; we're intrinsic to the process . . . but that's by the by. Moving on . . .

"There isn't any noösphere either, in the sense that you used to imagine it: no great mental fusion into a single individual Megamind. The plants *could* have done that—they're capable of vegetal reproduction, so they *could* have fused into a single great world-tree, with a single thinking consciousness—but they didn't. They chose not to. They chose to retain individuality, both at the physical level—including sex, the ability to shuffle the genetic deck—and at the mental level, thus preserving diversity, disagreement, argument, controversy, etcetera. It was an esthetic decision, maybe a hedonistic one, but it had its rationale.

"The point is, I think, that the individuals of seventh generation don't see themselves as any kind of end-point in Earthly evolution—quite the reverse. They see themselves as the true beginning, and everything that went before as mere prelude, nothing more than a matter of laying groundwork for true intelligence. They see themselves as something requiring further variation, further progress, and have always been anxious not to narrow that potential.

"True intelligence, you see, in their view, is dynamic and multidimensional, involving an understanding of what's going on within and without—the without in question extending all the way to awareness at the planetary level—and an understanding that's always reaching, always changing. This awareness of what it is to orbit the sun, to harvest its energy, and to harvest dust, is active, seeking, striving . . .

"I wish I could describe for you what that ongoing harvest feels like, Walter, but it would require a whole new phenomenology as well as a whole new vocabulary. Moving on . . .

"The members of the seventh generation, as I said, consider the real story of Earthly life as something not yet properly begun, which still has billions of years to run, but is nevertheless working to a deadline, with a sense of urgency, because the universe won't last forever . . . not, at least, in its present physical state, condemned to eternal expansion and eventual heat death. For them, the Earth is an active agent, like the enzymes that maintain their physiology, the substratum of their intellectual being, but one that operates, obviously, on a much larger stage, on a much more extensive timescale, on which the evolution of the expanding universe is a perceptible process, and its entropic heat death an authentic source of *angst*.

"The intelligences of the seventh generation are aware, you see. They're aware of other life forms elsewhere in the universe, exactly as we've just begun to suspect. The Coincidence senses evidently make that possible. They communicate with other intelligences, at least empathically. They harmonize with other intelligences. But they're not God, in the sense that Marie thinks of a Cosmic Mind, an ultimate Unity, a planner and a legislator. Far from it. I really do mean *they*, and how.

"The plant-descended intelligences see evolutionary processes within the universe, and the apparently fated dead end of entropic exhaustion, as a problem, which they think they need to solve, and on which they're working hard individually, even though they know that others are working on it too. They know they're not alone, and they're in sympathy with the others, but they feel that they have to strive all the harder in consequence, not in a spirit of competition, but in a spirit of demonstrating their worthiness, their entitlement to be a part of the narrative in the particular chapter that they've reached.

"I think, on reflection, that the Rats and the generations that come after them also think like that. We dirty monkeys are the odd ones out, the genuine primitives, the mere animals . . . but we shouldn't be too hard on ourselves, because we too are part of the pattern, we too have our role to play, we too have our contribution to make to the eventual evolution of the Plant intelligences and the sentient Earth. We've brought about our own Day of Judgment by being criminally stupid and irresponsible, but we've also done our bit, Walter. We're not unworthy. That's how I feel, at any rate, and I suspect that, at this moment, although I don't know for how long, I'm in sympathy with the seventh generation, in sympathy with the Earth as it really is, as it's destined to become.

"The Earth is collecting matter as it follows its long orbit round the remade sun. It's processing that matter, and expelling it again—not as waste, except for a tiny fraction, but as spores: spores designed to withstand the rigors of interstellar travel, drifting on the initial momentum of expulsion and a boost borrowed from the solar wind. I can actually feel that process of expulsion—that process of reproduction—not simply as a physical emission but as the ghost of a kind of pleasure, a kind of ecstasy. That, more than anything else, I think, is what the members of the seventh generation are trying to communicate to me . . . to us . . . trying to help me perceive . . . in some small measure, to share . . ."

"Why?" asked Halleck, finally unable to resist the temptation to butt in, even though he must have feared that breaking Corcoran's monologue might break his train of thought.

"Because they can," Corcoran told him, sure that it was something more than a mere guess. "The fifth generation and sixth generation didn't have it, and couldn't have communicated it if they could, but the seventh generation do and can, and they know that they won't be able to do it for long. They know that no matter how cleverly we fish, we'll never be able to contact an eighth generation."

"Why not?" Halleck demanded, defiantly, seemingly insulted by the slight to his beloved Sling.

"Because the particles will be dispersed. The Earth is a body now, accumulating, assimilating, excreting, reproducing, not in a confined way but on a universal scale. Soon—in another billion years or so—it won't be possible to find enough particles in close association to resonate, to form a ghost. You and I, Hal, and everyone else possessed of present-day intellect, will be reduced to infinitesimal fractions of seeds, on our way to the stars, one or a handful of atoms at a time."

There was silence then. Corcoran knew that Halleck was thinking about it, but the physicist didn't make any comment on the suitability or otherwise of his ultimate fate. He had regained his self-control, and that wasn't his style.

"By the way," Corcoran said. "I think I can come back to myself, now. The ghostly planet is gently fading out. I have no idea whether they think they've succeeded or not, but I guess they've done what they can, for now. They're letting me down, gently. I can feel their grip relaxing. Give me a few more minutes, though. I'll tell you when."

"The instruments agree," Halleck told him. "Your body and brain seem to be reverting to normal patterns."

Corcoran ignored that, because he already knew it. He was still grasping at the last echoes of the experience, trying to commit them to memory: not just the Earth's sight and the feel of the Earth's body and all its wondrous intricate, indescribably internal workings, but also its attitude: the way that the seventh generation operator, in securing him that link with the megastructural surrogate, had sought a measure of empathy, a kind of amicable handshake, even though he was a mere flibbertigibbet animal, a dirty monkey, a representative of a suicidal species.

After billions of years, they still cared. They still had a sense of kinship. They had been glad to see him, to touch him, to shake his hand. If they had been able to accept an invitation to tea with his Mum, they would have come, and they would have eaten the biscuits.

"Everything seems stable this end, Mr. Corcoran," Halleck murmured, stepping back into protocol.

"It's okay," Corcoran confirmed. "I think I'm home. I think you can unplug me now, without any risk."

Halleck didn't take any action, of course, until he had double-checked all his monitors, but in the end he was as satisfied as he ever was, on that score at least.

"Fine," he said, eventually. "Just keep still, until we can dismantle the hood."

"Is Denise still there?" Corcoran asked.

"Yes, of course. Everyone's still here."

"Give her my love, will you. In fact, give them all my love— and the sincere regards and thanks of the seventh generation."

XVIII

"Good day?" asked Corcoran's mother, when he and Denise arrived to visit her on Friday evening. She didn't even bother to look round, at first. She was busy in the kitchen, cooking something

180

exactly the way she had cooked it fifty years before, even though the ingredients were mostly synthesized and processed in such a way as to be more easily prepared. Habits die hard.

When Mrs. Corcoran did look round, and saw the flowers that he was holding, she nearly fell over with amazement.

"*You*, bringing flowers?" she said. "I never thought I'd see that. Denise told you to hold them for her, didn't see?"

Corcoran felt that his mother was overdoing the sarcasm and skepticism a bit.

"I could never quite see the point, back in the old days," he said. "It seemed an essentially absurd custom—like so many others."

"And now you can?" she queried. "See the point, I mean."

"*A* point," he said. "Dimly." *But that's how we see everything*, he didn't add. *Things only seem bright occasionally because of the woefully inadequate equipment of our senses.*

"It really was Zeph's idea," Denise put in, trying to help out even though she had to know that their mother wouldn't believe her.

"Well, thanks, then," said the old lady.

"If they could talk," he said, "they'd say the same."

"What for?" she said. "And how do you know?"

"For our appreciation," he told her. "And I know because their billion-times-great grandchildren told me so."

She didn't laugh, and she wasn't astonished. She knew that he'd spent a lot of time trying to talk to the plant-descendants of the far future, for months on end, seven years before. She knew, too, that Halleck had attempted some kind of crucial experiment only a few days before, although she had no idea what had been at stake, or even that it had been carried out in the shadow of yet another postponed Judgment Day. She had watched the news on Sunday night, but she had had no access at all to the news behind the news, and had gone to bed at her usual time, thinking that it was a great pity for all those poor pioneers in northern Greenland, but that with regard to the end of the world, it was bound to be yet another false alarm.

"You finally got them to talk to you, then?" she said, calmly, as she put the flowers in a vase and arranged them carefully.

"After a fashion," he said. "Not easy, mind, but we do have things in common. Communication is difficult, but not impossible."

You find communication difficult even with your own mother, she didn't say, even though he wouldn't have blamed her if she had. What she actually said was: "It doesn't make a lot of difference, though, does it—not to us. We still have to live our lives in the present—and according to you and Mr. Halleck, it'll all be for nothing in the end. We're going to become extinct, aren't we? Then the rats are going to take over, and after them the insects. Not a lot to look forward to, is there, even though it won't happen for billons of years?"

"You and I will be long dead," Corcoran agreed. "As you say, it doesn't make any difference to us, and the way we live our lives in the present."

His mother stood back and admired the flowers. As she did so, she seemed to absorb something from their charm, and their perfume. She smiled.

"It might," she said, "if you could be bothered to use your time machine for something sensible—like discovering next week's lottery numbers."

Corcoran sighed, at the fleeting thought that his mother really did think that discovering next week's lottery numbers was a "sensible" way to use a time machine—but he put the critical thought out of his mind, because he didn't want it in his head just then. He could have pointed out that if the Sling were capable of obtaining information that might actually change the future, the changes thus caused could easily lead to paradoxes that might prove too much for the logical fabric of spacetime, so it obviously couldn't be capable of doing that, in order that it could exist at all. It was a circle they had been round before, though, and there was no point in repeating it.

"Sorry about that," he said mildly. "Halleck will keep trying, I'm sure—indefinitely, if the Americans will let him—that and everything else. He's not the kind of man to let up while there's still breath in his body. For the time being, we've been given the green light to take a couple more shots, but the plug might get pulled at any moment."

His mother poured the tea she had made, set out the biscuits, and sat down. "The way you say that Mr. Halleck will keep trying *indefinitely* implies that you won't," she said. "So, the big news that you've come to tell me is that you're going away again?"

In her own fashion, their mother was really quite smart.

"Yes," Corcoran confirmed. "Both of us. Not immediately, but soon."

"Both of you?" she glanced at Denise, who nodded. "Together?"

"Yes," said Corcoran. "Together."

"Well, at least that'll be nice . . . won't it?" She seemed slightly uncertain.

"Yes," he said. "It will."

Again, his mother glanced at Denise. "It really will," his sister said. "We wouldn't want it any other way."

"Well, that's something. Where?"

"In the first instance, to Alaska," Corcoran told her.

"Alaska! What on earth for?"

"It's now the most go-ahead of the United States, and the one least battered by climate rage."

"Well, at least it's not Jupiter. For how long?"

Corcoran hesitated, but Denise had more courage. "We won't be back at all, Mum, once we've gone. It's permanent."

Their mother studied them one by one. "Not at all," she repeated. "You mean, I'm never going to see you again . . . once you've actually gone?"

"Not in the flesh," Corcoran put in. "But we'll be in touch over the screen for as long as possible."

"For as long as possible?"

"We might not be staying in Alaska for very long. There's another project."

"Another space project?"

"Yes."

"And you're both going?"

Denise picked up her mother's hand. "I want to go, Mum. I want to go with Zeph. You know how much I missed him, last time. I didn't think I would, and I'm not entirely sure why I did, but the fact is that I did, and since he has to go away again, I want to go with him. It seems that I'll be allowed to go, if the project does come to fruition."

"Has to?" her mother echoed.

"Yes," said Denise. "Honestly, Mum, he really does have to go . . . and to be honest, I feel that I really have to go too. I hope you can forgive us both."

"Why?" her mother countered. "There's nothing to forgive, is there? If you have to . . . and you needn't worry about me. I'm fine. Have I ever tried to stop you living your own lives?"

"No, of course not," Corcoran put in. "But thanks for understanding."

"Oh, I can't begin to *understand*. I've never understood either of you. But that's life, isn't it? The world changes, children move on. You can't understand it—all you can do is accept it. One of the neighbors has a little boy who's every bit as weird as you used to be, Zeph. You'd probably like him. But understand him? Nobody can—not even his mother."

"Emily Saverne's little boy?" Corcoran asked. "Luke, isn't it?"

"That's the one. How do you know?"

"I met him when I was staying here. He asked me a lot of questions."

"He does that. You're probably the only person he's likely to run into around here who can answer them. But that's the way it goes, isn't it? His own mother doesn't understand him, but some stranger can. That's just the way it goes."

"It seems to be," said Denise.

"Well, it would have to *seem to be* to you," her mother said, a trifle peevishly, "as you never seemed inclined to have any of your own. And now, if you do, I'll never get to see them."

"I'm sorry," said Denise.

"What for? There's nothing to apologize for." Deliberately, their mother changed the subject. "How's Mr. Halleck?"

"A trifle distraught," Corcoran said. "He's fighting tooth and nail to keep his project going, but the odds are against him."

"Because you're going to let him down again?"

"I'm not letting him down, Mum. Neither of us has had any real control over what has happened."

His mother turned to Denise, and groped for a change of subject. "And how's your friend Marie?"

"Oh, she's delighted. She thinks that Zeph's seen and talked to God—and she got to watch, although I was there too, and I have to say that there wasn't a lot to see, if you weren't looking with the eye of faith."

"And did you talk to God?" Corcoran's mother asked him, point-blank.

"No, but I think I had a brief communication with some exceedingly smart flowers—the flowers that are going to save the Earth from being swallowed up by the Sun when it expands into a Red Giant."

"You've been away with the fairies again, then?"

"Yes, Mum, I've been away with the fairies again."

"Chris Kemmering was there too," Denise put in.

"What, the space-captain? The handsome one?"

"Yes. We're going to Alaska with him."

"You've got no chance of hooking him, girl—a real Don Juan. Use you up and cast you aside like a worn-out sock. Trust me, I can tell."

"You certainly can. Don't worry—Zeph will protect me."

"Ha!" said Mrs. Corcoran. "Brothers can't protect you against men like him. Do you know that he slept with all seven of the women on that Jupiter mission?"

"Yes I did," said Denise, "but I'm surprised that you know. I didn't know you followed those kinds of gossip-casts."

"I'm an old woman who lives on my own. Of course I watch gossip-casts. They're my only company. And don't you smirk at me, Zeph. I know what you got up to aboard that spaceship, too.

Everybody does. Why you couldn't find a nice girl on Earth, God only knows. At least that would have been *private*."

"When I was doing it," Corcoran muttered, "I thought it was."

"And now it's going to happen all over again—except that you're dragging your little sister along with you."

"It's not like that, Mum," Denise said. "And I don't think that the project we're involved with now will involve the same kind of scrutiny . . . or if it does, I hope to God that the recordings are hacker-proof. I don't want to be remembered on Earth as some kind of space-bound slut whose life aboard ship was carefully mined for pornographic detail."

"Remembered?" her mother said. "You're really not coming back, then?"

"I'm afraid not."

"It's the starship, then? You're going on the starship? That little boy of Emily's will be green with envy when I tell him."

"You're not supposed to know that the starship exists, Mum, let alone who might be part of its crew, so it would probably be best if you didn't say anything to the neighbors."

"Oh, well then, my lips are sealed."

Of course they are, thought Corcoran, sarcastically—but he didn't say it. Instead, he said: "The starship might never reach completion. It might be better to wait until it does, and actually lifts off, before speculating about who might or might not be aboard. Civilization as we know it might not survive that long. And even if the ship does take off . . . who can tell whether it will ever get anywhere?"

He deliberately failed to mention that he was the one who was supposed to know, or at least to find out. He was the man who had shared the sensibility of the far-future Earth-organism, who had caught a glimpse of the pattern and distribution of life and intelligence within the galaxy, and within the universe. He was blind again now, or at least dazzled, but he had seen, just for the space of a single flash of celestial light . . . and he was no longer the same.

186

No one knew, as yet, least of all him, to what extent his hypothetical sixth sense had been stimulated by the seventh generation contact, or to what extent it could be trained, coaxed or persuaded to develop, but some kind of potential was undeniably there. And even the Dancing Rats, who were very nearly human, had been able to get to know the cloud-whales well enough to dance their dances.

Corcoran was confident now that he was well worth the price of his ticket on the starship, even if Halleck didn't get the chance to send him out again as far as thought and the Sling could reach, and he was confident that he was well worth the price of Nise's as well. He might only be a tiny atom of hope, but to be frank, in the dark shadow of Armageddon, anything of that nature was far better than nothing.

He hoped that he might get the opportunity to take a handful of further shots, of various temporal ranges, but that wasn't his choice, and he had no idea how the people trying to make the calculation would weigh up the options. For the moment, everything was uncertain . . . except, unfortunately, the end of human earthly civilization. That was already written, even though the exact date had still to be filled in.

"Well, if you ask me," said his mother, "not that anyone's going to, I think it's silly. A starship! When there's so much that needs doing here, that's crying out to be done. And you might want me to think that you're heroes for going on the starship, just as you wanted me to think that Zeph was a hero for going to Jupiter, but I don't—so there!"

"It might be a foolish enterprise," Corcoran admitted, "but if it is, that's only to be expected. We humans are addicts of futility, after all: just dirty monkeys working for our own destruction, so that the Dancing Rats can take over and add the next chapter to the story."

"Don't be so gloomy, Zeph," his mother chided him, not for the first time. She never seemed to notice the downbeat tendencies of her own world view, but never missed any evidence of pessimism on his part, and never resisted the urge to attempt to alleviate it.

"I'm not gloomy," he assured her, and meant it—but she wouldn't have believed him even if she'd taken any notice of what he'd said.

"You ought to make more effort to look on the bright side," she told him, following her familiar train of thought. She couldn't help adding, semi-automatically, not even as a joke: "Who can tell what the future might bring?"

PART TWO

RENDEZVOUS WITH SATURN'S RINGS

I

Denise Corcoran was fast asleep when the door buzzer sounded. There had been a time—even while she knew full well that the world was ending, and even after she had received the famous sealed envelope containing the instructions that she was supposed to follow in the event of a code red notification—when her immediate, instinctive reaction to being woken from deep sleep would have been an annoyance. Times had changed, however, and that change had even infected her instincts. She was to longer capable of feeling anything but panic when she heard an untimely alarm signal. She was no longer capable of any other thought than: *This is it; the Crash is going bang.*

And yet, it wasn't a screen alarm; it was someone at the door: a person. So her second thought was: *Who the hell can that be?* And that, at least, permitted a resurgence of annoyance, a flash of resentment; but it didn't slow her down as she leapt out of bed and ran to the intercom.

She didn't even have a chance to articulate the word: "Who . . ."

"It's Chris Kemmering, Denise," said the voice at the far end of the link as soon as it was open. "Let me in."

Then she knew. The Crash *had* gone bang, and she was getting an advance warning. She was getting a warning even before her own government had sent out the call telling her to open her instructions as to what to do, if there was still time, when the world ended.

She and Zeph had an invitation to dinner at the American Embassy the next day—or, more likely, that day. They had both assumed that the agenda of the occasion would include the signing of a formal contract binding them to the mission that had been their only topic of conversation for days. Now, it seemed, there was no more time for formalities.

While thinking all that, she was already grabbing some clothes, because she slept naked, but she had not had time to start putting them on before three curt, authoritative raps sounded on the door of the flat.

Somehow it would have seemed the height of absurdity to call "Just a minute," but there was no way that she was going to open the door to the American while stark naked except for a shell-suit that she was still clutching in her hand, trying to use as a fig-leaf.

She scrambled into the trousers and pulled the top on; then she opened the door.

The Captain didn't waste time.

"Code Red," he said. "Grab your bag. Let's go."

The height of absurdity arrived anyway, in spite of her efforts.

"I have to use the bathroom," she gulped.

No objection; no comment: just a nod of the head.

She disappeared at a run, and tried to take advantage of the brief interval to pull herself together. No chance.

When she came out again, Kemmering was already holding her end-of-the-world bag. It hadn't been difficult to find—it wasn't the sort of thing one locked away.

She cast a rapid glance around the flat that she was undoubtedly seeing for the last time. It had been home for six years. Zeph had never even seen it.

The Captain stood aside to allow her to lead the way downstairs. He closed the door himself. She heard the locks clock into place, and realized that she had committed the most absurd of all domestic errors and left her keys inside, in the clothes she had been intending to wear when she went into Imperial in the morning. It didn't matter now.

Outside, illegally parked, was a limousine with diplomatic plates. Kemmering opened the rear door for her and invited her to get in with the most minimal of gestures. The light inside the rear section of the vehicle had come on when the door opened, and Denise saw that it was empty.

She froze.

"Where's Zeph?" she demanded.

"The copter's picking him up in Kensington," the Captain replied, his voice perfectly level, under strict military discipline. "You'll see him at the base. Get in."

It was an order, and not the first he had issued to her in the last few minutes. Denise had always had problems taking direct orders; there was something in her nature that was inherently mutinous. Nevertheless, she obeyed.

As soon as Kemmering was inside and had closed the door, the car took off. Denise had become used to fancy cars being described in terms of their capacity for acceleration but she had never actually been in a vehicle that accelerated so rapidly that it shoved her rudely back into the cushions and made her feel as if a massive lead weight had just been dropped on her chest.

The Captain sighed with relief. The spotlight above his seat had stayed on, although the one above Denise's was out; he had his palm-unit in his hand and he was hitting the keys with an expert finger as well as reading the screen, but everybody nowadays—except Zeph, obviously—had mastered that species of multitasking, so he was able to talk to her with only a slight hint of absent-mindedness.

"Truly sorry," he said. "Thanks for being so quick. It caught us all on the hop, but the procedures seem to be working so far. I can't tell you not to be scared, because I'm utterly terrified myself, but we're doing all we can."

There was a slight pause while he had to concentrate, presumably not merely because he was texting but became he was encrypting the message, which required extra brain-work of which "everybody" would definitely not have been capable.

Denise looked out of the windows, which were tinted so as to be opaque when viewed from without, and which offered a somewhat dim view even from the inside, given that it was pitch dark outside and the street lights were on economy level. That gave her an approximate idea of the time, but in order to get a precise indication she took her own palm-unit out of her pocket.

"Please don't do that," Kemmering's voice cut in, perhaps interrupting his own encrypting.

He had said "Please," so it wasn't, strictly speaking, an order. Indeed, so far as she could judge from the glow of the spotlight over his head and the faint reflection from his screen, his expression was imploring rather than commanding. In any case, she was so far out of her depth that she didn't feel that it was a good time for mutiny. She didn't bother to tell him that she had only been going to check the time. She put the unit back in her pocket, cursing herself for her weakness even though she knew that it was the right—the only—thing to do.

The glass isolating the rear compartment of the vehicle from the front was raised, and that was tinted too, but she could see that there were two heads in the front; there was a second man—she assumed it was a man—in the passenger seat beside the driver.

Kemmering lowered his phone. "Sorry," he said, again. "We have time, now, while we drive to the base, but there's a lot I need to cover. If we'd only managed to get in tomorrow's— tonight's—dinner at the Embassy, we'd have been able to get a lot of explanation out of the way. Now, everything's a mess and I'm improvising furiously."

"It's bad, then?" Denise said, although she knew that it was a silly question.

"Worse," was the reply. "It might be touch and go whether we can even make it to Alaska. I can't go into detail yet—I have to take the most urgent matters first. At this moment in time, you're still a free agent. Right up to the moment when you see Zeph, you can still walk away. I know you have your own envelope in this bag"—his eyes flicked to her end-of-the-world bag, which he had placed on the floor of the vehicle between the two of them—"and that you have a ticket to the Snowdonian Enclave. If you decide in the next two hours that that's where you'd rather go, you can. But once the jet takes off, if you're aboard it, you'll be effectively committed to Fairbanks and the Cabal. There won't be any coming back. And the worst of it is that I can't give you any firm promises in return, as to what will happen to you or Zeph in Fairbanks, except that you'll have a right of entry to the innermost enclave. Any other opportunities are now up to . . . well, not me. The point, for now, is that you still have a choice, for a little while longer."

"And Zeph?"

"He's already made his. He was fully briefed on the situation last night, and agreed to the terms set out, whatever they were. I was due to be briefed today, as you were—before the apocalypse jumped the gun."

Zeph accepted terms without consulting me! Denise thought. *Without even ringing me to tell me what was going on! Is the old Zeph coming back, then—and where the hell does it leave me?*

"You have to think about what's best for you, Denise," said Kemmering, "and you have to think very carefully, very quickly."

"What do you think?" she demanded, forthrightly. "And don't tell me that it's not your place to give advice, because you're the only person who knows what's going on and we both know that you and your employers think they know far more about me and Zeph than we know about one another, or ourselves. So, what do you think?"

Kemmering didn't smile. In fact, he looked distressed and disconcerted, not at all like his on-screen image. He held up his phone, but his thumb wasn't active, and he wasn't really looking at the glowing screen. It was a shield.

"I'm biased in so many different ways, Denise," he said, using her first name with obvious deliberation, "and I'm also under orders. To be perfectly honest, I don't know what I'm allowed to tell you, or what I'd be supposed to tell you if I could—which leaves me in something of a quandary. Zephaniah will probably be able to tell you more, but you probably won't have more than a matter of minutes to talk to him before the plane takes off."

"That's not good enough, Captain," Denise snapped. "Am I allowed to call you Captain, on the assumption that you will be the Captain of the starship on which, I assume, my brother has just signed up for a berth?"

Kemmering looked positively agonized, plainly not relishing his situation at all. Denise decided to give him a few moments to think about it. She looked out of the window again. The car was heading north, through streets that were almost deserted. She had no idea where they might be going, but it didn't seem to be worth asking. One US airbase on UK soil would doubtless be pretty much like another.

"Who's the guy sitting alongside the driver?" she asked, simply as a stalling measure.

"He's riding shotgun."

She almost retorted: "I can see that," but bit her tongue as she realized that he meant it quasi-literally. The passenger was a soldier: a heavily-armed soldier.

"Are you expecting trouble?" she asked.

"No. If anything were to crop up . . . well, the drones are deployed and there are patrols on all the approach roads to the base." He checked the phone that he was still holding up defensively. "We still have two hours in hand before your government issues its initial code red, and they won't broadcast emergency instructions to the general public for another two hours after that . . . if they have the time."

"If? You mean it's *that* bad?"

"If I'd been able to give you this talk tonight, I'd have felt obliged to tell you that in all probability the Snowdonia Enclave would enable its inhabitants to survive for at least another thirty years, even if the oxygen levels in the atmosphere drop below the level of breathability for that entire time. Now, I honestly can't guarantee that you'll be safe anywhere on Earth for another thirty days. Within forty-eight hours, the Enclaves will probably be sealed. Whether that will save them, how many of them, and for how long, is anyone's guess."

Denise wanted to emit an expressive expletive, but it died in her throat. All she could say, when she found her voice, was: "Zeph . . ."

"He'll get to the base before us. He's not on his own—Mireille's with him. He knows that you're with me, and that we're on our way. He'd be insane if he weren't frightened, but so far as he can have resources, he has them."

Denise started to say: "Who's Mir . . ." but broke off halfway through the name as she realized. Mireille Angevot was an atmospheric chemist who had been the French representative on the crew of Olympus Five. She was suddenly glad that her half of the rear seat was unlit, because she felt herself blushing, even though she knew that there was really no need.

"I asked her to fly over from Paris today . . . yesterday, I mean . . . so that she could sit in on the briefing at the Embassy. She was at Zeph's flat when the panic started, so the copter picked them both up. You didn't know?"

"Zeph hasn't called me all day," Denise said, colorlessly. She knew that Kemmering wouldn't need a light now to gauge the extent of her confusion. She almost hoped that he did know her better than she did, because she couldn't keep track of the confusion of her own emotions, and thought a little sage guidance might be an asset.

"Zephaniah has explained the relationships aboard Olympus Five, hasn't he?" the Captain asked, uncertainly.

"There are some explanations Zeph can do, and some he can't," Denise said, weakly. "But I know that Mireille was one of the three women he slept with during the mission. So good, I'm glad he has someone with him who can be . . . a resource." Silently, she cursed, hoping that she didn't sound as crazy to Kemmering as she sounded to herself . . . all the more so as one of the other things she knew was that Mireille Angevot, along with every other woman on the crew, had also slept with the Captain of Olympus Five.

"That's unfortunate," said the Captain in question. "But you do understand the logic of the situation, and the importance of that aspect of the project. There were fourteen of us locked in a narrow, sealed environment for seven years. Among our needs was a need for sex—and not just the kind of assisted masturbation that VR can provide. We needed closeness, real contact. And we needed it in a social context that didn't facilitate, or even permit, the generation of dangerous obsessions and jealousies."

"He got that far," Denise admitted. "You needed a mini-utopia, complete with free love."

"In a nutshell, yes. I know what the media have made of the leaked data, and how many lewd jokes have come out of it, because I've been the butt of most of them, but you have intelligence and imagination enough to know what was really happening, and what was really at stake. Do you know how many people took it for granted that a crew like ours, confined to close quarters for seven years, would end up hating one another? But we didn't. Quite the reverse. I can understand your being jealous, but . . ."

"Jealous?" Denise snapped, the discipline breaking at last. "I'm his sister, and I can assure you that there's nothing incestuous about our relationship."

"I'm not talking about sexual jealousy," said Kemmering, mildly. "The whole point of the mini-utopia . . ."

"Okay, I get it," Denise, interrupted, furious with herself. "The world is ending; we don't have time to analyze the precise depth and nature of my sisterly feelings. Is it the Arctic Sea clathrates—the massive methane release we all feared last week when northern Greenland caught fire?"

"That release is still slow," Kemmering told her, "although there's every chance that it will accelerate very soon. We don't know yet exactly how far the chain reaction will extend, but the experts seem to be unanimous that it will be worldwide. It's already affecting the entire Ring of Fire. The volcanoes that were in the process of erupting have gone into overdrive, and the fault lines are splitting catastrophically. It started in the south, so that's where the quakes and the tsunamis are concentrated for the moment, but it's spreading northward on both the Asian and American fronts. Fortunately, the eastern coasts of the Americas had already been evacuated long ago, but the so-called safe zones aren't safe any longer . . . in fact, there aren't any safe zones any more and the seismologists have raised the danger level on Yellowstone to one point below critical. If, or when, that goes . . ."

"No more United States."

"Pretty much. Anyway, Europe, like Alaska, probably has thirty-six hours before the hard rain really begins to fall, but after that . . . the whole atmosphere will go bad, and even the people who've made it to the enclaves will have to start praying."

"Are the Enclaves ready?" Denise asked, knowing what the answer would be.

"Some are better prepared than others. Hopefully, Fairbanks is readier than most . . . if we can make it before the seals are applied. In theory, we have time. In practice . . . well, the most direct route involves flying over the Arctic Sea, which has its unique dangers, and taking a more southerly route will probably swathe us in a dangerously toxic dose of windswept volcanic ejecta before we land. It could be touch and go . . . which is another reason you might want to think very seriously about Snowdonia, given that you have a ticket. Zeph didn't, remember . . . but I think he knew that you have one, whether you told him yourself or not."

Denise hadn't. She wasn't entirely sure why not.

"But even if the Arctic Sea methane release turns catastrophic," she objected, "we'd be able to fly over it at thirty thousand feet, with our own oxygen supplies?"

"Probably, but . . ."

"There's more?"

"Yes. Nobody knows exactly how such distant events are connected, but there's a definite connection of some sort. There's a bad solar storm building. The jet will be shielded, obviously, but all shields are permeable if the intensity of the radiation becomes sufficiently intense, and the particle density . . . well, let's just say that the auroras are going to be spectacular."

Yet again, Denise strangled an impulsive expletive.

"And it's not a coincidence," she murmured. "Not with a small c, at any rate. Damn Halleck for screwing up the language with his casual terminology. The Earth-Sun simultaneity might be an effect of Coincidence-with-a-capital-C?"

"About that you'll have to consult Arkheimer."

"Helen Arkheimer?"

Kemmering looked surprised "You've heard of her?"

"In fact, I have," Denise said, oddly glad to be able to score a point. "I'm not actually in Imperial's Eavesdropping Circle, but I have friends who are. She's America's answer to Walter Halleck—one of the half-dozen people in the world who claim to have a neuronal configuration capable of permitting mental comprehension of Coincidence Theory. Reputed to be as crazy as a sack of monkey-nuts, as one of my colleagues put it, in his typical indelicate fashion."

"That's as may be," Kemmering replied, unsmiling, "but if you decide to stay on the jet and take a trip over the Arctic Sea, or northern Canada, at the worst time in living memory, so far as you and Zephaniah are concerned—and me, for that matter— she's God. Our fate will be in her hands. And you ought to pray that she, like Zephaniah, isn't nearly isn't as crazy as some people think, because if she is that crazy, she might well be the death of him . . . and perhaps all of us."

"You mean she's built a Sling of her own, and can't wait to try it out on Zeph?"

"Nothing so simple—that's why she was so desperate to get the data from Halleck's final Slingshot. Like Halleck, she'd have preferred half a dozen more, but the one she wanted *desperately* was the first genuinely productive seventh generation shot . . . a crucial piece in the jigsaw she's been building for ten years, com- bining data stolen from Halleck with her own. In a sane world, of course, she'd have supplied Halleck with her data, and worked in collaboration with him, in which case, if two heads really are better than one, they might both have a much better grasp of something that seems to be on the margins of their understand- ing, and way beyond those of common mortals like us. In fact, she's funded by the Cabal, whose inner circle have been obsessed with secrecy ever since the conspiracy originated in the twentieth century, so . . . well, in sum, Halleck doesn't have her data, but she's always had his. She believed that Zephaniah was something special even before he did, and if he hadn't yielded to the gentlest persuasion, she'd probably have been capable of trying to have him press-ganged aboard Olympus Five. She's never set eyes on him, but she thinks she knows him inside out and sideways . . . and she probably thinks the same about you."

"And she's running the starship project?"

Again, Kemmering looked pained, but he seemed to have made up his mind. "Okay, let's talk about Proxima. You need to know if you're to make a rational decision as to whether, if Arkheimer wants you on it, you ought to accept the offer. I have no idea what the word 'starship' conjures up in your head, but if you're imagining something big, with a human cargo in the hundreds, or even dozens, forget it. When the project was initially planned, Proxima was just going to be one more excursion in the same series as Olympus and Cronos, involving a ship built on a very similar model. The original mission specs called for a crew of fourteen, exactly the same as Olympus Five, and a provisional mission time of thirty years—time enough to take a look at the exoplanet in the so-called Goldilocks zone of Proxima Centauri and come home. Since then, though, and especially in the last seven years, there's been considerable . . . well, the polite way of putting it is *mission creep*."

"And how far has it crept?" Denise asked, sarcastically.

"God alone knows—by which I mean that Arkheimer, educated by the Cabal since infancy, has secrecy written into her neural programming. So far as I can tell, the project was nearly aborted while I was away in the vicinity of Jupiter, but instead of simply closing it down, the Inner Circle allowed Arkheimer to take it over—not because they had any faith in what she wanted to do, but simply because it allowed them to pretend that they were still exploring every avenue of escape and survival. To cut the story short, it's become a reckless gamble, and the crew members are now reckoned expendable. So, if you want . . ."

Denise cut him off. "We've done that. Tell me more about the ship."

"Well, you've doubtless seen media reports on Olympus Five or Cronos, and Proxima is built on the same basic plan. Its life-support systems and AIs are more advanced than those on Olympus and the drive is supposed to be more efficient, but any advance since Cronos has been tiny. In fact, if it weren't for the restricted mission plan and the label, you could just as easily call Cronos a starship, even though its mission plan doesn't take it any further than Titan. Arkheimer's made modifications in order to fit in her own equipment, but they'll be minor, in structural terms, and please don't ask me what her equipment is supposed to do. All I know for sure is that she's desperate to hook Zephaniah's supposedly special brain up to it, even though it isn't a time machine.

"Arkheimer has evidently decided that she wants you on the crew too, although that decision might have changed now that there's no longer time for you to go through the training program—which is another factor you ought to consider—but if the offer is still open, what you have to envisage is spending the greater part of the rest of your life locked in a tiny tin can, breathing recycled air, drinking recycled water and eating food grown in thermosynthetic vats, in the company of a dozen people. Whereas, if you were in an Enclave in Snowdonia, or Fairbanks, you'd at least have space to move around, potentially renewable air and water, vats the size of houses, and an authentic society of thousands of people . . . a life, in short."

"But you're going," she pointed out.

"Of course, if the role's still on offer—but it's been my life's work, and I've had practice, not to mention intensive training. So has Zeph. If Arkheimer hadn't been given *carte blanche* to run the mission exactly the way she wants to, there would have been absolutely no possibility of your being offered a berth. If you are—and I'm not in any position to confirm that—there's a whole set of good reasons why you might not want to take it."

Denise frowned. "Are you trying to tell me that you don't want me on your starship, Captain?"

"That's not what I said."

"I know. Is it what you meant?"

Kemmering only hesitated briefly before saying "No"—and Denise figured that, given the situation they were in and the fact that he hardly knew her, it probably wasn't a white lie designed to spare her feelings.

So it's real, she told herself. *It's not just castles in the air any longer. Everything's real, and I have to make the most important, and the craziest, decision of my life in a matter of hours . . . minutes . . . while the world is literally falling apart.*

She couldn't help turning her head again to look out of the murky window, but all she could see was the placid, sterile motorway, and darkness that seemed to extend forever.

II

"*Why* do you want me on your ship, then, Captain," Denise said to Chris Kemmering, because, ridiculous as it undoubtedly was, that seemed for the moment to be the most important of all the questions that were queuing up in her head, "given that I'm untrained, and that an evolutionary biologist would be as much use on a starship mission, however creepy, as a fifth leg on a donkey?"

The Captain sighed. "Partly because, if Arkheimer wants you, it's my job to want you too. And assuming that, if Arkheimer does still want you, in spite of the fact that she might be putting your life in danger by taking you aboard without the necessary scrutiny and training, it's because she thinks your presence would be an invaluable asset to Zephaniah, and . . . well, to put it simply, I'd like Zeph to be happy. I consider him a good friend."

"And is that why Arkheimer wants Mireille Angevot, too . . . because she wants him to be as happy as possible? Or was Mireille always going to be one of the crew?"

"She's fully qualified. She might have jumped the queue . . . but you'd have to ask Arkheimer about that. It's her show now. She wasn't supposed to be one of the mission crew herself, until quite recently—but in fairness to her, she has gone through the full training program in the last few months."

"And she definitely won't be as superfluous as a fifth leg on a donkey?"

"That, I don't know. I'm not privy to the secrets of her damned machine, even though it's now lodged on my ship . . . her ship, of which I'm still the Captain, it seems . . . unless I'm replaced too."

Denise had no interest in exploring Chris Kemmering's resentments regarding the changes to his situation and authority brought about by mission creep. Instead, she picked up the essential point. "So she has some kind of machine," she said, by way of recapitulation. "Not a Sling, but something related . . . something intended to employ Zeph's supposed talent in a spatial context rather than a temporal one."

"That's one way of looking at it."

"What's the other?"

Kemmering seemed profoundly uncomfortable. "I can't tell you," he said, "because I don't know . . . and if I reported the casual rumors that I've picked up I might be giving you ludicrous misinformation. I'm assuming that she intends to brief you herself, as she's briefed Zeph, and I really think it's a job best left to her."

"Okay. You mentioned the Cabal—what's that?"

"It's one of several semi-serious terms used to describe the organization that runs all the major projects in Alaska. It's notionally affiliated to both the US government and the US military, although it's more multinational and more independent than that. Some people say that the relationship is actually the other way round and that it's the government and the military that are merely affiliates, but that's probably an oversimplification. At any rate, it's something lurking behind the democratic facade, which has been pulling strings with increasing force and authority for well over a century, since the mid-twentieth century. They'd probably call themselves the Salvation Army if the label hadn't already been claimed, because their primary purpose, their overriding obsession, has always been preserving an elite fraction of the human race from the ecocatastrophe, which they've long foreseen as an inevitable consequence of the toxic spread of industrial development, population pressure and democracy. At any rate, they control practically everything that goes on in Alaska, almost all of which is part of their grand design."

"And you're a member of this Cabal?"

"Good God, no. Even Arkheimer isn't a *member*. I'm just a pawn; she might be a knight or a rook, but we're all just pieces in the game. No member of the Cabal will be aboard the ship, if it actually gets to take off. They're all fully committed to saving humankind on Earth, if it's possible . . . no matter what the Dancing Rats might think. We were always a sideline, and Proxima was a twig on the branch. Arkheimer's obviously talked them into keeping it alive, but in their grand scheme, it's still a minor issue. Survival on Earth is their primary objective."

"But that might change, depending on what the starship actually finds . . . and whether the Enclaves can survive until it gets back from Proxima Centauri?"

"How can I know? How can even Arkheimer know that . . . unless her machine can look into a much nearer future than Halleck's?"

"I could never understand why Halleck's couldn't," Denise admitted. "Zeph tried to pass on the explanation Halleck gave him, but I didn't understand a word of it. Nor did Zeph, I suspect. Maybe Arkheimer will be able to do better."

"I wouldn't bet on it," said Kemmering sourly. "Not that she's even bothered to try with me. I'm only the captain of the ship, after all, not a mathematician . . ."

"But given that you *are* the captain of the ship, once you take off—if you do—you'll be the one in command. Even Arkheimer will be under your orders."

"Technically, perhaps . . . but I doubt that she'll see it that way . . . which is a recipe for trouble in mini-utopia, if ever there was one. And thirty years is a *long* time."

"But if the ecosphere were actually devastated to the point that long-term survival became impossible on the Earth's surface, you and she would effectively be in charge of the future of the human race? You'd be humankind's last chance of surviving for a few more decades . . . or longer?"

"Very nearly," Kemmering admitted. He was still holding his phone, but his hand was resting on his knee; he was meeting her interrogative gaze squarely, as a hero should. "Cronos is already out there, and theoretically capable of sustaining life aboard for at least thirty years, maybe a hundred. There's even a contingency plan for the crew to have children . . . but what would be the point? Proxima—the ship, not the star—isn't a viable lifeline either, even if, by some extraordinary miracle, it could find a habitable planet . . . something a hell of a lot more promising than Proxima b—the star, not the ship—is likely to be."

"But Arkheimer thinks that, with the aid of her machine, we—Zeph, that is—might be able to do that?"

"I don't know—but I'd be willing to bet that it's what she's told the Cabal. They probably don't believe her, but they're doubtless at a stage where no gamble, however crazy, can be neglected—and if she's right about the data supplied by the Dancing Rats . . . but all I know about that is rumor and leakage."

"That, I can guess," Denise said dryly. "Even Walter Halleck, genius as he considers himself to be, doesn't think that he and his AIs have unraveled all the coding of the Rats' transmissions, but Zeph has always believed that the reason they're so excited about him is that they consider him to be a representative of the final generation of humankind. Nobody's ever wanted to take that literally, and nobody's ever wanted to believe that the Rats could date the extinction of humankind to within a hundred thousand years, let along a few decades, but . . ."

"Not that data," Kemmering countered, equally dryly.

"Ah! You mean that she's deciphered something that the Rats know about more distant spaces?"

"Apparently. You'll have to ask Arkheimer. But whatever she thinks she's found, any sane and serious student of probability would have to reckon that the chances of actually reaching a destination out there in Proxima are infinitesimally close to zero."

He was still looking into her eyes, apparently measuring her while she was trying to measure him.

"And how do you feel about the mission, at present, Captain?" she asked.

"Terrified, obviously. And not just because the chances might still be slim that the ship will actually get off the ground, or function as specified if it does. Managing a mini-utopia on a seven-year excursion, much of it spent coming home, with a home to come back to, albeit a precarious one, is one thing. Managing the fragmentary society of Proxima for decades, even if Arkheimer and Zephaniah can persuade us that we have a destination that might provide the slightest glimmer of hope, or even the promise of some kind of discovery, is something else. Maybe it will outlast Snowdonia, or Fairbanks, and maybe it won't—my guess is that it won't—but what you have to ask yourself is . . ."

"Is where the best quality of life might be obtainable," Denise said, cutting him off. "I get it. How long before we reach this base?"

Kemmering looked at his handheld screen and pressed a few keys. "ETA fourteen minutes," he announced. Then he glanced out of the window, presumably to check the traffic. The car had been on the motorway for some time; Denise hadn't been paying enough attention to the route they'd followed, but an economically lit sign told her that it was the M40. It seemed less deserted than she might have expected in the early hours, with a higher proportion of trucks than on a "normal" night, presumably making all kinds of nocturnal deliveries, but there was no evidence yet of any panic in the traffic flow. The UK government had not yet announced its Code Red.

"Why did you pick me up personally?" she asked the Captain.

"Your flat was on my route. It was the most efficient way of deploying the local resources. It's not such a tremendous privilege. In the Cabal's scheme of things, I'm a small cog, easily replaceable. Zephaniah is the number one priority, at least in Arkheimer's estimation, so he and Mireille got the copter. If she thinks that you're essential to him, you probably have a higher priority score than me."

"She must reckon that you're essential to him as well, or at last a significant asset, given the relationship you established aboard Olympus Five."

"We've bonded, but it's not the same."

"I'm only his sister," Denise said, pensively. "We weren't close before, and since he got back . . . well, as you doubtless have the Kensington flat bugged, you presumably know that things haven't run entirely smoothly since. Your mysterious Coincidence theorist might easily take the view that you and Mireille are more important as potential psychological props for her pet freak than I am."

"It's possible," Kemmering said, carefully. "Is that what you think?"

"I don't know what to think. I don't really know Zeph at all."

"I can't tell you what Arkheimer or her psych-analysts think, but I can tell you what I think, not on the basis of documentation and eavesdropping, but on the basis of having been locked in a tin can with your brother for seven years. Firstly, he's not a freak, and I, at least, am prepared to take his theorizing about alternative sanities very seriously. He has, or had, difficulty forming social relationships, problems with reading non-verbal communication and conventional verbal implications, but those weren't innate psychological incapacities and the Olympus mission helped him, in very large measure, to get over them, at least with regard to his fellow crew-members.

"When he began to make manifest progress in that regard, his first concern was to try to rebuild—or perhaps build for the first time—his relationship with you. That was important to him. It still is. I'm not going to offer any deep psychological analysis of the fact, I'm just stating it. It seems to have been similarly important to you—again, just a statement. I love him, and so does Mireille, and each of us, because of the particular character of our different relationships with him, can supply him with something the other can't, and which you probably can't either—but there's something about his relationship with you, however imperfect it might have been in the past and however difficult it might seem at present, that seems to be unique."

"God alone knows what it is," Denise observed, wishing that it wasn't so.

"Probably," Kemmering agreed, "although Helen Arkheimer probably thinks that she does too—but whatever it is, my impression is that in his current state of mind, he considers it vital. And although I've only met you a couple of times, and have hardly had an opportunity to form a sound judgment, my impression is that you think the same, probably without knowing why. So if I had to bet, even though the sane and rational thing for you to do is to cut and run, and head for Snowdonia at top speed as soon as you can, and hunker down there with your fellow national assets, there probably isn't any chance of your actually deciding to do it. Does that seem to be a fair summation of the situation?"

"Yes it does," Denise admitted. "And thanks for being honest, if that's what you were really doing."

"I'm a soldier, not a cunning mastermind," said the Captain. "Believe me, Olympus Five couldn't have functioned for seven years if I'd been putting on an act. Zephaniah trusts me."

"Yes," said Denise, "but he trusts me too, and I'm not sure that qualifies him as a good judge. He can be a trifle naïve . . . sorry, that sounds terrible. I'm his little sister, but I always felt, when we were in our teens, that he was the one who needed protection, and guidance, even though it was so difficult to give it to him. We weren't close, as I said, and even though that was partly a lack of effort on my part, it was frustrating. He does seem to have made progress in the seven years he was away, but to me that was just absence, and . . . well, you can work it out. The main thing, from your point of view, is that you're right. There's no possibility of my opening that envelope. I probably wouldn't have anyway, even if Zeph were out of the picture. National asset! I'm an evolutionary biologist, for God's sake! I'd be no more use in a post-holocaust world, if there is one, than I will be on a starship. When I got the call, if I knew that Zeph was out of reach, I'd probably have tried to get home to Mum, to hold her hand while the world ended. Pathetic, I suppose, but . . ."

She left it there.

"If you're interested," Chris Kemmering said mildly, "I can tell you why you were classified as a national asset, in spite of the seeming irrelevance of your specialism. It might not be entirely irrelevant to your situation *vis-à-vis* Proxima."

Denise looked at him suspiciously. "Go on," she said.

"Your age, in combination with your high intelligence and robust constitution. You were considered ideal potential breeding stock, from a eugenic point of view that the planners couldn't admit publicly to holding. Younger women are more fecund, of course, but they haven't had the opportunity you've had to demonstrate your intellectual capacities. Three years down the line, of course, your status would probably have been revoked, even without your alcohol problem."

Denise was astonished, mostly at herself for never having thought of that. "I don't have an alcohol problem," she said reflexively.

"Not from your point of view," Kemmering replied, dryly, "but you can bet your life that the people monitoring your consumption can see what they take to be worrying signs."

Denise had already stopped worrying about that, her attention having shifted to a different part of the argument. "And you think that the Cabal might take the same view, and let me aboard the starship as *breeding stock*?"

"It's possible. As I say, some of the contingency plans drawn up in the past, for Cronos as well as Proxima, involved the possibility of having children. I don't know how far Proxima's mission creep has gone, or how the thinking might shift in future, depending on what Arkheimer and Zeph can discover, but . . ."

"But?"

"Well, if they'd ever got around to planning an actual colonization project—which they never will, now—they probably wouldn't have wanted all of you, although they might conceivably have accepted you as a convenient envelope for your ovaries. Arkheimer might well have a slightly different view."

That was genuinely startling. "Because I'm Zeph's sister, you mean? You think it might not be just him she's interested in, but his genes . . . and the copies I'm carrying?"

"I don't know."

The Captain checked his phone again, presumably to monitor their progress; he didn't modify the ETA. Then he looked out of the window again. The traffic was no worse.

Denise suppressed an urge to ask him to open a window, so that she could feel a breath of wind and fill her lungs with an authentic sample of the atmosphere that might only last for a matter of days, or hours, before the pollution levels made the fuel residues typical of motorway driving seem the epitome of freshness. She suppressed yet another impulse to curse, thought that she could really do with a drink, and then thought that that was the kind of thought that it might be better to banish from her mind from now on.

"This is all completely crazy," she muttered. "I don't know which way's up any more."

Chris Kemmering reached out then, and took her hand. She was tempted to snatch it away, but she felt too frightened and too alone. Even so, her tongue ran away with her slightly, and she muttered; "Easy, Don Juan. Anyway, we don't have time any more."

"You know that I'm not a Don Juan," the Captain said, quietly. "Even if Zeph hasn't told you much, you know that the media caricature is just that. But Olympus Five taught me how precious physical contact can be, in stressed situations. I thought we'd both benefit from the touch, trivial though it is and will remain."

She almost said "Pity," but swallowed it in time. She couldn't help remembering, though, that when the world had seemed to be teetering on the brink of its final collapse the previous week, when she'd thought that the only potential partner available to her if she had to try to seek that kind of solace in her last moments was Walter Halleck, she had regretted the fact that although Zeph and Marie MacLaughlin had both seen Chris Kemmering only a couple of hours earlier, he wasn't with them any longer.

"Thanks," she said.

He seemed slightly surprised, and glanced down at the hand that was holding hers, assuming that that was what she meant.

"No," she said, "I mean, for picking me up. You didn't have to do it. You could simply have told Zeph that it wasn't practical, and flown off, leaving me behind."

"No," he said, "I couldn't. I had to follow orders. Just a pawn, remember."

"That's not the most flattering reply you could have made."

"Strictly speaking, it's the most honest one—but Zeph would never have forgiven me, and I couldn't let him down. He trusts me."

"Good. I'm glad. So, assuming that we manage to fly over the pole, in spite of the bubbling methane and the rain of deadly particles, what happens when we land?"

"We'll go into a strip that's within the enclave site, although not actually under the dome—think of it as the drawbridge. We could be inside in a few strides, but we'll probably be sent straight on to the Proxima site. Assuming that Arkheimer does offer you a berth, and you take it, you'll go straight into whatever pre-launch training can still be contrived—full briefing on the pods, the life-support system, any specific duties assigned to you, centrifugal adaptation, etc., etc. That depends, though, on how long we have before launch, which could be anywhere between forty-eight hours and a couple of months. If the worst comes to the worst, and it's forty-eight hours, you'll simply have to be stuck in the pod unprepared, and I'll improvise as best I can to bring you up to speed thereafter. It won't be easy either way, but if you have to go through take-off and initial maneuvers without at least some artificial-gee training, it'll be hard. All of which is assuming that you get to take the ride, which is Arkheimer's call. I can't guarantee that she'll still let you aboard, in the changed circumstances. Even though I've . . . well, in short, I hardly know her. Nobody does. Maybe nobody can—she probably thinks so. She seems to consider herself to be something more than a genius, more like a superhuman, mentally if not physically."

"You mean she's puny?"

"Wiry would better be a better description. She's shorter than you, and thinner, but she's tough, and spiky. She's not nearly as old as Walter Halleck, by the way—no older than Zephaniah, in fact. Lots of math geniuses burn out before that age, especially the female ones, but she seems to have bucked the trend in a spectacular fashion."

"Popular mythology suggests that it's female hormones that disrupt precious female genius," Denise proffered, tentatively.

"I wouldn't know, but she certainly doesn't give the impression of being sexless or quasi-masculine, just . . . well, as I said, spiky."

"You mean she offered herself to you, like the majority of the female population of the world, but she didn't simper when she did it?"

The Captain shook his head, refusing to recognize the intended humor of the gibe. "Not exactly. She's not one for flirtation, though. She might try to be less . . . authoritarian with Zephaniah, but I doubt it."

"And has she donated her ovaries to the survival project, for eugenic reasons?"

The American condescended to smile wryly at that idea. "I don't know. Anyway, I really can't advise you on how you ought or might be able to handle her—you'll have to make up your own mind when you meet her."

"And you can't tell me exactly what she expects of Zeph or what plans she has for him," Denise continued, trying to sort it out in her own mind rather than speaking to her interlocutor, "but she deduced years ago, long before Zeph or Halleck, that the Dancing Rats had—will have—knowledge suggestive of a Coincidence-based sense, or a Coincidence-based technology, that works across space rather than time?"

"Seemingly. I suspect the initial deductions she made from the theory pointed her in that general direction, for some reason. But there might be more to it. She seems to have been particularly interested in Zephaniah from a very early stage in Halleck's experimental runs, so it might have been something she saw in his reports rather than the data that the Rats and the third generation Insects transmitted . . . something he registered without realizing its significance himself."

"That's what Marie MacLaughlin thought," Denise mused, "even on a superficial reading of the material Halleck put into the public domain—but she thought of it in terms of Zeph having intuited the presence of God. I assume that Helen Arkheimer, like Walter Halleck, wouldn't think of it in those terms?"

"Probably not. On the other hand, there were deists aboard Olympus Five, and some esoteric theological issues were introduced into our discussions—not by me."

"Astrotheology."

"That was one term that was bandied about. Arkheimer might not have been behind that, but on the other hand . . ."

The car was slowing down, and it came to a halt at some kind of checkpoint. The driver lowered his window in order to speak to someone outside, and then tapped on the glass separating the two compartments. Kemmering lowered his own window and held out his palm unit, having presumably summoned up an ID display. A face wearing black greasepaint peered into the bare compartment, scanning Denise with a penetrating gaze. Then the soldier stepped back; Denise got the impression of a strict salute, and the car moved off again.

Fifty yards further on there was a heavily armored gate, another halt and another check. This time there were searchlights mounted on the tower beside the gate, and Denise could see the sentinels on guard very clearly. They were clad in full battledress and carrying automatic rifles. There was a brief exchange between Chris Kemmering and the sergeant in charge of the detail before the gate swung open, and then the sergeant stepped back, saluting in an obviously deferential manner that had no hint of fake ostentation about it.

"The jet's already on the tarmac," Kemmering told her. "Zeph's already on board. If there's any possibility that you might want to get off again, I can give you five minutes to say goodbye."

"There isn't," said Denise curtly.

The Captain nodded. "Had to check," he said

Two minutes later, the car stopped again, at the bottom of a ladder leading to the door of a militarized executive jet. Chris Kemmering picked up Denise's end-of-the-world bag, but as soon as they were outside he handed it to her. "Go on up," he said. "I'll join you shortly."

And he turned away, leaving her to make her own way up the ladder.

It was still pitch dark; the sky was overcast, with not a hint of first light in the east. Denise felt oddly glad about that, because she was fearful of what the daylight might reveal, when it eventually dawned.

III

The plane was not fitted out internally like a normal executive jet, although it was not entirely fitted out as a military transport either. The front section was fitted with functional seats and cargo space, and was presently unlighted, but there was an illuminated section at the back where there were four reclining seats set in two facing pairs, with a table in between, which was evidently adapted for comfort and conference, if not for luxury.

The two window seats in the block of four were occupied, the one facing forward by Zephaniah Corcoran. The passenger in the other was briefly hidden from Denise's view as she made her way toward the back of the plane, but she was in no doubt as to the identity of its occupant.

Zeph saw her coming, got up and ran to meet her. He threw his arms around her, demonstrating the surprising extent to which his antipathy to physical contact had evaporated as he had adapted to life on Olympus Five, and his recent presence in London and the associated encounters with old acquaintances.

"Thank God," he said. "I was afraid you might not get through. Some kind of coded text came through to say you were on the way—or so the copter pilot said—but I wasn't entirely sure that I could trust it. They're maintaining strict call silence except for encrypted texts, trying to keep the preliminary code red under wraps."

"It seems to be working," she said. "We had an armed guard aboard, but he spent the entire journey twiddling his thumbs. Is this plane literally just for the four of us?"

"I gather that the other passengers are all military personnel, who don't require first-class seating—except for the Captain of course, who's . . . well, the Captain."

He drew her back into the lighted area.

"Mireille," he said, "this is my sister Denise. Nise, this is Mireille."

The Frenchwoman stood up and extended her hand to be shaken, slightly uneasily. "I've heard a great deal about you," she said.

"I'm afraid that I haven't had the opportunity to hear anything about you," Denise answered, with what she hoped was perfect politeness. She refrained from adding: *except what I've heard on leaked tapes*.

She scanned the woman up and down as she spoke, and was surprised to find that she was considerably shorter and slimmer than Zeph, but by no means puny; the Captain's description of Helen Arkheimer as "wiry" immediately sprang to mind. It occurred to her, now she was forced to think about it, that Zeph was a good deal more muscular than he had been seven years ago, and that although Chris Kemmering was taller than any of them and thus more gracefully slim, he too was very solidly built. The somatic engineering to which space travelers were routinely subjected presumably had side-effects that she had not considered consciously before. That might well have had something to do with the fact that Mireille Angevot's face was free of any of the usual signs of aging, even though she gave the impression of being older than Zeph, and perhaps considerably older. Denise suspected that the Frenchwoman did not owe her berth on the ship to her childbearing potential.

When Zeph had resumed his seat Denise sat down next to him.

"Did Chris get any information as to how bad it is?" Zeph asked, curiously. "No one's telling us anything."

"Very bad," said Denise. "Massive eruptions, quakes and tsunamis in the southern sections of the Ring of Fire, volcanic ejecta spreading northwards, increasing all the while. The British Isles might still be in a highly favored spot, survival-wise, as is Alaska, but the whole atmosphere will be seriously fouled up, perhaps for some time. If the enclaves can survive the rain of fire, there's a good chance that they'll last thirty or fifty years. After that . . . well, I guess it depends on how conditions outside evolve."

"Shit," Zeph muttered. "When the communication blanket's lifted, I'll try to call Mum."

"That might not be easy if we're airborne and heading for the Arctic. There's a massive solar storm building. Some kind of Coincidental trigger, Chris thinks."

"I can believe that," said Zeph.

"Really?" Mireille Angevot put in. "Why?"

"Because something's been triggered in me, too. I can't describe it, but it's not just fear and anxiety."

"Mine, I suppose, *is* just fear and anxiety," Denise said, "but I have to admit that I don't feel good at all. I suppose we all feel that way—even heroes like the Captain." Mechanically, almost without being aware of it, she put out her hand and grasped Zeph's. She thought that she caught a glimpse of envy in the physical chemist's gaze, although her face seemed quite serene—probably due more to her somatic engineering than her state of mind.

Yes, Denise thought, in spite of herself, *but you'll probably get to screw him, if you haven't already—which is also comforting, it's said.*

Immediately thereafter, however, she thought: *What's wrong with me? I can't really be jealous of her, can I, because the fact that she's not his sister means that she can get closer to him than I can?*

She made a deliberate effort to calm the strange turbulence that was fermenting within her. "Chris Kemmering invited you over so that you could take part in some sort of briefing in Grosvenor Square this evening, I understand," she said, addressing the Frenchwoman. "I'm not sure we'll get the same standard of catering in Alaska, if we get there, but who can tell?"

"I was very fortunate," the chemist agreed. "If I'd still been in Paris when the US Code Red was declared . . . but they must have had other personnel there warranting emergency extraction, so I expect they'd have squeezed me in, if . . . although I'm not entirely sure why I suddenly qualified for emergency extraction, and a reunion with the Captain and Zephaniah."

"But you knew you had a ticket for the starship?" said Denise, without really thinking.

Suddenly, Mireille Angevot's engineered face took on the expression that it had seemed strangely lacking, and Denise realized that the other hadn't known that at all, and that it had just come as a tremendous shock to her. The Frenchwoman's first impulse, in response to that surprise, was to look accusingly at Zeph.

He put up his hands in a gesture of apologetic defense. "I didn't know what I was allowed to say and what I wasn't," he protested, "and I wasn't told in so many words that you'd been drafted on the Proxima crew, so I didn't think . . ." He looked at Denise, slightly reproachfully, either accusing her of speaking out of turn or wondering how she came to know something he didn't.

"Nobody told me, either," Denise said, her heart sinking. "I just . . . assumed. You were both on Olympus Five with the Captain, after all. I assumed that the whole crew had probably been reassigned, given that Olympus Five was such a successful training exercise."

"*Training exercise?*" Again, Mireille Angevot's face registered shock.

Denise wished there was somewhere to hide, or even a bathroom to run to, but if there was, she had no idea where it was located, and she didn't want to start running around at random, especially now that the front section of the cabin seemed to be filling up with men wearing military fatigues.

One of them detached himself from the rest, and was revealed as Chris Kemmering as soon as he stepped out of the gloom into the bright light.

"Belt up," he instructed them, as he practically pushed Mireille Angevot back to the window seat and took the seat beside her. "We're off."

Zeph and Denise hastened to occupy their own seats. The jet had already begun to taxi on to the runway, and Denise, glad of the distraction from the slightly touchy situation, fastened her belt.

"There seem to be things that I haven't been told, Captain," the Frenchwoman said to her neighbor, a trifle resentfully.

"Indeed there are, Angevot," the Captain retorted, in a conspicuously military tone. "You were to be briefed this evening. I'm sorry if Corcoran has been speaking out of turn."

"It wasn't Zeph," Denise was quick to put in. "It was me. I didn't know . . ."

The Captain raised an authoritative hand, although the gesture was slightly spoiled by the fact that the plane rose steeply into the air, tilting him forward in his seat involuntarily.

"No harm done," he said. "In the circumstances—which are extremely confused—security protocols have become a trifle redundant."

"You're really going to take command of the legendary starship?" the Frenchwoman asked him, clearly amazed.

"I am," Kemmering confirmed, with a hint of pride.

"And you've requested me for the crew?"

The American winced slightly. "Not exactly," he admitted. "And you haven't exactly been added to the crew, as yet, but it has become increasingly obvious since the Olympus touchdown that Zephaniah would be a valuable, not to say vital, addition to the starship team, and the organizers of the project have been . . . let's say gathering materials . . . that might assist him to be . . . more comfortable. But nothing's been finally decided yet."

Mireille's gaze switched to Denise. "But you can't possibly be involved," she said, bluntly, albeit not in a hostile fashion.

"Why not?" Denise snapped, unable to keep a hint of hostility out of her own voice.

"Because you haven't had the training, let alone the somatic engineering. You'd be lucky to survive the launch. MAEs are light years ahead of old-fashioned rockets, but they still go up initially with a hell of a gee-force."

"In fact," said the Captain, in a soothing tone, "the somatic engineering is more a precaution than a necessity, and anyone who's physically fit and reasonably robust should be able to survive the lift off. It won't be comfortable, but if an invitation is offered to Denise, and she decides to accept, I see no reason, as Captain, to object to her inclusion."

The Frenchwoman looked as if she were about to shake her head, but thought better of it. Instead, she picked up another train of thought. "And the reason you brought me over from Paris, and the reason I'm here now, is because of the . . . relationship that Zephaniah and I formed on Olympus?"

"Yes," said the Captain simply.

"But . . . meaning no insult at all to Zephaniah, that was part of . . . well, everyday routine. We all slept with one another, at one time or another. We were strongly discouraged from playing favorites."

"True," said the Captain, "But that doesn't mean that all the bonds that were formed were identical, or even similar. It appears to have been judged that you and he had a particular affinity. But let me add that there's no compulsion here. At the most—and perhaps not even that—you might be invited to join the Proxima team. You have every right to say no—and to be perfectly frank, that would probably be the sane and wise decision. The Alaska enclave can't be guaranteed safe against the unfolding catastrophe, but if anything on Earth survives, it's the best bet of all . . . and the ship, if it even gets off the ground, is a very long shot indeed."

The physical chemist lay back in her seat. "*Merde*," she murmured. "Excuse me while I digest all this."

"That's the trouble with the end of the world," the American observed, relaxing just a little. "You're never ready for it, even if you've been expecting it all your life."

"Can we use our phones yet?" Zeph asked.

"Not until we land," said the Captain flatly. In a rather less firm voice, he added: "If we land . . ."

They were sitting on the right-hand side of the plane, so Denise calculated that the window on Zeph's other side would be facing eastwards, or north-eastwards, depending on the initial route it took, but there was no sign yet in the darkness of a breaking dawn. There were windows on the other side of the fuselage, but their blinds were lowered, so nothing at all was visible in that direction.

"What's the latest?" she asked the Captain.

"From the southern hemisphere, nothing," he said. "All communications down. Code Reds have now been officially declared all over Europe. There seems to be less chaos than one might have expected, in most places. A kind of resignation seems to have been built up. Mostly, people are following instructions, private and public. It might not last, though. Some of the enclaves are bound to be besieged, and the designated individuals trying to reach them attacked. Fairbanks is safe, though—nothing but projects for miles around, and a massive army presence, which will be steadily reinforced as planes land." He flicked his head to indicate the men gathered quietly behind him.

"In any case," he added, "the Cabal has been preparing for this for decades—far more than a century. Democracy has had nothing to do with it . . . with the result that there's been far less corruption in the allocation of places. I don't say none, but less. We'll hold firm, however many others fail. So will the Chinese, at least in the Kuen-Lun Mountains. Even if hardly anywhere else pulls through, I'd bet my life on Fairbanks and Shangri-La for the duration. Snowdonia has a good chance, mind, relatively speaking . . . and the Jura."

"I had a ticket for the Auvergne," Mireille Angervot put in.

"Not such a good bet," the Captain observed. "The volcanoes have been asleep for a long time, but . . . things have changed."

"I suppose I ought to thank you, then." She didn't sound unduly thankful.

"No need," said Kemmering. "I was following orders."

"Whose?" asked the Frenchwoman, looking at Zeph.

"Not mine," Zeph was quick to say.

Kemmering said nothing, so Denise decided that she might as well complete the full set of indiscretions. "Helen Arkheimer's," she supplied. And before her interlocutor could ask *Who?* she added: "One of a handful of people in the world who thinks she understands Coincidence Theory, and probably the only one crazier than Walter Halleck."

"That's the guy you were involved with?" the Frenchwoman asked, addressing Zeph.

He nodded.

"Does she want you to travel into the far future too?"

"I didn't actually travel in time," Zeph said, correcting the common misapprehension. "All I did was peer through a kind of window . . . a particularly intimate kind of lens."

"And what you saw proved to you that this really is the end of the world . . . that humankind can't and won't survive . . . at least on Earth."

"In the long term, no. But in the shorter term . . . maybe survivors of the present catastrophe will be able by cling on for hundreds, or even thousands of years."

"And what has this to do with the starship?"

"I'm still not entirely sure," Zeph said, a trifle wearily, "in spite of my long and rather surprising conversation with Dr. Arkheimer last night. Obviously, though, she thinks that I really do have an innate talent for establishing some kind of a rapport with aliens, and that it might not be limited to those that will replace us in the

Earth's evolutionary sequence. She thinks that, with mechanical assistance and practice, I might be able to sense echoes of particle coincidences that go all the way back to the origins of the solar system, and even the initial creation of matter in the wake of the Big Bang, and pick up faint whispers of life on other worlds . . . maybe in other galaxies . . . who can tell?"

"And that's why you were on Olympus Five?"

"Ostensibly, I was on Olympus Five in order to attempt to make empathetic contact with the cloud-whales. If there was an additional secret agenda, I didn't know anything about it at the time, and I still don't, although I have my suspicions."

"Captain?"

"Me neither," said Kemmering.

"But you have met Helen Arkheimer," Denise put in. "You know far more about her than the rest of us."

"I've given you all I can, Dr. Corcoran," said the Captain, formally. "In future, I suspect that we'll all have to look to Mr. Corcoran for further information."

"I'm not really a prophet," Zeph hastened to say, "except of doom—but that's easy. All you have to do is look out of the window."

He matched his action to his words, and frowned. The sky was blue, and the cloud beneath the plane was white—but the cloud did seem unusually turbulent, and the jet was lurching slightly.

All four of them checked their seat belts, which were still fastened.

"It could get bumpy," said Chris Kemmering, "especially if we try to go across the Arctic Circle."

"On second thoughts," said Mireille Angevot, "maybe I shouldn't be thanking you. If we're all going to die, it would prob-ably have been better to do it in Paris than taking a dive into the Arctic Ocean."

"Oh, I don't know," said Denise. "Plunging into an Ocean while it's bubbling up like boiling milk as it releases millions of years' worth of stored methane, while the sky's on fire with the biggest particle storm in living memory, does have a certain apocalyptic grandeur. And if we want to spend our final moments in hectic debauchery, you and I have a whole planeful of virile young men at our disposal."

She felt Zeph's hand squeeze hers, but couldn't tell whether the gesture was motivated by surprise or reproach—neither of which, in her estimation, would have been justified.

Mireille Angevot laughed, though. "I've already had the Captain," she said, "so be my guest. Don't worry about Zeph—I can take care of that."

"This plane," said Chris Kemmering, authoritatively, "is *not* going down, whatever happens up above or down below."

"The Captain has spoken," said the Frenchwoman, her voice falsely light. "Don't take it as a rejection, *cherie*."

To Denise's amazement, Zeph leaned forward and said: "Behave yourself, Mireille." Even more amazing was the fact that Mireille Angevot actually seemed to take the rebuke meekly.

"Sorry," the Frenchwoman said, looking at Denise. "Tense situation, too many surprises, too far from home."

"Me too," said Denise.

Chris Kemmering unbuckled his seat belt and stood up. "It's terribly irritating being a passenger when you're used to being in command," he said. "I'm going to have a word with the pilot. Does anyone want breakfast, or coffee?"

"Please," said Denise.

Zeph nodded.

"Couldn't make it a bottle of Cognac, I suppose?" asked the Frenchwoman.

"I fear not," said the Captain. "Military regulations apply."

"Coffee, then—double espresso."

"Me too," said Denise, "as long as you can tell me where the bathroom is afterwards."

Kemmering disappeared again into the gloomy part of the plane, where most of the military personnel appeared to be sleeping peacefully, or making the attempt. Denise assumed that they were all coming off long shifts of duty.

"You had to go and mention the bathroom, didn't you?" said Mireille Angevot. "Now I'll have to go and look for it."

Denise was not sorry to see her stagger off in the Captain's wake.

Denise turned to Zeph, with no intention at all of being aggressive, but was surprised to hear herself say: "I suppose you were too busy fucking her yesterday evening to call me and let me know what was going on?"

Zeph blushed deep red, but not because he was confirming the conjecture. "I'm sorry I didn't call," he said. "I was in private conference with Helen Arkheimer for several hours, wearing earphones and goggles. And for what it's worth, although it really isn't relevant, Mireille and I weren't even in the same room. We hardly had time to shake hands beforehand, or afterwards, before we were told to rendezvous with the copter in Kensington Gardens."

Denise squeezed his hand. "No, I'm sorry," she said. "Sometimes these things just pop out, without warning. I'm glad you had someone to keep you company, and I hope they give her a berth on the ship, if it will help. This Arkheimer woman certainly seems to be willing to move mountains to ensure every comfort for you. What does she know that I don't? Does she really think that you can steer the starship to an earthlike planet by means of interstellar telempathy?"

"I don't know exactly what she thinks, or wants, but I'm certain that it's not that simple. We'll find out soon enough. What Mireille said worries me, though—I hadn't thought about that."

"About what?"

"About your not having had the somatic engineering or the centrifuge training. Look, Nise, I can't tell you how much I want you with me if I really do get a place on this crazy expedition, but I can tell you that the one thing I want more is for you to be as safe as it's possible to be while the world's going to hell. If you got hurt because I'd dragged you into something for purely selfish reasons, I'd never forgive myself."

"Oh," said Denise, not knowing what else to say.

"I was a terrible brother back in the day," he continued, speaking rapidly, presumably because he thought that time was severely limited. "I can't even claim that it wasn't intentional . . . but I really wanted to make up for it when I got back. It would be too terrible, though, if my yearning to make amends only resulted in more damage. You have to think about this very carefully, Nise. Find out, if you can, what the risks really are—and if you think it best to stay behind, you really won't be letting me down. In fact, maybe it would be better if we both stayed on Earth. We'd be in the safest of all the enclaves, after all."

With Mireille, apparently, Denise couldn't help thinking, although she was able to refrain from saying it. *My God,* she added. *I really am jealous, aren't it? Maybe I do have repressed incestuous urges that have been carefully buried by some censorious fraction of my mind. Oh shit, not only is the world ending but now I need psychoanalysis.*

"You're not saying anything," said Zeph.

"Sorry," said Denise. "Just thinking it over. Now I have—and if the mysterious Dr. Arkheimer offers me a berth on her Ark, there's nothing on earth that will stop me being on it—certainly not a few minutes of weighing three times as much as normal. I don't say I'm as strong as an ox, but believe me, I'm strong enough, and even the uncomfortable awareness that I'll be as useful aboard the starship as a fifth leg on a donkey, except perhaps as a brood mare, is not going to stop me grabbing the chance to take part in humankind's last great adventure. Okay?"

He didn't get the chance to do anything but nod, because Mireille Angevot arrived back, followed swiftly by Captain Kemmering carrying a tray laden with plastic-wrapped *pains au chocolat* and lidded cups containing hot black coffee. Neither of them sat down immediately.

"Nothing new," Kemmering reported, as he distributed the meager food and drink. "Still the calm before the storm, hereabouts, but we're taking the longer course to avoid the region of the magnetic pole. It'll take us over northern Greenland, which won't be a pretty sight and might generate some turbulence of its own, but the Captain reckons it's safer. It's his call."

"Permission to swap places, Captain?" said the Frenchwoman.

"With me? Granted." Kemmering slid along to the window seat and left the one opposite Denise to Mireille.

Instead of refastening her seat belt the latter leaned forward. "We got off on the wrong foot just now," she said, extending her hand. "My fault, I'm sorry. Can we start again?"

"It was my fault too," Denise said, obligingly. "We're all strung out. It's difficult to form friendships while the world's literally falling apart around you. If Zeph's told you a lot about me, he must have warned you that I can be sharp without really meaning to be."

"No, he didn't. He can be very careful, can't he?"

How would I know? Denise couldn't help thinking. *You're the one who was teaching him about the joys of sex while I didn't even see him for seven bloody years.* Aloud, she said: "He was very guarded as a boy, but he seems to be growing out of it."

The Frenchwoman leaned even further forward, conspiratorially. "How dangerous were those experiments with the Sling that he did?" she asked. "He says not, but I'm not sure I believe him."

"He does say that," Denise agreed, "but I was always worried about them, to tell the truth. I didn't like Walter Halleck, and I didn't trust him. Monstrous ego . . . not a man to put the welfare of his employees ahead of his own crazy ambitions . . . except that, to be fair, they turned out to be far less crazy than everyone thought. This Arkheimer woman's rumored to be even crazier, but who can tell? She and Halleck are the ones that understand things way beyond the capacity of the ordinary human brain."

Mireille nodded. "I see," she said. "Thanks." She hesitated, but didn't withdraw from the *tête-à-tête*. "I'm sure Zephaniah hasn't said anything about it, but the Captain must have explained to you how things were on the ship? You know that I really do care about your brother, no matter how many other crew members I screwed?"

"The Captain did explain," said Denise, in a neutral tone.

"Good. So . . . if you need help protecting him from any mad scientists, you can rely on me, okay?"

"Okay,"

Mireille sat back in the seat and buckled her seat belt. Denise turned back to Zeph, whose hand she was still holding. He was ostentatiously looking out of the window, pretending not to have heard a word of the conversation, although she suspected that he hadn't missed a single one, in spite of the low tone that the Frenchwoman had been employing.

Reflexively, Denise followed the direction of his gaze . . . and her heart lurched.

IV

Denise told her heart, sternly, that there had been no rational reason for the lurch, given that she had known that the world was ending, and that there were volcanoes in the rest of the world as well as the Ring of Fire. As usual, however, what the head knew and how the heart reacted were two different things. Automatically, she tried to calculate how far south of the densely packed eruptions they were.

"My God!" said Mireille, realizing from her unspoken reaction that she and Zeph had seen something, and looking past him. "What the Hell is *that*?"

"Iceland," said Zeph, tersely. "Coming apart at the seams—literally."

"The wind's blowing toward Scandinavia," Chris Kemmering put in. "It shouldn't cause us too much trouble in our current flight-path . . . but that's the main reason that the pilot decided not to take a more northerly route."

"Ah," said the Frenchwoman.

Denise agreed with her. There didn't seem to be anything else to say. For a few minutes they watched the distant soaring fire and the mists from the boiling sea.

"The island's been evacuated for decades," the Captain remarked. "No casualties there."

"No," said Denise, "they all moved to Greenland and died there last week—except for a few in the south. You were lucky to get out in time, Zeph."

"Yes," said Zeph, baldly, and deliberately turned away from the window before adding: "I wish I felt tired, so I could copy the soldiers. This coffee might have been a mistake."

"The boys aren't going to be able to sleep for long," muttered Chris Kemmering. "We're already lurching ominously. It might be the bread that was a bad idea, if we start feeling queasy. Better hang on to the plastic wrappers."

"When we're somewhere out in interstellar space fifty years from now," Denise observed, looking down at the remains of her hasty breakfast, "and our grandchildren ask us what we were doing when the world ended, let's try to think of something better than this to tell them, shall we?"

"Let's be thankful for small mercies," said Mireille. "For once, nobody's taping us, are they? Maybe we ought to take the opportunity to indulge in some serious debauchery, confident that nobody's going to be hawking it all over the world as sleazy porn in two years' time?"

"I wouldn't bet on that," said Chris Kemmering. "If there's still a world to hawk it all over." He was staring out of his own window, trying to scan what little could be seen of the western horizon, toward which they were heading, where the cloud still resembled an infinite white sheet and the sky that met it seemed a perfectly normal blue. All in all, everything in that direction looked uncannily peaceful. If it hadn't been for the storm of fire and cloud in the north, which appeared to be limited seen from their present distance, everything would have seemed reassuringly normal.

"How long will the flight take?" Denise asked.

"Seven, eight hours on our present course," Kemmering replied. "In theory, that shouldn't be enough time for too much dust to drift into our path, but . . . the atmosphere has been a lot more active of late, and the jet stream . . . but there's no cause for anxiety."

Nobody bothered to point out that the lie was blatant.

"There are times," Zeph remarked, "when being a prophet isn't the most comfortable of vocations. When I first encountered the Dancing Rats, and realized that the human species was well and truly doomed, without posterity . . . well, in a sense it wasn't telling me anything I didn't know already, but still . . . there was an interval when I would really have liked to believe, as everyone else wanted to believe, that I was crazy, or hallucinating . . . but I couldn't. I knew. The other future generations were just icing on the cake.

"As soon as I'd made contact with the Rats, long before we established any kind of sign language for exchanging rudimentary information face to face, I *knew*. But it shouldn't really have made any difference, should it? I mean, as Mum is so fond of saying, in personal terms, in terms of the scale of our own lives and destinies, we have no idea what the future might hold, or how long it will last, and we still have to decide how to live our lives from one day to the next. We still have to find a sense of purpose for the time we have, a mission. We're by no means the first people in history to have been confronted with the imminent end of our own civilization, the world as we know it. And however bad things get, there's still a will to survive, a will to persist, built into our essential make-up."

He raised his left hand—the one that Denise wasn't holding—into the air to make a gesture that might have signified anything, except despair.

Denise had never heard her brother make such a long speech before, but it wasn't the length that astonished her so much as the abstraction. He'd learned that, she knew, aboard Olympus Five, where the entire crew had become accustomed to discussions of that philosophical dimension, and even greater breadth.

"So tell us, prophet," Denise said, "how is this all going to work out? If the four of us do get to take off in a flying coffin, with ten other people, including a mad mathematician and her mysterious machine, and a life-support system theoretically capable of sustaining us for fifty or a hundred years, how it is actually going to work out? What are we actually going to find when we get to Proxima Centauri?"

"We don't really want to go to Proxima Centauri," Zeph told her. "We already know too much about Proxima b to know that there's no point. Alpha Centauri A and B remain options, but Tau Ceti might be better. If or when we get to that phase of the mission, our selected destination might depend on the information I can collect, if any, with the aid of Helen Arkheimer's machine."

"Arkheimer really believes that her machine will enable you to make some kind of sensory contact with inhabitants of a world orbiting one or other of those suns?" Denise asked, trying to suppress her automatic skepticism.

"It's not as simple as that, but she does hope that I might be able to recover intuitions that might indicate which stars in proximity to the solar system have life-bearing planets . . . planets theoretically capable of supplying the raw materials for continued human existence. It's plausible. I'm no Dancing Rat, but their species is a close cousin of ours, with a brain whose neural architecture isn't so very different. They knew . . . will know . . . about the Jovian cloud-whales—and a hell of a lot more."

"Wait a minute," said Chris Kemmering. "What do you mean, *if or when we get to that phase of the mission*? What other phase is there?"

"This is presumably something that Dr. Arkheimer would have told you herself this morning," Zeph said, "so there's probably no reason why I shouldn't . . . in the first instance, Dr. Arkheimer wants to take the ship to Saturn."

"Saturn! But Cronos is already there, or should be."

"Yes. She wants to rendezvous with Cronos."

"Why?"

"Because the Dancing Rats won't just know something significant about Jupiter, apparently—they'll know something even more significant about Saturn. Something to do with the rings."

"Are you saying that there's life in Saturn's rings?"

"*Life* might be stretching the definition, but yes, something like it. Something . . . well, sentient might be stretching the definition too, but, given what I found out about the seventh generation of earthly life . . . who can tell how far we might have to stretch the definition of life and intelligence, even to accommodate the phenomena within the solar system, let alone beyond it. The universe is a much stranger place than our ancestors, even as recently as the twentieth century, could imagine. The Sling has already taught us that we have to think in much broader terms than our own image: about insectile intelligence, about megaplant intelligence and about seventh generation intelligence . . . and that's not the end of the universal spectrum, even if it's the terminus of earthly life. So, the first phase of the mission as Dr. Arkheimer presently conceives it, assuming that we can actually get off the ground, will take us to Saturn's rings. After that . . . well, phase two will depend on what phase one tells us, but if it's possible, we'll head for the stars . . . for *a* star."

"And then?" Denise wanted to know.

"Who can tell?" Zeph countered. "But *something*. If we're still alive, and still *compos mentis*, there'll be something further to do, something further to find. And we'll be able to send the information home, if there's anyone here to receive it. Maybe they'll be able to do something with it, and maybe they won't, but they'll surely want to know. The species might be doomed to extinction, but before we go, we'll surely want to understand, to the extent that we can . . . and there won't be anyone better placed than us to add to that understanding, unless Walter Halleck can build a new Coincidence machine of his own, in Snowdonia or wherever, and find someone else like me . . . which he will be absolutely determined to do, until his dying breath, if only to prove to himself and others that he was always a bigger genius than Helen Arkheimer, and that he really never needed me at all."

Chris Kemmering reached out a hand to pull the blind down over the window beside him. After glancing through the transparent plastic of his own window, and hesitating briefly, Zeph did the same.

One of the officers from the contingent at the front of the plane made his way along the aisle and slipped in behind the

Captain's chair, in order to whisper something in his ear over the back of the seat. Kemmering nodded, and the soldier returned to his seat, staggering slightly as the plane lurched.

"They've sealed all the enclaves in the southern hemisphere, most of Africa and Asia north of the equator, and Mexico too," Kemmering reported. "Britain probably has another twelve hours in hand, and Alaska too, but the overall situation doesn't look good. The Pacific is boiling in several locations, and the whole of Indonesia is a disaster zone. The methane release from the Arctic Ocean is accelerating, and it could reach flash-point within twenty-four hours. If it does . . ."

"*Merde*," said Mireille Angevot.

"If any of you are theists," the Captain said, "now might be a good time to start praying. I can't, alas." He looked at Zeph.

"It wasn't God that made contact with me via the seventh generation lens," Zeph whispered, "whatever Marie MacLaughlin thought . . . but there is one thing that might offer grounds for hope."

"What's that?" demanded the Captain.

"It wasn't omnipotent . . . far from it . . . but if my intuition can be trusted, it was *good* . . . kind . . . benevolent. Like the Dancing Rats, it wished me well."

Mireille Angevot looked at Denise. "May I borrow your brother's free hand?" she asked.

"You don't need my permission," Denise pointed out.

"I know—but I'd like it anyway."

Denise didn't even bother to nod her head. Zeph was already reaching out with his free hand to grip Mireille's left hand. Captain Kenmering reached out to take the other—but he didn't complete the tangle by reaching across to invite Denise to link her free hand with his. Whether in order to pray or not, the Captain closed his eyes and settled back in his seat. Denise didn't think that there was any possibility of any of them going to sleep, and not simply because of the coffee they'd drunk. She didn't close her own eyes, but she put her head on Zeph's shoulder.

Once upon a time, he would probably have flinched, but not now. He tilted his own head so that his cheek was cushioned by her hair.

Without opening his eyes, Kemmering spoke, in a soft and level voice, addressing himself to his companions, if to anyone, rather than God—but there was nevertheless a sense in which seemed to be praying.

"The United States," he said, "is still the most powerful nation in the world, in spite of the inexorable tide of history and the damage it sustained in the Crash. As well as the national enclaves, there are hundreds of survivalist communities who have made their own private arrangements to survive the apocalypse, and hundreds more individual bunkers. Even if . . . when . . . Yellowstone blows, there will be survivors, for years, for decades. Even if it takes centuries or millennia for algae and primitive plants to bring the oxygen levels in the atmosphere back to breathable levels, they'll sustain sufficient activity to permit the enclaves and the bunkers to renew their supplies of water, air and organics. This is the twenty-second century—early days yet, admittedly, but we have the biotechnology, and we have the will. The ecosphere has already survived at least two catastrophic extinction events on the same scale as this one, as Denise can confirm. And Zeph can confirm that the day of the Dancing Rats is still tens of millions of years in the future. We are not done yet. Not yet."

"Amen," Denise couldn't help adding, not even as a joke.

And then silence fell, as the plane continued its slightly unsteady flight through the aerial wilderness.

Denise took the opportunity to take stock of her situation, reviewing all her past decisions, including those taken by default, and wondering if she could have and should have made better ones. She assumed that she probably could have done and should have done, but she also assumed that there was no use crying over spilled milk and that she really ought to forgive herself, no matter how foolish, in retrospect, she turned out to have been.

On the whole, she thought, she could not possibly claim to have done well, but that was not entirely her fault, given that circumstances really had not given her a lot of scope to do any better.

Like many of the young women of her generation, she had decided early in life, probably before reaching puberty, that she would not have any children, because it would be a crime to bring children into a world that was already doomed and manifestly deteriorating at a rapid pace. She had decided to live selfishly, extracting what she could from the declining situation for her own pleasure and her own idiosyncratic satisfaction.

She had never been tempted to join the so-called Promiscuous Tendency, not because she saw any particular reason for moral disapproval, but simply because her own experience of sexual intercourse had never given her reason to think that it was a goal worth seeking in undue profusion for its own sake, and she could not see any significant advantage to be gained simply from multiplying the number of partners involved. She had settled for steady but relatively desultory relationships that had supplied a physical need of sorts but had never seemed more than a minor feature of life and had never come close to resembling the mythos of romantic amour.

She did not think that there had been any particular virtue in dedicating herself to academic study, as she had, as obsessively as she could, because it had simply been a matter of native temperament. Her particular frame of mind, within what Zeph had once been fond of calling the "multidimensional array of alternative sanities" had equipped her with a capacity for absorption in contemplation and the exercise of the intellect in the attempt to understand, and she had taken selfish advantage of that capacity.

Perhaps, in retrospect, it had been a mistake of sorts to choose evolutionary biology as her specialism, but not because it was a science of the remote past, founded entirely in relics, fossils and retrospective deductions based on genomic analyses, with no apparent practicality for the future, and no possible contribution to make to the slight prolongation of the life of a species she had known to be doomed even before the advent of Walter Halleck, the Sling and the discovery in the wilderness of the far future of the post-human inheritors of the Earth. No, she had been born into an era when that kind of practicality no longer counted for anything, in any sane calculation, and when any kind of intellectual contemplation that provided even an illusion of comprehension and aid to resignation could be reckoned as good as any other. What had made it seem like a mistake, in hindsight, was the accident of being Zephaniah Corcoran's sister.

Without meaning to, and without even making any effort, Zeph had turned her entire science upside down. Thanks to Walter Halleck's astonishing discovery of a means to open windows into the far future, Zeph had been able to add a futuristic dimension to her field of study that it ought not to have been logically capable of possessing. Zeph had completed, albeit sketchily, a vast picture on a canvas that ought to have remained serenely and comfortably blank, and in so doing, had reduced her much more detailed and painstaking study of the ecosphere's past to virtual irrelevance.

When she had briefly taken her brother to task for that, after his return to England following his seven-year jaunt to Jupiter, she had charged him with making her looking like a fool by removing the inside track that she ought to have had to the information that he had collected during his glances through Walter Halleck's windows, but the sense of injury she felt actually cut far deeper than that. It was not just that he had taken away an oracle to which she might and ought to have had privileged access, but the fact that, in merely becoming that oracle, he had rendered all the understanding she had so carefully gleaned regarding the evolution of life on earth trivial and redundant. In so doing, he had, in effect, rendered *her* trivial and redundant, a waste of intellectual space—and that had hurt, more than she could express.

Obviously, he had not done it deliberately. Indeed, in a sense, it was not something he had *done* at all, but merely something that had happened to him. He had never had the slightest intention of injuring her science, let alone her self-esteem. He had always been a difficult person, in some ways, by virtue of his various quasi-autistic traits, but he had never wished her any

234

harm. In his way, he had always loved her, even though he had found it difficult to express that love in ways that were considered appropriate by the self-styled neurotypical individuals who had attempted to usurp and reserve the concepts of sanity and normality for themselves. There was no malevolence in him. Like the mysterious quasi-cosmic consciousness with which he had made empathetic contact through the seventh generation lens, he was fundamentally good, if largely impotent. She could not and did not blame him for wrecking the obsessions that, for lack of viable alternatives, had provided the framework and the foundation of her steady but desultory life—but wreck them he had.

Was he even aware of that fact? She suspected that he was not. He did not have a sufficient capacity to place himself in another person's shoes to glimpse that kind of effect. She suspected that she couldn't even have explained it to him—that if she had tried to tell him how the effect of his discoveries had pulled the rug out from beneath her existential feet, he would not have been capable of understanding, because his own mental configuration was different.

He had not made the same kinds of choices as she had. While still a teenager, he had had artificial neuronal contacts fitted into his flesh that would enable him to work in the field of sophisticated telepresence, manipulating machines by remote control. In a way, that was just another kind of exploration, but it was not the same kind of exploration for which Denise had been psychologically pre-adapted. In another way, it was the very opposite: while Denise's quest for intellectual understanding had taken her away from direct sensory experience of the world into the remoter realms of abstract consciousness, his had attempted to extend and enhance his own senses and project them further into the physical, into the material. Perhaps it had led him to a similar existential isolation, but he had gone by a different route.

Given, though, the fact that they had moved in such divergent directions when they were young, when they had never been close, effectively living parallel lives in the same house but never really interacting to any significant degree, why had seven years of separation changed their attitudes so much? Why had Zeph felt a need to make contact with her while Olympus Five was still distant in space, and why had she been so glad that he had? Why had they both looked forward so much to their eventual reunion in the flesh? It was surely not surprising that the reunion had not lived up to her hopes—or, in all probability to his—but it surely was surprising that, in spite of its awkwardness, it had still seemed enormously important.

Perhaps on her part, it had been the very circumstance that he had created such a void in her life, which needed filling somehow, and that holding him responsible had somehow directed her attention to him, as if he had owed it to her to make good the deficit as best he could. On his part, presumably, the fact that the obligatory adaptations he had had to make to life aboard Olympus Five, which had introduced him to the rewards as well as helping him to overcome the difficulties of social contact, had created an urgent desire to build relationships, and that his sister had simply seemed like a natural or convenient starting-point.

Both arguments seemed vaguely plausible, but also a trifle insufficient.

Then again, there was another factor that might have to be taken into account in that particular equation: Helen Arkheimer's willingness—eagerness, even—to keep them together. That surely could not be a simple reaction to Zeph's attempts to rebuild their relationship, begun while he was still on Olympus Five. Nor could it be, as Chris Kemmering had suggested, manifestly in jest, that it was the genes she shared with Zeph that interested her . . . unless, of course, she was not merely thinking of those genes of something usable in reproduction.

Was it possible, she wondered, that Helen Arkheimer thought Zeph's attempts to build a relationship with her were connected with his slow and as-yet-uncertain development of a Coincidence sensibility? Did she think that there was some mysterious special affinity between them? Might there, in fact, be such an affinity, given that she seemed so absolutely determined to stick with him, in spite of all the good reasons there might have been for her not to have taken this plane, but to be on her way to Snowdonia instead?

But were those reasons really good, given that the difference between eking out the rest of her life on the starship and eking it out in the somewhat larger groundship that a domed but mostly subterranean enclave comprised, was not really that great? There would be more space in Snowdonia, and a better chance of one day emerging into a wider world, but was a population of thousands really much preferable to a population of little more than a dozen, given that the number of intimate acquaintances that any life could reasonably contain could hardly be more than a dozen? Doubtless she would have found a role of some sort to play in the daily economy of the Enclave, but would she not find one aboard the starship too? Perhaps, in either case, given her biological knowledge, she would have been forced to assist in maintenance of the enclosed life-support and food-supply systems, or go into medicine or culinary chemistry. Again, those facilities would be more varied and on a larger scale in Snowdonia than on a spaceship, but they would be essentially similar in kind.

But that was a dead issue, and, in any case, a trivial one. The real point was the one that she had just abandoned in order to follow the digression: the question of whether there might be an affinity between herself and Zeph, to which his supposedly burgeoning Coincidence sensibility might be reacting, or which it might even be enhancing. Was that conceivable?

As she had told Chris Kemmering, she didn't understand the first thing about the mathematics of Coincidence. In fact, according to Walter Halleck and Helen Arkheimer, hardly anyone could, because a human brain had to be configured in a particular way in order to permit the mind to which it played host to grasp its particular multidimensionality.

But that's not good enough any more, is it? Denise thought.

She looked at Mireille Angevot, who was evidently deep in meditation of her own. Her eyes were open, but her gaze seemed unfocused.

Without turning her head, without moving anything but her eyes, Denise glanced at Zeph and Chris Kemmering, who seemed similarly entranced, withdrawn into private worlds of thought.

But we're holding hands, she thought. *We're connected.* And that, she realized, was perhaps the point, both materially and psychologically. Something was going on between them—perhaps something ordinary, or even trivial, but nevertheless *something*.

There really was, she thought, Coincidence as well as coincidence in their being here, together . . . and suddenly, Denise had the distinct impression that if she couldn't concentrate her thought, if she couldn't at least begin to make sense of what was happening to her, she might be lost forever in the psychic wilderness . . .

V

I have to think, Denise told herself. *After all, this might be the last chance I get to meditate, to weigh things up, because once we land . . . everything will start to move again, hectically.*

Deliberately, she returned to the frayed edge of the broken train of thought.

All she really knew about Coincidence Theory was what everyone knew, thanks to the media: that it was a way of accounting for, or at least of modeling, the fact that subatomic particles that had once been associated retained some kind of affinity when separated, so that the effects of detectable forces on one of the separated particles found a kind of echo in the other. Thus, the "lenses" that Walter Halleck had established in the present in his Sling could, when manipulated in a particular fashion, produce echoes over time that permitted the same particles, at a distant point in time, to produce the "phased echo" of the lens, of limited but temporarily stable duration.

In Halleck's view—his original view, at least—that kind of echo phenomenon could only supply images from the future Earth, because that was where the particles associated in the present still existed when they had been sufficiently separated by the accidents of time, to be subject to the controlled echoing. And the phenomenon was bound to grow weaker over time because some of the separations were irremediable, and the distant associations uncollectable, although a certain amount of temporal distancing was necessary because the Sling's "lenses" could not be focused over intervals of mere thousands, or even hundreds of thousands of years.

Some aspects of that view, however, now seemed to be obsolete. Some kind of Coincidence echoes were, it seemed, detectable across space—interplanetary, and perhaps interstellar space—because associations that had existed between particles in the very distant past, perhaps including the original associations implicit in the initial creation of matter, still permitted some kind of resonance: resonance that might, in principle, be amplifiable by machinery, and could also lend itself to some kind of quasi-sensory or hypersensory perception.

The five senses traditionally attributed to human beings were, of course, all varieties of touch, all involving some kind of physical contact capable of exciting nerve cells. There had long been speculation, however, about a "sixth"—or, strictly speaking, a second—sense that was not a subcategory of touch, but involved a different kind of intuition. There was a rich mythology of extraordinary mental powers, including the precognition of oracles and prophets and the telepathic or telempathic distant awareness of the thoughts or emotions of others. Such ideas were conventionally dismissed as delusions precisely because it was difficult to accommodate them to the subcategory-of-touch model— but what if there were a whole set of alternative pseudosensory perceptions based, not on touch, but on something much more nebulous and uncertain, but nevertheless real: the essentially puzzling but mathematically ordered phenomena of Coincidence?

Perhaps such phenomena were much more commonplace than people realized, or, at least, much more common than positivistic scientists were able to admit. Given that positivistic scientists found it so difficult, in fact, to come up with a plausible account of the nature of mind and the fundamental physics of such everyday phenomena as thinking, feeling, imagining and dreaming, perhaps there was a whole sector of the psyche missing from their conventional account.

Odd mental affinities had often been observed between identical twins, although some of those might be in the minds of beholders, but Zeph was not her twin, let alone a clone derived from the same fertilized ovum. They were just an ordinary brother and sister, with approximately fifty per cent of their genes in common—but were genes even relevant, given their own crude physicality? Doubtless, some pairs of siblings had slightly more than fifty per cent of their genes in common, others slightly less, but if particular limited sets of genes were relevant in some way, then the chances of those limited sets being duplicated might occasionally produce coincidences-with-a-small-c . . . and some apparent coincidences-with-a-small-c might actually be effects of Coincidence-with-a-capital-C.

Was it possible, then, that she and Zeph really did have some special kind of affinity, long dormant even while they were living in the same house, but now beginning to burgeon? And if so, what might its implications be? Did Helen Arkheimer have some kind of hypothesis, or was it just something that she would be interested to investigate? And if it were the case that the recently developed affinity between herself and Zeph were some kind of Coincidence phenomenon, might the same be true of the affinity that had apparently formed on Olympus Five between Zeph and Mireille Angevot? Might the same be true of all the affinities that had apparently formed aboard Olympus Five . . . and, in fact, between many, if not all, the affinities that formed somewhat haphazardly between human beings in general, and sometimes between humans and animals? Might amour be, essentially, a phenomenon of Coincidence, since that too seemed somewhat resistant to reductionist positivist analysis?

But that, Denise told herself, was surely broadening the argument too far. The point was not to provide a hypothetical catchall explanation of affinities in general but to discriminate between affinities, to determine, if possible, what it was about Zeph that equipped him for empathy with the likes of the Dancing Rats . . . and what might be special about her that was drawing her to him as his powers of prophecy and understanding seemed to be developing, albeit slowly and awkwardly . . .

A hand touched her on the shoulder, and she flinched. Her eyes, which had been open but staring into infinity, seeing nothing, suddenly focused, and she found herself staring diagonally across the table at Chris Kemmering, who seemed anxious. He immediately put the forefinger of his free hand over his lips, and then, without moving his head more than slightly, he directed his eyes first to the left and then to the right: at Mireille Angevot and at Zeph.

Denise looked at them in turn, with similar minute care, although she already knew what she would see, having realized it before the Captain.

Neither Mireille not Zeph was asleep, but they both still seemed to be lost in the same kind of quasi-hypnotic trance she had observed before . . . exactly as she must have been, she realized, before the Captain had tapped her on the shoulder, and as the Captain must have been himself before the officer commissioned to relay information to him had tapped him.

Perhaps, she thought, it was coincidence-with-a-small-c, or perhaps involuntary imitation. They had all had a sleepless night, and were all in a similar state of high anxiety; it was understandable that they might all be in a suggestible frame of mind, as well as a state of imminent exhaustion.

But she didn't believe it. She didn't even believe, in retrospect, that they had elected to hold hands simply for the sake of comfort and moral support. Chris Kemmering was evidently anxious about it, though, and not just because all three of his companions had been temporarily entranced. Denise felt oddly flattered by the fact that she was the one whose attention he had tried to attract, the one he wanted to consult.

"What is it?" Denise whispered—or, at least, formed the words ostentatiously with her lips.

Kemmering used the forefinger of his free hand to touch his ear, bidding her to listen.

She listened, and couldn't hear anything.

It took her three seconds to realize that she ought to have been able to hear the sound of the twin jets.

She almost panicked, but the Captain's eyes were bidding her not to do that.

"Clogged," whispered the Captain. "Volcanic microparticles. We're gliding."

"Oh shit," Denise murmured. "You've been updated?"

The Captain's eyes flickered to confirm that one of the soldiers had brought news back, as before. He leaned forward, and Denise moved her own head toward his, conspiratorially.

"We've flown over the Mackenzie and we're heading directly toward Dawson," he whispered. "If necessary, we could land there, but the pilot has sent word that he's sure he can make the Alaskan border and find a place to put us down without actually crashing. They're sending airtight vehicles from Fairbanks to meet us—they could cross into Canada if necessary, but every mile we can save will be precious. Conditions at ground level are pretty filthy, though—it'll be a nasty drive to Fairbanks, but at least the road won't be busy. A State of Emergency is in force and travel prohibited to all non-military vehicles. The ejecta shouldn't have got here so quickly, but there's a hell of a wind blowing on the west coast of Canada. The Juneau Enclave's sealed, and Fairbanks is partly sealed, but the area around Fairbanks is pretty clear, for now, and we should be able to reach the subterrains in an hour or two. After that, we should be okay."

Denise flicked her eyes sideways, in both directions. "Shouldn't you be telling us all?" he whispered.

"Maybe," he agreed, "but they're even further out of it than you were . . . and me. Do you have any idea what's happening?"

"No. Stress? Subconscious imitation? Involuntary somnambulism?"

"The pilot's messenger snapped me out of it." Kemmering said, thoughtfully. "I figured that it was best to take it one step at a time. Were you dreaming?"

"No, just thinking—miles away, but perfectly lucid."

Although they had been keeping their voices low, the sound

had penetrated the daze in which the others were languishing. They both shifted slightly, and came round.

"What's going on, Captain?" Mireille asked, dully.

"We've lost the engines," Kemmering explained, curtly. "We'll have to cover the last eighty or a hundred miles of the journey on the ground. We'll have to put on protective clothing and breathing apparatus before we land, but the vehicles will be protected. We'll be fine."

Zeph looked at the window-blind.

"No point," said the Captain, although he pushed up the blind anyway. "It's daylight, but you'd hardly know it," he added, although that was perfectly obvious. Beyond the window there was nothing but gray mist.

"How are things in Europe?" Mireille asked.

"Not as bad as they could be, all things considered," the Captain reported, passing on what he had been told. "The evacuations and relocations are proceeding smoothly, no riots, let alone revolutions. Aircraft are still flying in Britain and France; the weather's bad but not too dire yet." Presumably adding his own inferences or conjectures, he went on: "London and Paris still have another twelve hours' grace, at least. People will mostly be resigned, or at least obedient to discipline. They all know the score. It's not like the first Crash, when too many people were unprepared and there were too few procedures in place. We've learned from our mistakes."

"Hurrah for us," said Denise, dryly.

"We were in some kind of trance just now," Zeph observed, belatedly.

"Yes," said Denise. "For a long time, apparently—longer than it seemed."

"Did you drug that coffee we drank?" Zeph asked the Captain.

"No," was the Captain's curt reply. "The phenomenon was spontaneous, I assure you."

"What were you thinking about?" Denise asked Zeph, curiously.

"Things in general: the situation; Coincidence."

Denise suppressed a temptation to say: *That's a coincidence—me too*. She looked toward the front of the plane, where the military personnel were quietly fitting thin rubber suits over their fatigues, and adapting oxygen cylinders to their backs, but without applying the masks to their faces as yet.

Chris Kemmering craned his neck in order to follow the direction of her gaze.

"We'd better do likewise," he said. "I'll show you all how to fit the masks and control the oxygen supply—go gently, the stuff's poisonous in excessive doses, and even a small excess can make you dangerously intoxicated. The supply should be easily adequate to get us to Fairbanks, even if we have to keep them on inside the vehicles. I've asked the pilot to request a small vehicle for the four of us as well as a truck for the boys. They're built to handle much worse conditions than we'll find, so the only slight problem will be visibility. If the pilot can put us down where he intends, though, it's a reasonably good road."

Denise wasn't unduly alarmed by the prospect of donning the protective suit, especially as the scanty clothing she'd thrown on when she leapt out of bed was so elementary. She had to excuse herself first in order to go to the bathroom, though, and a queue immediately formed behind her.

Eventually, however, they were all fully equipped.

The plane seemed to be lurching quite badly now, as they were in denser and more turbulent air. Denise felt distinctly queasy, and experienced a slight hint of *schadenfreude* in seeing that Zeph and Mireille both looked distinctly pale and distressed. Chris Kemmering was still maintaining the iron discipline that was appropriate to a military man, but even he looked distinctly tight-lipped.

Considering that the plane had lost its engines some time ago, it still seemed surprisingly buoyant. Obviously, it was capable of gliding a long way.

"The landing is going to be rough," Kemmering warned them, when they were all firmly strapped in. "As soon as we've come to a halt, fit your masks and open the oxygen tap. Then I'll open the emergency door, and we'll all go down the emergency slide, Zeph first, then Denise, then Mireille. Don't argue! Just do it. With any luck, you'll be able to see the vehicles that will come to meet us. If you can, move toward them. If you can't, move away from the fuselage in a straight line. Either way, stay together. I'll signal to you with my hand like *this* to tell you when to stop, and then you stand still. If I signal like *this*, you drop flat; otherwise, stay upright. Got that? Now, by the way, might be another good time to pray, if you can."

Denise couldn't. She took Zeph's hand again. "If we get killed," she muttered in his ear, "I'll never forgive you."

"Me neither," he muttered back.

Then the lurching started in earnest. Denise was convinced that they were going to hit the ground any second, but they didn't. They flew on, and on, until she had almost given up expecting that they were ever going to touch down—at which point, perhaps inevitably, they did.

Touch, was, however, putting it mildly. The undercarriage was down, but it snapped almost instantly, and the jet pancaked. Denise had no idea whether they were on an airfield, a highway, or just a big patch of flat ground, but whatever it was, it was far too bumpy for her liking, without the aid of wheels. She lifted her feet off the floor of the plane, frightened that the shocks might break her ankles.

Eventually, though, the plane came to rest.

"Masks on!" ordered the Captain, and set the example. Then, seemingly in the same smooth movement, he opened the emergency door and deployed the inflatable chute. He practically grabbed Zeph and pushed him out. Denise made haste to follow in order not to be seized and tossed like a parcel. The trip to the ground was unexpectedly smooth, and there wasn't far to go. When she landed on her backside, Zeph immediately pulled her upright, and then moved her to one side in order to do the same for Mireille.

Automatically, like a marionette, Denise started moving away from the plane, her eyes searching the gloom for vehicles—of which there was no sign. The darkness was intense, but did not give the impression of a void. Indeed, there was a fierce wind blowing in gusts, and Denise could hear a strange whisper, which she assumed to be particles of some kind making contact with her mask. There was no landscape, no sense of place at all; but the world was still there; she could feel its gravity, its substance and its sullen turbulence.

After she had taken thirty hesitant paces, there was an urgent tap on her shoulder, and she stopped. The deeper shadow of a tall man was just about visible in the gloom. If Kemmering said anything, she couldn't hear him inside the mask. Anxiously, she fiddled with the oxygen valve, but she was moderately sure that the flow wasn't excessive.

Her eyes gradually adapted to the obscurity as best they could, but the touch sensations caused by the violent and shifting wind seemed more informative than the vague shapes that her eyes could make out through the goggles of the mask. She looked up, but the cloud cover seemed to be uniform. To judge by the weakness of the strange whisper, there didn't seem to be overmuch dust in the atmosphere, but it had started raining. Was that good? she wondered. Might the rain wash the air clean of dust?

There was another tap on her shoulder, and the shadow that was the Captain's outstretched hand showed her four headlights in the distance. As they drew closer, the light they projected gradually illuminated her surroundings. She was vaguely aware of the soldiers forming up in ranks to either side of her—to either side of the four of them—like an escort, or a squad of bodyguards. When they marched off, she tried to match their stride, but the Captain was the only one who could do it. She, Zeph and Mireille gradually fell back, but not so far as to emerge from the back end of the tunnel formed by the two ranks of soldiers, whose rearmost members slowed so as to stay level with them.

By the time the three stragglers had caught up with the head of the column, however, the Captain appeared to be engaged in a violent argument with someone who had emerged from the vehicles: an argument conducted with the aid of some kind of wire connecting their two helmets, which presumably enabled them to hear one another clearly, although all that the onlookers could hear was a muffled hum.

The person with whom Kemmering was arguing was much shorter than him, and thin—but not frail. The word "wiry" came to Denise's mind again, and she realized that the person with whom the Captain was quarreling, and who was very obviously disputing his authority, must be Helen Arkheimer herself.

For a few seconds, Denise couldn't imagine what the two of them could possibly be arguing about, but then it became obvious, as the smaller figure gestured imperiously to order her, Zeph and Mireille to go to the smaller of the two vehicles, and left the Captain standing where he was, apparently deeply frustrated by the fact that he wasn't quite able simply to pick the diminutive figure up and plant her somewhere out of the way.

As the three of them paused before the vehicle, Helen Arkheimer signaled graphically that they were to keep the oxygen masks on. Then she ordered Zeph and Mireille Angevot to get into the back of the armored car, and indicated the front passenger seat to Denise.

Nobody thought of querying the orders, or even hesitating to obey them.

The soldiers were still being loaded into the back of the truck, and Chris Kemmering was still standing on his own, watching the smaller vehicle in an attitude that clearly displayed frustration and annoyance, as the car pulled away.

VI

Helen Arkheimer picked up the trailing end of a long piece of wire dangling from her helmet, and stuck it to the plate of Denise's mask, to which it adhered easily enough.

"Can you hear me, Denise?" she asked.

Until the other woman used her name, Denise had wondered whether she had been placed in the front seat by virtue of a case of mistaken identity. "Yes," she said. "Can you hear me?"

"Loud and clear," said the other, who had both hands on the steering wheel now. "I fear that I've just annoyed the dear Captain profoundly, but he really ought to be better able to obey orders. I drove the car out here, and I have every intention of driving it back. He can take the truck with the rest of his men. The chain of command has to be respected, don't you agree? I'm Helen Arkheimer, by the way—but you've realized that, of course?"

"Of course," said Denise, figuring that it would stand as an answer to both questions.

"Good. If the world had only continued to behave itself for one day more, I'd be talking to you right now in your flat in Kilburn, briefing you as I briefed your brother last night, ahead of your conference at the Embassy this evening, but the best laid plans of rats and men gang aft agley, as the poet nearly has it. Damn it, the rain's getting worse, and all the lights on the road are out—but no matter. I'll have you through the airlock and into the subterrain in little more than an hour. The air outside isn't short of oxygen, in fact, but the microparticles are already a problem, even at ground level, and I don't want any of you breathing in that kind of stuff—it can cause serious long-term problems. An evil wind, alas, blowing from the south. We have urgent matters to discuss, though. Presumably the captain gave you the option of not getting on the jet, and conscientiously spelled out the reasons why you might not want to?"

"Yes," said Denise, tersely.

"And twenty minutes ago, you were probably wishing you'd taken the advice; but I'm glad you didn't. He told you about the Proxima, of course—although we'll have to change its name, now—and exactly what it is you're volunteering for."

"Exactly would be a wild exaggeration," Denise said, "but I'll stick with Zeph all the way, if you'll permit."

"Permit? The dear Captain must have overdone the caution. I want you aboard the ship, and I'm very grateful to you for agreeing to join the crew, in spite of the risks. I'm not taking too much for granted, am I? When you say that you'll stick with Zeph all the way, you do mean *all the way?*"

248

"To the stars," Denise confirmed, tersely.

"Good. It would have been better, obviously, if I could have spoken to you first, so that we could at least have paid lip service to the principle of informed consent, but I think we understand one another well enough. You know Walter Halleck, I believe."

"Yes."

"A great man . . . a truly great man. I wish I'd been able to meet him, or at least talk to him, but that's not the way the Cabal works. Did the Captain explain the Cabal?"

"Very sketchily."

"That's the only way it can be explained. He and I are both its creatures, body and soul. It's been exercising covert eugenic selection for generations, in the context of its plan for the salvation of the race. He was picked out for his present role before he was sent to the military academy; I was designated for mine while I was still a child, as soon as they could make an approximate calculation of my mathematical ability. I wasn't out of my teens when I was introduced to Coincidence Theory. I assume that they handed Halleck's initial analyses to half a dozen of us, but it only took a matter of months for them to realize that I was unique in being able to get a proper handle on them. Ever since, I've been his doppelganger, with the specific mission to step out of his shadow as soon as superhumanly possible, and overtake him. As for the Sling—magnificent; the moment I saw the initial plan, I wanted us to build one, but the committee men dragged their feet and decided to let him do the work, because it was beyond the scope of their feeble imagination to think that it might actually work, even though I assured them that the math and the physics were absolutely sound. A stupid hesitation on their part . . . except that it might have turned out for the best, no credit to them, because the Sling itself turned out to be only half the equation, and luck . . . or perhaps Coincidence . . . dropped the other half into Halleck's lap."

"Zeph," said Denise, colorlessly.

"Exactly—but before we talk about him, and what I need him to do, I'd like to explain myself a little more clearly. Had you even heard of me before today?"

"Yes, but nothing substantial."

"And probably insulting. I understand. Well, I suppose mine has been a strange life, in a way—some people might think I'd been robbed of a childhood and exploited as an instrument, but to me, living in a mental world of abstruse mathematics, I've been in paradise. Obviously, you can't simply take my word for it that I'm not mad, but I need you at least to consider seriously the possibility that I might not be, and that everything I'm going to ask of you and your brother has logic behind it and a purpose in view. Can you do that?"

"Yes," said Denise, because it was what her interlocutor wanted to hear. Privately, she reserved her judgment.

"Good. My immediate handlers, mercifully, have always paid me the compliment of taking me seriously, even though they couldn't follow my thought processes, never suggesting for a moment, at least to my face, that I might be mistaken in my calculations or conclusions. I think they sometimes had a hard time convincing their fellows, who were initially very reluctant to believe my endorsement of the Sling data, but they always backed me.

"Nobody, to begin with, wanted to believe in the Dancing Rats, let alone the Insects and the Megaplants. A lot of people, given confirmation of the inevitability that the human race would have ceased to exist in twenty or thirty million years and replaced by rats, could have shrugged their shoulders and deemed it utterly irrelevant to them and their foreseeable posterity, but the Cabal didn't like it at all, and they were desperate for me to tell them that Halleck's machine didn't really work, and that the lens wasn't really providing a window into the future, or, if it was, that it was only a contingent future that could still be avoided—a kind of timely warning. How they would have loved Zeph to be hallucinating! But when the data began to come back from the Rats, encrypted as it was . . . I knew right away that we were dealing with something radically new, something unhuman.

"Math is math, the only pure and objective aspect of thought, but it needs minds capable of grasping it, and only a handful of human minds are capable of seizing the tail end of some of its exotica. I could see instantly that the Rats were possessed of what your brother would call an alternative sanity. Like a lot of human geniuses, that doesn't necessarily mean that they're capable of getting the buttons in the right buttonholes when they put their pajamas on, but it certainly meant that they weren't a figment of any human imagination.

"My handlers believed in me, though. They defended me to the rest of the Cabal, at the risk of their own positions, and I paid them back in gold when I began to decrypt the Rats' data, and indicated some of its possible applications. Then, when the Insect data added a further dimension . . . well, to cut a long story short, I proved myself, in spades. I proved Halleck and I proved Zeph . . . to the extent that, in the end, when I demanded the starship in order to put Zeph to the absolutely crucial test, they made up for not letting me build a Sling fifteen years ago by letting me have it. To most of them, of course, space exploration had always been a minor issue, a kind of folly, a disposable plaything, but even so . . . can you imagine acquiring that kind of authority, Denise? To be able to ask for the ultimate product of human technology, perhaps the future of the human race, and to have it handed to you, meekly?"

"Not really," Denise confessed.

"Well, believe me, it goes to your head a little—but don't think I'm overdoing the oxygen, because I'm perfectly sober at the moment. You do realize, I assume, that your brother is presently the greatest asset that the human species possesses?"

"Don't tell him that for God's sake," said Denise, trying to make a joke of it. "His head is big enough already."

"Really? I got the impression last night that he's rather modest—perhaps unduly so, in fact. And shy, too. I'm less than a year older than he is, but he brought out maternal instincts I didn't know I had."

"I know the feeling," Denise remarked. "I'm younger, but I always used to feel that I had to look out for him. I still do, even if he did wreck my career by devastating my science."

"You haven't lost anything, dear. Just look out of the window at those clouds. It's just rain and dust for now, but tomorrow it will be fire and brimstone. Your science had no future—Zeph has. At least, he will if I can get that bloody starship off the ground. I'm sorry that you won't have a chance to go through the training program, or even get a proper briefing on the ship, but you understand the situation, don't you? You're willing to take the risk?"

"Yes."

"Good. I need you aboard. Zeph needs you aboard."

"Because of some kind of weird Coincidence affinity?"

The masked head turned abruptly to look at her. "You've been thinking about it, I see," said the mathematician. "That's good. That's very good, in fact. Yes, that's it, exactly. I don't say I understand it, mind. The math I can see in all its beautiful purity and perfection, but the psychological connotations are beyond my remit, and perhaps beyond anyone's remit, as yet. I don't understand the bond, but I know it's real."

"And Mireille Angevot? Does she have a Coincidence affinity with Zeph too?"

The mathematician laughed, briefly. "I doubt it," she said. "I commandeered her to provide him with . . . relief, having noted what the reports said about their compatibility aboard Olympus. I'd have been perfectly happy to provide it myself, obviously, but physical interaction isn't really my forte. I didn't want to run the risk of disappointing him, and creating an unnecessary awkwardness between us, so I figured that it might be better to keep our relationship strictly scientific, for the time being."

"You could always take lessons in technique from the Captain," Denise suggested, keeping her voice scrupulously level. "He's said to be something of an expert."

"I did try that," the other replied, matching her matter-of-fact tone perfectly, "but it didn't go well. Anyway, once we're on our way to Saturn, we'll all have plenty of time to refine all the things we couldn't master while we've been on Earth. Did Zeph tell you about Saturn?"

"He mentioned it, but he wasn't very clear about what you expect to find there."

"I'm not entirely clear myself. The Dancing Rats' encryption processes are fiendishly complicated, but the data really are a godsend, once interpreted. Some of the material they've sent us . . . it could take years to unravel it all, even for the Cabal's entire team of math geniuses, but it's already been well worthwhile, not just from the viewpoint of pure math, but technological applications too, especially the biotech. The genomic analyses and manipulations were almost the first things we worked out, given that we already knew the genetic code of DNA. The programs are rat-centered, obviously, but potentially useful even in themselves without our having to work on their transposition to the human genome. If we had another hundred years to work out all the potential . . . but as you can see, we don't."

She waved a hand vaguely, and Denise obediently looked out of the window, but as on the plane, the world outside the vehicle had been reduced to a mere dim blur. She wished that the impression didn't seem so aptly and ominously symbolic. She tried, once again, to construe the raindrops streaming over the windshield and the side window as a possible cleansing agent, striving to rid the air of insidiously deadly dust, but the imaginative leap wasn't easy.

In the meantime, Helen Arkheimer continued her lecture. "The optimists of the Cabal still hope they might get something out of the transtemporal data capable of changing the rules of the game, and I try not to undeceive them, but I'm convinced that the Rats know exactly what they're doing. They know perfectly well that history can only be completed, not changed, that reality's tolerance for paradoxes is very limited. They're working for themselves, not for us—but I believe Zephaniah when he says that they do love us, him most of all. And they understand that in working for themselves, they're working lovingly for all the future generations too . . . and perhaps even for the extraterrestrial intelligences. They can only have a rudimentary idea of how it all fits together, to be sure, but they do sense it, they *feel* it, as Zephaniah does, and they're doing everything they can, from their vantage point tens of millions of years in the future, to help Zephaniah feel it too. That's their gift to him, to me, to us . . . by which I mean all of us, but I also mean you and me. I think you and I might be able to achieve great things, Denise."

"Me? I'm an evolutionary biologist, possessed of minor expertise in a science that's about to die. I hope that I can be useful in some way aboard the starship, but . . ."

She left it there rather than actually saying that she was just along for the ride. Somehow, that seemed insulting to the project—even if, as she was beginning to suspect, Helen Arkheimer, for all her mathematical genius, didn't really have a clue what she was doing, because the psychological connotations were beyond the remit of her particular brand of supersanity.

"Don't sell yourself short, dear. The fact that you're Coincidentally linked to Zeph is at least interesting, and could prove vital. I know that you've only been back in physical proximity for a matter of days, and haven't had the chance to spend that much time together, but tell me: during those days, and especially since the seventh generation slingshot, have you noticed anything . . . odd."

"Odd, how?"

"Anyhow . . . but in particular . . . how can I put it? . . . let's say, unusual similarities in your mental state?"

"No . . . although, yes, I suppose so . . . but we all did, I think."

"What do you mean, you *all* did?"

"The four of us, on the plane. We were in a state of stress, shocked, fatigued, but strung out. We were holding hands, for reassurance. Then, when the Captain snapped me out of it to tell me that we'd lost the engines, we all seemed to have been in the same peculiar mental state: *entranced.* I haven't checked with the others, but objective time seemed to have passed more rapidly than my thought processes, which had seemed perfectly lucid, if a trifle rambling. The Captain had only been dragged back to reality by a message from the pilot."

"*All four* of you were . . . entranced?" The mathematician seemed to be having trouble believing it.

"Yes, but it was nothing," Denise said. "Probably just induced suggestion, like group meditation. There was nothing supernatural about it."

"Of course not," Helen Arkheimer retorted. "Everything that happens is, by definition, natural . . . it's just a matter of figuring out the logic and mathematics of the nature. You were holding hands, you say—in a circle?"

"Not quite. Zeph was holding my hand and Mireille's, and Mireille was also holding the Captain's, but the Captain and I each had one hand free."

"Linearity, connection, separation . . . quite lucid, you say? It didn't feel like dreaming?"

"Not at all. I was trying to weigh up my personal situation, things having happened around me too quickly for me to get to grips with where I figured in the evolving situation. I was rambling a little, as the train of thought ran on, but no, it didn't feel at all like dreaming. It was just . . . normal self-absorption. Normal, at any rate, for me. Maybe I'm more self-absorbed than . . ."

Helen Arkheimer cut her off, obviously following her own train of thought, and obviously no stranger to self-absorption. "I seriously doubt that, my dear. This is something I hadn't anticipated, but it might fit . . ."

The mathematician turned around then, to look at Zeph and Mireille Angevot in the back seat of the vehicle—not at their faces, but at their hands, to see if they were linked.

Unfortunately, although the road was level, the region was hilly, and the road, following the contours of the hillsides, was far from straight. The momentary inattention to the way ahead, given the limited visibility that had not allowed her to see the bend at a distance, caused Helen Arkheimer to drive straight off the road and on to an uneven downslope.

Denise thought that the landing of the jet had been bad, but the way the short trajectory down the hill bounced her about was far worse. Fortunately, her seat belt held her in place, and prevented her from smashing her head against the roof of the vehicle or the dashboard, although the oxygen cylinder on her back, even though it wasn't metallic, dug into her spine painfully.

When the vehicle came to a stop, in fact, she was still fully conscious and was initially convinced that she had escaped essentially unscratched, except for a nasty headache . . . but that was before she started gasping for air, because the connection to the oxygen cylinder in question had been squeezed and blocked, and the nastiness of the headache increased by an order of magnitude, in what seemed to be no time at all.

VII

When Denise opened her eyes, the first thing of which she was conscious was a strong sense of irony. She did not have amnesia. She remembered the fact that immediately before the stupid genius who was driving the vehicle had driven off the road because she was distracted by the idea of their ridiculous moment of collective self-absorption, she had been quizzing her about entrancement and the loss of subjective time, and now, here she was, without the faintest clue as to how much time had passed since then, except that it *felt* like . . . well, it was impossible to set a yardstick on it, but a duration that was definitely not trivial, spent in some kind of trance.

Had she been capable of belief in God, in fact, she might even have wondered whether she was on earth or in Heaven, but her brand of sanity did not permit the possibility that there was anywhere to be but in reality or a vulgar dream.

And, bizarre as her surroundings seemed to be, she was morally certain that she was not dreaming. She supposed that she might have been buried alive, but she knew that she wasn't dead.

She seemed to be in a box that bore a vague but uncomfortable resemblance to a coffin—except that there were no lights in coffins capable of allowing glimpses of translucent but confining walls and an exceedingly low ceiling. She couldn't see much more than that, in fact, because the angled light shifted, so that it was shining directly in her eyes, dazzling her, and forcing her to close them again, confining her briefly to sensations of touch: sensations of touch that reminded her, in rapid succession, of other things with which coffins were not conventionally equipped, like the drip inserted into her left arm, and the catheter attached to her nether regions . . .

Hearing intervened then, as a voice, speaking through a gap in the right-hand side of the incomplete coffin said: "Please open your eyes again, Dr. Corcoran, if you can. I need to check both pupils."

She managed to open her eyes again, and keep them open long enough for the assumed physician to check the reactivity of her pupils.

Inevitably, the ritual did not stop there; indeed, it had hardly begun. It took several seemingly precious minutes to prove to the professional imbecile that she knew her full name and date of birth, that she could count backwards in threes from a hundred, that she could raise her arms, touch her nose with the tip of her forefinger, recite a tongue-twister and perform several other essentially meaningless tasks, all the while being uncomfortably aware of the fact that she was naked beneath a light sheet, before she finally got the opportunity to explore the questions whose answers were actually of some significance to her.

"Where am I?"

"In a pod aboard the *Proxima* . . . although I think its name might have been changed."

"How long have I been unconscious?"

"A little longer than two days."

"Two days! Was I badly hurt, then?" She realized that she didn't even have a headache. She remembered having a headache before . . .

"As it turns out, no—but you had a narrow escape. Your oxygen supply was compromised . . . which has a certain irony about it, I suppose, given that the entire world's oxygen supply has now been compromised. Your brain was deprived for long enough to worry the army paramedic at the scene, so he followed protocol by putting you into an induced coma until you could be given a proper diagnostic examination. That's the fashionable kneejerk reaction nowadays, although it turns out in most cases to have been quite unnecessary. Medical AIs are programmed to err on the side of caution, so this pod AI has kept you under . . . and me waiting. Everything seems fine to the machine now, though, and as you've just seen, the final ritual check has endorsed their findings. You owe the Captain a massive thank you, though. If he hadn't pulled you out of the vehicle, realized that you weren't able to breathe and hooked you up to his own tank . . . ten more seconds of deprivation and there could have been serious damage."

"How's Zeph? And the others?"

"Plenty of bruises. Your brother suffered a mild concussion, but nothing serious. Dr. Arkheimer escaped even more lightly. Mademoiselle Angevot broke her wrist, but it's not a complex fracture. You all had to come back in the truck, though. The jeep didn't make it."

"And I'm on the starship?"

"Indeed. Dr. Arkheimer had you all brought directly here, and she's already trying to identify a launch window, so I'd better get out before she finds one."

"You're not crew?"

"Do I look crazy? No, sorry, scratch that . . . I didn't mean to imply that you're crazy."

"Bad bedside manner," Denise observed. "Don't worry—even I think I'm crazy. My brother and Helen Arkheimer would call it alternative sanity, but that's only because they don't want to admit that they're both as crazy as a sack of monkey nuts. The Captain's sane, though . . . assuming that he's still the Captain."

"He is. Look . . . I really do have to get off the ship, if I don't want to run the risk of being press-ganged for a thirty year expedition, and my presence here is just a token gesture to human chauvinism, given that your pod's AI has the entire heritage of human medical knowledge in its databanks, monitoring devices far more sophisticated than anything human senses can use for amplification, and nanotech surgical capacities that boggle the mind. If there's any dispute between me and the AI, it's the AI that has the crucial vote. Although . . . well, the AI has passed you fit to fly, and I wouldn't have. I don't suppose you'll listen, but I want to have it on the record; if you take my advice, you'll come with me, off the ship."

Denise was startled, as much by the abruptness of the advice as its content. As the doctor seemed to be pressed for time, though, she simply said: "Why the disagreement?"

"Because AIs are fundamentally stupid, however much they know and whatever tricky things they can do. The AI can only take into account the physical parameters of the situation. It can calculate that your body is capable of withstanding the acceleration of take-off, but it can't take the psychological factors into account. You haven't had any somatic modification, you haven't been trained, you haven't even been properly briefed, and you've just been in a plane crash and a car crash. Believe me, Dr. Corcoran, by any sane, non-mechanical standard of assessment, you are *not* fit to fly."

Denise laughed, slightly surprised at her ability to do so. "But it's my decision," she said, "and if I'd rather trust the AI's calculation than your human chauvinist hunch . . ."

The doctor didn't exactly take offence, but he didn't seem to relish the comparison either. "If there's any truth in the rumors," he snapped back, "you wouldn't be here at all if it weren't for the craziest human chauvinist hunch in history. But I've said my piece, and as I say, I really don't want to be aboard if the order to start the launch sequence comes through. I wish you the very best of luck, because I think you'll need it . . . anyway, your brother's waiting to see you, and he's just the man at the head of the queue. The AI has passed you . . . and all I can do is offer you my advice and register a minority report. Adieu."

And with that, the redundant human physician disappeared, allowing Denise to obtain a brief glimpse of the space that seemed to contain four "pods" like hers, stacked two by two with a narrow gap in between, before her view was blocked by Zeph.

Instinctively, her hand gripped the edge of the sheet that was shielding her naked body.

"Thank God you're all right," said Zeph. "The machines said you were, but . . . well, I'm glad they're right."

"Can you find me some clothes?"

"The orders are that you stay put for the time being, with the drip and the catheter in place. The doctor didn't have to be in that much of a hurry—we'll have a couple of hours notice if a launch window does come up today, but even so, we're on high alert."

"Things are bad, then?"

"Bad doesn't begin to describe it. I managed to talk to Mum, though, on-screen."

"How is she?"

"For someone who probably has not much more than forty-eight hours to live, uncannily serene. She says everything's working smoothly. The army evacuated all the young women and children, including her neighbor Emily and young Luke, but the shelter to which they're being taken, so far as I can judge from what she said, is a tokenistic makeshift. The National Enclaves are sealed, with only minor rioting. Almost everybody's following the government guidelines religiously; Mum and several other residents are gathered in one flat in the block, with water, food supplies and oxygen, and the windows and doors taped up, but they know full well that it's a cosmetic gesture—all they have to do is look out of the window. Not that they'll be able to see much, as the sun isn't going to be shining for a long time. Anyway, Mum says that she's had her life, and doesn't have any cause for complaint . . ."

His voice broke, and he paused in order to hold back tears.

"Has Yellowstone gone up?" Denise asked, when he seemed to be reasonably composed again. She wanted to say more about her mother, but she didn't want him to break down in an embarrassing flood.

"It's in the process, but not explosively, as yet. There are millions of people still alive in the other States, hoping that the pressure release will be slow enough not to crush them like bugs. The southern hemisphere's a write-off, except for Antarctica, but large swathes of Europe and northern Asia are still doing quite well,

260

relatively speaking . . . except for the diminished oxygen pressure, of course, and the dust. The microparticles get in practically everywhere, invisible but deadly. There's a thick plastic sheet over the entirety of Fairbanks and the projects, but it won't hold for long, and everybody's ready to retreat to the solid shelters at a moment's notice. Our cover won't come off until the last minute, but once we get a launch-window . . . and if no eye in the storm materializes overhead, we'll just have to blast through it. Chris and Helen have at least managed to agree on a deadline."

"All is not sweetness and harmony between them, then?"

"It's been one long battle ever since the Captain tried to stop her driving the armored car, and the fact that events proved his judgment right made things worse. She seemed very pleasant when she was talking to me onscreen, but she has a hell of a temper, and seems to snap easily . . . but I can understand that, remembering the way I used to be. Chris pulled her out of the wreck before he got to you—I was too slow, and too dazed, and poor Mireille couldn't help—but she doesn't seem grateful to him. Perhaps it might have been better if it had been her life he'd had to save instead of yours . . . maybe she's even jealous of you because it was. Anyway, it's safe to say that, compared with Olympus Five, this is not a happy ship. I'm trying to keep out of it, but it's hard. I'm truly sorry that I dragged you into it, Nise. I had no idea . . . and you could have made it to Snowdonia with ease . . ."

"You didn't drag me into anything. How's Mireille?"

"Her wrist's strapped up, but she's up and about. She's an atmospheric chemist, so she's tracking the incoming data intently, with avid morbid interest. It's probably the only opportunity she'll ever get actually to observe a planetary atmosphere in metamorphosis."

"And what's her verdict?"

"Uncharted territory, no reliable prognosis possible. Until we know how low the oxygen pressure will ultimately sink, it's impossible to judge the probable timescale for its recovery."

"But on the bright side," Denise suggested, "we already know that it won't be terminal for all of mammalkind. We already know that plants and insects, and even rats, will survive the cataclysm. It's not the end of *their* world. The news you brought back from the future is gloomy for the human species, but not for the ecosphere as a whole. That will soldier on . . . and since the rats, at least, will come through, the adaptive radiation of the last sixty-five million years hasn't been a total loss."

"True," Zeph agreed, "although that seems to be a thornier issue than you might think. The news I brought back from the future . . . might not have been as irrelevant as most people imagined to begin with."

"Really?"

"In fact, there seems to be a growing body of opinion that considers both me and Helen, and Walter most of all, to be traitors to the human race."

"Why?"

"The thing is, we know that the rats will survive, but we don't know exactly how or where. Maybe in the sewers, and maybe gone to ground in remote areas of wilderness . . . but there are rats inside the enclaves, Nise, and not just vermin that couldn't be kept out."

"What do you mean?"

"I mean that there are genetically engineered rats inside the enclaves, both here in Alaska and, perhaps more relevantly, in China . . . rats genetically engineered, in various ways, on the basis of data recovered by me and deciphered by Walter and Helen. Initially, Helen was only interested in applying it to prove that her calculations and decoding methods were correct, but the Chinese . . . well, obviously, they stole Walter's data, and hers too; they doubtless have their own mathematical geniuses working on it, and they're more than capable of developing applications at least as fast as the Americans."

"What's your point?"

"The Chinese are developing engineered rats as livestock, for food, and God only knows how many other purposes."

Denise connected the observations with what Helen Arkheimer had said to her about the Dancing Rats knowing exactly what they were doing . . . and that they loved humans, and Zeph most of all.

"You think the rats have supplied us with the data to engineer their own ancestors? To set in train the evolutionary process that will initiate their creation?"

"Possibly . . . probably . . . and it's not just me who thinks so. Hence, traitor to humanity. Not the majority view, but Helen's worried about its spread. One more reason why she's eager to get a launch window."

"But even if the biotech data the Rats sent us really is enabling us to lend a helping hand to their evolution, it doesn't necessarily mean that we're paving the way for our own extinction?"

"Not necessarily, no—just that we're giving a helping hand to those who'll replace us when we're gone, however and whenever we eventually go . . . just as the Rats will do themselves, voluntarily and gladly, for their own replacement species, if my reading of their situation is correct, and just as all the other generations will do thereafter. If we are using our final years as a species to help the rats, we won't be the odd ones out in the long-term sequence, except in the sense that, thus far, we're only doing it accidentally . . ."

"You mean Coincidentally? And not with a small c?"

"Maybe. Who can tell?"

"If you can't, nobody . . . but Arkheimer seems to have high hopes for you . . . did she quiz you about what happened on the jet, while we were holding hands?"

"Yes, and Mireille too, and she didn't seem to believe us when we told her it was nothing—that we were just taking stock and lost track of time. What did you tell her to make her think it was something more?"

"The same thing . . . but she probably read more into that than coincidence-with-a-small-c. It's the way she's programmed to think, after all. She was already convinced that you were in the process of forging some kind of a special Coincidental bond with me—now she probably thinks that you're radiating psychic influence in all directions. Maybe there was a reason for the fact that you spent the first thirty years of your life with a phobia about physical contact."

"It wasn't a phobia . . ." Zeph began but broke off, presumably realizing that the label really didn't matter, and already beginning to think about the possible corollaries of the fact that life aboard Olympus Five had broken his barriers down. "I'm not a psychic medium, Nise," he added, defensively, "and I'm not the Messiah, either."

"I'll agree to the second half of that assertion," Denise told him, "although I'm not even completely sure about that."

"Fundamentally," Zeph told her, "Coincidence is simply a matter of a connection between subatomic particles that extends through multidimensional space in a pattern that requires bizarre mathematics to describe it. I don't see how, in that scheme, there can be significant individuals more important to the underlying pattern than others."

"But there are," Denise pointed out, "at least in mental terms. The underlying pattern of the universe might be the same for everyone, but that doesn't mean that everyone is equally capable of understanding the conceptual geometry of the pattern, nor does it mean that everyone is capable of sensing, or intuiting, its connections. Walter Halleck isn't unique, as he likes to believe, but he's still very special. You're probably not unique either, but just as he and Arkheimer have a particular mental configuration that allows them to understand the mathematics of the pattern, you have a mental configuration, if not to be the Messiah or actually to commune with God, at least to be a prophet, and commune with . . . well, who can tell? Not Arkheimer, even though she thinks she's built a machine that will help you do it more effectively."

"I see," said Zeph, pensively. "I already knew the direction her thought is heading, but hadn't looked at it from that viewpoint. I wonder if she thinks that, as well as there being special individuals within the pattern, there are also special places . . . or does she just think that the rings of Saturn are, in some sense, an individual or group of individuals? Or, I suppose, both . . . ?"

"That's a good question," said Helen Arkheimer, speaking from a vaguely discernible slit in the ill-lit room that was presumably its door. "Forgive me for interrupting, dears, but I thought that you'd had your ration of family time, and as you seem to have moved on to discussing abstract matters anyhow, I felt that my turn had come. You don't mind, do you, Zephaniah?" She didn't bother to wait for Zeph to testify as to whether he minded or not before continuing; "Would you mind leaving us alone for a few minutes, dear? I'd like to speak to Denise in private."

Again, it didn't seem to matter whether Zeph minded or not. She practically shoved him through the slit, and then sealed it.

"Forgive me, dear," she said to Denise, "I . . ."

Denise felt that she had every right to interrupt. "I'll think about it," she said, "but for what it's worth, the masquerade of bonhomie really isn't working. It takes a lot more than simply addressing everyone as 'dear' to simulate even the most elementary fellow feeling. It just adds an annoying element of contempt to the rudeness and the harassment."

The mathematician did not seem unduly distressed by the rebuke. "Fair point," she said, insouciantly. "You're beginning to sound like the dear Captain, my dear . . . but I really can't blame either of you. I'm truly sorry about crashing the jeep, and not simply because it made me look like a perfect fool and an incompetent. I'm sorry for having put you in danger, and for not being able to stop that stupid paramedic from putting you into an entirely unnecessary temporary coma, and the stupid pod AI for not bringing you out of it immediately. And I'm not simply being selfish in that regret. However awkward my means of expression might be, I'm not incapable of empathy, sympathy, love or whatever, any more than your brother was before I kidnapped him seven years ago. Maybe seven years aboard Minerva will do as much for me as his excursion did for him, but in the meantime, *dear*, I'll just have to ask you to take me as I am, warts and all." As the speech continued the tone had shifted from insouciance to sarcastic aggression. Denise could see what Zeph meant about her tendency to snap.

"Minerva?" Denise queried, trying to calm things down and bring the conversation back to safer ground. "You're really going to rename the starship *Minerva*."

"I already have. I contemplated Eris and Nemesis, but decided to avoid irony. Do you think that, for both our sakes, you can learn to tolerate me, if not to like me? It's going to be a long journey, if we can ever get a launch window, and blast a way through it. Although I suppose you still have time to desert the ship if you want to. Do you?"

"No," said Denise. "And I apologize for being a little sharp. I have a nasty habit of venting. I'm all yours, Dr. Arkheimer."

She tried to sit up in the bunk, in spite of the fact that it would make wrapping the sheet around herself more awkward than it already was, especially with the drip in her arm. She realized that there wasn't actually room in the pod for someone of her height to sit up straight, but she managed to raise herself enough to prop herself up on her elbow, and meet the other woman's gaze on slightly more level terms.

"Helen," said the mathematician. "Even the dear Captain admits that we can't maintain the ridiculous military custom of only using surnames, given that two members of our mini-utopian community have the same one. Fortunately there's no duplication of forenames among the twelve of us."

"Twelve?" Denise queried. "I thought the crew was supposed to number fourteen?"

"That was before I had my equipment installed. Two pods had to be modified—including the Captain's, I fear. I'm sure you'll be flattered to learn that his first choice for an alternative berth was this cabin, but I overruled him. I think I can make peace with him, though, once I can get around to taking those lessons in sexual technique you recommended. Would that work with you, do you think?"

Denise decided to misunderstand her, and said: "I haven't quarreled with the Captain."

Arkheimer smiled faintly, to show that she wasn't fooled. "Oh, you and I will be just fine," she said. "I'm not that bad when you get to know me. My heart's in the right place. I've had to be a trifle assertive these last few days . . . well, longer than that, actually . . . in order to get things done as they need to be done, but once we lift off, the pressure will be off. I'll revert all authority to the dear Captain, at least in appearance, and I'll even stop referring to him as the dear Captain. I have as much interest in the mini-utopian aspect of our mission as anyone. The only thing I want more than for everyone to be able to like me is for me to able to like them. I've had difficulty with that in the past, but I haven't given up hope. I like Zephaniah already . . . and you too, Denise."

"You might want to be careful about that," Denise advised. "I've known a lot of biologists in my time, and they generally tell me that it's not a good idea to become fond of your lab rats."

"That's not venting, Denise, that's just insulting. I don't know what Walter Halleck's attitude to Zephaniah was, but believe me, I do not think of him as a lab rat. I think of him as a collaborator—and that's the way I'd like to think of you, too. I need you, Denise, not simply because you have some kind of Coincidental connection with Zephaniah, but to help me explore, examine and understand it. I'm a mathematician; I've always had slightly dubious qualifications as a human being. Perhaps I can learn . . . but I suspect that you'll always have the advantage. So I need you, because you're already closer to Zephaniah than I can ever be. You might be the only person aboard capable of figuring out what's going on in his head, if I really can amplify his spatial telempathy. I'm certain that I can, in fact . . . the last Slingshot proved all my calculations. I wish that we'd had time for half a dozen more, but . . . well, we're not setting the timetable, are we?"

Denise decided that it would be one insult too many to point out to the mathematical genius that she was beginning to ramble like a loquacious idiot, so she said: "I'll do what I can to help Zeph, and you. I'd really like to get dressed and get up, though. I surely don't need the drip any longer, and I'd like to get rid of the catheter too."

"I understand—but, like the doctor, the Captain and I are both a little worried about how the launch might affect you, given your lack of preparation. I don't feel strongly about it, but precisely for that reason, this might be a good time for me to defer to his judgment and begin to patch things up between us. He's waiting to see you too, and it's arguable that perhaps I should have let him come in first, but I'm having difficulty at present being patient, as you've doubtless noticed."

"Well, thank you for making time to call in and see me," said Denise, only a little sarcastically.

"I owed you an apology," the mathematician said, "and perhaps I also owe it to you, since we never did achieve properly informed consent, to give you one last chance to opt for the Enclave. The Captain will tell you, if I don't, that ours is the more dangerous option, and that conditions for take-off will be far from ideal even if we can find a gap in the storm. That doctor might be right, and you really might not be fit to fly, in spite of the expert AI opinion." The tone of her voice made the observation sound more like a challenge than a suggestion; Denise was certain that the mathematician would never have made it if she had thought that there was any chance of her lab rat chickening out.

"We could all stay on the ground," Denise pointed out. "You could postpone the launch for weeks . . . even months . . . and test your machine here."

"Actually, we can't," Arkheimer replied, soberly. "Minerva is too exposed. If she doesn't take off within forty-eight hours, she probably never will. And whatever initial results my machine produces, I still need to go to Saturn, and Chris needs to go to the stars. Neither of us wants to wait that long."

"And Zeph?"

"He needs to go to Saturn *and* the stars."

"Then so do I. And your apology is accepted. Anyone could have gone off the road like that, in the circumstances. It wasn't your fault." She was being generous, she knew, but she felt that the situation called for it.

"Good," said the mathematician. "We'll talk again, in much greater depth, about Coincidence, Zeph and Saturn's rings, but I'll send the captain in now, or he'll be getting wound up too tightly again, and he's surly enough as it is. Thank you, Denise."

She left, and was replaced almost immediately by Chris Kemmering. That renewed Denise's anxiety regarding her state of undress, but she remained propped up on her elbow, even though she still had to look up to meet Chris Kemmering's eyes, given that he was so much taller than Helen Arkheimer.

"How are you feeling?" he asked.

"Fine," she said. "I understand that you saved my life."

"Not really. I just happened to get down the slope first. If I hadn't pulled you both out, someone else would have."

Denise decided not to press the point. "I'd really like to put some clothes on and get up," she said. "Maybe you could give me a tour of the ship, and introduce me to my fellow crew-members?"

"It's up to you," he said. "I'm not going to order you to say there—but I have to say that I do have some concerns about your ability to tolerate lift-off, and there really isn't time to give you a tour, or even a briefing, given that we'll only have two hours notice if the meteorologists can identify a window. For myself, I'd prefer it if you stayed put, even if you do get dressed. If you insist, though, Zeph or Helen can show you over the ship—it's not exactly a long tour."

Since he'd put it so politely, Denise decided to defer the decision at least until she'd asked him a couple of questions. "How's the situation outside?"

"Bloody. Everyone, all over the world, is hunkering down as best they can. Mireille's monitoring the atmospheric data, and although she won't say anything specific, I can read her well enough to know that it couldn't be much worse. The oxygen levels are still dropping fast, and the temperature's still rising. The temperature will fall again once the dust has blotted out the sun completely, but . . . well, no shelter built to hold for less than a generation is going to be able to release its inmates. Fairbanks will be completely sealed within forty-eight hours, and we have to blast off before then. The news from Cronos makes it all the more necessary for us to get off the ground."

"What news from Cronos?"

"The ship's pod AIs have gone into hibernation mode. No one knows why—the crew didn't manage to send an explanation, if they have one."

"Hibernation mode?"

"It's a standard contingency plan, incorporated into the ships in more optimistic times. The crews can be put into artificial hibernation in the pods if the life-support system is compromised. The idea was to buy time to allow the AIs monitoring the shipboard environment to deploy their nanotech capabilities, or perhaps to wait for the possible launch of a rescue mission. Now, of course, there's only one ship remaining that can possibly play that role relative to Cronos."

"Minerva."

"That seems to be what we're called now."

"So we'd have to go to Saturn anyway, even if Arkheimer didn't want to?"

"We need to know what happened to Cronos."

"Can we rescue them, if they need rescue? Can our life-support system actually support a double crew?"

"Temporarily, certainly. In the longer term . . . various things would have to be recalculated. But even if the crew were to be taken off the Cronos, if that proves to be necessary, where can we take them? First, we need to know what we're dealing with."

"Did they actually reach Saturn?"

"Nearly. The ship continued its course, obviously without the active involvement of the crew, and will complete the existing flight plan. It should be in a stable powered orbit, in the gap inside the C-ring, within a year. What we'll find when we get there, which will be at least two years after that, even at maximum thrust, is anyone's guess."

"I see. Can you get me some clothes, Captain?"

"They're within arm's reach inside the pod," the Captain told her. "Everything is. I'll ask Zeph to brief you quickly on the pod's facilities, and to show you how to operate them. I'd do it myself, but . . . duty calls."

"I understand. How are things between you and Arkheimer?"

"Tense—but that's mostly the situation. Once we lift off, and we're facing at least a three-year stretch with only routine work to do, save for her precious experiments, her sense of urgency will presumably fade, and everything will settle down. I think we can achieve a satisfactory working relationship."

"Especially after you've screwed her?"

His immediate response to that was a wry smile. "We tried that once before," he said. "That will need work too—but as I say, when things settle down . . ."

"The burden of command will become more manageable."

"Indeed."

"And if the crew's been reduced to twelve, you'll only have six of us to take care of in that particular fashion."

"Seven," he said. "The strict balance of the sexes has been abandoned . . . unless Arkheimer's counting herself as a man."

"Cutting," Denise observed. "Well, I'm sure you'll cope. Zeph will do his best to help, I'm sure. What's life without a challenge, after all?"

"If you could look outside," said the Captain, glumly, before leaving, "you'd probably have stopped that sentence at 'What's life?' Believe me, we're beyond challenge now."

VIII

It was quite a relief for Denise to find herself on her feet again and detached from the apparatus of the pod, although the clothes she'd found in the locker that Zeph had pointed out to her were not much different from the top-and-trousers that she'd hastily put on when Chris Kemmering had interrupted her in her sleep, a world away in Kilburn, and the slippers on her feet seemed extremely flimsy by comparison with the sturdy rubber-soled shoes she had donned then. Her present costume appeared to be standard wear aboard ship, if not exactly a uniform, given the variety of colors available and slight variations in style.

Then Zeph showed her the multiple functions of the pod, which was, in effect, almost an entire house collapsed into a space whose internal dimensions still seemed to her to be uncomfortably similar to those of a sarcophagus. Getting rid of the catheter seemed less of a relief once the standard lavatorial features of the pod had been explained to her and she had been introduced to the glorified plastic bag that constituted the horizontal shower.

Mercifully, the space did not have to double as a kitchen as well, although it did accommodate the laundry facilities for clothing, but the lack of headroom seemed an awkward inconvenience, even for employing the VR apparatus. The hood and goggles offered a better facility for looking outside than the screen beside the bedhead, but as the Captain had indicated, one glance at either was enough to assure her that there was nothing to see in that direction, for the moment, but chaos.

"It's a bit cramped for . . . entertaining," Denise observed to her brother.

"I thought you already knew that," he said, tersely. "Didn't you make an intense study of the spicier bits of the leaked tapes from Olympus Five?"

"Long on data, short on visuals," she said. "It wasn't exactly authentic video-porn. The grunts take on a new significance when you see how close you always are to bumping your elbows, even when you're not attempting anything athletic. And the range of viable positions seems distinctly limited."

It was obviously not a subject that Zeph was comfortable discussing with his sister. "I'll show you the gym cabinet," he muttered. "There's room for two in there, and space for acrobatics if you're that way inclined. Can I continue showing you the controls now?"

"Go on. Discretion rules."

He showed her the screen properties and the virtual keyboard, and ran through the various programs and data retrieval facilities.

"I can't promise that you'll have all of human knowledge at your fingertips," he said, "but you won't run short of reading or video material, even in thirty years—or games to play if you're that way inclined."

"So when we were talking on-screen during the last phase of your homeward journey, you were actually lying down, and you rotated the image through ninety degrees?"

"You didn't realize?"

"Well, yes, I suppose I did, to begin with—but then I just forgot, and figured you'd developed a funny habit of tilting your head. Can I still make calls from this unit?"

"Only to Fairbanks, at present; communications are down all over the world. Once we get into space, it might be possible to communicate with at least some of the Enclaves while they're in line-of-sight. You won't have a chance to say goodbye to Mum, though. I'm sorry about that."

"I'm sure you did a good job for both of us," Denise observed, baldly, hoping that she sounded more convinced than she felt.

They went out then, so that Zeph could introduce her to the basic layout of the living quarters of the ship, which was, in effect, just a four-story tower with ladders connecting the various floors. What was effectively the bottom floor, although it also had a hatchway leading down to the matter-annihilation engine and all its subsidiary apparatus, was the most cluttered, containing the food production and reprocessing devices, the general organic recycling machinery, the air-renewal facility and numerous equip-ment-lockers. The floor above was the least crowded, embodying a common space where all the crew members could gather in reasonable comfort, to eat or converse or make collaborative use of various screens, at least while the ship was accelerating in such a way as to simulate earthly gravity. The next floor up contained the cabins, including the one that had been adapted to contain Helen Arkheimer's experimental apparatus, and the facility that Zeph had called the "gym cabinet." He didn't take her up to the topmost cell, which he described variously as "the Captain's eyrie," or "the control room," which contained links to both the engines and telepresence equipment allowing the deployment of all external apparatus, currently folded away into various internal spaces in order not to disrupt the streamlining of the ship during the vertiginous lift-off.

"It really is a control room," Zeph told her, "but it's arguable that Chris isn't really the one in control. The AIs do everything during normal operations, unless and until there's a top-level executive decision to be made, in order to supply them with a goal. I don't expect to be using the telepresence equipment in the near future, although I might have some tricky work to do when we reach Saturn, if Cronos is in bad trouble."

"I've already had the standard conversation about the stupidity of supposedly omniscient machines with the doctor," Denise told him. "I understand that when the crew call themselves that, it's just human chauvinism. Really, we're just passengers—except that we have to ask the machines, politely, to take us where we want to go. If the human race really can be saved from the present worldwide disaster, it will be the AIs that actually work the miracle, at our behest."

The argument was too familiar to need any supplementation, so Zeph reverted to more practical instruction while introducing her to the various systems. There was a great deal to take in, and Denise knew that a great deal of it would need repeating, more than once. She reminded herself, however, that the expert medical AI had passed her fit to fly. The rest of her belated training could take as long as necessary, once they were out of chaos and into outer space.

In the course of the tour, particularly when they passed through the common space, Zeph introduced Denise to the seven crew members she had not yet met, calling each of them by his or her Christian name, as the new protocol now required. Most seemed to be American by birth or adoption, the most obvious exceptions being a theoretical physicist named Alessandro, who had apparently volunteered in order to make a heroic attempt to supplement Helen Arkheimer's burgeoning comprehension of the New Multidimensional Manifold, which incorporated

Coincidence Theory into the latest model of the universe, and Mellita, the ship's biochemist and nutritionist. Birstan was the chief technician, with notional responsibility for the MAE and all its associated apparatus. Victor was a cosmologist of international reputation, Savina a xenobiologist, Paula a librarian and Gabrielle a psychologist. All seven seemed to be in their thirties; Victor and Paula were the oldest, to judge by their appearance, but it was a close-run thing. None of them was taller than Denise, and they all gave the impression of being sturdier and more muscular.

So, Alessandro, Birstan and Victor, together with Chris and Zeph, now constitute my entire male society, from today until I die, she thought. *And I'm not permitted, in theory, to make a selection among them, but have to strive to love them all . . . and I suppose, the women too, at least in a sisterly fashion, including Helen.*

Three of the crew, however, were already known to her by different names as ex-crew-members of Olympus Five: Birstan, Savina and Mellita. They, at least in theory, already loved Zeph, even though she didn't think either of the women had been among those who had been physically intimate with him.

All of them seemed to greet Denise with the utmost politeness, and she couldn't detect an atom of hostility, but that didn't prevent her from feeling very much the odd one out. She was the person who didn't really belong, who not only had no experience of space flight but had never even gone through the training program, the person who was only here because she was someone's sister—albeit the sister of the man to whom the others, whether they had known him before or not, were now manifestly looking for some kind of guidance or some kind of inspiration: the prophet who might be able to guide them, by occult means, to the right star, where there might be something to be found worth finding.

When the general meet and greet was over, Denise asked: "Where's Mireille?"

"Up top with the Captain, monitoring the situation."

"With Helen?"

"Probably, but she might be in her so-called lab. We'll check."

When they did that, they found that Helen was, indeed, in her "so-called lab"—which, not unnaturally, looked exactly like a two-pod cabin in which both pods had been modified in order to be integrated with a battery of electronic apparatus that only bore a faint resemblance to Walter Halleck's Sling—a resemblance considerably diminished by the absence of the hooded chair in which Zeph had taken his excursions into the far future.

For a moment, Denise almost asked where the chair was, but then realized the obvious answer. One of the modified pods had presumably been adapted, along with its VR apparatus, to stand in for the rather brutal chair. Instead, she asked the mathematician, who was standing by, waiting for her to express suitable amazement and admiration: "Why leave the other pod in position? So that you can sleep on the job if necessary?" No sooner had she said it, though, than she realized that it was a stupid remark.

"That would be possible," said Helen, blandly, her keen eyes squinting slightly as she tried to measure Denise's reaction to the realization that she had made a mistake.

"Or for a second person to use the apparatus simultaneously?" Denise queried, too late, feeling a slight sinking feeling.

"That would be possible too."

"Me?"

"If you'd care to volunteer, when we reach that phase of the experiment."

"And you?"

"Certainly, at some stage."

"And the others, too?"

"Perhaps—it depends on how the initial experiments go. But yes, if things go well, I'll certainly call for other volunteers too: ultimately, everyone, individually or in tandem. As Zephaniah learns from the machine, the machine's AIs will learn from Zephaniah. It would be optimistic to expect that it will eventually be able to give all of us a significant degree of spatial perception, but I hope that Zephaniah won't be alone in being able to benefit from the technology . . . and I hope that the rest of us might be able to benefit from Zephaniah's physical presence."

"You think it's not just me in whom he might be able to induce some kind of Coincidental affinity?"

"I don't know—but you've certainly given me reason to hope so, with your account of what happened aboard the jet."

Denise shrugged her shoulders slightly. She still didn't believe that what had happened aboard the jet had been significant of anything but collective anxiety and mutual suggestion. She resumed her study of the apparatus, but it made no sense whatsoever to her, any more than Walter Halleck's Sling had, when she had finally got to see it in all its dubious glory.

"But it's not like the Sling, is it?" she said as much to herself as to the mathematician. "The Sling actually induced the formation, at a distance of hundreds of millions of years, of a physical entity capable of registering at its surface an echo of electromagnetic waves and sound waves, permitting the AIs to reconstruct a kind of visual image, so that Zeph really did seem to be peering through a window into future time. But you can't do that with spatial perception, can you, because the particles to which particles located in our local space might still be linked because of associations formed during or prior to the birth of the solar system, or a few seconds after the Big Bang, would be too widely scattered now, and any visual information you could gather would probably be useless anyway—a mere nebular blur."

"That's essentially correct, save for one significant modification," admitted Helen. "But first of all, let's not underestimate the potential of what you call a nebular blur. If I'm right about Saturn's rings, Zephaniah will certainly be able to obtain visual information there, even if it's a trifle vague. In fact, I'm hoping to produce more than one kind of nebular blur, which might not in themselves convey much information to Zephaniah's consciousness via the VR hood but might nevertheless be useful. The AIs might be able to detect more than he can see, not so much by examining electromagnetic radiation impinging on the—let's call it a *scattered lens*, shall we?—as by interrogating the structural features of the scattered lens itself . . . but that's a secondary matter, in my view. To begin with, the point is not what the AIs might eventually be able to 'see' but what Zephaniah might be able to *feel*, or intuit, by means of his still-rudimentary but mechanically enhanced Coincidence sensibility."

"You mean that, although all he'll be able to 'see,' even with the aid of the AIs, is a blur, it might enable him to detect the presence of something . . . a mind."

"Hopefully, yes."

"An extraterrestrial intelligence of some kind."

"In Saturn's rings, possibly."

"And possibly, beyond that, *the* extraterrestrial intelligence: Marie Maclaughlin's God?"

"Your friend the chaplain? Yes, I suppose, what she would probably call God, or at least mistake for what she calls God. But she only made that mistake by ignoring the most important aspects of what Zephaniah reported during the seventh generation Slingshot. If she hadn't been so intently focused on her own preconceptions, she would have noticed at least two highly significant factors pointing in different directions."

For once, Denise managed to jump to the conclusion immediately. She had been there during the slingshot, after all, hanging on to Zeph's every word. "He insisted that they were many and not one—but he was talking about the population of the future Earth, not the universal mind."

"There might be less distinction than you think," Helen suggested. "Especially if you bear in mind Zephaniah's impressions of the Insect collectives—I know he has reservations about the term 'hive mind,' but he clearly recognized that the members of the fourth generation were both individuals and elements of a larger collective, mentally as well as physically, and he inferred that the same was true of the Megaplants. But the most important of all the aspects of the seventh generation contact wasn't so much what he saw when he looked into the abyss . . ."

Again, Denise caught on instantly: "It was what the abyss saw when it looked into him."

"And what the abyss *did* when it was able to bring him into focus: the vision that it took care to offer him, augmenting the power of the lens very considerably. As you say, that action was presumably taken by the population of the future Earth, acting collectively . . . but also as elements in a larger collective . . . a collective distributed in space, probably extended within the solar system, and almost certainly beyond it . . . but not God; many but not one, vast but neither infinite not eternal."

"And you think that your machine might allow Zeph to make contact with that vast intelligence again, enabling him to catch the merest glimpse of it, but, more importantly, enabling it to catch a not-so-mere glimpse of him, and to build a bond between them, allowing valuable communication."

"That particular intelligence exists, or will exist, billions of years in the future, the product of evolutionary processes that have not yet come to fruition, at least in local space. No, I don't want him to contact that intelligence again, but I hope that I might be able to allow him . . . let's say to be 'fished up' . . . by something similarly vast, but probably markedly different; a collective of different collectives. In fact, I hope to enable him to get some kind of empathic intuition of at least two such collectives."

Denise darted a sideways glance at Zeph, who was maintaining a studious silence, as if at least some of this were new to him too, and as if he might be anxious to derive what benefit he could from the information that the mathematician was imparting.

"Why *at least two*?" queried Denise, on her brother's behalf as well as her own.

"Because there are at least two phases in the game of Coincidence that's being played out here and elsewhere, and perhaps more. Firstly, and perhaps most conveniently, in terms of potential access, there are the Coincidences formed in the matter from which the solar system condensed, before the condensation into planets took place. Those might well be the Coincidences that allowed the Dancing Rats and their successors to intuit the existence of other sentient entities within the solar system, specifically in the clouds of Jupiter and the rings of Saturn.

"In addition to those Coincidences, however, there are more primitive ones, at least those that originated in the very early phases of the evolution of matter, in the few seconds after the Big Bang. Whereas the Coincidences formed prior to and during the origin of the solar system are probably confined to the solar system—although that depends to some extent on the ultimate sources of the matter concerned—the Coincidences formed immediately after the Big Bang must extend throughout the entire universe. As to what kind of collectives those Coincidences might offer access to, we can only conjecture at present, but there's probably good reason to expect a certain localization of effect there too: localization within the galaxy, and perhaps a much narrower interstellar region than that, permitting some degree of coherence in the calculable Coincidences."

"So you think that, with the aid of your machine, Zeph might be able to build up impressionistic maps of the distribution of 'sentient entities' both within the solar system and in local interstellar space?"

"It's not as simple as that, alas. Unaided, I don't think Zephaniah would be able to build up sufficient impressions even to construct the sketchiest of maps . . . but if he has help . . . ?"

"If your machine's projection can enable him to bring himself to the attention of one or more such sentient entities, you think they might be able deliberately to feed him information in the way the collective of which the seventh generation earthly life forms will be a part was able to do?"

"Yes. There are no guarantees, of course, but I'm hopeful. I certainly don't expect to succeed at the first attempt, any more than an angler expects to succeed with his first cast—but with patience, application and practice . . . eventually, I hope, we'll catch a fish. And then . . . well, who can tell? But everything that Zephaniah has brought back via the Sling thus far suggests that such entities tend to be both interested and benign . . . that at least some of them would be glad to make contact with him, just as the Dancing Rats were. Thus far, at least, he hasn't found monsters, no matter what some of his prejudiced critics think of the prospect of our being replaced on the Earth's surface by the descendants of rats and ants."

At that moment, there was a slight buzz in the headset that Helen was wearing, which must have sounded much louder and more urgent to her than it did to Denise.

The mathematician readjusted her earpiece and said: "Go ahead."

Half a minute later, she looked at Zeph and Denise again. "I have to go confer with Mireille and Chris," she said. "Feel free to continue your tour, but be ready to return to the pods for the initiation of the launch sequence if the alarm sounds. Have you briefed Denise on that, Zephaniah?"

"Succinctly," said Zeph. "It might be as well to go through it again, though."

"Yes, it might," said Helen, as she showed them out of her lab and scampered up the ladder to the chamber above.

"Best step in here again, then," said Zeph, indicating the door to their cabin. "I'll run through the procedure again."

"It's not complicated," said Denise, dismissively. "Did you know all that stuff that Arkheimer just told me?"

"Some of it. Things have been so confused lately that I don't think she's sure of what she's told me and what she hasn't—but it certainly didn't hurt to run through it again."

"What was the *one modification* she mentioned?"

"Sorry?"

"When I summarized the situation—the difference between what she had to do and what Halleck had done—she said that one significant modification had to be made to it, but didn't specify what it was."

"Didn't she?"

"No. All the stuff about collectives was based on the assessment I offered, or could have been."

"Then I don't know—you'll have to ask her what she meant. I'm not sure I like the image of being a fly baiting an angler's hook, though, waiting to see what swallows me. The entity with which I made contact during Walter's last Slingshot might have been an angelfish, but that doesn't mean that there aren't nasty pike out there."

"But what harm could they possibly want to do you? And what harm is there left that anyone could want to do to the human race, whose nature-assisted suicide is all but complete?"

"Good point," said Zeph, with a sigh. "I suppose there really is no need to be afraid. The worst that can probably happen is that I spend several hours a day for months on end staring at *nebular blurs* and not intuiting anything. That could become exceedingly tedious."

"It's not going to happen," said Denise.

"How do you know?"

"Would you believe me if I told you that I feel it in my bones?"

Zeph laughed. "No," he said. "If it were that simple, I'd probably feel it there myself."

"Don't imagine that your empathy is the only kind there is," she admonished, "any more than your sanity is the only kind there is." And immediately she wondered if she might have just said something profound, purely by accident.

"You're probably right," Zeph agreed, promptly. "I never had much of the common-or-garden kind. I was even worse than Helen once, wasn't I?"

"It's not a matter of better or worse," said Denise sharply. "All of that is pride and prejudice. We're beyond all that now. This is utopia, remember, a petty paradise in a tin can. We're all equals now, and forever."

"Try telling Helen that," Zeph muttered. "Or the Captain, for all his theorizing."

"You're the one who's the first among equals now, Zeph," Denise told him. "The Captain is only the Captain, but you're the Prophet Zephaniah. On your word rests the hope of the human race."

"It's not the hook I'd hang it on," Zeph persisted, still muttering, "if I were the human race and I had a choice."

"God, she's right," Denise bemoaned. "You are modest, after all."

"Who's right?"

"Helen. I told her you were big-headed and she pulled me up, and said you were actually modest. Not as modest as her, mind, at least about her physical attractions." But she stopped then, not wanting to explain further what she meant by that.

Zeph took it as a general remark. "Well, you are much better-looking than she is," he observed. "Or any of them, in fact."

"Flatterer," she replied—but she didn't make any attempt to search for a counter-example. It was something, even if being the best-looking woman in a mini-utopia of twelve people was a very tiny claim to fame, and about as much use in context as a fifth leg on a donkey.

A bell started ringing then, and Zeph and Denise stood staring at one another, stunned by the shock. They were still staring when Mireille came through the door, agitating her heavily bandaged wrist.

"Well," said the newcomer, "don't just stand there. Pods, *now*, and initiate the safety procedures—especially you, Denise. This is going to be seriously rough. Believe me, you have *no* idea."

Denise climbed back to her pod while Zeph inserted himself into the one below, Mireille took the bottom pod on the other side of the cabin.

When Helen came through the door she looked around with satisfaction before climbing up to the pod above Mireille's. "Good," she said. "All neat and tidy."

"Considering the state of the atmosphere we're going up into," said the Frenchwoman, before sealing her pod and lying down, "this might be yet another good time for anyone who can pray to do it."

But she knows perfectly well, Denise thought, *that we can't.*

She sealed her own pod, lay down and went through all the procedures that Zeph had just rehearsed with her, with patience and precaution.

Then, suitably cushioned and immobilized, she waited.

She seemed to be waiting forever, and wished that she could hold Zeph's hand, and fall into a trance that would detach her from the flow of time and leave her alone in a private universe with her perfectly lucid but slightly rambling thoughts.

Then Minerva lifted off, and Denise just had time to think, quite lucidly, that Mireille Angevot had been absolutely right. She had known perfectly well what was about to happen, and understood the theory of it with perfect clarity, but she had had *no* idea.

The force of the ship's acceleration seemed to squash her flat, like a bug. And then she blacked out.

IX

Denise woke up feeling surprisingly well, perhaps even a trifle euphoric. She immediately drew the conclusion that the pod's medical AI had fed something into her system that had given her no choice about feeling that way.

As she began to take stock of herself, she realized that "fed" might be the operative word, because she had a feeding-tube inserted into her mouth as well as a venous drip stuck in her arm. As well as a catheter, she was fitted with some kind of complex loincloth whose functions she did not care to think about.

What the hell? she thought. *Have I been in an induced coma again? I know I blacked out during lift off, but surely the bloody pod could simply have brought me round again. I can't spend my entire life lying around waiting for some over-cautious machine to consent to my waking up.*

She moved her arms then, and realized that they felt peculiarly mobile.

I'm light, she thought. *Not weightless, by any means but not as heavy as I am on Earth. Which means that our current acceleration isn't sufficient to simulate one-gee. Why not? If anything, it ought to be slightly in excess, in order to get us to Saturn a little bit faster.*

She ripped out both the drip and the feeding-tube, and turned on to her side, propping herself up so that she could see the two pods on the opposite side of the cabin. They were both empty, for the moment.

She felt strange—not bad, but strange, and not simply because she was disorientated. Slowly, she contrived to detach herself from the glorified loincloth, and put on some clothes, assuming that that would help her feel better psychologically.

Then it occurred to her to obtain some information from the screen in the pod. She tried to activate it, but it didn't respond. She cursed herself for not having listened with sufficient attention to Zeph's instructions, assuming that there was some step in the activation process that she was omitting. The pod's seal responded in a more obliging fashion, though, and she stepped out with great precaution.

Unlike the opposite pods, the one below hers was occupied, by Zeph. She knelt down in order to peer through the transparent envelope.

He too had a feeding-tube, a drip and apparatus for dealing with his excreta. He was unconscious, as she had been a few minutes before, and quite motionless.

That discovery worried her considerably more than the fact of her own unconsciousness. She was untrained and modified; it was easy enough to credit that the shock of lift off had been too stressful—and, in fact, the doctor who had examined her when she came out of the first coma had warned her that it might be—but Zeph was fully trained and experienced. There was no way that lift off should have required him to be put in an induced coma . . .

Unless something had gone wrong.

"Shit," she muttered.

She had been warned about that too. All the ship's systems had doubtless been tested thoroughly on the ground, but they had never been properly tried. They were fundamentally very similar to the systems aboard Cronos . . . but the systems aboard Cronos had apparently gone wrong themselves, so that knowledge was far from reassuring.

She tried to activate the wallscreen situated between the two top bunks at head height. Like the one in the pod, it didn't respond—but that didn't make sense. It was just an ordinary wallscreen, activated by the simple push of a button. Except that something had obviously gone wrong . . .

Fortunately, the door opened just as easily as the pod, and she eased herself into the space between the various cabins. The area was unlit, but there was a door-slit opposite that was open, through which light was filtering, and sound: the sound of voices, seemingly in contention. Denise recognized them: Chris Kemmering and Helen Arkheimer. The chamber they were in was Helen Arkheimer's "laboratory."

Before moving across the intervening space, Denise steadied herself. She felt mentally spaced out, in addition to her purely physical lightness. The euphoria introduced by whatever the pod had dosed her with was beginning to wear off, and her mouth was beginning to feel sore, although the feeding-tube hadn't seemed to cause any undue friction when she pulled it out.

She made it across to the open door-slit without any incident, although it almost seemed to her that she had somehow forgotten how to walk. She paused in the slit, supporting herself against the jamb.

"It's too risky," Chris Kemmering was saying to the mathematician. "I can't permit it. I don't care what Halleck says. After what happened to Zephaniah . . ."

Denise stepped forward reflexively at the mention of Zeph's name, and the two interlocutors turned to look at her. They were both apparently dumbstruck by her appearance, which gave Denise time to say: "What have you done to my brother, you crazy bitch!" before her legs buckled beneath her and she began to fall.

Chris Kemmering leapt forward and caught her, but he still seemed to be incapable of saying anything except: "Denise!"

"Sorry about that," Denise muttered. "Not used to the change in gravity, I guess. You look terrible, by the way. Both of you."

"I dare say we do," said the Captain. He eased Denise toward the wall, where there was a collapsible divan, extended it, and sat her down.

"Well," she said to Helen Arkheimer. "You haven't answered my question."

"No," the mathematician agreed. "I haven't. But I don't suppose you'd believe me if I said that I haven't done anything . . . and I *was* the one who hooked him up to the machine, and you're not the only person present who thinks I'm a crazy bitch." She glanced resentfully at the Captain; her impatience and ill temper were showing again.

"You've already started your experiments?" Denise queried. "While I was in another bloody induced coma?"

Helen Arkheimer and Chris Kemmering exchanged a glance, before the Captain redirected his attention to his palm unit, but neither answered the questions, perhaps considering them to be rhetorical.

"Mireille," said Kemmering, "can you come down? Denise is awake and I need you to check the other pods to see whether anyone else is back."

"What do you mean, *back*?" Denise demanded, bluntly.

Instead of answering, the Captain switched his screen to mirror and held it out to Denise, so that she could see her own face.

"Okay," said Denise, after a pause of alarm. "I look terrible too. What the hell is going on? Why is Zeph in a coma? Why was I?"

"We don't know why Zeph in a coma," Kemmering told her, in an ominously level voice. "Technically, you weren't, although it started out that way. You were in hibernation."

"Hibernation?" An awful suspicion began to dawn on Denise, as to why the Captain had shown her the mirror, and why he and Helen Kemmering did not look as fit and well as when she had last seen them. "How long have I been out?"

"A little over three years," the Captain informed her, bluntly.

"*Three years?*"

"I'm afraid so, dear," said Helen Arkheimer. "Nor are you the only one, although you were the only one who was unconscious before you were put into hibernation mode. And we have no idea why. In fact . . . well, it might be grasping at straws, but I'm rather hoping that you might be able to explain it, given that I can't immediately think of any other reason why you've been woken up."

"Me? How the hell can I possibly know, if I've been asleep ever since lift off?"

"It does sound strange, put like that," the mathematician admitted. "But you have been . . . dreaming, haven't you?"

"Dreaming? Not that I remember. The last thing I can remember is you coming to the cabin and climbing into your pod. Since then, nothing. *Three years?*"

Arkheimer and Kemmering exchanged another significant glance.

"Zephaniah is still asleep? You saw him in the pod?" The queries came from the Captain.

"Yes," said Denise, "but I didn't know he'd been asleep for three years . . . or has his hibernation been more recent?"

"He's not in hibernation," Kemmering told her. "Not technically. We're not even certain that he's in a genuine coma. The pod AI seems puzzled by his condition, which is worrying in itself. It's possible that he's merely asleep, or even entranced, but whatever you care to call it he's been that way for a very long time. Helen didn't do it . . . not deliberately, at any rate. Her attempt to put him in contact with . . . something . . . seems to have succeeded far too well. Not only did his brain go into an abnormal state, but we seem to have lost control of the AIs too. I don't think they're being actively or continuously controlled, but while Zephaniah was hooked up, they went into emergency mode. Either they've invoked a series of unfamiliar emergency protocols, or some new directives have actually been imported to them. The fact that we can't tell is worrying in itself.

"Anyway, we haven't been able to retake control of some of the systems that have gone rogue. The AIs have put most of the crew into hibernation mode and closed down so-called non-essential systems. We unhooked Zephaniah as soon as we realized that things had gone awry, but he didn't wake up. His brain is active, though—very active, in fact. Yours was much less so, but far from being shut down—hence the question about dreaming. It's possible that the AIs have allowed you to wake up simply because we're in the final phase of deceleration toward Saturn orbit, but you can't blame Helen for hoping that they—or something—had some other purpose . . ."

"You mean you were hoping that *something* might have wanted me to serve as a messenger, by narrating my dreams?" Denise made no attempt to conceal her incredulity.

"It does sound absurd," Helen Arkheimer admitted, "but we've become unashamedly fanciful in our quest for explanatory hypotheses. We don't know what the contact that Zephaniah apparently made has done to his brain, or what it might have been able to do, indirectly, to the AIs monitoring his brain. After three years we're a trifle desperate."

Desperate enough to cause an argument, Denise thought, remembering what she'd heard as she came into the room. *Desperate enough to argue about which desperate measure to try next.*

Mireille Angevot appeared in the doorway then, and stared at Denise as if she could hardly believe her eyes. "No change in any of the others," she reported.

"You three are the only ones awake?" Denise asked.

"Yes." Again, it was Helen Arkheimer who answered. "We've been assuming that there was some kind of logic or purpose in that, since there doesn't appear to be anyone aboard Cronos awake . . . although it's possible that their AIs are controlling their communications more rigorously and only giving that impression. Unfortunately, in three years, we've had no inkling of what that logic or purpose is. Mercifully, our AIs have kept a communication channel to Earth open. Conversation has become difficult because of the time lag, and some of the Enclaves won't communicate, for fear that if our AIs have been corrupted, they'll somehow manage to infect theirs, but we're exchanging information regularly with Fairbanks, and two of the British Enclaves."

"They all survived the volcanic mayhem, then?"

"Yes," Mireille Angevot put in. "The data they've fed through isn't encouraging, though. Photosynthesis is still going on, although the continental plant dieback was well over ninety per cent, but for the moment, it doesn't look as if the oxygen levels can be restored to a level capable of sustaining mammalian life for decades, probably centuries. There should be enough useful raw materials to enable the Enclaves to sustain themselves, but it won't be easy."

Denise nodded, and swallowed. "I think I need a drink," she said. "For thirst, mainly, but I certainly wouldn't refuse a stiff Cognac."

"Can you make it down to the common room?" Chris Kemmering asked.

"I think so . . . yes, I'm sure I can."

She stood up, and moved to the door, without the need for active support, although the Captain remained on hand, just in case it became necessary. The ladder down to the floor below was trickier, but she managed to negotiate it, slowly.

All four of them sat down around a table. Mireille passed a tube of water to Denise, but didn't start a search for Cognac that would presumably have been futile.

After moistening her mouth, Denise looked at Helen Arkheimer, and said: "You mentioned Halleck before I started abusing you?"

"That's right," said the mathematician. "We weren't allowed to collaborate while I was still on Earth, but it's a different ball game now. He's been trying to help me solve the conundrum, after his fashion, but he's annoyingly prone to distraction, as you'll see when you read the messages he's addressed to you. There are other messages waiting for you too, but you'll have to play them on the screens in the control room or the VR hood in your pod. The rest have been closed down."

"Other messages?" Denise queried.

"Just junk," Arkheimer opined, loftily, "including the ones from Halleck, and the one from Marie MacLaughlin."

"Marie! I didn't even know she had an entry permit to an Enclave."

"She didn't," Chris Kemmering explained, "until the last minute. She's in the Highlands. How much that decision was due to the fact that she witnessed the Seventh Generation contact, how much to the fact that she has a friend aboard the starship, and how much to centuries-old Scottish/English rivalry, and the fact that her name indicates a Scottish ancestry even though she was born and raised in England, is anybody's guess. Anyway, I assume she was fishing for a reply, rather optimistically when the message was sent. You've had other contact requests from people who used to be at Imperial, so you haven't quite left your old life behind."

"And you still have the Cabal on your back?"

"Chris and I prefer to think of it as having them hanging on our every word," Helen Arkheimer supplied, "except, alas, that we haven't had anything substantial to tell them for quite some time. Your waking up might be big news, if we can only figure out why it's happened. Are you sure you can't remember any dreams you had?"

"Certain."

"I'd better go up top," said the Captain. "We ought to keep monitoring all communication channels, especially now. If the people of Cronos begin to wake up too . . ." He left it at that, and walked to the ladder, his gait only slightly peculiar because of his reduced weight.

"This isn't exactly the way he was expecting the mission to go, is it?" Denise observed, to no one in particular.

"It's not exactly the way any of us expected it to go," said Mireille, with a sideways glance at Helen Arkheimer.

"No, dear," said the mathematician. "Although . . ."

"Although what?" Denise demanded, when the other trailed off.

"It's always easy to be wise after the event," said Arkheimer, "But . . . it's possible, if there has been some kind of active sabotage, that I should have guessed that the Saturnian intelligences wouldn't be quite as delighted to hear from Zeph as the future inhabitants of Earth, and that their own agenda might be . . . unhelpful."

"Should you? Why?"

"It's a long story, and I never got the chance to prepare the groundwork back on Earth, thanks to my stupidity in crashing that armored car. I fear, though, that you might not be in any condition . . ."

"If you're going to suggest that I lie down, forget it. Having been asleep for three years, I can assure you that I want to make the most of being awake, at least for a while."

"Well," said the mathematician, "do you remember when you told me that you couldn't see how my attempt to enhance the perception of spatial Coincidence in Zephaniah's brain would allow him to perceive anything but a nebulous impression of once-associated particles scattered over interplanetary or interstellar distances?"

"Yes. You said there was a significant modification to be made to the argument but never got round to specifying what it was. I hazarded a guess, but I never got a chance to ask."

Helen Arkheimer seemed interested. "What was the guess?" she asked, instantly.

"Well, the obvious amendment that the kind of continued associations detectable on Earth would also be detectable on other planets—that a Sling, or something similar, or even some kind of weird natural sense, employed on or near Saturn might be able to get glimpses of Saturn's future, and if there really are Saturnian intelligences, on the planet or in the rings, to map their evolution in the same way that Walter Halleck and Zeph contrived to map the evolution of intelligence on Earth."

"That's the seed of the argument," the mathematician conceded, "but only the seed. I hoped that you might be able to take the argument further, being an evolutionary biologist."

"Evolutionary biology isn't a predictive science," Denise pointed out.

"You're missing the point, dear. It's not a matter of going forward but going back. I know they're unorthodox, but you must be familiar with theories suggesting an extraterrestrial origin of life on Earth . . . and since you were actually present when Zephaniah reported back on the account he'd been given of the nature of the seventh generation of that life, you must surely have realized that if the story Halleck and Zephaniah had put together was typical of the evolutionary development of planetary life, then the extraterrestrial hypothesis becomes much more plausible? At least, you would have done if you'd had more time to think about it."

Denise could not find it in her heart to feel grateful that Arkheimer had added the final phrase to let her off the hook of her assumed failure, given the condescension in the other's tone. Helen Arkheimer was a seriously annoying person when she wasn't making strenuous efforts to be pleasant, although she probably couldn't help it. Zeph had been the same way when he was a child, and probably still required a similar effort not to fall back into old habits.

"Okay," she said to the mathematician. "I can buy that. If other planetary life systems evolve, even occasionally, let alone typically, in the fashion mapped out by Zeph's discoveries, then yes, the universe might already be infested by Arrhenius spores, and it's conceivable that one such spore delivered life to Earth. But the panspermia hypothesis doesn't really solve the problem of the origin of life . . . it just pushes it back in time."

"Only in its most simplistic form," put in Mireille Angevot, perhaps trying to be helpful.

"True," Denise admitted. "If you regard the formation of planetary life forms as a kind of secondary phase, after an initial origin of proto-bacterial self-replicating systems in loosely aggregated gas-clouds—but so what?"

"The way I extrapolated the fundamental data I'd assembled," Helen Arkheimer said, "even before the final seventh-generation slingshot and Zephaniah's enhanced perception of the spore-producing mechanism provided the confirmation I was desperately seeking, was that if the fundamental elements of life really can be found in some cosmic gas-clouds, then it's possible that the kinds of spores produced and expelled by the seventh generation of Earthly life or analogues thereof, might be able to initiate or enhance variant evolutionary sequences in locations other than planetary surfaces."

"The rings of Saturn?"

"That was the example foremost in my mind, obviously. I was trying to explain the puzzling data transmitted by the Rats, to figure out how there could possibly be some kind of intelligence in such a hostile environment—but if the lifecloud hypothesis is correct, it's possible that the kind of life and intelligence that evolved on Earth isn't the most common kind distributed through the solar system or the universe."

"But the rings of Saturn are inorganic, and very cold. It's difficult to imagine how any kind of life and intelligence could evolve there, even if the lifecloud hypothesis is invoked to suggest that interplanetary space might be rich in exotic self-replicating systems."

"They're mostly inorganic," Arkheimer agreed, "and, as you say, extremely cold. Cold enough, in fact, for the exotic forms of matter predicted by theoretical physics not only to exist there, but to engage in metamorphoses and transactions, much as solids, liquids and gases do at the Earth's surface."

"Simulating life?" queried Denise, skeptically.

"If you wish . . . or producing what might be better regarded as an alternative kind of life. Definitions become difficult or questionable in such exotic circumstances."

"Quasi-life, then. Intelligent quasi-life?"

"Indeed . . . or quasi-intelligence, if you like that kind of terminology."

"Intelligence, or quasi-intelligence, based not on the kind of senses that earthly organisms possess, those being adapted to high-temperature existence, but on a different range of senses? Coincidence senses?"

"Again, indeed. And if so . . ."

Denise had no difficulty following the train of thought to its conclusion. "If so," she said, "then not only might some such intelligence be distributed over a space as vast as Saturn's rings, attaining sizes that analogues of earthly organisms could never achieve, but it might be distributed over much, much vaster distances: cosmic distances. So the rings of Saturn might not simply be a quasi-living entity in their own right, perhaps—or even perhaps not—possessed of a quasi-intelligence of their own, but they might be at least in contact with, and perhaps even a part of, much vaster quasi-intelligences. Perhaps even a panspermic mentality . . . what Marie Mclaughlin would call God."

She became aware that the two women were both looking at her in an oddly quizzical fashion, and guessed why.

"Oh no," she said. "That was just my own imagination, I can assure you . . . I'm not operating under the guidance of any kind of revelation left over from dreams I can't remember."

"How would you know?" asked Mireille, mildly.

"Because I know what my imagination is capable of, and even if it needed a bit of prompting from you, it was always perfectly capable of following a train of thought like that. Not that it matters how I came by the thesis, or even whether it duplicates yours. The point is, what might it tell us about what happened to Zeph . . . and why, if the quasi-life of the rings of Saturn, or some greater intelligence, is operating through his intermediary, their interference with us is so . . . unhelpful?"

"Precisely," said Arkheimer, with an apparent satisfaction.

"And you think that you might have guessed . . . and perhaps ought to have guessed, now that you can look back with the aid of hindsight?"

"Zephaniah obtained an impression of benevolence on the part of the future intelligences of the earthly ecosphere, including those of the seventh generation. But that makes perfect sense, in a way, because, even though humans aren't the direct ancestors of the Dancing Rats, any more than the insect or plant generations, humans might well have played—or from our temporal viewpoint, have yet to play—a crucial role in enabling the ancestors of the Rats to become the ancestors of the Rats. If that's true, then of course they think of us fondly, and wish us well in our present tribulations. But the spatial intelligences have no such motive. That doesn't necessarily mean they're not interested in us—one would surely expect quasi-intelligences to be quasi-curious—and it probably means that they don't wish us any harm . . . but they surely can't feel the kind of affection for us that comes naturally to future forms of earthly life. To them, we're probably just . . . microbes who have wandered into the field of their microscope."

"So they might poke us a bit to see how we react, but they won't talk to us?"

"I doubt that they *can* talk to us. Even the Dancing Rats couldn't *talk* to us, as such, because they had no way of establishing a common language, except in terms of mathematics, as in the coded data they sent us, and mime, as in the cavorting that earned them their nickname. The spatial intelligences won't even be able to do that. If they can communicate with us at all . . . if only with the rare individuals among us who have the rudiments of some kind of Coincidence perception capable of mechanical augmentation, they won't be able to talk to us. If, however, they can provoke, and perhaps even learn to influence, the dreams or ideas of those individuals, there's just a chance that they might be able to communicate more than a mere benevolent blur."

"And that's what you think is happening to Zeph?"

"We hope so."

"And you thought it might be happening to me too?"

"We hoped so, given the possible involvement of Coincidence in the particular bond between you."

"But it didn't," Denise concluded—although she could see, even as she said it, that they might not accept her conviction as evidence, let alone as proof. Quickly, she changed tack: "But they might be able to communicate, after a fashion, with the ship's AIs."

"They can evidently communicate, *after a fashion*, with Zephaniah," Helen Arkeheimer supplied. "It's just that he hasn't been able to report to us yet what the results of that communication have been. It's probable that any indirect effect their contact with him had on our AIs was limited and brutal, but we have to remember that machine quasi-intelligence is digital and binary, and thus bear in mind the possibility that it's far more easily graspable by alien intelligence than the kind of analytical processes that go on in our neural tissue."

Denise nodded, pensively. "I'll have to think about all this," she said. "I'll need time to sort it out."

"Of course," said Arkheimer. "And you have it, now."

Another thought occurred to Denise. "What were you and Chris arguing about when I woke up?" she asked. "What is it that you want to do that he thinks is too dangerous?"

"I want to hook someone else up to my machine, of course. I'd have done it long ago if we hadn't been a little short of candidates, and Chris hadn't taken the view that we have none to spare for the experiment."

"Given the effects that the first experiment had, I'm not surprised that he thinks it's too dangerous."

"But that's assuming, as he does, that the spatial intelligences haven't learned anything as a result of the first experiment and its aftermath. They might be able to do better second time around."

"Or if not, third time around, or fourth?"

"Perhaps," said Arkheimer, with perfect equanimity.

Denise looked at Mireille. "And you're the guinea-pig?"

Mireille smiled, wryly. "I was," she said.

Denise had no difficulty extrapolating that inference either. "But now I'm awake, you think there's a more promising candidate? In fact, you're wondering whether that's *why* I'm awake?"

"The thought had crossed my mind," the chemist admitted. Helen Arkheimer didn't bother to confirm that it had crossed hers—of course it had.

"And if I say no?"

"I wouldn't blame you," said the mathematician. "As the dear captain says, it would surely be dangerous . . . even though we don't really know exactly what the risks would be, or what the potential reward might be. It would be a shot in the dark . . . rather like volunteering for the Minerva mission, without any preparation, in order to follow a brother you don't really know very well."

My God, thought Denise. *She not only thinks I'll do it, she thinks I won't have any choice . . . in fact, come to think about it, she might be right. And her impatience has been building up for three years.*

Aloud, she said: "I need time to think about it. It's not the kind of decision one can make in a hurry." She was uncomfortably aware, as she proffered the excuse, that the risky decision that had brought her here had been made in a tearing hurry, even though it was the kind of decision that shouldn't be.

"Of course," was all Helen Arkheimer said. "Take all the time you need. By all means talk it over with the Captain."

Denise looked at Mireille. "Oh, don't mind me," the chemist said. "I only volunteered because I was bored to death, but now things have started happening again, I might be able to dispel the ennui without taking extreme measures."

"I suppose life aboard must have become a trifle tedious, if none of the screens work and there are only three of you awake," Denise observed.

"Oh, the VR equipment in the pods still plays stored tapes," the chemist told her, "and the quality of the company compensates for the lack of quantity. I shouldn't exaggerate."

"I'll try not to diminish the average quality too much," said Denise, sarcastically.

"There's no danger of that, my dear," said the mathematician, "although it isn't very becoming to fish for compliments like that."

"I'll try to be more decorous too." Denise wondered whether she was up to the task of climbing all the way up to the Captain's eyrie, and decided that there was no harm in trying. "But I think you're right—I do need to talk things over with the Captain, in order to figure out how to make myself useful now that I'm finally able to report for duty."

And with that, she stood up, and began to make her way uneasily—but thankfully not unsteadily—to the ladder.

X

Mireille got up as if to help Denise climb up to the control room, or at least to accompany her, but at a signal from Helen Arkheimer she sat down again. As she climbed, Denise marveled at the expertise of the pod AI that had maintained her muscles and nerves so well while they lay idle. The relative lightness of her body doubtless helped a little, but, considering the duration of her hibernation, her organism seemed to be functioning admirably, and her mind too seemed to have clicked back into gear without any difficulty.

But why? she wondered. *Why are so many of the crew in hibernation—and why not all of them, since the AIs can maintain and steer the ship perfectly well without human intervention?*

On the other hand, she reflected, the one thing that the AIs couldn't do, except in a mechanical fashion, was maintain an intelligent conversation with Earth. That conversation must have become exceedingly slow, given that the information still had to travel the old-fashioned way, riding electromagnetic waves, and must have suffered even longer interruptions while the Earth moved behind the Sun on its annual round trip, but the exchanges of information between the Captain and the Cabal, and even more so between Helen Arkheimer and Walter Halleck, were something for which there could be no mechanical substitute.

And Mireille? She was the shipboard expert capable of interpreting and extrapolating the data received from Earth relating to the condition of the atmosphere, but it was possible that she had a more valuable function in balancing a relationship between Chris and Helen that was to some extent adversarial. The AIs undoubtedly had data culled during Olympus Five and previous long haul space missions relating to the necessities of maintaining viable interactivity among the active crew.

Behind the efficient AIs, however, there might, as Helen Arkheimer suggested, be a further intelligence: an alien intelligence, which had gained access to the AIs via Zeph's brain, briefly at first, but evidently for long enough to establish a permanent connection with Zeph via his dreams.

Was it possible, she wondered, that information of a sort was still feeding through an established connection, doubtless in a very vague sense on the very margin of comprehensibility, akin to the communication he had established with the Dancing Rats or the Insects, but capable of refinement? Even his communication with future Earth had been amenable to the kind of sophistication of which the seventh generation minds had contrived to take advantage.

Helen Arkheimer might be right, she decided. If there really were quasi-intelligences in Saturn's rings, they wouldn't be able to communicate with Zeph in words, but they might well be able to enable him to see visions of some sort in the private arena of his imagination, and also to feel emotion.

The real question, however, she thought, as she reached the top of the ladder—the part of the ship that she had not seen during the desultory tour that Zeph had given her when she woke up from her first induced coma—was not what Zeph might be able to learn about the Coincidence Intelligences by way of the enhancement of his Coincidence sense lent to him by Helen Arkheimer's machinery, but what they might have been able to learn from him, and what they might have done, or might be doing, or might yet do, in consequence.

The top of the ladder gave direct access to the space in which Chris Kemmering was located; there was no further stairwell, nor any subsidiary door. The hatchway giving her access made no noise as it dilated, with a soft click, and the Captain had his back to it, so she was in the chamber before he realized that she was there. As soon as he did he took the three strides necessary to take her hand, although she didn't really need the support or the steadying interest.

The space was equipped with three chairs at separate work stations, all three of which still had working screens receiving and displaying information from within and without the ship.

"How are you feeling?" he asked.

"Quite well, even though the induced euphoria has worn off," she told him. "No matter how hard I try to distract myself with the ideas that Helen Arkheimer's thrown at me, however, I'm having difficulty getting my head around the notion that I've lost three years of my life. *Three years!* Even though it only seems that I've had a single night's deep sleep!"

"I was worried about you," he told her, as he sat her down at one of the work stations before resuming his own command post. "We all were. I'm still worried about the others. If the AIs have allowed you to wake up . . ."

"Why not them?" Denise finished for him. "Why not Zeph? It might be only a matter of hours, now, though, with luck."

"I've notified Fairbanks of your awakening," he told her, "but it's a pure formality. More pertinently, I've tried to contact Cronos, with which we could have a real conversation if there were anyone aboard capable of talking, but Fulsom and his crew all seem to be still in suspended animation. All I've got back from the ship so far is AI babble."

"Can I get a visual of Saturn on this screen?" Denise asked, when she had made herself completely comfortable in the seat to the Captain's left.

"Sure," he said, "but we're still some way from orbit—and I'd better warn you that once we've decelerated sufficiently for the lateral jets to start the final maneuvers, you might begin to feel very peculiar. Your weight will vary, and you'll begin to feel sideways tilts—your brain will have difficulty making sense of the information coming from your semicircular canals, and you might well feel dizzy and sick. Eventually, you'll adapt, but you might find it easier, at least to begin with, to ride out the worst in your pod, where the AI can counter the symptoms. I'll give you fair warning of any course changes if I get any myself, but the AIs have become a trifle uncommunicative, so I might not."

While he was speaking, he pecked his keyboard in order to bring up an image on Denise's screen relayed from a camera in the nose cone. Saturn was a measurable disk, far bigger than any of the other points in its vicinity standing out from the stellar backcloth by virtue of their brightness, but it was still little more than a glorified dot, and the celebrated rings were mere lateral smudges.

"I'll magnify it," Kemmering said.

The magnification made a considerable difference, giving Denise a much clearer image of the planetary surface and its vague features, but she had seen others just as good relayed by unmanned probes over the course of more than a century of space exploration. The rings were more discernible, but looked more like streaks from the present angle of vision, far less majestic than their representation in old "artists' impressions."

"And this is a magnified view from Cronos," the Captain said, bringing up a third image, in which the planet looked bigger, but the rings were hardly visible at all, because the ship was orbiting in the same plane as the particles making up the rings, within one of the gaps.

Denise nodded to tell him that she had seen enough.

"How are you feeling, really, though?" he asked again, solicitously, obviously not for the sake of politeness, this time, but fishing for some sort of clue as to what had happened to her.

"I wish I knew," she told him, and not merely as a quip. "Mostly, I suspect, I'm feeling after-effects of psychotropics the pod pumped into me, but . . . I can't help wondering whether there are other possibilities, and whether I'd be able to detect them if there were."

"Helen's been probing, then? Trying to detect some evidence of a continuing link with Zeph?"

"Not directly. Mostly, she was trying to bring me up to speed with her theories as to what we're dealing with, and why her attempt to boost Zeph's Coincidence sensibility produced such a screwed-up result. But she wants to put me into her machine for a second run. She seems quite gleeful about the possibility—and to be in something of a hurry."

"I didn't think she'd waste any time. She'd have had Mireille wired up months ago if she'd been able to talk her into it, orders or no orders."

"Your orders?"

"Anyone's. The Cabal are thousands of millions of miles away and I'm right here, but she's equally capable of ignoring everyone, except maybe Walter Halleck, and probably him if they didn't see eye to eye so much. At least the time lag has interrupted their weird meeting of minds . . . no, forget I said that. It was petty and stupid, and directly contrary to my duty as captain. I have to stop thinking of you as an outsider rather than a crew member."

"Easier said than done," Denise muttered, still studying the magnified image of the planet toward which they were heading.

"You don't have to let her wire you up to her machine," Kemmering pointed out. "If she doesn't have to take anyone else's orders, you certainly don't have to take hers."

"It's what I'm here for," Denise said, a trifle dully.

"From her point of view, undoubtedly," the Captain agreed. "But you've always had your own agenda."

"Have I? I'm not so sure any more that it really is mine. I know that what you said to me in the car, what seems like only a couple of days ago, was mostly following a script, and probably had an element of reverse psychology in it, but you know as well as I do that all the arguments you put to me as to why I shouldn't get on that plane were perfectly sound. Rationally, I should be in Snowdonia—but I don't regret that I'm not. Even after having just lost three years of my life to some stupid AI that deemed that I'd be better off asleep, possibly because its programming had been screwed up by a momentary brush with an alien intelligence, I still don't wish that I was in Snowdonia. Which makes me crazy, I guess."

"You're here because you love your brother," Kemmering observed.

"That's the convenient and flattering label for the impulse that drove me, but again it's not rational. Zeph and I lived separate lives even while we were kids. Then he went off to be a telepresence operator, and then a human bullet fired from an electronic sling, and then he spent seven years on a jaunt to bloody Jupiter. You and Mireille know him far more intimately than I do. It makes sense that you love him, but me? Why do I love him?"

"Why does anyone love anyone?" Kemmering countered, solemnly.

He wasn't simply being glib, Denise knew. He meant it as a philosophical problem that might possibly have a new dimension in the light of Coincidence Theory. From one point of view, Coincidence Theory was fiendishly abstruse math that the normal human mind could not begin to comprehend—but from another it might be a philosophical key to the universe, and to the arcane springs of human motivation.

Wouldn't it be ironic, Denise thought, *if the only two people who had ever gained any genuine insight into the mechanics of love were Walter Halleck and Helen Arkheimer?* But perhaps not, she reflected. It would be petty and stupid, as Chris Kemmering had just pointed out, to fall in with the conventional neurotypical opinion that mathematical geniuses who found smooth talk difficult were incapable of love. It was just as plausible if not more so, that it was the smooth talkers, the pretenders, who were incapable of the reality of the sham behind which they hid . . . except that that thought was probably petty and stupid too.

"I don't like feeling like a pawn in this weird game," Denise said, "but at the end of the day, that's what we are, isn't it? And we have no more appreciation of who the players are, what the rules of the game are, and what their objectives might be, than the pawns on a chessboard used to have of the self-styled human grandmasters, in the days when humans could still beat AIs."

"Actually," said the Captain, "we do have a better appreciation, thanks to your brother. You were there, remember. Perhaps the fact that you were there—that it was just one more incident in your busy day—made it difficult to realize exactly how important those two hours were, but what your brother perceived during that final slingshot told us a great deal about the nature of life, from a cosmic perspective. Helen claims that she'd already worked it out, theoretically, but she's never been one for modesty, and even she was desperate for the confirmation and the elaboration. Thanks to Zephaniah, we do know far more, now, than any pawn ever knew about any self-styled grandmaster . . . and let's be fair to our species: we knew a hell of a lot even before he put the icing on the cake."

"I suppose so," admitted Denise.

"It's true," Kemmering insisted. "Even while we had no inkling of Coincidence Theory, we'd made progress. It's not just Helen's math that got us where we are now; it's three thousand years of collective scientific and technological endeavor, which has to be reckoned, from an objective and rational point of view, utterly spectacular. And in spite of all the breast-beating about the suicidal contribution we made to the ecocatastrophe, in the final analysis, it was a purely natural disaster. We hastened it a little by overstimulating the atmosphere, but we didn't lay down the clathrates and we didn't pump up the volcanoes.

"You, of all people, understand how impotent the species that have lived on the surface of the Earth were in the context of the forces that existed beneath and above them, and drove so many of them to extinction. You know as much as anyone about the major cataclysms of the past, and you know perfectly well that the kind of intelligence we have would have been impotent to put up any resistance to any of them. Even if the Enclaves only manage to hold out against this one for decades, or centuries, at best, we'll have achieved something truly heroic."

"You're right, obviously," Denise conceded. "But even so . . ."

"We're going to die," the Captain finished for her, having worked up a head of steam, and having a new audience at hand, in the flesh, for the first time in three years. "But that's not the point—and again, thanks to Walter Halleck and your brother, we know that. Thanks to them, we can see the greater pattern, and, thanks to them, we can play our role in its progressive thrust. We know, thanks to the Sling, that the extinction events of the past are merely part of a pattern that is going to extend into the future for billions of years. We know that we're far from being the only intelligent species doomed to be wiped out by the brute force of all the environmental factors implicit in matter and radiation.

"We know that humans are doomed, that mammals are doomed, and at least two generations of invertebrate intelligence are doomed before the symbiotic sequence that will bind the vegetable and mineral realms together and produce the hybrid intelligences of the seventh generation emerge, having survived the first explosive phase of the stellar evolution that will eventually doom the Earth itself, and the Sun. And we can be sure, too, even though we haven't actually seen any further, that the seventh generation won't be the last. So yes, the human species is going to die, just as you and I, as individuals, are going to die, but, just as my individual death is part of the progressive evolution of the species, so the death of the species is part of the progressive evolution of earthly life, and the eventual death of the Earth and all the life on its surface is part of the evolution of cosmic life. And we all have our roles to play, our moves to make.

"Most of the moves made by individuals are irrelevant. Most individual human beings are absolutely correct to deem themselves utterly insignificant, and to think that their only possible purpose within their nasty, brutish and short lives is to squeeze what meager personal satisfaction they can out of quotidian existence. But that's not true of everyone, and it's not true of you and me. Maybe that's a matter of pure chance or coincidence, rather than anything we deserve by virtue of personal merit, but it's a fact, and it's a circumstance for which we ought to be extremely glad."

"Amen," said Denise, with a wry smile.

Having run out of breath, Kemmering paused to collect himself. Then he said: "Sorry, I guess all that had been stored up for a while, waiting for release. I love Mireille dearly, and I even love Helen, in a somewhat perverse fashion, but sometimes . . . well, particular rants need particular audiences."

"And you don't love me . . . yet," said Denise, although she knew that wasn't the relevant issue.

"Of course I do," he countered. "It's my duty, my job . . .and, truth to tell, my pleasure."

"But I shouldn't fish for compliments like that," said Denise, with a sigh. "Tell me, since we were on the subject a moment ago, how much do you think our role, relative to that of the evolution of the human species, has simply been that of a dupe . . . a patsy, I suppose you might say, as an American?"

"Ah," said Kemmering, taking the inference instantly. "The rat question. Helen obviously hasn't wasted any time updating you. Well, the simple answer, I guess, is not so much. It's a big issue in the Enclaves right now, as you can imagine. Not surprisingly, there's a contingent of humans for humanity, who consider the Dancing Rats to be sly and treacherous, and believe that they took Halleck and Zephaniah for a ride, pretending to be enlightening us by means of the data they sent back to us, while actually feeding us precisely, and only, data that would inevitably lead us to lay the foundations for the evolution and eventual world dominance of their own species. There's no shortage back on Earth of humans who favor the genocidal solution: death to all rats.

"Even if we assume, however, that the Rats' motivation is—will be—purely self-serving, or even frankly malevolent, let's try to look at it from their point of view. Isn't it, from their standpoint, not merely the rational thing to do, but the necessary thing to do, and the moral thing to do? Aren't they absolutely correct and justified to be delighted by the opportunity that the Sling offered to them—although some of them, at least, presumably take the view that it had to happen, because if it hadn't, they might not even exist. We can't be sure about that, of course, and in all probability, neither can they. Probably, if they hadn't sent the data back, and we hadn't used it, they'd have evolved anyway, once humans were out of the picture. Maybe all that the loop in time has achieved has been an accelerating impulse. But maybe not. At any rate, at the opposite end of the ideological spectrum back home, there's a party that asserts that humans ought to do everything humanly possible, before they die, to smooth the way for our heirs—in brief, to be good midwives to the Rats."

"Can we really make that much difference?" Denise asked, skeptically.

"Oh yes. We probably couldn't do anything much to inhibit the rats' evolution, let alone prevent it, but we're certainly in a position to give it a helpful boost. Mireille's the expert, so she can give you a much fuller and more detailed explanation, but the point isn't so much that rats genetically engineered in accordance with specifications transmitted via the Dancing Rats' data dumps are playing significant roles in some of the Enclaves as auxiliaries and even as livestock. The crucial issue is the role that deliberately adapted rats might, and almost certainly will, play in the reconstitution of a breathable atmosphere—what Mireille calls the reterraformation of Earth.

"Put simply, rats can be adapted, using the modification mapped out in the data transmitted from the future, to operate in atmospheres with a considerably lower oxygen pressure than adapted humans. Humans have sufficient genes in common with rats for much of the Dancing Rat biotech to be applicable to human beings as well as to rats, but rats have certain innate natural advantages that give them a long head start in being able to operate in hostile and toxic atmospheres. They'll be able to work outside the Enclaves, without protective suits, long before humans can—and if humans are ever able to emerge without diving suits, any agriculture and civilization that they rebuild will have to be a collaborative endeavor between humans and smart rats, in which case it will be impractical, or even impossible, to reduce the rats to the status of slaves, let alone livestock. From this point in time onwards, according to rational calculation, the survival of humans in the medium term will depend on the survival of rats modified according to Dancing Rat specifications."

"So, in that scenario, we have just as much reason to be grateful for the contact Zeph made as the Rats do?" observed Denise, savoring the irony.

"That's what the wise money says, in my judgment. As I say, Mireille knows all the details, because she understands the fundamental biochemistry, but I'm with her, and so was Zephaniah, before the aliens disrupted or abducted his brain. The Dancing Rat contact was a win-win situation. They had—will have—every right to be delighted about it, and arguably, so do we; and also, by logical extrapolation, all the subsequent generations in the sequence. Even those who don't have anything much to say to us will be glad we got in touch. It makes perfect sense that Zephaniah should have got the strong impression that they'll feel benevolent toward us, not just because of the inherent intellectual interest of the contact, but because they really will see it as heroic, something for which they can and ought to love us."

Denise nodded, pensively. "An argument that, as Helen just took the trouble to explain to me at length, doesn't apply to the extraterrestrial intelligences . . . which might have, as you put it, abducted his brain."

"We had assumed," Kemmering suggested, mildly, "that they might have abducted yours too. It was active, although not as active as Zephaniah's. The fact that the activity in question seems to have left no memory trace is . . . disappointing."

"You were hoping I'd come down from the mountain carrying the tablets of the law?"

"Hardly—but we were hoping that you'd come back with *something*. Information, insight . . . the possibility that Zephaniah might eventually wake up, after years of hard mental labor, and remember absolutely nothing is . . ."

"Disappointing," Denise finished for him. "Not to mention puzzling, frustrating and numerous other participles with negative correlations. But we surely have grounds for hoping that not only will he remember, but that he'll at least be able to begin to make sense of what he remembers."

"Do we?"

"Of course. He's done it before. The other agents Halleck went out via the Sling couldn't make head nor tail of what they saw through the lens. Without Zeph, the returns of the experiment would have been rather meager. But Zeph has the kind of alternative sanity that can begin to grasp that kind of communication, just as Walter Halleck had the kind of alternative sanity required to grasp the math underlying the Sling, and Zeph could remember enough to begin to string the narrative together. He's done it once, so there's reason to hope that he can do it again. That's why we're here, after all. In fact, now I come to think about it, that *is* why we're here, isn't it? Not just him, but *us*. There's another dimension to the matter that you might not have considered properly . . . although Helen has certainly begun to realize its significance."

"The catalyst thesis," Kemmering supplied, obviously having discussed the matter with the mathematician. "Initially, she thought it was just you, because you were his sister: that as his Coincidence sensibility developed under the stimulus of the various contacts—including the contact with the cloud-whales, and perhaps especially that one, although it seemed the least productive from our viewpoint—it drew him to you more forcefully than it ever had before, and provoked a reciprocal reaction. Then she began to think that it might be more general, and that it extended to other relationships . . . specifically, to Mireille and to me. At first, she decided to co-opt Mireille to the crew for trivial reasons, but after that moment the four of us had on the plane, the first time we'd all come together, she began to think that the potential nexus was wider, that Zephaniah's innate sensibility was being enhanced, even before she added an electronic boost, by the proximity of . . . well, his nearest and dearest."

"All right," Denise conceded, "so you had begun to consider it properly, and it's just me who's slow catching up."

"That's not your fault," the Captain pointed out, "and you certainly seem to be making up ground hand over fist."

"Yes, I do, don't it?" Denise mused. "Is that a compliment to my intelligence, or my evolving Coincidence sensibility, I wonder?"

"Is there really a contrast there, or even a difference?" Kemmering suggested.

"Maybe not." She paused before adding: "But there has to be a reason, doesn't there, why I've woken up? It's unlikely to be just happenstance."

"Perhaps," Kemmering agreed.

"It's the next point in an evolving schema, which is reaching its denouement as we get nearer to Saturn and journey's end . . . to the rendezvous with Saturn's rings. Because physical proximity is important, isn't it, even within the context of Coincidence Theory, which maintains relationships over vast, perhaps limitless distances? It's not just past physical associations that are important, but all of them. When we reach the rings . . . things will happen. Zeph will surely wake up, for one . . . and hopefully, he'll be able to tell us *something*. Maybe it will fall a long way short of a full explanation of what the hell is going on, but *something*."

"I'd like to believe that," said Chris Kemmering.

"You have to believe it," Denise corrected him.

"Yes," he admitted.

"But not the tablets of the law. Not that it would matter much if it were, given that the originals have always been far more honored in the breach than the observance."

"That might be unfair cynicism," said the Captain. "We always notice the breaches more than the observances, but that very sensitivity indicates a certain fundamental respect. But no, I don't believe, and certainly don't hope, that what Zephaniah might bring back from the Cosmic Mind, will be a set of commandments. I can't believe that the Cosmic Mind, if the extraterrestrial intelligences can indeed constitute a universal superentity, has any interest in being the kind of God that religions have always feared or requested. Can you?"

"No," said Denise, "but I know a woman who can. Didn't Helen say that there's a message from Marie waiting for me?"

"Among others, yes. She didn't think much of it, though."

"She's seen it, then? And you too?"

"Yes." He didn't elaborate as to the reasons for that prying but added: "Do you want me to put the message up on our screen?"

"Yes, please."

"Would you like me to leave while you listen to it?"

"Don't be ridiculous. You've already seen it."

Kemmering's practiced fingers danced on the virtual keyboard appended to his own screen, but it was the screen in front of Denise that replaced the magnified image of Saturn with an image of Marie MacLaughlin's face, with a flicker that seemed oddly, if arbitrarily, significant.

Denise was slightly surprised to feel a pang of gladness at the sight of a person to whom she had never felt particularly close—although she immediately recognized, as soon as she experienced the surprise, that it might not be surprising at all, given that Marie had intruded herself so rudely and so effectively into her reunion with Zeph, and hence into the evolving pattern of its Coincidence.

XI

"Hello, Denise," said Marie, speaking direct to camera. "Obviously, I don't know when, or even if, you'll receive this, but I hope you will, at some stage. Apparently, you're in hibernation, because the starship's AIs have been disrupted or subverted by the alien intelligence that Zeph was able to contact via Dr. Arkheimer's Coincidence Machine. Walter is sure that you'll wake up, though—I'm in continual on-screen contact with him, even though we're in different Enclaves. My hosts have their own reasons for encouraging that, and it is, in a sense, why I'm here.

"We never talked about the sealed envelopes of course. People didn't, did they, even people who knew one another more intimately than you and I did? But you probably assumed that I didn't have one, not so much because of the limited demand in the Enclaves for chaplains as because of the way the Renewed Church hierarchy works in distributing its privileges. Just as your status suddenly shifted when Zeph arrived back on Earth, though, so did mine—thanks entirely to your kindness and my pushiness. For years, the official position in the UK had been, stupidly, that Walter was probably a fantasist, and even if he wasn't, that his findings were essentially irrelevant to the immediate problems of surviving the impending catastrophe. That perception changed overnight, though, the moment that the Americans commandeered Zeph.

"The fundamental thinking didn't change, obviously, given the notorious stubbornness of official opinion, but the one thing politicians can't stand is the idea that the opposition might have stolen a march on them, and in the political context, everybody is the opposition, within as well as outside official alliances and parties. When the Americans stole Zeph, the British parliament instantly moved to make sure of Halleck. He already had his envelope, but they also instituted emergency measures to take possession of the Sling.

"Within the context of the parliament, though, there had been an internal contest between the English and the Scots going back centuries, unamended by the Act of Union and exaggerated by all the concerted attempts to break that Union made in the twenty-first century. The controllers of the Highlands Enclave inevitably decided that if Snowdonia had Walter, they needed, if only in order to save face, someone who could either rival him or maintain some kind of fruitful contact with him. As you can imagine, there weren't very many candidates, even among his techs, and to cut a tangled story short, their dragnet caught me. Absurd, you'll doubtless agree—but not unsuccessful, as it turned out. Walter and I have formed an on-screen relationship that suits us both, and he's in continual, if somewhat belated, contact with Helen Arkheimer, so I'm still able to cling on to the periphery of this enormously intriguing affair.

"Opinion is inevitably divided within the Church as to whether my contacts with the affair and the theological conclusions I drew from it are a hotline to revelatory truth or whether they merely qualify me as one more whore of Babylon tempting true believers to the false faith of the Antichrist, but one way or another, I've become notorious enough to have an audience—so, the first thing I want to say to you is thanks. I know you helped me on a whim, not because you believed in me, but it was still an act of kindness on your part to introduce me to Zeph, and I appreciate it.

"I'd like to be able to tell you that the entire world, or what survives of it now that the atmosphere has turned toxic, is waiting with bated breath for the next phase of the new revelation, but it isn't. Ninety-nine people out of a hundred are almost entirely focused on immediate issues of getting by in the world beneath the domes, and even those who go to church or look to any religious faith for some kind of consolation are mostly told that what Zeph has discovered is at best irrelevant to their particular faith, and at worst an instrument of the Devil, or some equivalent thereof. So it has always been. But I'm not alone, Denise. Some of us are intensely interested in the Revelation so far, and avid to hear the next phase: the one that will complete it. We've had the revelations of Time; we're now awaiting, expectantly, the revelations of

Space. Zeph's first series of expeditions has confirmed the reality of God and given us a few additional glimpses to his nature, but we have every reason to hope that a more direct contact and confrontation between God and his latest prophet will produce further insight and consolation.

"When I say 'every reason' I mean, of course, in addition to reasons based in religious faith and the threats and promises of previous prophets, the productions of Walter's theories, now supplemented by and fused with Dr. Arkheimer's. Walter doesn't use our terminology, of course, and maintains an obstinate and absurd insistence that he's an atheist, but the difference is simply a matter of terminology. Even there, the overlap is considerable; religious men were using such terms as 'cosmic intelligences' long before physicists began to reappropriate them from the despised wilderness of science fiction. I know that you feel, as Walter does, that there's some kind of strange shame in admitting a belief in God, and that you cling to the same terminological resources of denial, but believe me, it doesn't matter. We're talking about the same thing, and are involved in exactly the same quest: to determine and enhance the appropriate intensity of awe and adoration.

"I won't try to take persuasion any further than that, given that I was obliged to accept as a fundamental condition of our friendship that I could only attempt to convert you by stealth, and not by overt confrontation. What I'm primarily interested in talking to you about—and in regard to which I hope that you'll eventually be willing and able to reply—is what my jargon calls theodicy, and vulgar parlance calls the problem of evil.

"Put crudely, the issue comes down to the deceptively simple question of why, if God is both omnipotent and good, evil exists. Superficially, at least, it seems that in order to account for the existence of evil, belief has to compromise either on the matter of God's omnipotence—in which case, he is somehow unable to prevent the existence of evil—or his benevolence, in which case, although he could eliminate evil, he chooses not to do so. I won't bore you with a summary of the long history of attempts to weasel out of that puzzle by arguing for a kind of authority that is limited but somehow still qualifies as omnipotence, or one that has devastating consequences for the most virtuous of human beings, while still somehow qualifying as benevolence.

"Not unnaturally, even those of us who accept the fundamental truth of Zeph's initial sketchy revelations regarding the nature of God disagree with regard to their theological implications. There's a contingent, obviously, that clings hard to the traditional idea of the present ongoing apocalypse as a punishment for original and ongoing sin. There's also a party that is attempting to integrate Coincidence Theory into a quasi-Leibnizian theodicy that argues that God's omnipotence was and is compromised in the creation and maintenance of the universe by the inherently flawed nature of the materials of construction: the nature of matter and its possible transactions.

"Let me say right away that I don't belong to either of those parties, even though the arguments they have elaborated on the basis of the present scientific conception of the universe are ingenious. Insofar as I'm affiliated to any party rather than thinking independently, it's the third major party that has formed in relation to the Zephanian revelation, which might be described as the party of compensations: the party that believes in some kind of balancing of the moral account books, which compensates the virtuous for the effects of evil that they have suffered, and perhaps also punishes those individuals who have chosen to be instruments of evil.

"Personally, I'm not interested in going in search of possible cosmic hells, but I *am* interested in the quest for cosmic heavens, and I believe that Zeph's discoveries do provide scope for a reimagination of heaven, which will hopefully be endorsed and further elaborated by the news that he will impart when he wakes up from his present trance. Perhaps, while in your own trance, you have received some such news yourself, but if not, I have confidence that Zeph will make up the deficit.

"The point is, it seems to me, that Coincidence Theory, and the principal ramifications of that theory sensed by Zeph—and

315

other prophets before him, although they didn't have the terminology to describe their perception appropriately—point us in the direction of a more sophisticated notion of the soul than we have previously been able to possess, and the nature of its survival of the material body, and indeed, its eternity. It seems to me that what Dr. Arkheimer's machine has done, in enhancing what she and Walter call Zeph's Coincidence sensibility, is to put him directly in contact with his own soul, and that soul's cosmic connections, giving Zeph an awareness of an existing and enduring relationship with subsidiary cosmic intelligences, both in multiple terms—angels, in Christian parlance—and in terms of the ensemble: the Monad, or God.

"We already know, thanks to Coincidence theory, that the atoms constituting a body will retain an association of sorts even when physically dispersed after death, and we know, therefore, that a component of the association formed as a unique individual is formed survives after that individual's death. What we hope and expect to learn from the completion of the Zephanian revelation, is some further explanation of the operation of God's goodness in securing and shaping a future for that component, in the realm of the angels, and the consequent privileges attached to the fact of having lived a virtuous life.

"I know, Denise, that you and Zeph will use different terminology to describe what has been revealed to him when he wakes up from his trance, and that's perfectly all right. But what I'm asking, of you and, indirectly, of him, is that you both pay some heed to the new aspects of the revelation that I hope and expect you to discover, and that you'll communicate the relevant information to me as soon as you can. I'll be eternally grateful—and I think you can understand, now, how sincerely I mean that. If you head out of the solar system after your rendezvous with Saturn's rings, as your mission plan intends, I'll never see you again in this life, and two-way communication will become increasingly difficult, but whatever might happen, I hope to encounter you again, by means of Coincidence sensibility, in Heaven. God bless you, Denise, and I hope to hear from you soon."

316

Denise, somewhat taken aback, shook her head. She sat back in her chair and looked at Chris Kemmering. "That wasn't a message for me," she said. "It was a reading from the pulpit. She was actually using an autocue, damn it. Did she even write it herself, do you think?"

"I presume so," opined the Captain, "but I dare say that it was carefully vetted and perhaps rewritten in accordance with comments made. You're right, of course—your name is merely a convenient cover for an address to an earthly congregation. That shouldn't surprise you overmuch, knowing the nature of on-screen communication in a world of eavesdroppers."

"I suppose not," said Denise. A thought struck her. "When I was communicating with Zeph during the last phase of Olympus Five's homeward run, was everyone on the ship playing back the tapes?"

"Certainly not," Kemmering replied. "Fourteen people living in a narrow tin have to sacrifice a good deal of privacy, but a certain respect for personal space remains essential. Nobody on the crew listened in on anyone else's personal communications; any eavesdropping that was done on yours—and I don't doubt that there was some—was done at your end, by people on Earth tapping all of the ship's communications. Helen and I listened to that message because you were asleep, and because we knew that it wasn't really, or at least simply, a personal communication. Most of the other messages waiting for you are unopened, although they're probably no more genuinely personal."

"How many are there?"

"Only a dozen or so addressed to you—very few, by comparison with the hundreds that have stacked up for Zephaniah's attention. We've read a number of those, but nothing interesting, and they're probably all junk. The people who genuinely have something to say address themselves to me, Helen or Mireille, and will continue to do so until they receive news that he's awake."

"I see. And any message I might transmit, to Marie or anyone else . . ."

"You might as well be transmitting to the entire world—or what's left of it. Even Zephaniah's last call to your mother, which was presumably about as personal as you can get—and of which I have no knowledge personally—has probably been viewed by tens of thousands of people on Earth."

"So the only people that the four of us can talk to confidentially, at present, are one another? On the brighter side, though, given that we're not planning to go home for a very long time, it will be decades before your next set of bootlegged sex tapes hits the black market."

"They only had a certain novelty value," the Captain replied, evenly, "as you presumably know."

Denise blushed. "I didn't know you then," she said. "And I didn't know, until Zeph explained it to me, that you were just doing your duty."

Kemmering sighed, but didn't bother to tell her that she knew better than that.

"I'm sorry," she said. "I haven't had the training, remember, or the indoctrination. It might take me a while to adapt."

"That's fine."

"I know. How long will it take us to catch up with Cronos?"

"The AIs haven't shared their flight plan with me, in spite of requests, but if Cronos remains in her present orbit, and we follow what seems to me to be the logical deceleration and maneuvering sequence, about five days."

"And what happens then? Do we send out a boarding party?"

"In a manner of speaking. Obviously, in the first instance, we'll use surrogates manipulated by telepresence. If Zephaniah's awake by then, his in-flesh contacts make him the ideal man for the job, but I can maneuver a surrogate well enough, even without inlays. It's not hard to pass through the locks and take a look round. With luck, it won't be necessary. Given that the AIs woke you up, presumably in response to some kind of cue, they can probably do the same for the Cronos crew, and the rest of ours—unless they have other plans, which require the sleepers to stay asleep."

"Such as?"

"Your guess is as good as mine. We have no idea why any of them are asleep—especially as you don't seem to have retained anything consciously of the brain activity you manifested while asleep."

"Which implies, I suppose," Denise said, pensively, "that I wasn't so much thinking as having the contents of my mind scanned."

"Possibly. Personally, in spite of having had so much time to ponder the question, I simply don't know what to think. I don't like the idea, but I can hardly deny the possibility that the cosmic intelligences—or the intelligence contained in or constituting the rings of Saturn, at least—might have been trying to mine all our minds for information, trying to figure out exactly what we are. At least it doesn't seem to be doing us that much harm, if that really is what's happening. On the other hand, the AIs might simply be following their original directives in keeping the sleepers as healthy as possible while they're out for the count, and might have put them all into hibernation simply because they perceived a threat and didn't know how else to respond."

"Well," said Denise, "if I was being psychically probed, I wish I could be sure that I made a good impression; I'd hate to think that the examining angel had looked into my soul and found nothing but sin and weakness."

"As to that," said Chris Kemmering, "I'd be prepared to bet that my nine sleepers and the fourteen aboard Cronos are as flattering a sample of the human species as could plausibly be assembled: all highly intelligent, perfectly sane, and thoroughly virtuous. I have no reason to suspect that you might have let the side down. If we were to be judged and found wanting, at least it will have been on the basis of our best examples."

"I admire your confidence—and I'm grateful for it. But still, even if the Rings give us top marks for mere planetary intelligences devoid of Coincidence sensibility, it doesn't necessarily mean that they'll like us or that they'll want to return the favor by letting us know what's on their mind, or by furnishing us with a traveler's guide to the galactic arm. How many humans have ever been inclined to lend a helping hand to the microbes they examine down heir microscopes?"

"That's a false analogy, although Helen seems fond of it," said her interlocutor. "Your friend in the Highlands is probably wrong to think in terms of angels, whether as messengers, guardians or avengers, but if the inference is correct that they're reading our minds, or trying to find a means of doing that, they certainly can't see us as microbes. Marie might be over-optimistic in assuming that they feel benevolence toward us, in spite of what Zephaniah intuited about the future generations of Earth, but there's absolutely no reason why they would be hostile. The probability is that they'll wish us well, simply because there's no reason not to do so. They're not angels, in my opinion, but they're surely not demons either."

"Well, naturally, we'd like them to be scientists, in search of truth for its own sake . . . assuming that they don't already know all that there is to know, by virtue of having existed since a couple of seconds after the Big Bang and filling the universe with their distributed selves. That's because we want to see them in our image, though, just as Marie wants to find souls there whose existence can guarantee us some sort of immortal and rewarding afterlife."

"You're the scientist," Kemmering pointed out. "I'm just a military man . . . but for all that, I'd rather not find the ultimate captain or general out there. I'm only a pragmatic disciplinarian; idealistically, I'm an Anarchist."

Denise laughed, although she wasn't certain that it was a joke. "You don't have any orders for me, then, in your capacity as my captain?" she queried.

"Not at present. I could make a couple of suggestions, though."

"Go on."

"First of all, think hard before you let Helen put you in her machine, as she's doubtless avid to do."

"No problem—I'll take my time before I let my own curiosity get the upper hand. Secondly?"

"Secondly, go and get yourself something to eat down in the common room. To be perfectly honest, what passes for shipboard food isn't so very different from what the AI will have been shoving through your feeding tube for years, but at least it will be tastier, and you can swallow it at your own pace."

"The thought had occurred to me. Any more?"

"Yes. Thirdly, and most importantly, when you've had something to eat, go back to your cabin, sit on the floor next to your brother, and talk to him."

"Talk to him?"

"Yes. Maybe it's just superstition, but it's always been recommended that people talk to their loved ones while they're in comas, just in case they can hear, or the sound of a familiar voice can provoke a purely physical reaction. I'm not suggesting that you make any strenuous effort to wake him up, but simply to let him know, if he's capable of knowing anything, that you're there. Hold his hand, too."

"Did anyone come to talk to me and hold my hand while I was in hibernation?" Denise asked, sarcastically.

"As a matter of fact," said the Captain, "I did, regularly. So did Mireille, and even Helen."

Denise was taken by surprise, although it immediately occurred to her that she shouldn't have been. "Oh," she said. "In that case, I'm, sorry I don't remember. Duty, I suppose?"

"Not really, although I suppose you could argue that it was my duty. It wasn't Mireille's or Helen's though."

"And you've all done the same for Zeph?"

"Yes."

"And the other sleepers?"

"Sometimes. Mireille and I have, at least. Helen, not so much. We don't have a rota. We've tried other things, obviously, such as putting their VR hoods on—those still work, although the screens are dead—and playing them familiar and personal tapes. Thus far, obviously, nothing's woken them up . . . but that doesn't necessarily mean that it had no effect. If you talk to Zeph, you might not have any more luck pulling him out of it than Mireille has had, but it's not inconceivable that he might take some comfort from it—or that you might."

"Do you?"

"Sometimes."

"You're a strange man, Captain."

"Am I? I seem perfectly normal to myself—but then, I suppose we all do."

"Not all," said Denise, soberly. Seeing a note of surprise in his expression, she added: "Oh, I do, obviously—I was thinking of Zeph. Helen too, I suspect. You and I can't ever have been made to feel different the way that they always have. I doubt that either of them was ever allowed to feel *normal*. The best they could manage was to claim an alternative sanity."

"And rightly so," said the Captain. "That's all the more reason for you to talk to Zeph, given your unique connection."

"I will, and I'll hold his hand too—I'd better leave the magic kiss to Mireille, though . . ." She paused, her eyes searching the Captain's eyes. "My God," she murmured. "You did, didn't you? You played Prince Charming while I was the Sleeping Beauty?"

He shrugged his shoulders. "It works in fairy tales," he said.

"But not aboard starships."

"Not so far. But it seemed to be worth a try . . ."

"Well," she said, a trifle coldly, "thanks for making the effort."

"You're welcome," he said, with an equanimity to which she supposed, on due reflection, that he was perfectly entitled. He had, after all, been doing his duty.

Denise went back downstairs, all the way to the common room. Mireille was still there, but Helen was gone, presumably back to her lab.

Mireille showed Denise how to select and order food from the dispenser. "It's not what you'll have been used to in London," she said, "but you'll get used to it. I have, and I've lived in Paris."

"I'm told that it tastes better than the carefully calculated nutrition that I've been fed for the last three years, bypassing the tongue," Denise observed. "Not that I remember any of that. To me, London was only a couple of days away. You're the one who's had to put up with three years of tedium."

"It hasn't been that bad," the chemist assured her. "I've had practice, though, aboard Olympus Five. Tedious, yes . . . but there are worse things than tedium. All in all, I'm not so sure that the Auvergne would have been better, although the Puy-de-Dôme Enclave seems to be doing well, in spite of being constructed on and inside an extinct volcano."

"I'll try not to disrupt your equilibrium," Denise promised.

"As I already told you," said the Frenchwoman, "I hope you do. Indeed, I hope your awakening is only the first of many, and that things will soon be buzzing. There are worse things than tedium, but there are much better ones as well."

"Chris reckons that I ought to talk to my brother, and maybe hold his hand."

"You should," Mireille told her, without hesitation. "I've tried . . . I'd like to think that it might have helped, even though it didn't wake him up, but you might well achieve more than I did."

Denise hesitated for a moment over several possible sarcastic remarks, but in the end, she said. "Thanks for trying. I appreciate it."

The Frenchwoman must have been tensed in anticipation of the sarcasm, because she relaxed visibly.

"I hope you can get through," she said. "I really think you might. He and I have been close, in the past, but you're . . . well, you know all that. He used to talk about you a lot, on Olympus."

"I honestly don't know why," Denise admitted. "Until we started talking on-screen when the ship-to-Earth time lag became tolerable, I really thought that I hardly knew him. I talked about him a lot, I suppose, but having a brother on a long-haul space mission is a more inherently interesting conversational topic than having a sister who studies fossils at Imperial College."

"He felt a bond," Mireille said, "but I suppose that's not surprising, given his special sensibility. That's why I think you might be able to make a connection with him even while he's entranced. He won't wake up, I fear, until the AIs let him—or whatever's pulling the AIs' strings, if something is—but if he can hear you, and feel your touch, I really do think it might comfort him, more than I could."

"Even with a kiss?"

The Frenchwoman was not in the least embarrassed by that remark. "I doubt if he found it very stimulating," she said. "Have you ever tried kissing someone with a feeding-tube sticking down your throat?"

"Apparently, yes—but I don't remember it."

Mireille actually laughed at that. "Well, now you can try without," she said.

For a moment, Denise almost asked whether she meant with Chris or with her, but suddenly realized that she would doubtless be told, with perfect equanimity, that it was her choice. This was still a fragment of a mini-utopia.

"Chris says that you've been keeping a close eye on the atmospheric data from Earth," she said, retreating to safer ground.

"I've been trying. I'm not convinced of the accuracy of their measurements, or the extent to which one can generalize from readings taken in the vicinity of the Enclaves, which have some odd inconsistencies, but if you want a summary in one word, I'd have to say: *merde*. It's going to take a long time to become breathable again, if it ever does. I can't rule out the possibility of a runaway Venus Effect, as it migrates to a different and utterly hostile equilibrium."

"Yes, you can," said Denise.

"Because of the Dancing Rats? Well, okay . . . but the window Halleck opened is a long way in the future: tens of millions of years. A lot might have happened in the interim—not a full-scale Venus Effect, but it could still be dire, for hundreds of thousands of years. Yes, the descendants of the rats will surely pull through, but perhaps sorely tested."

"Chris seems a lot more optimistic."

"Chris always seems optimistic. He thinks it's his duty. I shouldn't complain, though. I've had relationships with pessimists, and optimists make better lovers, don't you agree?"

"I don't know," Denise replied. "Now that I come to think of it, I don't think I've ever had an intimate relationship with an optimist. They've been rare birds in London for quite some time."

"Probably in Paris too," said Mireille, "but a higher proportion felt obliged, or thought it politic, to pretend . . . and then there was Olympus. Pessimists were the rarity there."

"There was Zeph," said Denise, almost without thinking.

"Zephaniah? He was sweet—positively radiant."

Denise blinked. "I guess you brought out the inner optimist, then," she said. "I never met him, until . . . but you're right. When he got back, he'd changed."

"I wish I could claim the credit," Mireille said, "but I think it was a collective effect. He loved it, you know—the whole experience."

"So he told me," murmured Denise. "Oddly enough, I never quite believed him, until now. I thought he felt obliged to pretend . . ."

"No," said the Frenchwoman, "he's genuine. So's Chris, really, duty aside. In fact, the only pessimist aboard and active these last three years, has been me. I hope they don't . . ." She didn't finish the sentence.

"Well, now there's me," said Denise. "Although, I sometimes think I'm just a common-or-garden coward, and not a genuine pessimist at all. Let's hope someone else wakes up soon, so the optimists can outnumber us again, and help keep us back from the brink."

"I've survived three years," the Frenchwoman said. "Another five days won't be a challenge, especially as things have already begun to happen again. I really have no idea how this is going to unfold, but Zephaniah can't sleep forever, can he?"

Denise got the impression that the question wasn't rhetorical. She also thought that it was her duty not to be pessimistic. "No," she said, firmly, "he can't. If your kiss didn't wake him up, I doubt if my holding his hand will do the trick, but one way or another, I feel morally certain he'll come back for the rendezvous with the rings. And even if I don't have Marie MacLaughlin's faith that he can bring us news of Heaven, I feel it in my bones that the news isn't going to be bad."

XII

Denise did talk to Zeph, and she unsealed the pod in order that she could reach into it and take his limp right hand. At first, she didn't know what to say, so she began by simply giving him an account of what she had found when she woke up, and what her impressions were of what she had found. She spoke in a low voice—almost a whisper, even though she had closed the cabin door, and didn't suppose for a moment that any of her three active companions were listening in order to discover what she might say about them.

At first, she felt uncomfortable, because the situation was strange. She had never talked to an unconscious person before, and although she had had occasion when they were both children to try to console Zeph when he was hurt or upset, sometimes holding his hand, he had been awake then, and she had had a model to follow. She could still remember how her mother had talked to him when she was trying to calm him down—and to her too, on occasion—but the present situation was quite different. It wasn't consolation for physical and emotional woes that Zeph needed this time, but something else—perhaps moral support of a different kind, but at any rate, something she couldn't pin down, and something she didn't know how to provide.

"I don't know what to tell you, Zeph," she told him, apologetically, while he continued to lie placidly asleep, and she continued to extend her right arm through the unsealed flap of the pod in order to clutch his right hand in hers. "I don't know why the pod AI allowed me to wake up, or somehow received permission to wake me up. Perhaps it's so that I can do this, and try to nudge you back in the direction of consciousness, or perhaps it's so that Helen can use me as a guinea pig, as she's avid to do, because she's been idle far too long and is desperate to do something . . or perhaps there's no reason at all, and it was some glitch in the AI's functioning—but whatever the reason, I'm back, and I wanted you to know that, if you're capable of knowing anything at present, so I came to tell you, and I've told you, and I really don't know what to do next, because I don't understand what's happening, to the ship or to me. Nobody does, although I suppose we're each trying to work on it in our own way.

"To be perfectly honest, I feel very uncomfortable here, in the present company, even though they're all amicable, and even kind—including Helen, in spite of her occasional spikiness. They seem so very comfortable with one another, perfectly relaxed in the troilistic relationship they've been maintaining, apparently without much effort or strain, for three years, while I . . . well, I just feel embarrassed with all three of them. I haven't had the training, you see, or the practice, although Helen didn't seem to think that her practice had done her much good when she was trying to explain herself to me in that stupid armored car, and she seems to have adapted well enough, in spite of her quarreling with Chris over mission matters. The problem, obviously, is with me, but I don't know how to break through it.

"If you were here . . . but I really shouldn't be selfish. There are an infinite number of reasons why everyone wants you back, and the fact that you might be able to make me feel better about my personal hang-ups really doesn't figure very high on the scoreboard, especially by comparison with discovering the truth about life, the universe, and everything, including love. Compared with what Marie is already calling the Zephanian Revelation, mere brother-and-sister stuff doesn't seem very important at all . . . except that I'm still stuck in my stupid body, unable to travel to the end of time or the far side of space, and can't help being imprisoned by my own petty problems . . . which shouldn't even be problems at all, really, as they're so utterly trivial.

"Anyway, whatever brought me back, I really hope that you can come back too, and soon, because I feel that I really need you. I'm not entirely sure why I feel that, but I do. Do any of us really know why we have the feelings that just rise up to the surface of consciousness from the complex and murky depths of the unconscious? Does it have something to do with Coincidence sensibility, do you think? Perhaps such feelings, such impulses, such cravings, really do come from outside us, echoing from distant regions, because of things that are happening to the particles that composed us millions or billions of years ago . . . on Earth, mostly, I suppose, but perhaps before the Earth even formed, when the heavy elements composing it were blasted out of a supernova trillions of miles away . . . or even before that. And if the mysterious workings of Coincidence really can support some kind of distributed intelligence that extends over the entire universe, as well as a local one inhabiting the rings of Saturn, well, maybe some of our feelings come from much further afield than we've so far been prepared to imagine.

"Logically, I suppose, any echoes of Coincidence that our consciousness translates as feelings emerging from the unconscious must relate to associations formed in the relatively recent past: the Earthly past of thousands, or millions, of years, that is . . . but if the aggregation follows something akin to a Poisson distribution it must have an exceedingly long tail. After all, the particles making up the atoms composing us go back all the way to the mysterious second following the Big Bang, and if the associations formed then still persist, however weakly . . . and there's actually no reason to presume that such associations get weaker over time, or even over distance . . . then it must be the case, mustn't it, that our bodies, our minds, and our selves really do retain a connection to the entire universe, to the moment after creation, to the initial form of creation, to the initial mentality of creation. And because our bodies retain that connection, so do our minds, even though the conscious part of our minds has difficulty apprehending it, let alone comprehending it . . . because the only way that the unconscious part of our minds can feed anything into our conscious minds is via the fringes of rationality . . . not just the feelings that I'm trying in my inept way to explain but dreams, fancies and whims, illusions and hallucinations, the vagaries of free association . . ."

She stopped suddenly.

Where is this coming from? she thought.

And then she knew.

My God, she thought, then, *I'm telepathic . . . or at least telem-pathic*. But then she laughed. "But of course I am, stupid," she whispered, voicing her thoughts again so that Zeph could hear her, because she knew that it helped—that the support of en-coded sound was, in fact, necessary, even when the sounds were imaginary, produced silently inside the mind by people talking to themselves.

"For people," she went on, "language is vital, whether directly coded in speech or indirectly in writing. It's the instrument of the kind of thinking we do, the organizer of all the kind of sanity we have. It's an instrument of the senses, an instrument of touch. We think of it as something intangible, but it's not; it's merely the refined essence of tangibility. But the internal monologue isn't the whole of mind, by any means, or the whole of matter. We're not just subject to the fundamental forces that hold matter together and determine its transaction. We're subject to the Coincidence effects too, which aren't forces, although we don't have an alterna-tive term with which to describe them, any more than we have alternative terms for all the further effects and the side-effects of the phenomena of Coincidence. We don't even have a term for the thing itself except a borrowed term that forces us into endless confusions trying to distinguish the new concept of Coincidence from mere coincidence . . . except, of course, that there's prob-ably no such thing as *mere* coincidence, merely uncomprehended side-effects of Coincidence . . .

"So yes, I'm telempathic. My body is capable of perceiving effects of Coincidence that originate elsewhere and elsewhen, mostly close at hand—relatively—but also from anywhere and anywhen. But it's all, even at best, liminal, because it has no language of its own, and it's exceedingly difficult for us even to begin to make a language out of it. If it were just a matter of translation . . . but it isn't. It's something much harder than that, something that requires a particular talent, a particular frame of mind, a particular neuroarchitecture . . . a very particular alterna-tive insanity.

"You don't have an extra sense, Zeph, any more than Helen has an extra sense enabling her to perceive mathematics. What you have is a gift for . . . not translation, and not perception, but something that allows your mentality to find a handle on something of which everybody is subconsciously aware but hardly anyone can grasp. Just as Helen Arkheimer and Walter Halleck are able to grasp with consciousness a kind of math that is objectively logical, and sensible, and descriptive of the real, but which simply makes no sense to common-or-garden consciousness, you can wrap your mind around at least some of the effects of Coincidence that are happening within our constituent particles . . . within everyone's constituent particles . . . within every*thing*'s constituent particles.

"We can all hear—literally *hear*—echoes of Coincidence effects, but we can't make sense of them, and we think that's because they don't make sense, but what we really mean is that we can't *make sense* of them, no matter how hard we try. But we do try, Zeph—all of us, all the time. We may not try to make sense of the echoes in our dreams—and consciousness, as it grows and develops, rapidly develops the art of forgetfulness, which allows us, most of the time, literally to rid our minds of the traces of those echoes—but we try to make sense of our feelings, mostly without much success, because we're really not very good at it. Even so, we do try. We grapple constantly with the aspects of our mentality that don't seem to belong to us, trying to appropriate them, or at least trying to orientate ourselves in respect of them.

"If we could *make sense* out of those effects of Coincidence, or the echoes they produce in our consciousness, then there really is a great deal we might learn, isn't there? Because those echoes really do reflect something that extends in both time and space to their ultimate limits. It's not a matter of *getting in touch* with what Marie and her fellow members of the Renewed Church call God, because we already *are* in touch with It. It really is within us, and everywhere, always has been and always will be. The problem is that every time we try to make sense of that presence, that existence, we're ensnared by our preconceptions and our desires.

"We issue warnings to one another about the danger of raising idols and worshiping false gods, because we know that it's wrong, but we just can't help it, because there's no other way to approach the problem except by analogy. So we keep on smashing the old idols and sculpting better ones, and we call it progress, because it is, because every error smashed gets us that much closer to the truth . . . except that the *that much* in question isn't really very much at all, and the distance still separating us from a viable understanding, a productive understanding, is still vast. But it *is* progress. It *is* productive.

"Little by little, we're creeping up on the truth, on better ways of understanding. It's not easy, by any means, because the quest keeps taking us in unexpected and puzzling directions, but it *is* productive. Walter Halleck's new math, which seemed so utterly abstruse at first that it couldn't possibly have any practical application or value, laid the groundwork for actual technology, not just for the Sling but the machine for which Helen Arkheimer hasn't taken the trouble to borrow an existing analogy on to which she can stick a pretentious capital letter and a new meaning. The machines really do work—but most of the Sling operators weren't able to make much more use of them, if any, than they were able make of the innate capabilities of their own mentality. A machine is only a machine; to do its work it needs a skilled operator . . . and to work miracles, it needs an operator with talent, an operator with genius. And genius, as someone is rumored to have remarked once, needs perspiration as well as inspiration, and a great deal of the former to capitalize on a mere dash of the latter.

"So it's taken you time, hasn't it, to work through the flash of inspiration that Helen's machine gave you. It's taken you a long time, and fierce concentration. It really wasn't the rings that put you to sleep, was it, let alone the Cosmic Mind—not deliberately, at any rate. It was the AIs, following their programming, reacting to what they perceived as dangerous symptoms, in your brain and in the space around the ship. That's what happened to us, isn't it? The AIs were following their programming . . . not alien programming but the programming fed into them by their human designers. When the rings attempted to make contact with us . . . and I really do mean *make contact* . . . the physical side-effects were alarming. Aboard Cronos, which is actually within the body of the ring-entity, close to its heart, the effect was so alarming that the shipboard AIs put the whole crew into hibernation and shut down all of the ship's non-essential systems. In effect, they went into panic mode.

"With us, with the effect channeled through you, the reaction was less extreme; the AIs left an emergency crew awake . . . and they left scope for you to work, for you to labor in your dreams in order to get a grip on the reason the ring intelligences had for trying to get in touch with us. And not just you, because you aren't *just* you, are you? You're part of us, and that gestalt assists your talent in some way, which the rest of us don't understand, because we don't understand anything much, consciously, and which involves processes that I can't even remember experiencing . . . but the connection really does *help* you. Not just the connection to me, but to Mireille and Chris . . . and Helen too, or at least her talent for math. We've all been perspiring, haven't we, in our various ways and to our various degrees, although we haven't even been conscious of it, because we aren't conscious of our own telempathy.

"But now, we're almost there, aren't we? We're almost inside the ring-entity—perhaps already on the fringes of it, and the message *has* got across, at least in part, assuming that the sense you've made of it really is the right sense. You think you know what the ring-entity wants of us, and why. I get that now, just as you do. And you think you know what might happen next, what we might do next, if we have a mind to do it . . . even though I can't quite glimpse or grasp it yet. But I don't have to, do I? You can grasp it, and all you have left to do now is to wake up . . ."

"Nise?" said Zeph, then. "Is that you?" He hadn't yet opened his eyes.

"Yes," said Denise, in the grip of an enormous surge of re-lief, and gratitude, and love, and perhaps a few other feelings, to which she couldn't put a name, "it's me." She had no idea why she was surprised, given that she had known, somehow that he was about to wake up, and that it was inevitable, and vitally necessary, that he would.

"Where am I?" he asked. At least, that was what he tried to ask; his speech was slurred. He removed his right hand from Denise's grip in order to pull the feeding-tube out of his mouth and work his jaw and tongue a little.

In the meantime, Denise said: "In your pod, aboard Minerva."

"The starship?" His diction was gradually becoming clearer.

"Yes."

"That's right," he said, slowly, obviously still struggling a little in order to bring the memories back to consciousness. "Helen's machine . . . it was supposed to amplify my Coincidence sensibility, allow me to see . . . or at least to feel . . . it didn't work, then?"

His speech was clear now. The words made sense—except that they didn't, quite.

A cold shiver ran down Denise's spine. "What do you mean, *it didn't work?*"

"I mean that I blacked out . . . and here I am. Somebody must have carried me to the pod. How long have I been out? Why did I have that damn tube stuck down my throat."

Denise swallowed saliva, momentarily unable to get her own thoughts in order. Eventually, she said: "Can't you remember?"

"Remember what?" he countered, clearly having no idea that the remark, and its implication, was the next worst thing to a stab in the heart for his sister.

"Think hard, Zeph: you were dreaming, Can't you remember your dream?"

The light in the cabin was dim, as usual, and Zeph was in shadow; it wasn't easy to make out the expression on his features. He really did seem to be trying to do as he was bid. After a few seconds of intensive concentration, though, he said: "No, it's gone. Whatever dream I was having, it's gone the way of all dreams. Does it matter?"

There was an edge of anxiety in his voice; clearly he had some inkling that it did matter, but Denise knew that that might simply have come from his reading of the expression on her own unshadowed face—which, she suspected, must be distraught.

"You need to try, Zeph," she told him. "It's important."

Perhaps he did try, or perhaps he had already given up.

"Why?" he asked, curiously.

"Because I have reason to think that you might have been dreaming something important . . . something very important."

"I'm sorry," he said, blandly, without bothering to ask what reason she could possibly have for thinking such a strange thing.

Is it me who's dreaming? Denise thought. *Am I insane? Was it just a delusion that I was sharing his ideas, his thoughts . . . that all the things I was just thinking were his as well as mine, his rather than mine? Was I just rambling? Or was the feeling right, and we've just fallen victim to the hoary old joke about the man who dreamed that he'd discovered the secret of life, but then found when he woke up that he couldn't remember it anymore?*

Denise remembered, with a severe pang of discomfort, that almost the first thing she had been asked when she woke up was whether she had been dreaming, and that the only answer she'd been able to give was that she couldn't remember.

We're all telempathic, she thought. *But not only can't our infantile minds develop ways to enhance and exploit that alternative perception as they develop and mature, they automatically build defenses against it. They develop the ability to screen out most of the echoes, to banish them from consciousness, in order to stop them troubling it. We cultivate the art of forgetfulness, and we apply it, assiduously and reflexively, to our dreams. We simply can't help it . . .*

That, she knew, was her own thought, her own mental perspiration, whether or not the initial inspiration had come from elsewhere.

But I didn't extract enough inspiration, she thought. *I sensed that he knew the answer, but I didn't manage to sense what it was . . .*

"You haven't answered my question," Zeph said, mildly, interrupting the train of thought.

"What question?"

"How long have I been out?"

"Three years," she replied, with reflexive, unthinking honesty.

He started like a jack-in-the-box. "Three years!" He didn't accuse her of joking, though. He leaned forward, propping himself up on his elbow, and stared into her face.

"Sorry," she said. "Yes, that's why I look terrible. The others look even worse—they've been awake, poor sods."

"They?" Zeph queried.

"Chris, Mireille and Helen. Everybody else has been in hibernation mode."

"Except you?"

"Me too—I only got a few hours start on you. If I read your mind right, everyone else will probably wake up now—not just you, Alessandro, Mellita, Victor and the rest but the Cronos crew too. We've arrived, you see."

He didn't bother to ask where they had arrived. He had worked that out. He focused on a different matter: "What do you mean, *if you read my mind right?*"

"I thought you and I had a moment," she told him. "I was talking to you, because Chris and Mireille suggested that it might be a good idea, and I was rambling, and I found myself . . . well, this is going to sound absurd now, perhaps because it is, but I found myself saying things that didn't seem to be entirely mine, as if they were coming from outside—specifically, from you. Reading is the wrong word for the mental connection, although one of the things I was rhapsodizing about was that all the words are wrong, because we don't have any right ones, but at any rate, I had the enormously strong impression that I was intuiting your thoughts . . . the thoughts you were having in your dream, that is . . . the ones that you now think you've forgotten . . . I really do sound crazy, don't I?"

Zeph didn't get a chance to answer that, because the door opened and Mireille stuck her head through the slit. She took in the situation at a glance, and turned round to say to someone else: "Yes, Zephaniah too. They're all back!"

For a moment, she almost withdrew, but then changed her mind and stepped into the cabin. "They're all back," she repeated.

"Yes," said Denise, dully. "I had an idea that they might be."

Before Mireille had a chance to react to that remark, she was shoved rudely forward, stumbling over Denise's seated body, as Helen Arkheimer barged into the narrow space between the pods.

"Thank God!" said the mathematician.

Denise had struggled to her feet, and she helped Mireille back to hers.

"I wouldn't thank the divinity yet, dear," said Denise, grimly. "He doesn't remember anything."

She had obviously anticipated the question correctly. Helen Arkheimer looked at her in frank disbelief. "What, *nothing?*" she said.

"Nothing," Denise confirmed.

"All that furious mental activity, and he doesn't remember *anything?* He wasn't even in a real coma. It was bad enough that you . . . but . . ." Words failed her.

Zeph was looking at everyone as if they were all mad. "Apparently," he murmured, "I've disappointed you all. How, exactly?"

"It's not your fault, Zeph," Mireille put in, before Denise could formulate an answer of her own. "We had . . . unrealistic expectations. Has Denise told you how long you were asleep?"

"Three years," said Zeph, as if he still couldn't believe it.

"Yes. Apparently, it was the extraterrestrial intelligences who . . ."

"No," Denise interjected, "it wasn't. It was a defensive reaction on the part of the AIs. The ring intelligences were the indirect cause, but it wasn't deliberate. The ring intelligences and Zeph have been doing some pretty intensive intellectual labor, and the ring things seem to have figured out how to back off sufficiently to let the AIs relax and call off the emergency—which is good news, I think, because it means that the ring intelligences have probably figured out other things as well, which they aren't in any danger of forgetting. Even if Zeph can't tell us what they want from us, they might be able to figure out another way of telling us."

Helen and Mireille were both looking at her in amazement, but neither of them seemed to think that she was mad.

"What makes you think that?" Helen asked her.

"I think Zeph told me, before he woke up. If he'd only stayed asleep a little longer, I think he might have told me what it is the ring intelligences want of us, given that they do seem to want something, but . . . it was probably my fault. I was praying so hard that he would wake up . . . who was it who said that you have to be careful what you pray for, in case your prayers are granted?"

Helen and Mireille exchanged a long, significant glance.

"You knew!" Denise guessed. "You've been talking to him too, and holding his bloody hand, and picking up his thoughts. You all knew that before you sent me in here!"

"Calm down, dear," said Helen. "We didn't *know* anything. Mireille thought that his close presence might be having an in-fluence on her, and we talked about it. She thought it was an illusion, but I wasn't so sure, even though I didn't feel it myself. When we compared notes with Chris . . . well, I thought there was a possibility, but I couldn't convince either of them. We all thought, though, that if something really was happening, then you would surely feel it much more strongly, so yes, we were curi-ous to know what you'd have to say when you came out again . . . except that you didn't come out again, and now . . . how much more did you pick up?"

"I honestly don't know," Denise replied, trying to do as she was asked and calm down. "I don't know how much was the overflow of Zeph's dream and how much was my own conjecture . . . my own mental manufacture . . . but I'm pretty sure that he really did think that he's worked out the truth about the ring intelligences' motives for trying to make contact. In a sense, that's why he woke up . . . not realizing, while he was in his dream, that when he did wake up, he'd lose the information he'd been looking for."

"But you got enough to work it out?" Helen queried. "You might not have got the Q.E.D., but you got enough of the working out for us to be able to complete the argument?"

"I wish I had," said Denise, "but I don't think so."

"But you have help now—not just me, but Zephaniah, Mireille and Chris. Zephaniah might not be able to remember—yet—but if we put our heads together, we can . . ." She stopped dead. A thought had obviously occurred to her.

With or without the aid of telempathy, Denise guessed what it was. She didn't know whether or not to be terrified.

"He's only just woken up," she complained, letting a little of the terror leak.

"We don't have time to waste," Helen countered.

"What are you talking about?" asked Mireille, whose ability to jump to conclusions was evidently lagging a little bit behind.

"She wants to put him back in her machine," Denise told her. "She wants to put him back in contact with the ring intelligences, right away, in the hope that the contact won't overwhelm him second time around . . . that whatever he and the ring intelligences concluded in his dream, they'll now be able to communicate while he's conscious. But if all that the ring intelligences succeed in doing is triggering the AIs' defense mechanisms again, we could be back to square one."

"Great minds think alike, dear," said Helen. "But with your consent . . . your informed consent, naturally . . . there's an extra measure of our own that might boost our chances. I was thinking of it anyway . . . in fact, it's always been on my agenda of possibilities."

Again, with or without external aid, Denise had no difficulty in jumping to the conclusion. "You want to wire us both up," she said. "You want to amplify our Coincidence perception simultaneously."

"It has a certain arithmetical propriety," the mathematician pointed up. "Even conventional wisdom has always suggested that two heads are better than one. I know you're not twins, but

". . . in a metaphorical sense, I suspect that you are. At the very least, again in a metaphorical sense, you can hold his hand. He really does draw strength from you, Denise . . . more than Mireille could provide."

"You really are a crazy bitch, you know," Denise observed.

Helen Arkheimer actually seemed surprised as well as offended. "No I'm not, dear," she said. "Alternative sanities, remember."

"Really? You were already thinking about it, you said. Which means, I assume, that you weren't just thinking of hooking me up to your machine, but thinking of hooking Mireille up in parallel, even though we're not twins, even in a metaphorical sense, and have never even slept together."

Once again, the mathematician's innate waspishness burst through her customary self control in response to momentary annoyance. "Well, dear," she said, "*that* could have been arranged."

"Why bother?" Denise snapped back. "You could have told me which lever to pull, and the two of you could have hooked yourselves up."

"I had considered all the options, obviously," Helen retorted, "and revised the list continually as better ones came along. But now we have Zeph, and you, the others can't really compete, can they?"

"I don't suppose," Zeph put in, "there's any possibility that I'm still dreaming?"

"Just get out, will you," Denise said to the mathematician. "You too, Mireille. Sorry if I'm being rude, but I'd like a few minutes alone with my brother, if that's okay. We hadn't really caught up before the two of you barged in. You'll get your turn, but for now, it's not a request. Get out."

Helen Arkheimer shrugged, nodded, and stepped back through the slit. Denise made room so that Mireille could follow her. She sealed the door again, but if there was any way to lock it, she didn't know how.

XIII

Denise sat down on the floor again so that her head was on much the same level as Zeph's.

"Sorry about that," she said. "Things are a little bit crazy at the moment. Helen and Mireille will have plenty to do bringing the others up to speed. Chris is probably overwhelmed already, making contact with Cronos and taking a full inventory of his crew. There's no reason for anyone to disturb us for a while. I'm glad you're back, and I'm not going to regret having prayed for you to wake up."

"Actually," he said, "one of the most recent memories I still have is praying that you'd wake up from the artificial coma that the pod AI had put you into after lift off. You must have blacked out under the acceleration. I thought the AI was being over-protective, just as it was the first time. I gather that it seems to have become a general problem."

"And how," said Denise. "That's the trouble with continually updating your systems—new bugs always crop up. Except that it's not really a bug; you can't really hold it against the AIs if they err on the safe side rather than taking risks. They've been trained to consider human life precious . . . and now there's so little of it left, it surely is."

Having removed the drip from his arm, Zeph was going through a disciplined routine of physical self-investigation, stretching his limbs and testing his muscles. It was obviously a routine he's followed before, and into which he had slipped with automatic ease. Not that he'd had a chance to forget his training, during his brief spell on Earth, which must now seem like a mere intermission, a brief holiday from real life. Unlike her, he probably felt that he was home again.

"How bad are things on Earth?" he asked.

"Bad. But we already knew that they would be. We already knew that the rats would make it through but that, ultimately, we wouldn't. The starship can't help with that, of course, even if contingency plans have been made for children to be born aboard, and even if the ring intelligences can make use of their Coincidental contacts to point us in the direction of a world that could support human life. There aren't enough of us."

"Really? Wasn't there a time in the past when the human population was reduced to a mere handful of individuals?"

"No—that's a myth. The monogenetic theory of the single Adam or Eve emerging in the midst of a population of ape-men is a myth too. The recent paleontological evidence and genomic analyses give us a rich assortment of ancestors of overlapping species, always numbered in the hundreds of thousands, all the way back to the lemuroids and beyond."

"But there must be hundreds of thousands of people, at least, in the enclaves. If they can pull through until increasing photosynthesis can begin to replenish the atmospheric oxygen . . ."

"But they can't. Not without the active support and aid of the rats. And once the rats have the evolutionary bit in their teeth . . . well, I can't foresee the future, but I don't think they'll even have to commit genocide. I think we'll simply die out, quietly. In fact, we already are, for lack of reproductive effort, of which Mireille and I are only two examples among a host. Although the eugenicists can let the breeding stock into the enclaves, overtly or surreptitiously, they can't make them procreate if they decide otherwise."

"I see," said Zeph. After a momentary pause, he added: "Do you really think that I dreamed an answer to the question of what the intelligences contained in the rings of Saturn want of us? A correct answer?"

"I'm absolutely sure that you dreamed an answer, although that certainty might conceivably be based purely in my own insanity. As to whether it was correct . . . your guess is as good as mine. Probably better."

"But I've definitely been dreaming for three entire years, even though I can't remember anything?"

"Definitely. If only AIs could read minds as well as detect neuronal activity . . . but they can't. Human minds can't be *read*, by machines, alien intelligences or one another. Any meaningful communication established has to be done a different way."

Zeph nodded. "Figuring out signals that I could exchange with the Dancing Rats was hard enough," he observed, "and I could see them, after a fashion. Even then, the AIs did better than I did, in recording visual and digital data."

"But without your insight," Denise reminded him, "what the AIs recorded would probably have remained opaque and indecipherable. And even if the formulae the rats send back had been decoded, we wouldn't have been able to estimate their significance without the context you provided."

"And that's the square one we're back to, isn't it?" Zeph said. "If I picked up the correct inferences from your slightly contentious dialogue, Helen believes that I'm the only person that has a realistic chance of providing the right context for whatever the ring intelligences can send us through the medium of her amplifier. She wants me for exactly the same reason that Walter Halleck wanted me for the final seventh generation shot . . . except that she seems to want you too. I'm not sure you should do that, Nise—not right away, at any rate. Obviously, I'll have to let her hook me up again, the sooner the better, otherwise everyone aboard will just be twiddling their thumbs waiting for something to happen, but there's no need for you to hook up with me, at least the first time. Let's see what happens to me first."

"The AIs would probably agree with you," Denise observed. "Indeed, they've already set an example by allowing me to wake up first, to make sure that worked out, before they woke up the rest of the sleepers. They've been programmed always to err on the side of caution. So has Chris Kemmering, I think. Helen Arkheimer clearly hasn't . . . not that we'll be putting the matter to a vote. This isn't a democracy. It's my decision."

"The way you say that," Zeph observed, "suggests to me that you're not thinking of saying no."

"You never used to know me so well," said Denise.

"That was then; this is now."

"Fair enough. You probably know why, then."

He looked her in the eyes. "You want to go with me," he said. "That's why you're here, after all. You want to be with me, all the way. You've never forgiven me for signing on to Olympus Five and leaving you behind, even though we hardly ever spent time together even while I was working with Walter, hardly a stone's throw away from Imperial. You always felt connected . . . until I left Earth. Now, you're determined to keep the connection on a tighter rein. If you hadn't been in a precautionary coma after suffering the shock of lift off, you'd have asked Helen to hook you up to the machine with me the first time. And if she'd been capable of patience, she'd probably have waited for you to come out of the coma before hooking me up . . . which you would have done, if the contact I made—or to be strictly accurate, the contact the ring intelligences made with me—hadn't thrown the AIs into a panic."

While he was speaking, Zeph had detached himself from the remaining medical equipment. He stepped out of the pod, stark naked. Denise knew that the unselfconsciousness of the action was not because she was his sister, but because he was aboard a spaceship again, where quasi-utopian norms and conventions applied. He slipped on a light uniform, having rummaged round in the pod's lockers.

And he's right, Denise thought, *except for one small supplementary point. He's ready and willing to lie down in Arkheimer's machine again at a moment's notice, even though the first run put him in a three-year coma from which he's only just woken up, because he's back in a familiar environment, where special disciplines apply. And I'm ready and willing for precisely the opposite reason: because all this is utterly alien to me, and I'm a fish out of water, and I don't have anything to which to cling that might make me hesitate.*

"I feel light," Zeph observed, as he carried out a new series of gymnastic exercises in a standing position, while Denise remained seated on the floor, tucking up her knees to give him space.

"We're decelerating with less force than that required to simulate one-gee," Denise explained. "You'll feel even lighter soon, and then we'll begin to experience tilts as the lateral jets begin to maneuver us into an interception trajectory with Cronos."

343

"That's okay," Zeph said, "I've done that before, in the vicinity of Jupiter. It's odd, but you get used to it."

"So I'm told. Chris had planned to get you to operate a surrogate to explore Cronos, if she were still playing derelict, and that would probably have started a fight with Helen over who got to exploit you most immediately, but if the Cronos crew are all awake again, that won't be necessary . . . which will give Helen free rein."

"The Cronos crew presumably have little or no idea what happened to them?" Zeph queried.

"I don't know. They might not even have known before the AIs put them out, though, that Earth had been hit by catastrophe. If so, it's probably shaken them up to discover what they'll find when they get home. There's probably some confusion over there."

"I doubt it," Zeph said. "Shipboard discipline will keep their upper lips stubbornly stiff. Not that that will alter the situation. I suppose things won't get much better on Earth during the five or six years the journey will take them?"

"Mireille says not. She's the expert."

"And in the thirty or forty years that it will take us to make a minimal round trip to another star?"

"Again, she says not."

Zeph nodded, as if it merely confirmed what he had already assumed. Denise had to admire the way that he was limbering up with such methodical efficiency. She wondered whether the disciplined crew of the Cronos were going through similar routines, in unison, already in the grip of "shipboard discipline" as soon as they had woken up.

I just staggered around, she thought. *Fish out of water.*

"I need a drink," Zeph said, as if it were simply the next step in the sequence of his readaptation to upright life. Denise knew that he meant water. He was a seasoned astronaut; he knew that there was no wine aboard, let alone Cognac. He had never had the merest shadow of an "alcohol problem."

"Do you feel up to going down the ladder, or shall I fetch you something?"

"Actually," he said, "my legs feel surprisingly fit, considering that I've been in a coma for three years."

"It's the AIs," she told him. "They have some very clever nano-tech. No muscle wastage; you're practically as good as new. I had to go gingerly, until my mind and my semicircular canals got used to the unusual lightness, but you're an experienced space-man, so you probably won't have any difficulty at all. I could do with a hug, though, before we go out to face the crowd."

There had been a time when Zeph would have hesitated, but not any more. They hugged—and Denise realized as they did, that she really had needed it, that in an odd, and perhaps implausible way, it brought her back into her element, into her own world.

She turned to the door then, and opened it.

The space between the cabins seemed crowded, although there were only four people there, including Helen Arkheimer and Mireille, who were obviously waiting for Zeph, Helen with the more obvious urgency. Birstan and Savina were with them, but they seemed a trifle disorientated, as if, in spite of the exercise program they had presumably put themselves through, they had not quite adjusted well enough yet to wakefulness and their altered weight to descend the ladder into the common space below, where the rest of the awakened crew seemed to have gathered.

Denise knew as soon as she took a step toward the ladder that she wasn't going to get there uninterrupted, but Helen Arkheimer's rapid move to cut off Zeph's path was itself interrupted as Chris Kemmering stuck his head through the hatchway leading to the upper deck.

"Zephaniah," he said, in his finest voice of command, "would you mind stepping up here, please? I need to talk to you."

Presumably, Denise thought, Zeph still needed a drink, but he raised no protest.

Helen Arkheimer did, but she only got as far as "I need . . ." Before the Captain snapped: "Debriefing first, Helen. There's a protocol."

Doubtless there was a protocol, but Denise had no doubt, either, that it was a protocol for which Helen didn't give a damn.

The merest glance, however, must have told the mathematician that Zeph had no intention of snubbing the captain in her favor. It was probably her imagination, but Denise thought that she could actually hear Helen Arkheimer's teeth clenching, as she turned abruptly, and disappeared into the cabin that had been converted into her laboratory, probably in search of some practical application for her restless mind and hands.

Denise cleared a path to the ladder for Zeph by means of a suggestive gesture, to which Mireille responded perfectly meekly, and as soon as his slightly tentative feet reached the level of her head, she followed him.

Chris Kemmering made no move to shut her out, but once she was in his eyrie he sealed the hatch with a soft but peremptory click.

The Captain ushered them to the chairs. Then he handed Zeph a tube of liquid that he had ready and waiting.

"Sorry I couldn't be there when you woke up, Zephaniah," he said. "The AIs did consent to alert me to the fact, but as they were busy with so much else, there was something of a temporary information overload. Then Cronos signaled, and I had to give Captain Fulsom my complete attention for a while. Now that things have begun to settle down a little . . . how are you feeling?"

"Fine, Captain," said Zeph. "Fit and well and reporting for duty."

"Much obliged," said the Captain. "Unfortunately, I don't have any orders to give you, for the moment. I was rather hoping that you might provide some assistance, when you woke up, as to what orders it might be reasonable to give everyone, once the regulation checks are completed. Unless you've remembered something further since Mireille made her report, it appears not."

"I'm sorry," said Zeph. "Have you, by any chance, received any useful information from Cronos . . . or our own crew?"

"About any dreams their crew or our hibernators might have had while in hibernation mode? When I raised the question their

Captain reacted much as my own people did, although he had slightly less inhibition about wondering visibly if I were mad. He's promised to take a census and get back to me, but I'm not holding out much hope. None of our sleepers remember any more than you did . . . which leaves Denise."

He looked at her enquiringly, but she didn't have any advice ready to offer him. She hadn't processed the puzzling features of her monologue herself yet, but she was fairly certain that it didn't offer any basis for strategic action, or any other substance for possible orders of command.

"You told Captain . . . Fulsom about the situation on Earth?" Denise queried, to parry the expectation.

"Of course. Mireille has transmitted all her data for independent checking, but he's respectful of her judgment. He's a military man, like me—perhaps with a trifle less charisma, but with the same sense of discipline . . . or lack of imagination, as Helen might put it. He sees no reason in the news from Earth to change his interrupted mission plan, in the short term. He's going to pick up at the exact point that the AI emergency measures obliged him to interrupt it. He'll employ drones to explore the Saturnian atmosphere and some of the smaller satellites, and eventually carry out a landing on Titan with a view to longer exploration. He'll doubtless pay a little more curious attention to the data regarding the rings whose collection was on his agenda anyway, but he isn't going to attempt any further investigation until he's completed his schedule. Once he's completed the Titan program, he says, he'll consider his options."

"Options?" asked Zeph.

"His mission plan did take aboard the possibility of the impracticability of a return to Earth. Cronos could remain on Titan for decades, if necessary, and still have the capability to make a return journey. It's damnably cold there, obviously, but there's a plentiful supply of organics to replenish the life-support systems and internal ecology. When he enquired about my plans, I told him that I have certain investigations to carry out in the vicinity, which won't overlap with his, and that if nothing materializes therein to change my mind, I'll continue with my original mission plan and head for Proxima Centauri."

"And will you?" asked Denise.

"Of course. Helen Arkheimer might not like it, but I still have the power of decision, and that's what I'll do. However unpromising Proxima b might seem, it'll be warmer there than on Titan. In the unlikely event the red dwarf's system is utterly devoid of organics, we won't be able to replenish our own elementary supplies, but we should get back easily enough, barring accidents."

"And then return to Earth?" Zeph put in.

"However bad things are there, it will still be more hospitable than Titan, or, in all likelihood, Proxima b. But that's just the fallback position. If you can point me at a different destination, and a different spectrum of possibilities . . . well, I trust you. It might be grasping at straws, but we're close enough to drowning for straws to start looking good. You don't have to match Helen's breakneck pace, though, if you'd rather take things more gently. We have time in hand."

Zeph was content to nod, but Denise judged from his slight frown that there was something in what the Captain had said with which he wasn't entirely sure that he could agree.

"Anyway," Kemmering added, when he was sure that Zeph wasn't going to make a more elaborate response, "for the moment, the AIs are still following the same course that they'd plotted to rendezvous with Cronos in the vicinity of the C-ring. I've seen that flight plan, at last, and there doesn't seem to be reason to change it for the time being, even though Cronos no longer needs our help . . . unless you know of some reason why it might be better to steer clear of the rings?"

"No," said Zeph. "Probably better not to, in fact, if we're going to make another attempt imminently to contact the ring intelligences . . . or any other intelligences . . . via Helen's machine."

"Are you actually certain that there are any ring intelligences? Helen's given me the benefit of her theories, but I can't say that I'm totally convinced."

"I am," Denise put in, quietly.

"I can't honestly say that I'm convinced by Mireille's hypothesis that she picked up echoes of Zeph's dream, either," the Captain added, "although I might take it more seriously coming from you. The question is, are you sure that anything you might have thought you picked up was real, and not a figment of your imagination?"

"Not absolutely," Denise confessed. "Presumably you have a tape of what I said, though. What do you think?"

"In fact," said the Captain, "I don't, although I wouldn't have had time to look at it if I had. The systems that the AIs considered non-essential didn't come back to full capacity in time to record your conversation. But I'll take your 'not absolutely' to mean that there's still a margin of doubt."

"Fine," said Denise. "Hopefully, we'll be able to settle it soon enough."

"When Zeph hooks up to the machine again?"

"When we both hook up to the machine again."

Kemmering frowned. "Is that really wise?" he asked

"I don't know," Denise replied. "But I do think it's necessary, even if it's reckless. Recklessness got me this far, and I told you just a couple of days ago—from my point of view, at least—that I intend to be with Zeph all the way, no matter where it takes me."

"And if you both get kicked back into a coma along with the rest of the crew—perhaps including me this time?"

Denise glanced at Zeph, looking for support.

"It's a risk," Zeph conceded. "Not even a calculated risk, I fear. But now you're forewarned, surely you can instruct the AIs not to do that. You have control again, and you presumably have some way of amending or blocking the oversensitive element in their emergency protocols."

"Presumably," the Captain agreed. "I'll have to consult the manuals—it'll be a matter of 'AI, heal thyself,' as it were, but yes, it must be possible, and practicable. Have you considered the possibility that if I can instruct the AIs not to evoke the emergency protocol next time, that might leave you—and Denise—vulnerable to the effects from which the AIs were trying to protect you when they put you to sleep three years ago?"

"It's a risk," Zeph repeated, "but it's what I'm here for. You have your mission specifications; I have mine. I have no intention of giving up because of an initial hitch. You understand that, I'm sure."

"And Denise?"

"It's her decision . . . which she appears to have made. Unless, of course, as Captain, you're going to order her to stand down."

"No, of course not," said Chris Kemmering—but his gaze switched to examine Denise with such care that she felt vaguely uncomfortable.

She felt obliged to say something, so she said: "As Zeph says, it's a risk. I don't trust Helen to weigh it up accurately any more than you do, but if I can trust the leakage from Zeph's dream that I picked up while I was talking to him—and I think I can, even though I can't be entirely sure—then there might be a good deal to gain, and in our present situation, I really don't see that I, or Zeph, or you, have anything much to lose. And there isn't just us to think about, is there?"

"What do you mean?" the Captain asked.

"If I'm right about what I picked up, or conjectured, or fantasized, the ring intelligence, or intelligences, has something at stake too. It wasn't Zeph's attempt to contact the aliens that caused the problems, any more than it was anything the Cronos crew did that caused their shutdown. It was the alien's spontaneous attempts to contact us, which it did because it had a motive, because it wants something from us."

"What can it, or they, possibly want from us?"

"I don't know. That's what we need to find out, if we can. We need to find out more about its nature before we can even make a guess . . . and before we can calculate exactly, if we can do something for the aliens, what they can do for us in return."

That was obviously further than the Captain's own speculations had so far taken him. He frowned. While he was frowning, his screen lit up and Helen Arkheimer's image appeared. "Permission to come up, Captain?" she asked, with only a slight hint of sarcasm in her voice.

Kemmering smiled wryly. He glanced at Zeph, but Zeph simply shrugged his shoulders. He didn't bother to consult Denise. "Granted," he said.

XIV

Helen Arkheimer was through the hatch within five seconds.

"The equipment's all set," she said, the arc of her glance taking in all three of them, with a hint of challenge. "Ready when you are."

Denise couldn't tell whether the Captain was really taken aback, or just putting on a show of surprise. "Now?" he objected. "Poor Zeph's only been awake for a couple of hours. He hasn't even had a meal yet."

"Time," said the mathematician, more than a trifle truculently, "may be of the essence. The AIs will have kept his nutritional levels topped up, he hardly knows the other members of the crew, and Denise even less so, so they have little or no need to make a fuss about saying hello or goodbye . . . and if they want to get laid beforehand, Mireille's standing by, and I'm sure you can take care of Denise, so what's the point in hanging around?"

Denise was uncomfortably aware of her blush, but nobody was looking at her. Helen Arkheimer was trying to stare the Captain down, and everyone else was looking at the mathematician, mildly surprised by her aggressive manner.

"Are you really in that much of a hurry?" the Captain asked.

"Yes," she replied. "Aren't you? How much longer do you want to linger in uncertainty, when we have a chance of getting answers? You're obviously no mathematician."

Denise felt certain that Chris Kemmering wanted to retort: "And you're obviously no Captain," but he was too good a Captain to allow himself to be carried away.

"I don't see any harm in waiting a little while longer," he said. "Zeph has a lot of messages piled up, and he'll surely want to take a look at some of them, and perhaps answer a few."

"I've read almost all of them, including the ones from Walter Halleck and that stupid chaplain," Helen Arkheimer informed Zeph, loftily. "Believe me, it isn't worth the trouble."

"Chaplain?" said Zeph, genuinely taken by surprise. "You mean Marie?"

"That's right," Denise put in, swiftly. "She got a belated berth in the Highlands Enclave. She seems to have become an important, if somewhat controversial, figure in the Renewed Church."

"Why?" asked Helen, having long thrown all diplomacy to the winds. "Have you got a soft spot for her?"

"I suppose I have, in a way," Zeph replied, pensively. "For purely accidental reasons, she played a considerable part in what turned out to be my last few days on Earth. She's practically the only human being, apart from Denise, Chris, Walter and a couple of Walter's techs, with whom I made human contact in that strange interval."

"Well, it's not a love letter," Helen snapped. "It's a sermon and a prayer, asking you to look out for evidence that we have immortal souls, and begging you to tip her off first if you find any. As for Halleck's missives, they're mostly catalogues of complaints about how badly he's being treated in Snowdonia, considering that he's the most important man on Earth. He sends me longer ones, and more of them, with hardly a word about the math we're supposed to be working on together. The man's a paranoid egomaniac."

The words "pot" and "kettle" sprang to Denise's mind, but she didn't voice them. Nor did she remark on the fact that the mathematician had previously waxed lyrical about Halleck's intellectual greatness.

"You've read all my mail, then?" Zeph queried mildly.

"Everything that looked as if it might be important and might require attention."

"It's perhaps as well that there weren't any love letters, then," Zeph observed.

"Oh, I didn't say there weren't *any*—just that the one from the ex-college chaplain wasn't one of them. Mind you, you should see the Captain's mailbox . . ."

"Which you accessed why, exactly?" Chris Kemmering asked, although he seemed more amused than annoyed.

"Are you saying you haven't read mine?" she retorted.

"I didn't read your love letters, Helen," said the Captain, with a slight smile that informed Denise that there hadn't been any to read.

"This is a waste of time," said the mathematician. "Zephaniah can have all the time he thinks he needs, I suppose. How long will that be, do you think, Zephaniah, bearing in mind that . . . ?"

"Time might be of the essence," Zeph finished for her. "I get that. What do you think, Denise?"

"I haven't got many messages piled up," Denise replied, "and I've already read Marie's little polemic—the copy addressed to me, that is; I haven't touched your picmail. So it's up to you. Say the word, and I'll be there."

Zeph glanced at a time-display in the corner of the screen in front of him. "Give me six hours," he said.

"Six hours!"

Considering that she had been waiting for three years for Zeph to wake up, Denise thought, Helen Arkheimer's sense of urgency seemed a trifle overdone.

"My mail isn't the only thing I want to look at," Zeph replied.

"The screen in your pod should be working now, and the VR hood too," the Captain put in, "or you can use the equipment here if you prefer. If you find anything in your mail or in the news from Earth that causes you to ask for an extension to your six hours, I'm sure that Dr. Arkheimer will be patient."

"Aren't we supposed to be on first name terms, Captain, according to *protocol?*" the mathematician riposted.

"Of course, Helen—my apologies."

Helen Arkheimer's parting shot, as she disappeared through the hatch again, was: "I'll tell Mireille to keep standing by, then."

When the hatch had clicked shut, Denise said: "What on Earth's got into her?"

"Frayed nerves, I fear," said the Captain. "These last three years have been . . . well, she had the requisite physical training, but she would never have passed the psychological scrutiny required to get aboard Olympus Five or any other long-haul mission. I really have done my best, but . . . she doesn't take contradiction well.

When her mathematical mind reaches a conclusion, she considers it something established and written in stone, even if it's just some petty item. She thinks that Mireille and I *gang up* on her, although, in truth, Mireille's been a real saint in dealing with her. If there'd been more of us awake to reduce the tension . . . but there weren't. Don't let it bother you."

"As a matter of interest," Zeph put in, "how did I pass the psychological scrutiny required to get aboard Olympus Five?"

"Technically," said Kemmering, "you didn't—but I swore to the panel that you wouldn't pose any problems, for yourself or anyone else, and I was right. Arkheimer and I were on the same side then, because she was the one who wanted you aboard."

"Why?" asked Zeph.

"Why what?"

"Why did you swear that I wouldn't pose any problems, if I hadn't passed the test."

"Because I had confidence in the logic of the situation. I only met you briefly, I know, but I knew you weren't going to be any trouble to anyone else, and I was pretty sure that among the thirteen of us, we could find a few people capable of making a connection. Then again, you were a top-flight telepresence operator, and the only chance we seemed to have of making any kind of contact with the cloud-whales. If ever we were going to bend the rules a little, you were a prime candidate."

"So, if you'd stuck to the rules, I wouldn't be here now?"

"If I'd stuck to the rules, *none* of us would be here now. Believe me, Zeph, I don't regret it." His gaze flickered briefly to Denise—not, she assumed, because he thought that she might regret it, but because he felt a trifle guilty about permitting her to indulge her recklessness, in spite of the fact that his orders had given him no choice.

"Don't feel guilty on my account," she told him. "In six hours' time I might be doing the most worthwhile thing I could ever have done in my pitiful end-of-days life. I wouldn't have missed it for the world . . . not that the world's worth much at present, of course."

"Do you mind, Captain, if I take advantage of your offer to use this screen here to read my messages?" Zeph asked. "I think I find the sitting position more comfortable than the horizontal one, at present. My body seems to be aware of the fact that I've been lying down for three years, even though my memory isn't."

"As long as you don't mind company. I have work to do here."

"Not at all. You'll stay too, Nise?"

"I'll come back," Denise said. "I just have to go down to my pod for a few minutes to use the bathroom."

Zeph was already pecking his keyboard.

When Denise had finished in the pod she went down to the common room, which was crowded with awakened crew members—but Helen Arkheimer was not among them. Denise had hardly finished the visual scan that assured her of that fact when Mireille Angevot materialized by her side.

"Helen's not here," she said, obviously having deduced the objective of the scan. "I hear she threw a tantrum upstairs. Don't hold it against her too much—she has difficulty with crowds, all the more so after three years *à trois* . . . and sometimes she seemed to think that three was too much of a crowd. The sudden influx caught her on the wrong foot. She'll be fine. Alessandro's taken her to bed."

Denise was startled by that. "Oh," was all she could manage by way of an embarrassed response.

"Sorry," said the Frenchwoman. "Forgot that sort of thing bothers you—thrown a bit out of my routine myself, I guess, with everything happening at once."

"It must have been difficult for you," Denise said, trying to sound sympathetic. "Three years, with just the three of you."

"Not that bad," Mireille said, with a Gallic shrug of the shoulders. "Helen's fine when there are no bones of contention in the air, and Chris would figure on anyone's list of people they wouldn't mind being stuck in a lift with. As I said before, it was tedious, but as I also said, there are worse things than tedium. Everything will settle down into the normal routine soon . . . unless Helen's machine allows Zeph to make a more fruitful contact second time around. I think there's a certain amount of nervousness about a repeat minicatastrophe, but the general consensus is that it will be easy enough for the Captain to order the AIs not to do it again."

"I think he's working on that as we speak," Denise confirmed.

"Good. Are you hopeful that the second shot might work, after what you picked up from Zephaniah's dream? I believe you, by the way, even if Chris is dubious. He couldn't pick up anything much himself, but I picked up enough to convince me that you could do a lot better. Zephaniah really does have a special connection to you, doesn't he? I thought it was just absent friends syndrome when he used to talk about you on Olympus, but it's obvious now that it was more than that. I'm an only child myself, and decided not to have any of my own, the world being what it is . . . was . . . so the closeness aboard Olympus was something new to me, and special. I suppose there's a bit of Helen in me, too, always having used my obsession with science as a way of avoiding contact with actual human beings."

"I'm familiar with the phenomenon," Denise said, wryly, "although I'd be reluctant to describe it as a bit of Helen in me . . . but I shouldn't criticize her. She really was making a sterling effort to be kind and friendly when we were in that armored car, before she ran it off the road and nearly killed me. I must try to forgive her for that."

Mireille looked down at her wrist reflexively. It had healed a long time ago, but the memory evidently lingered. "No," she said, "you're not like Helen. Nor am I, really. I would have said a little bit of you if I'd dared, but . . . I have to admit that you intimidate me slightly."

"Me? Why?"

"It's probably my imagination, but you sometimes seem to disapprove of me."

Denise knew that a reflexive denial would ring false. "It's my imagination that's to blame, not yours. There's no good reason for it, but I feel . . . well, slightly jealous of you."

"Because of Chris? Or Zeph?"

"Both . . . although, as I say, absolutely without rational justification. I'm glad that Zeph found someone with whom he's comfortable, and I understand about the Captain."

"Good," said the chemist. She hesitated, and then said: "I would have been willing to try the machine, you know, solo or with someone else . . . but I know that you and Zeph have an infinitely better chance than anyone else of making some sense of the amplification, if anyone can. For what it's worth, my thoughts and prayers will be with you."

"Thanks," said Denise, and left it at that.

She headed for the ladder but didn't make it.

"Excuse me, Denise," said a woman whose name she couldn't immediately recall, although she did so just in time to respond, without too long a delay: "Mellita?"

"That's right. I feel that I know you, even though we hardly had time to shake hands before lift off. I was on the Olympus Five, and Zephaniah used to talk about you, especially to me, because I'm a biologist, albeit in a different branch. Look, I won't beat around the bush. Some of us feel that Helen is . . . shall we say, rushing things a little. It'll be another three days, apparently, before we actually rendezvous with Cronos, and it seems a trifle . . . hasty to attempt another experimental run with her machine before then. I don't know her very well at all, but she has the reputation of being . . ." She hesitated.

"As crazy as a sack of monkey nuts?" Denise suggested.

"Well, I was going to say a bully, but that too. Frankly, I'm worried about Zeph, because he's anything but a bully, and I wonder whether he isn't being . . . well, rushed is putting it mildly."

"Thanks for your concern," Denise said, sincerely, "but Helen's insistence that time is of the essence might have some justification to it. Zeph thinks so too, and I must admit that they have a point. I can't explain it exactly, but there's one possibility that might be worrying, if we were to delay too long in trying to make contact again with the entity, or entities, that provoked our AI shutdown."

"Which is?"

"That if we don't open the door, *it* might take the initiative . . . and we can't tell what the consequences of that might be, although what happened to the Cronos crew stands as a warning. We have no idea what this thing consists of, but it's definitely capable of interacting with our kind of matter and . . . well, I think it wants to make itself heard as desperately as we want to hear it. It wants something from us, and although it's probably prepared to ask politely . . . I'm not sure how far it might go if it begins to think that we're no longer making an effort. I doubt that it knows that the contact it's already made with Zeph was lost because Zeph's automatic memory censor blotted out the dream. It might take our silence as a refusal. If only for politeness' sake, I think we need to make contact again as soon as we can, within reason."

"And *within reason* really means a few hours?"

"If that's what Zeph thinks, I'm prepared to trust him. Aren't you?"

Mellita nodded, seemingly a trifle reluctantly. "Well, I'll pass it on to the others—but the final decision will rest with the Captain, if he's called upon to arbitrate. What does he think?"

"He trusts Zeph," Denise said, firmly. "He was on the Olympus Five too, so he knows him well. You trust him."

Again, Mellita's nod was a trifle hesitant, but seemed to concede the point.

This time, Denise made it up the ladder.

Zeph and the Captain were still engrossed.

"Any love letters that will make you regret Earth?" she asked.

Zeph smiled wryly. "They're not love letters," he said, "just expressions of good wishes. There's a nice one from one of Walter's techs, who seems to be sorry that I wasn't able to stick around a little longer, although she's extremely glad that he got her into the Enclave with him—to help with the Sling that they then banned him from using, with typical bureaucratic inconsistency. I'm sorry I paid hardly any attention to her. If I'd known . . ."

"Is that what Walter's complaining about—that they commandeered his Sling and then mothballed it?"

"Mostly. The fact that there's a faction under the dome that think he's a traitor to the human race for having given the Dancing Rats the opportunity to lay the foundations for their impending emergence as the dominant species doesn't help. I suspect I'd have got some of that myself if the hate-mail filter hadn't blocked it Earthside. Walter wishes he was in the Highlands, although the people there are probably only supporting him because they automatically support anyone persecuted by the wicked English. Marie's message was interesting, though, in a prejudiced kind of way. She makes some interesting points."

"Surely you don't think that the existence of the Coincidence Force can be recruited to bolster the Renewed Church's model of the soul, let alone the idea of a posthumous paradise?"

"No, and I can't believe that Marie believes that either—she's obviously under pressure from her superiors. But the existence of a latent Coincidence sensibility will force us to rebuild our models of the mind, especially its unconscious component and the trans-actions between that unconscious part and consciousness. And if that sensibility really does give us a kind of liminal awareness of the distributed cosmic intelligences, their kinship and their sense of community . . . can't that qualify as a glimpse of Heaven? And although the fact that the particles making up the body and our consciousness will remain associated by Coincidence when the body and the consciousness have been disaggregated isn't the kind of immortality of which people dreamed and for which they wished, it's still a kind of immortality, isn't it?"

"And that's what you're hoping to get when Helen throws her switch is it? A glimpse of Heaven and a hint of immortality?" the Captain put in, sitting back in his chair, with the attitude of someone who has just completed one task and is pausing before going on to the next.

"In the background, maybe," said Zeph. "Certainly, in fact . . . but there's a reason why we're here, even though the ring intelligences didn't bring us here deliberately, and had no way of knowing that our coming would be a consequence of their crude attempt to make contact with Cronos . . . at least until Helen's amplifier threw my mind wide open to their telempathy. One of the reasons why time might be of the essence is that it might be a good idea not to get too close to the C-ring before knowing more about what we're dealing with. Jaunting through time on Earth, I encountered nothing but goodwill or blank indifference, and I don't expect anything else from the cosmic intelligences, whose presence is bound to seem vague and distant, but the ring is material. Exotic matter, to be sure, in states that can only exist a few degrees above absolute zero, with little in common with solids, liquids and gases, and probably hybridized with even stranger states of being, but nevertheless possessed of a brutal element, which we already know to be capable of doing harm even without meaning to do so."

"Helen said that it might be *unhelpful*," Denise remembered, "but she didn't seem to think that it might be hostile . . . or is that just wishful thinking?"

"No," said Zeph, "I can't see any logical reason why it might be hostile. Hostility is something that only makes sense between kindred competitors. Furthermore, intuition tells me, even without the support of my memory, that the ring intelligences are actually benign, that they don't have anything against us at all . . . but the mere fact that they think we can do something for them, that there's something they can request from us, and would like to request . . . well, benignity can turn. Nothing else generates hatred as easily as unrequited love. On the other hand, maybe I'm simply being ridiculous is making human analogies, and the ring intelligences are far more godlike than that."

"If so," observed Denise, "we'd better pray that they're not like the Old Testament God. Look what effects Jehovah's love for his chosen people had on him when he thought it was unrequited. On the other hand, we've already had the modern Deluge, so we don't have a lot to lose. I suppose we can be sure that it wasn't the ring intelligences who caused Earth's recent cataclysms?"

"I think so," Zeph opined. "Material beings, however exotic, have the innate limitations of matter. There's obviously more to the ring than the orbiting dust we can see, and insofar as it's analogous to an organized, thinking entity, those are attributes of the fraction we can't see, but it remains anchored to the dust, only able to affect other bodies of matter via electromagnetic radiation, gravity and so on. Earth is effectively out of its reach, just as Saturn was out of ours until we invented the matter annihilation engine and built long-haul spaceships. We actually had to come here in order to make it feasible for the ring intelligences to try to make contact with us. Their Coincidence sensibility presumably enables them to be aware of the existence of intelligence on Earth, but dumb and blind intelligence, metaphorically speaking . . . or perhaps *unfeeling* would be a better metaphor . . . excuse me, will you; there are some things I need to look up that might help me to get a better grip of this."

He didn't wait for permission, but immediately leant over his screen, in the unmistakable attitude of a screenbound individual shutting out the world.

The Captain meekly turned his entire attention to Denise. "If you need more time . . ." he said.

"No," Denise said. "Not me, anyway. If Zeph needs more, he'll doubtless take it." She glanced at her own screen, wondering whether she ought to eavesdrop on whatever it was that Zeph was "looking up." It was surely not a love letter, and in any case, he had no secrets from her. She decided that she would find out soon enough if he drew any conclusions, and if it helped with what he was about to do.

"Do you need anything?" Kemmering asked her.

Denise suppressed an urge to laugh. "No."

If the Captain judged that she did, but that she was in denial, he didn't press the point; he didn't even ask her whether she trusted him. He merely said: "It's a long way to the stars. When this little flurry of excitement is over, we'll all have a chance to settle down, and figure out a *modus vivendi.*"

"Unless I get kicked back into yet another coma," she remarked.

"I've desensitized the AIs," he told her. "Not that that's any guarantee, of course . . . but if Helen crashes the car again, they'll still be able to look after you, and you'll certainly wake up again. Believe me, Denise, you and I still have a long way to go, together."

"Amen," she said, dryly.

XV

The pods attached to Helen Arkheimer's Coincidence Sensibility Amplifier were just modified pods, and looked it. The VR hood that was fitted over Zeph's head while Denise waited her turn was simply the pod's original VR hood. The wires connected to the inlaid terminals he'd had fitted when still in his teens and interacting to be a telepresence operator were supplementary to standard equipment, of course, but in the same way that the contacts themselves were as unobtrusive as humanly possible, so the wiring connecting them to the machine was tucked discreetly out of sight.

When Denise had watched her brother being hooked up to Halleck's Sling, it had been an obvious matter of connecting him to something exotic and bizarre, to something that could have passed, in a pinch, for a time machine in an ancient science fiction movie, but while he was being wired up to Helen Arkheimer's apparatus it only looked as if he were being put to bed.

The immediate witnesses to the experiment had been restricted to those that the limited space could accommodate without anyone treading on anyone else's toes. The Captain was there, and so was Mireille Angevot, but that was it: the triumvirate that had been ruling the ship for three years would be restored to their Trinitarian glory as soon as Zeph was in position and Denise lay down in the pod beneath his, to be fitted with a cruder neural net and an identical VR hood.

Also restored, in terms of physical proximity, would be the nexus of four individuals that had briefly bonded during the flight into the deadly cloud of volcanic microparticles. Denise had no doubt, however, that the other ex-sleepers would all be keeping track of the procedure indirectly, and even more intimately, not simply by watching a visual feed of the room's interior but keeping track of whatever the scanning equipment could pick up of the exotic experience that Zeph and Denise were about to share.

They would not have unreasonable expectations, Denise knew. She had reviewed the tapes made during Zeph's first experiment, and knew that there was nothing at all therein that the AI monitors had been able to translate into visual or auditory imagery. Its secrets, such as they were, had remained locked in Zeph's mind, and not even its conscious component. The surface of the unconscious where dream imagery was generated could not be reflected by any kind of scanner yet devised; it remained available for subjective experience alone . . . unless the experiencing individual cared to give a verbal commentary. That was what both of them had to do, to the best of their ability.

Everything went like clockwork. Helen Arkheimer seemed, in fact, to have become a virtual automaton as she ran through the connection procedures and the multiple checks necessary to ascertain that the various components of the apparatus were functioning correctly. While that was going on, everyone maintained the obligatory quasi-religious silence—except for Zeph, who wanted to make a few checks of his own.

"Can you hear me, Denise?" he asked, once she was inside the hood.

"Loud and clear," Denise confirmed, ritualistically.

"Can you sense my presence?"

"Of course."

"I don't mean in the trivial sense that you know I'm here."

"What other is there, and how would I tell it apart?"

"I can't explain. For now, it's probably enough that I can sense you . . . and not just you, actually, but all eleven of you, with varying degrees of intensity. And beyond . . ."

"I haven't switched on yet," said Helen Arkheimer, keeping her voice scrupulously level and full of good will. "Don't let your imagination run away with you."

"I'm not," Zeph assured her. "To tell you the truth . . ." He paused.

"Why?" Helen replied, losing a fraction of the artificial good will. "Weren't you telling the truth before?"

Ignoring the interruption, Zeph continued: " . . . I've been aware of the human presences ever since lift off . . . but not the others. It's only since I've been awake . . . but I didn't know what it was, at first. I'm sure now . . . and it's a good thing. If I can focus on the ring even before you switch on, if I can forge a connection, however tenuous, before the amplification."

"Be careful, Zephaniah," Chris Kemmering put in, quietly. "We talked about the possible dangers of getting too close, remember."

Peering through the transparent side of the pod, forced by its position to look up at the people in the chamber, Denise noticed that the Captain and Mireille were holding hands, like lovers out for a stroll. Helen Arkheimer's hands were fully occupied for the moment, but she couldn't help wondering whether she would feel the urge, or the compulsion, to join in, once they were free, and whether it would make any difference if she did, to anything.

"That's it," said the mathematician, finally. "All set. Are you ready?" The last phrase was pure ritual, as were the affirmative responses that came from each pod.

There was no countdown, even from three. Helen Arkheimer simply reached out to her beloved machine, and triggered it.

Denise had had no idea what to expect, so there was no baseline by comparison with which anything that happened could qualify as a surprise, and she was perfectly familiar with the illusion in question, so there was nothing particularly odd about the fact that the pod, and the surrounding spaceship, seemed to dissolve, and gave her the impression that she was floating, bodiless, in space.

She could see stars, but that wasn't unusual either; she had already used the VR hood in her own pod to obtain a view from outside the ship, to examine the tiny sun and the fully illuminated disk of Saturn, and the blur of the almost-horizontal ring, and the multitude of stars that filled the sky . . .

What did seem strange, however, were the voices, which seemed to be screaming in the distance, a very long way away.

They overlapped and became confused, reducing their clarity, but she distinctly heard someone shout: "Shut it down, you crazy bitch! Can't you see that he's fitting!"—which couldn't possibly be the Captain, because the Captain never lost control to that extent.

And she heard, even more distinctly, though no less distantly, someone else shouting "No! No! No! Don't break the contact!" which, equally couldn't possibly be Zeph's voice, because she knew that Zeph was already incapable of speech, and seemed very unlikely to be her own, as she had no consciousness herself of activating her vocal cords, her tongue and her lips. But she knew that she did have to talk, and quickly, and keep talking, because if she didn't, if she couldn't, then the contact would be broken, and lost, and she would never know . . .

So she spoke. She didn't report what she could see, because she couldn't see anything at all except stars, because that was all there was to be seen if one looked past and through Minerva, ignoring her matter and its vulgar opacity, and outwards into the universe. She had to make something up, use her imagination. She had to tell them a story, and hope . . . just hope . . . that somewhere along the narrative sequence, that story would begin to become true.

"It's all right," she told them. "Zeph's safe, even if he's being shaken up a bit. Let the Bells learn . . . forgive the pun, but I can't keep calling them the Ring intelligences, because it's too cumbersome. Let them learn. They mean him no harm . . . absolutely the opposite, in fact. They know how precious he is, just as much as you do. They're clumsy as yet, but they're figuring it out and refining their touch. They won't do his neurons any damage if they can possibly avoid it—but he can't talk right now, so I'll have to do that for us. He's in a coma, of sorts . . . he has to be in a coma, of sorts, or a trance, or he can't feel them properly, and he has to feel them properly, because all he and they can do is feel.

"We can see them now . . . he can see them, that is . . . , no, *we* can see them . . . but we can still only see the fraction of them that can be seen, or translated into visual imagery by some transfiguration akin to the way your scanners are translating his brain waves. We understand what he meant now by sensing their presence, and his, and focusing. It's the focusing that's difficult—very, very difficult—but we think we can . . . we hope we can . . . we feel we can.

"You already know what we can see, in essence—the rings—and we're still looking at them almost edge-on, because the ship is still traveling along the plane of the ecliptic, and in order to see at all, even in the imagination, we need a position and a line of sight. Doubtless they look prettier from north of Saturn, where they'd be extended around the planet like a vast halo, but it really doesn't matter. All that matters, in terms of visuals, even enhanced visuals, is the size. The Bells are big . . . very, very big, by planetary standards . . . but they're also tiny: very, very tiny, by cosmic standards, although we're several orders of magnitude tinier. They're also widely distributed, by planetary standards, although very compact by the standards of the larger cosmic intelligence . . . although by no means as incredibly dense as we are.

"In terms of relative sizes, the analogy of the man looking down the microscope at a bacterium doesn't even begin to grasp the proportions, and that's why it's all so difficult. The Bells have senses, of course, including material senses physically akin to ours, including a kind of sight and a kind of electromagnetic sensibility, but they can't see us . . . they can barely even make out the Earth, which is less than a dot to them. They can see the Sun, obviously, and Jupiter, when the conjunction permits, but the rest is just dust, and microparticles within the dust. Not insignificant, of course, because much of the Bells' own bodies, at last in their conventional material fraction, is just dust, and microparticles within the dust, just as our incredibly dense bodies are made of cells, and atoms within cells, and particles within atoms. The point is that they can't see us, any more than we can see them. They can interact with us, matter to matter, but the idea of trying to do microsurgery on a bacterium viewed through a microscope with a pair of garden shears while wearing oven gloves hardly begins to model the difficulties in analogy . . .

"As for the others, the comic intelligences, there's absolutely no way that they can see one another. All they can see, and all anyone or anything can really *see*, of the universe and its constituents, is stars: just stars. Even with senses that correspond to our most powerful telescopes . . . and there are some senses, believe me, that can go far beyond that . . . all that anyone or anything can see are different types of stars and different aggregations of stars, and stars of various sizes at different stages in one or another of the fundamental stellar life cycles, because materially, sensibly, in the strictest sense of the term, that's all there is to be *seen*.

"But it isn't all there is, by any stretch of the imagination—and we can assure you that, at present, we're stretching our imagination as far as we can, although hopefully we'll get better with practice. It isn't even a tiny fraction of what there is. It's isn't even a tiny fraction of what can be *felt*, with the kinds of pseudosenses that answer to and manipulate Coincidence. By manipulation, though, I don't mean godlike manipulation, in the crude model of magical omnipotence; I mean the kind of micromanipulation that sense organs have to do in order to make sense data comprehensible, because you can't just *feel*. Feeling is complicated, awkward, and difficult, and requires clever manipulation, just as seeing, when you get down to fundamental analysis, is complicated, awkward and difficult, and requires clever manipulation.

"We wish it were simpler, we really do, but it isn't. True feeling—and we can assure you that, at present, we're feeling as truly as we can, though doubtless, etc.—requires art, and talent, and sympathy, and connection, and God only knows what else, which we simply don't have, or only have in the most primitive fashion imaginable. You probably think that loving, however difficult and awkward it might be in practice, is fundamentally simple, but it's not. It's complicated . . . we'd say fiendishly complicated, but there's nothing fiendish about it, because loving is good, and the relationships that exist between the cosmic intelligences, complicated as they are—more complicated than human imaginations can grasp, alas—are fundamentally loving, and hence fundamentally good. We know that, because we feel it, even though we are, not to put too fine a point on it, incredibly incompetent, and stupid, and lame, when it comes to any kind of feeling of which the cosmic intelligences, or the Bells—which are cosmic intelligences as well as local intelligences—are capable, and which they find necessary and fundamental to their existence.

"All of which is mind-boggling, we know, and there'll be a temptation for you just to say *no, it's too much for us, I can't understand it and I won't even think about it*, but that's a temptation we all need to resist, because if we can't resist it, and don't resist it, and won't think about it, we're cutting ourselves off, not merely from the universe, and one another, but from ourselves, because all of this is within us as well as without, and if we're ever going to feel anything meaningful—*truly* feel anything meaningful— we'll have to think about it first, and bring it into focus. There's a sense, we know, in which it's too late for mere humans even to try, because we're on the very brink of extinction . . . but there's a sense, too, that makes it all the more important that we do try, because when the future generations look back at us, all the way to the seventh and beyond, that's going to be the measure of our achievement; that's going to be the measure of the contribution that we were able to make, as a species, not simply to the evolution of true feeling on Earth, to the limited extent that the seventh generation will contrive to achieve it, but outside the Earth as well.

"You might think that all of that's absurd, that we're far too tiny and too insignificant to make any contribution at all to the life and feeling of entities as big and as complicated as the Bells, let alone entities on the scale and the complexity of the cosmic intelligences, but you'd be dead wrong, just as you'd be wrong to think that invisible bacteria and nanomachines can't make any significant contribution to the life and feeling of the thinking organisms we are. In fact, as we've known for some time, without our bacterial symbiotes, we wouldn't be alive at all, and we wouldn't be capable of thinking or feeling even at the crude level that we've learned to do such things. We're a lot tinier than that relative to the Bells, of course, but that doesn't mean that we can't and don't have a possible role to play in their lives, and a role that's potentially very important to them . . . a life-changing role, in fact.

"If you think about it, it's really quite simple, and if we'd had time to reflect, we'd have been bound to figure it out, because it's as logical as one-two-three-many. The Bells have always known that there was life on Earth, and, more recently, life with the potential for feeling, albeit in the most elementary imaginable fashion. But they've never been able to make any practical contact with that life because of the distance involved and the limitations that distance places on material communication. They could affect life on Earth, if they had a mind to do so, but only in slow and exceedingly crude ways. They could have destroyed us, for instance—but they had absolutely no reason to want to do that, and every conceivable reason for doing the opposite, because the harmony of the universe, the community and communication of the cosmic intelligences, is fundamentally loving and good. They never wanted to harm us in any way . . . but they couldn't do anything, either, to help protect us from the harm inflicted by the vicissitudes of violent nature. They didn't have the mobility.

"Neither did we, until very recently, but we do now. It's too late for us, of course, for that mobility to be of any constructive use to us, as a species, but it's not too late for it to be of use to the Bells. Obviously, when you think about it, the only thing they could possibly want from us is a service that only Cronos and Minerva could provide. The only thing that we can possibly do for them is to help them, or some fraction of their material component, to travel, with a celerity and pinpoint accuracy beyond their scope.

"We could help the Bells, or at least their offspring, to travel to Earth if we wanted to, and if they wanted to go, but they don't. That's the last thing they want. The inner system is way too hot for their kind of existence, for their kind of life. Our Goldilocks Zone is their Inferno. What they want to do is to go outwards, into the paradisal worlds—paradisal for entities of their kinds of exotic matter, which can only exist a few degrees above absolute zero—of their fellow Bellkin in the rings of Uranus, and their even stranger Bellfellows in the Oort Cloud.

"To some extent, of course, the Bells are already engaged in a community of feeling with those outsiders . . . but that's not the same as a material connection, however distant and disjointed and, in particular, it's not the same as the kind of community that could be contrived with the additional connections of feeling that it's possible to build with the aid of material transfer, because of the retained and manipulable associations of Coincidence.

"To put it very simply, what the Bells would like from us is a lift. They'd like us to take something of them—their seeds, if you like—on an outward journey away from the sun: a multi-targeted outward journey of the kind that only a spaceship can under-take, with a definite and detailed itinerary, taking in the rings of Uranus, and various locations beyond Neptune, but extending ultimately, all the way to the stars. And if we can help them with their itinerary, they're more than willing to help us with ours. If we can take them to meet their friends, and establish a more elaborate and more versatile community, they can take us to meet the strangers who might be willing, able and eager to become our friends, and establish a community of sorts with us.

"It's too late to save and preserve a fraction of the human race, in all likelihood . . . probably, in fact . . . but even if that's the case, it's not too late to add to our achievements, to the measure of our accomplishments. And even though it won't be easy, it won't be so very difficult. The fractions of the Bells that we carry won't be any trouble, except that they'll add to our mass. They won't take up any space inside Minerva, because they can't possibly live inside it, but outside . . . well, the hull isn't exactly paradisal from their point of view, by any means, but it's tolerable, maybe even verging on the comfortable.

"And while they're being carried, of course, it's by no means inconceivable that they might be able to help us out a little with our own agendas. They won't be able to talk to us, obviously, or show us pictures . . . but we will be able feel their presence, vaguely to begin with, with more intensity and focus over time.

We have the latent capability; all we need is the right kind of training and the willingness to make the effort.

"Only a few of us, at first, will be able to derive any benefit at all, but it won't end there, and it has already begun to extend, tentatively, beyond the mere minimum. In the years that it will take to reach Uranus, and the decades that it will take us to reach the stars, we'll all grow and develop. It will be slow, and it will be limited, but we're not incapable of feeling, of loving . . . we just find it direly difficult. The proximity of the Bells' offspring, and the other Bellkin we meet, will help us evolve, personally and as a community . . . as a species, in effect.

"What else they might be able to help us do, they have no idea; there are possibilities beyond their imagination, just as there are beyond ours, but once they get to know us a little better—the two of us, initially, but all twelve of us eventually, and perhaps twenty-six if we can persuade the Croons crew that we're not insane and that we have an option to offer them that might be better by far than the ones they're presently facing—all kinds of other opportunities might come into view. This will be a journey to discovery for all involved. It will be a difficult journey, as all journeys of discovery are, but you don't need us to tell you that it will be the most important journey of discovery that the human race has ever had the opportunity to make, as well as the last.

"Anyhow, that's the offer. It's up to us to decide whether or not to accept. We're for it, and we hope you will be too. Either way, politeness requires us to let them know. There's no desperate hurry, now that we've taken the first step and established the channel of communication, but it might be advisable not to wait too long; human life is short and the stars are a very long way away.

"We're truly sorry that it has been so difficult for us to receive and relay this message, contending with the inherent frailties of the human body and mind, and its awkward inbuilt mechanisms—not to mention those of our vessels' AIs—and we're sorry that we couldn't tell you more clearly ourselves what it was necessary to do in order to contrive its transmission, but we hope the fact that we seem to have got there in the end will make up for it . . . if we have, in fact, got there in the end, and if we survive the experience.

"There's so much more we could tell you, and so much more that we want to tell you, and so much more that we will tell you, in time, but we're rather afraid that one of our bodies might have taken something of a neural battering, and could probably do with some rest and recuperation. There will be time, we hope, and plenty of opportunity, to allow us to make up that ground.

"In the meantime, love to you all."

And with that, Denise fell silent, hoping that, inadequate as it obviously was, she had done enough, for a start. She could only hope, of course, that it was true, but she felt that it was, and felt that the feeling was probably enough, even given the woeful inadequacy of human feelings in general.

And then, with or without the aid of protective AIs, she fell unconscious, and slept. If she dreamed she didn't remember her dreams when she woke up.

XVI

Denise woke up with a distinct feeling of *déjà-vu*, although the first thing she noticed was that she didn't have a feeding-tube stuck down her throat, and therefore suspected that she hadn't been out for that long. On the other hand, she did have a drip, so it hadn't been a momentary blackout, and when she opened her slightly sticky eyes and tried to squint, she quickly concluded that she was back in her own cabin rather than Helen Arkheimer's hyperspatial telegraph office.

She wasn't alone this time, though. In fact, there was someone holding her hand. If he had been talking to her, though, she couldn't remember anything he'd said.

"How long?" she asked. "Not three years?"

"Not even three days," the Captain assured her. "The precautionary coma might have been over the top, but it turns out that when the responsibility is in my hands, I'm just as likely to err on the side of caution as the AIs."

"Zeph?" she queried.

"Still out. As you said, he took something of a neural battering, and the medical AI will probably keep him out for a couple of days more, but he's not in any danger. The automatic doctor has his situation well in hand . . . thank God. I nearly pulled the plug on him, you know, although I'd probably have been forced to lay Helen out to get to the switch, which would have been a serious black mark on my reputation as a competent captain. Luckily, I didn't."

Denise tried to sit up, and succeeded all too well, bumping her head on the ceiling of the pod.

"Careful," said the Captain. "You're a lot lighter now than you were last time we spoke, and we're matching orbits with Cronos. I'm used to it, but you'd be wise to take things very cautiously until you adapt. Stay where you are for the time being, Zephaniah's right here beneath you, so you can climb down if you want to hold his hand, but I wouldn't go much further until you get your space legs, if I were you."

Denise was concentrating on staying still, which seemed to be almost as problematic as moving. "You did hear me, then?" she said. "I really was talking, and not just to myself."

Chris Kemmering laughed. "Oh, I heard you," he said. "The whole ship heard you. And since then, I suspect, the entire population of Earth, such as it still is, has heard the tape."

"You're exaggerating."

"No, I'm not. Three years into Enclave life, the survivors of the human race are looking forward to a long and desperate fight to stay alive in unremittingly hostile circumstances; what they need more than anything else, it seems, is some kind of distraction—a sideshow. For three years we've been short-changing them, but not any more. Your news is an enormous sensation, and a considerable boost to morale, in spite of a certain amount of inevitable controversy. At this moment, you're world famous. You might only have accumulated a dozen or so messages in your first three years aboard, but you've already collected well over a thousand in the last few hours. They started coming through as soon as the two-way time lag permitted, and they're going to keep coming for a long time yet. You're not getting the full credit, though. Everyone's still calling it the Zephanian Revelation. Blame your parents. Denise! What were they thinking?"

"Dad was a neo-sexist," said Denise, absentmindedly, while she attempted to absorb the import of the revelation. "He thought the road to happiness for boys consisted in standing out, whereas girls would be happier if they blended in."

"He was wrong," the Captain stated. "Mercifully, since, now and for a long while to come, your little speech will make you stand out more than any other member of the human race."

"*Merde*," murmured Denise. "I hope they realize that it was off the cuff, in confused circumstances. If I'd had time to plan it, I'm sure I could have phrased it a lot better."

"I'm sure you could," the Captain agreed. "Bells! What were *you* thinking?"

"I wasn't," she said. "It was the only thing that came to mind on the spur of the moment. Isn't it your duty as captain to give your crew moral support rather than mocking them, though?"

"Admonition accepted. You do realize, I suppose, that the entire human race is going to be eavesdropping on this conversation too, don't you? All the recorders are back on, and all the ears are tuned in."

"Oh," she said, not having given the matter a thought. "It doesn't seem to be inhibiting you," she added.

"I'm beyond embarrassment, after the Olympus leaks. I think I can build a privacy screen, though, at least for the cabins. I'd have done it already, but I've been fearfully busy."

"Holding my hand?"

"Among other things. We've taken the vote, by the way. We recorded your ballot and Zeph's on the basis of your campaign speech. You got a unanimous yes aboard Minerva, but Cronos is still split. Fulsom's trying to put off a decision until the ship had completed its mission schedule, but things are apparently a little stormy over there. Opinions are deeply divided back on Earth as to what Cronos ought to do, apparently, but nobody here cares about that. The Cabal have reconstituted their space program, by the way; the construction of Minerva II will probably begin in a matter of days, but finishing it might be a different matter. The loudest voices are those calling you a fantasist and refusing to believe a word of it, but they're a small minority; the mood of the times is dead against them, and it was a good narrative move to promise more in future broadcasts. Always keep them wanting more."

"It wasn't a narrative move. I was just worried about going on for too long, with Zeph's nervous system having fits."

"You can remember the more you promised them, then?"

"I remember everything," Denise assured him. "I wasn't asleep, or dreaming—I might have been entranced, but I was perfectly conscious and lucid, echoing Zeph's dream faithfully. Dad was wrong, as you say—the optimum strategy for life isn't to find different and diverging paths for a brother and sister, but to find paths that will bring them together into a fruitful collaboration; you're right about naming me Denise, though. I really should have changed it—but how could I know that I was going to become a career prophet, or even an astronaut? How predictable was that, a subjective three weeks ago . . . or three years and a bit, objective time?"

"Fair point," the Captain conceded. "Look, now that I know you're all right, I'll go see what I can do about that privacy screen. You'll need to give me a couple of hours, at least, though, before the cabin can be made effectively bugproof. How close a watch you keep on your tongue in the meantime is up to you. I can order the others to stay out if you want to be alone with Zeph, though."

"There's no need to throw your weight about," Denise told him. "I presume that Helen's the first in the queue?"

"Obviously. If you'd rather see Mireille . . ."

"No, it's okay. After all, there's no reason for her to be hostile, is there? And we'll all have to learn to love one another eventually, if the shipboard society is going to work, while we and the Ringlets take our cosmic tour."

"Too late," he said. "We're stuck with Bells now, and all the puns that go with them. But before I go, though, I ought to say *well done*. As your Captain, I can say that on behalf of the entire crew, and the Cabal too. And I do."

He turned away then, because excessive effusiveness wasn't his style.

Helen Arkheimer came in as soon as Chris Kemmering had left. Before she could speak, Denise seized the initiative. "Congratulations, Helen," she said. "You've proved your math, proved your machine and proved that you were absolutely right to commandeer Minerva. You've changed the future of the human race, for the better."

The mathematician seemed slightly taken aback, having evidently not been sure what kind of reception she was going to get. "I had good help," she admitted.

"But the speech could have been better?" Denise suggested.

Helen shrugged. "Maybe," she said, "but it did the job. You're world famous—but I suppose the dear Captain told you that."

"Yes, but all the right people know that the triumph was yours. I'm just a mouthpiece. Walter Halleck must be green with envy."

The mathematician contrived a wry smile. "Actually, he's trying to claim all the credit for himself, asserting that I just followed in his footsteps and stole all his work. He's got the bigger public profile and he's on Earth, so he'll probably get away with it. I don't mind. As you say, the people who count know the truth—and if he can build a machine like mine and get some results from it, good luck to him. At least I'm in no danger of being assassinated by the Death-to-Rats brigade."

"That would be a tragedy," Denise observed. "I didn't like him much, but men of his ability are exceedingly rare—and he did make a crucial conceptual breakthrough with the Sling."

"True," conceded Helen, with an apparently sincere generosity. "Geniuses are entitled to be a little curmudgeonly and short-tempered . . . aren't we?"

"Of course," said Denise. "I'm no genius, but I have my moments of ill-temper, as you know. Let's forgive one another, shall we?"

376

The mathematician seemed genuinely relieved. "I'm not really a crazy bitch, you know," she said.

"Of course you are," Denise said, "and a bully, when you think you can get away with it—but it doesn't matter. You're still a genius, you still built the machine that not only facilitated humankind's first contact with extraterrestrial life but opened up a channel to universal love and goodness, and you had the foresight to draft me into your team as well as Zeph. What's a few minor bad habits compared with all that? In my moral account book, you're in the black forever."

Helen nodded. "As you are in mine," she said. "But for you . . . well, without you, it would all have come to nothing. I won't forget that. And you and Zeph can take all the time you need before the next run. No pressure. We can all be patient now."

"We'll need to be," said Denise. "It's a hell of a long way to the stars."

"It's quite a long way to Uranus, considering that the two planets aren't in conjunction . . . but we'll get to the stars in the end, and now, we have grounds for traveling hopefully, with every possibility that the arrival won't let us down. There are more people who want to see you, by the way—shall I send the next one in?"

"If you wouldn't mind," Denise said, "I'd prefer it if you could ask them all to wait a while, until I come out. If I can get out of the pod without banging my head on the ceiling, I'd quite like to float down and spend a little time alone with my brother first. I know he's still asleep, but . . ."

"I understand," said the mathematician, perhaps implausibly, although Denise decided to believe her. Helen helped her out of the bed, and made sure that she was comfortably ensconced before withdrawing and sealing the door.

Denise studied her brother's face or a moment or two before opening the face of the pod and slipping her hand in to grasp his.

"Well, Zeph," she said to him, "we're together now, forever. Two halves of a whole, although I might be overstepping the mark a bit claiming to be a half, when I'm really just an echo. We have a job to do, a mission to fulfill, and we're going to see the universe together . . . only a tiny fraction of it, of course, but an interesting one. Hopefully you'll remember this time, but if you don't . . . well, I guess I'll have a lot to tell you.

"You'll have a lot of work to do, of course, in and out of Helen's contraption, and we might both have a long road of personal evolution ahead of us if our Coincidence sensibility can be further enhanced . . . not to mention Mireille's and the Captain's and perhaps everybody else's. We might be locked in a tin can with two-way communication with Earth cursed by an increasingly dire time lag, but life probably isn't going to be nearly as boring as we feared, with an entire universe to explore by exotic means and some extremely exotic friends to get to know, only the thickness of the hull away.

"Poor Marie will be disappointed, of course, that the only paradise we've found so far is only fit for beings that can only live at a few degrees above absolute zero, but at least we've endorsed her claim that what she calls God is good and loving—and who knows what the future might yet bring? Just when you think existence has run out of possibilities, eh?

"I suppose I'd better go out and say hello, if I can keep my footing. Can't hide away any more, can I? And then I'd better start looking at all these messages that the world has addressed to us. Wake up soon, will you—I could do with some help, and some extra moral support . . . and we have a request to answer, and an offer to accept, and a mini-utopia to guide into the world of stars and cosmic intelligence. All in all, the end of the world aside, things could be a lot worse."

She let go of Zeph's hand, resealed his pod, and rose, very carefully, to her feet. It was probably an illusion, but she felt that she was getting the hang of it already, and that she would be an experienced spacewoman in no time at all.

Before she opened the door, though, she turned to look back down at the comatose form, and said: "Love you," even though she knew that he knew that already.